THE MADNESS OF GODS AND KINGS

Book V of the Northern Crusade

Copyright © 2020 by Christian Warren Freed

Excerpt from *Even Gods Must Fall* 2021 Christian Warren Freed
Cover design by Melissa Andres
Cover copyright 2021 by Warfighter Books
Author Photograph by Anicie Freed

Warfighter Books
Holly Springs, North Carolina 27540
https://www.christianwfreed.com

Second Edition: August 2021

Library of Congress Cataloging-in-Publication Data
Name: Freed, Christian Warren, 1973- author.
Title: The Madness of Gods and Kings/ Christian Warren Freed
Description: Second Edition | Holly Springs, NC: Warfighter Books, 2021. Identifiers: LCCN 2021913414 | ISBN 9781736804452 (trade paperback) Subjects: Epic fantasy | Military fantasy | Paranormal

Printed in the United States of America

10 9 8 7 6 5 4 3 2 1

She stabbed again and again. Ropes of blood whipped off the blade each time it ripped from the flesh. Anger, hatred, and pure malevolence dripped from her soul. She felt empowered each time she stabbed the helpless body pinned against the wall thorns before her. Pain echoed deep in those eyes, the wounding of the soul beyond compare. It inspired her. Drove her deeper into fits of delicious agony that only pain could satisfy. She continued to stab until the body hung limp. Blood pooled at her feet. With a last gasp, a gentle rattle, the body found peace through death.

It wasn't good enough. Maleela stabbed harder. Faster. Her intensity picked up as she expunged years of mistreatment. Years of neglect that had anchored deep within the wells of her heart. She became vengeance. She became hatred. Only when her strength faded did she drop the now dull dagger and look upon her work. Hundreds of deep stab wounds scarred the corpse. She reveled in delivering such damage.

Maleela looked upon the glossed-over eyes of her victim: her father. He'd gotten what he deserved. The same as all those ever snubbed her or ignored her when she needed attention the most deserved. A cold, painful death stretching for hours. Reaching out, she gently touched her father's mangled face and laughed. Vengeance was finally hers!

Law of the Heretic
Immortality Shattered Book I

'If you're looking for a fun and exciting fantasy adventure, spend a few hours in the Free Lands with the Law of the Heretic.'

Where Have All the Elves Gone?

'Sometimes funny and other times a little dark, Where Have The Elves Gone? brings something fresh and new to fantasy mysteries. Whether you want to curl up with a mystery or read more about elves this book has something for everyone. Spend a few hours solving a mystery with a human and a couple of dwarves - you'll be glad you did.'

<u>**War Priests of Andrak Saga**</u>
The Children of Never

SO, You Want to Write a Book? +
SO, You Wrote a Book. Now What? +

*Forthcoming   + Nonfiction

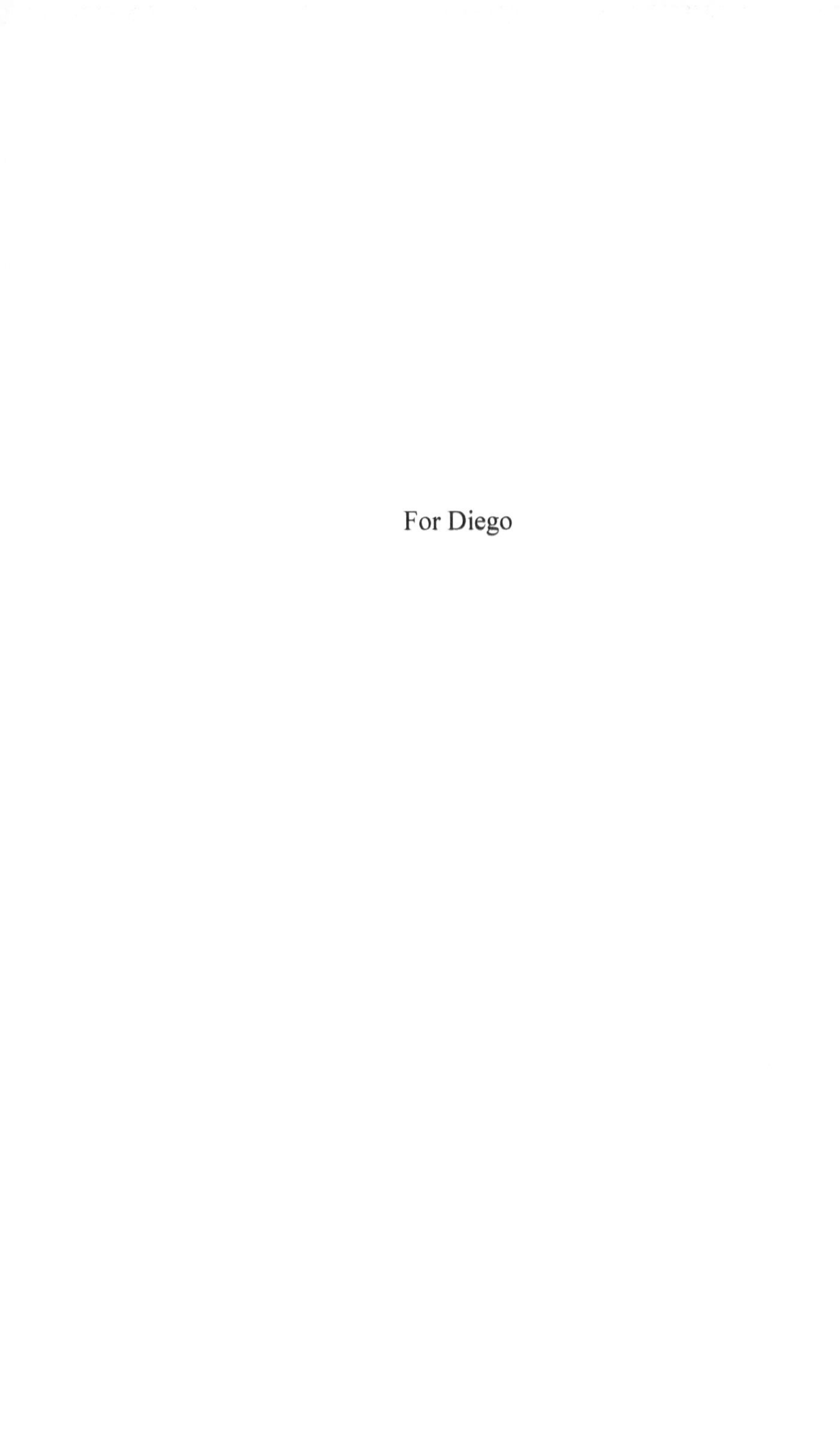

For Diego

Christian Warren Freed

THE MADNESS OF GODS AND KINGS

ONE

Ingrid

Black smoke mingled with dust as the handful of horses sprinkled through the battling infantrymen thundered across the tiny farmstead. A pair of dappled geldings already lay dead in the snow-covered fields, their riders having bled out shortly after. Spent arrows and broken spear hafts were jut up at random, turning the fallow potato field into a macabre scene. The old barn, rickety and half collapsed, blazed away. Flames licked high into the late winter sky as the sound of cold steel clashing sang its grizzly song across the tundra.

An arrow whistled past Ingrid's head, too close for her liking. The reluctant warrior knew she had nothing to prove by being caught in the middle of another battle but she'd vowed, not only to herself but to the others in the rebellion, not to stagnate like the previous council. Perhaps if they'd had more nerve to be seen on the front with their people the rebellion wouldn't have almost been destroyed by Harnin One Eye's forces. Her earlier crisis of faith abated after many long nights of deliberation with her shadows Orlek and Harlan. Their insights had thus far proven invaluable in keeping as many of her fighters alive as possible while Harnin continually spread his own Wolfsreik reserve forces thin across the breadth of Delranan in a vain attempt at stopping her. Ingrid felt momentum rebuilding with each passing dawn.

None of that would matter if she got herself killed out on this lonely farm. She accompanied a platoon-sized element out from their mobile bivouac site thirty leagues northwest of the capital city with the intent on seizing the farm to lay an ambush. Most of the rebellion was peasants and farmers, not like the trained professionals they were facing. She knew they couldn't go toe to toe in a pitched fight, leaving little alternative but to strike through guerilla tactics. A thick network of spies and local informants stretched from the far western coast to the base of the Murdes Mountains in the east. Every movement Harnin made was observed and reported back to the central command structure of the rebellion. Sometimes that meant delays of days, bordering on weeks. They were delays Ingrid was forced to tolerate as she struggled to keep one move ahead of the One Eye tyrant occupying the throne.

They'd arrived at the farm in the predawn hours only to find a Wolfsreik supply train reinforced with heavy infantry already camped out. Both the farmer and his elderly wife had been killed long before Ingrid arrived, under suspicion of treason. The lieutenant in command found the couple's winter stockpile and wrongfully assumed it was for the rebellion. Ingrid spied their bodies hanging from the barren branches of an old oak tree just in front of the farmhouse.

Faced with the tough choices of fleeing back to their camp without making contact or fighting an essentially losing battle, Ingrid reformulated the plans and struck just as fast as she could get her people into position. They fired the barn with flaming arrows as other archers targeted the wagon horses. Wagons couldn't move without horses. The Wolfsreik was either going to have to abandon their supplies or, after fighting a long battle, carry them on their backs. Neither prospect suited the wolf soldiers.

Ingrid gave their lieutenant credit for how quickly he roused his soldiers and formed a defense. She'd barely had time to send her meager cavalry, more akin to light raiders, around behind the farm while her archers continued an occasionally punishing barrage. A handful of wounded meant little in the enemy's capabilities, however. The Wolfsreik locked their heavy shields in a wall and effectively reduced any aerial assault to mere nuisance.

Any initiative the rebels once held dissolved like so much spring snow as Harnin's soldiers organized and defended. They made no move to go on the assault, content to wait for Ingrid to counter and make the next move. Any notion of a stalemate ended abruptly when Ingrid sent her cavalry in from the rear and infantry from the front under cover of archers. The battle remained stagnant for the first few minutes before the enemy lines cracked. Ingrid sent the largest men first. Their combined weight bowed the enemy line, distracting them enough for her cavalry to strike from behind. The Wolfsreik square broke and it quickly became a melee.

Hand-to-hand combat was fierce. Men, and an occasional woman, fell dead or wounded. Their rich blood painted the melting snow. Ever the opportunists, Ingrid's rebels snatched up the better-quality weapons from fallen Wolfsreik and surged ahead with renewed confidence. Ingrid was able to stay behind, barely, as her forces steadily overwhelmed the surviving enemy. She didn't offer quarter. Neither would they. This type of war didn't allow for prisoners. Each side bore that burden into battle every time. It was a sad fact that countrymen killed countrymen with ruthless abandon in the name of causes they didn't truly understand.

Ingrid didn't pretend to understand them. An officer's wife, she'd been around the army for as long as she could remember. Many of the men fighting her now seemed familiar, invoking fond memories turned painful by the war at the very least. She often wondered if any were once friends. Thinking of killing former friends didn't sit well. None of her previous emotions meant anything in the ongoing struggle for the soul of Delranan. She fought just as harshly as her enemy and expected the same from them.

She looked up, trying to find the archer that had come within a breath of killing her, spotting him just in time to catch Orlek plunge his short blade down between the neck and shoulder. The archer died with a grimace locked on his bearded face. Orlek's scowl prevented Ingrid from smiling.

His displeasure with having her on the battlefield was well known to everyone in the command cell.

The archer's death signified the end of the real fighting. Ingrid's rebels hunted down the surviving Wolfsreik, mercifully ending the suffering of the wounded with a quick swipe across their throats. She couldn't watch. Death was her boon companion, but she viewed their relationship in a foul atmosphere. Even after nearly a full winter she still couldn't stomach watching a man die, much less killing one herself. *All the more reason to return to the village and lead from behind the scenes. Getting yourself killed will only make matters worse for everyone. The rebellion's been through so much I don't think they could stand going through another restructuring.* She saw that sentiment echoed in Orlek's dark eyes as he stalked across the distance separating them.

"What do you think you're doing?" he fumed.

She held up her hands in protest while letting him vent. There wasn't much point in trying to stop him, not when his emotions were amped up. He was a man, after all. *Of course it doesn't help that we have feelings for each other.* She sighed. Romantic entanglements never worked out in these sorts of situations. One of them was bound to end up face down in a field, leaving the other a broken husk of a survivor. She almost prayed it was her dead in the fields, that way she wouldn't have to bear the heartache of seeing a second man she loved killed.

He paused momentarily after noticing her reluctance to engage. "Don't give me that silent treatment, Ingrid! I'm serious. War isn't a game. You're the leader of…."

"Of the rebellion. I know this, Orlek, but that doesn't negate my responsibilities in being a leader. These men and women need to see me out doing what leaders are supposed to do. We've had this argument a hundred times since fleeing Chadra. Inaella and the others were more politician than leader. How can I inspire anyone when they never see my face?" she fired back.

Ingrid placed her hands on her hips, daring him to give her further fuel for her to attack with. She had just as much passion for Delranan as her rebellion and would argue like a badger until her opponent saw her point of view.

"Ingrid, we're slowly turning the tide back against Harnin," he said, much of the earlier conviction bled from his voice. "But we can't maintain momentum if you get killed by a stray arrow."

"Only that wasn't a stray and you know it. He meant to kill me. I'm a recognizable figure now. Harnin has my description plastered in every village he has the tiniest grip on. I'm a target, Orlek. Hiding me away won't change that," she told him. "He'll stop at nothing to get at me and cut the head off the rebellion for good."

Orlek's shoulders sagged. "We should have made sure Inaella was dead before leaving."

"She's only a small part of the problem."

He barked a bitter laugh. "Women scorned are seldom small parts. I have a feeling she's one of the main driving forces in Harnin's new offensive."

"She is," Ingrid replied. There'd been rumors of a pockmarked, dark-haired woman at the front of Harnin's formations as the campaign waged across the western part of the kingdom. Until Ingrid had confirmation, there was little point in pursuing them. She wanted Inaella dead more than any other save perhaps Harnin himself. Once she pitied Inaella. The woman had lost everything and been stricken with the plague. Whatever remained was a shallow representation of the woman she'd been. Hatred fueled her thoughts, hatred for Ingrid. There was a reckoning coming and Ingrid could only hope something foul happened before it arrived.

"Inaella knows all your secrets. She'll stop at nothing to see you hanging from the gibbets over Chadra Keep," Orlek needlessly said.

Ingrid finally allowed some of her ire to calm. Living with Inaella's wrath was a burden only she could bear.

Anyone else caught in the path would either be swept aside or driven under. Their fire threatened to consume the northern kingdom all lost amidst the growing conflagration between good and bad. No one in Delranan knew anything about the coming storm between the gods and their minions here on Malweir.

Flashing a soft smile, Ingrid pushed a lock of blond curls from her face. "I can't let her stop our progress. She's only one woman and lacks any knowledge of where we've come since leaving the city. Her information is outdated. Harnin will see her for that and, from what I can guess, will have her strung up or sent to one of the labor camps in the east for wasting his time."

The camps were equally rumor. Ones she tended to believe. Even before the rebellion fractured and abandoned the major cities, Ingrid had heard mention of Harnin's troops fortifying the east against the eventual return of King Badron and his much larger, more professional army. No doubt Harnin felt trapped between two raging conflagrations. Dealing with the rebellion in a swift, efficient manner was his best option, especially with the ten-thousand-strong Wolfsreik returning from campaign in Rogscroft. Ingrid still had a chance, albeit a slight one with a closing window of opportunity.

"All I'm asking is that you bear with me until we can force this ordeal to a conclusion," she told him with all sincerity. "We can break Harnin. Leave him ineffective and bloodied when Badron returns."

"Where does that leave us, though? We've all heard dark things about the king. How can we trust him to treat us or the kingdom any better? For all we know he'll come after us the moment he's done crushing Harnin." Orlek frowned. Deep creases lined his weather-beaten forehead. A soldier, he'd chosen to keep his past hidden from Ingrid. There were some things she just didn't need to worry about. "For now we need to focus on mopping this mess up. We can't afford to let any of Harnin's men escape."

She felt the weight dragging her heart down get heavier. Killing was never easy, nor should it be. It took a different kind of man to take a life. Those rare few finding perverse pleasure in the deed left stains on all humanity. Ingrid ordered men killed because she had to. Because there was no other viable solution to ending the rebellion in Delranan without letting Harnin win. Too much had happened already. Too many depravities. Too few people standing up for what was right. The imbalance of social justice spurred her decisions. Her conscience would have to wait to be dealt with once the fighting ended.

"Order the cavalry to hunt down the survivors. As much as I'd like to take prisoners, we can't afford the manpower necessary to guard them," she instructed.

Orlek sheathed his short sword. "The men know what to do. I'll see to it. I suggest you get inside the farmhouse and try to get warm. It's a long ride back to camp and we need you with all your fingers and toes, if you take my meaning."

She forced a smile. Frostbite was a very real concern plaguing the rebels as they struggled through the deep snows previously untouched by anything larger than a bull moose. "Leave me a few to take care of the farmer and his wife. They didn't deserve to die, especially not at the hands of the same army sworn to defend them."

"Of course," was all Orlek said. The rebellion had seen its share of civilian casualties. A sad fact of war was that more civilians wound up getting killed than soldiers. This farming couple was merely the latest in a long line of victims.

Ingrid watched him walk away with mild interest. She couldn't help but wonder if they'd ever find the path back to normalcy or would Delranan suffer under the cloud of madness until the great fire went out of the world? Unwanted answers assailed her as she stalked inside with heavy heart.

TWO

A Last Meal

A flock of red ibis floated overhead, adding flavor to the endless sky of blue. Not a cloud could be seen, leaving the golden rays of sunlight to warm the ground. Nestled in the middle of a gigantic clearing rested the only temple of the gods of light in Malweir. Trennaron was a symbol of hope to some, myth to most. Only a select few were ever allowed admittance. Artiss Gran, the only Dae'shan remaining true to their original purpose, focused his thoughts on those few resting within the comforts of Trennaron.

The long war was finally ending. Centuries of careful planning and unseen manipulation to ensure the proper bloodlines were present at the right time were about to pay off. At least he hoped. Even one as powerful as himself couldn't possibly foresee ever potential future. Artiss struggled through centuries of solitude while his errant brethren scavenged the world in search of souls tainted enough to enact the return of the dark gods. The crusade ranging across northern Malweir was their final gambit.

Amar Kit'han and the other Dae'shan had armies at their disposal. Artiss had only a handful of collected heroes to counter the rising tide of darkness. His faith that all races would respond to the challenges facing them, while well intentioned, wasn't strong enough to rely on. The withered, old man closed his eyes and gently punched the top of the wall keeping him from falling off of the roof. So many uncertainties kept him from doing what he knew, or thought he knew, what needed to be done. How could he be sure he was indeed acting in accordance with the gods of light when he was trapped within the alabaster walls of Trennaron?

As much as he'd like to abandon the temple and see his band of heroes safely back to the holy site of Arlevon Gale, his oaths bound him to Trennaron. Should he leave, the magic of the temple would fail and his life would be forfeit. Artiss sighed again. Perhaps there were matters in life that meant more than one soul. He contemplated leaving his post, if for no other reason than to combat the other three Dae'shan. Nothing the races of Malweir had was sufficient to battle the servants of darkness.

Leaving Trennaron was a temporary solution to a permanent problem. The knowledge of the gods of light rested safely within the underground vaults. Who was he to risk losing the wealth of knowledge for all time just for the sake of exorcising the demons that had plagued him since the dawn of Man? He found it suddenly odd that after several mortal lifetimes the end game had begun. Years wasted thinking of the potential outcomes were stripped away, leaving him only with what was and what wasn't. Artiss Gran prided himself on being practical. Practicality stated all his efforts and hard work were ending, a grand finale from which there were only two possible conclusions. Those basest of all mortal designs: success or failure. He wished he could do more, but the gods of light had been specific with their charge. Reluctantly, Artiss turned from the dawn to confront his guests.

He found them shifting blandly through their meal of roast fowl, freshly baked cornbread, and a wheel of yellow cheese. Of them all, only Boen the Gaimosian and Ironfoot the Dwarf held an appetite. They ravenously set about devouring whatever food was laid out in front of them, washing it all down with fresh brook water and a pint of Trennaron's finest mead, an indulgence Artiss never managed to shake from his youthful, mortal days. He smiled at the memories, watching the pair consume his favorite drink produced. Artiss took a minor measure of pride in having some of the finest honeybees in the southern kingdoms.

"Our host returns!" Boen called raucously between bites of fowl and a rather loud, uncouth burp that echoed throughout the domed hall. Juice dribbled down into his beard. Older than most of them, the Gaimosian, named

Vengeance Knights by much of the world due to their curse of never having a homeland, was far too set in his ways to bother or worry about changing now.

Artiss forgave him his trespass and offered a curt bow. "Master Boen, I see you are enjoying what my cooks have prepared."

"Indeed. No finer a feast have I had since joining this damned fool crusade!" he said as he laughed and drained his mug. "Almost makes me forget what's to come. Almost."

"I'm afraid there is only so much I can do to alleviate your apprehensions of the future," Artiss replied smoothly, choosing to ignore the lack of manners. "How did everyone sleep?"

Bahr, once known across the northern part of the world as the Sea Wolf, ran a hand through his now silvered hair. Heavy bags darkened his face beneath his eyes, accompanying the fresh set of wrinkles he'd accumulated since the quest began. "Sleep has not been our ally in a long time, Artiss."

"Understandably so. It's not everyone's place in life to be asked to rescue the world from certain doom."

Bahr rubbed his chin and gave the Dae'shan a rueful glance. "You have a way with words."

"An unfortunate side effect of living in near seclusion for so long. I find that I've lost the subtle art of conversation. Perhaps, once this ordeal is finished, I'll be able to return to a normal life and open the doors of Trennaron to those wise enough to care for the knowledge." Sadness echoed in his words. The awful truth he wanted to conceal casually bled through his demeanor.

Bahr paused, making a mental note of Artiss's unspoken regrets before replying, "No worries, Artiss. We are in your debt for your hospitality." He left a natural pause at the end of the statement.

Artiss picked up on it immediately. "But you are more than ready to be about your business?"

"I'm afraid so," the wizard, Anienam Keiss added. Responsible for the majority of those assembled being included in the quest and the sole descendant of the order of Mages, his father had bestowed the knowledge of the dark gods' return on him at a young age. He was forced to live more than a hundred years with the burden of leading a handful of people into the worst possible situation conceivable. Their lives rested in his hands and he wasn't wholly convinced he was going to be able to keep them all alive. As it stood, one had been captured and another murdered on the journey to Trennaron. How many more would fall before they reached the end? "You of all people recognize the need for haste. We must get the Blud Hamr to Arlevon Gale before time expires on us."

"Long have I awaited this moment, Anienam Keiss. It has been so long I was beginning to think it would never come. I cannot say the way ahead will be easy, but whatever trials you undergo will be dwarfed by the rewards of a mission successfully accomplished." The Dae'shan glided across the bronze, marble floor to where the group sat. "You have all already proven your worth. Very few in all my years could have done what you have, and in the face of such adversity. I congratulate you all and wish you the best of luck on the final stage of your quest. The fate of all Malweir rests in your hands."

The Dae'shan struggled to think of what else he could say to alleviate the harshness of their final stage. Many of them would not make it out alive. It was a sad truth he'd known since the breaking of the Dae'shan. Victory demanded prices higher than many of those assembled knew they were going to have to pay. Righteousness was demanding and cruel. He snorted mildly. *No wonder so many found it easier to turn to darkness and let their emotions control their deeds. How many good souls have been corrupted simply because they lacked the conviction to preserve in difficult situations?*

Bahr held out his hands. "Little else needs to be said, Artiss. None of us, save the wizard here, have any inkling of what comes next but that hasn't stopped us from pushing forward. I think it's safe to assume that we are all dedicated to seeing this matter through to the end, whatever that may be. All I can personally ask is for you not to coat what we're about to face. We're all proven warriors, for the most part, and have been through too many exploits for our own good. I'd personally like to retire from this life."

His eyes darkened as they remembered the flames from his burning estate and those from his beloved ship, the *Dragon's Bane*. Harnin One Eye stole them both in the span of a single night. All he'd accumulated in nearly six decades of life wiped out at the whim of a man bitter with personal hatreds for a perceived wrong even he didn't understand. Bahr slowly began to regret the decision of placing his brother on the throne. Perhaps he should have taken the crown instead of wandering off to make his name in the wider world.

Then again, if he had, where would he be right now? Delranan was locked in a bitter civil war while his brother, the rightful king, busily destroyed neighboring Rogscroft. People in both kingdoms died by the scores with nothing to show for it. The entire north seemed to be collapsing in on itself while the rest of the world watched with bated breath, secretly hoping the conflagration wouldn't spread to yet more kingdoms while they declined requests for aid. Bahr quickly began to lose faith in humanity.

Artiss visibly relaxed. "Thank you for that, Bahr. I've imagined this conversation a thousand times if once. Each time it plays out differently in my mind, for I had no way of knowing the caliber of the individuals gathered to defend Malweir. You have far surpassed any expectations I once held. You are all truly champions of what the gods of light represent."

Only Rekka Jel remained untouched by Artiss's speech. Outcast from her native village of Teng for the supposed reason behind her former suitor's death, she struggled to find her new place in life. Always there had been the promise of returning home once her time served at Trennaron was completed. That way was now closed to her. Much had changed over winter's course. She'd found love in the sell sword Dorl Theed, who now sat beside her, oblivious to her internal deliberations. Unwanted complications seemed to plague her, making it exceedingly difficult to concentrate on her true purpose: find Bahr, escort him to Trennaron to retrieve the Blud Hamr, the only weapon capable of stopping the dark gods, and get him back to Arlevon Gale in time. Nothing else mattered. Life and death were relative terms she forced aside for the greater good of all life on Malweir.

Her eyes casually shifted over to Dorl and her heart warmed. Just being in his presence had a calming effect on the warrior woman. Years of servitude to Artiss Gran robbed her of the emotional stability normal people had. She became more of a machine, focused on protecting Malweir rather than developing as a person. The self-neglect threatened to prove detrimental to the others, unless she managed to fully understand what it meant to be human again.

Artiss slowly panned his gaze across the motley assortment of characters in the dining hall. A Dwarf from Drimmen Delf, Giant from long forgotten Venheim, a Gaimosian, a boy who had yet to realize his full potential, and a handful of false heroes from Delranan. Never in his dreams could he have imagined bringing them all together with common purpose. Despite his musings he knew there were no finer candidates for the appointed task.

"I will leave you to your meal. My instincts tell me it will be your last peaceful one in a long time," Artiss announced quietly. "Rekka, if you would escort them into the main courtyard when you are ready to proceed?"

"Yes, Master," Rekka replied curtly and watched with flint-hard eyes as the Dae'shan floated out of the hall.

Boen burped again. "Sure does like to make a show of things, doesn't he?"

Ironfoot the Dwarf wiped his mouth on the back of a sleeve. "People like that are well beyond my reckoning. Life is simpler without mystic ranting. Give me an axe and point me at the enemy."

Boen nodded his agreement. He and the Dwarf were kindred spirits. Gaimosians had roamed Malweir for centuries after the destruction of their kingdom. Deemed too powerful, a concentrated effort by a host of kingdoms tried to wipe their race from existence. It failed, despite Gaimos being destroyed, and the survivors spread across Malweir. They claimed the title of Vengeance Knights and slipped through the cracks as mercenaries. He'd lived a warrior's life, never stopping to settle down and have a family. His life was one of perpetual frustration of his own choosing. Boen was far from complicated. He went where the work was and lived with no regrets. Joining the quest to save Malweir from the dark gods had been on a whim but, after careful retrospect, he couldn't think of any place else he'd rather be.

The Dwarf captain's predicament came about through vastly different means. He was responsible for capturing Bahr and the others in the foothills outside of Drimmen Delf. Once Anienam Keiss made himself known to King Thord, Ironfoot was placed as an escort. Together they assaulted the enemy dark Dwarf lines and ended the siege of Drimmen Delf. Thord promised Ironfoot in tribute to Bahr's contributions in the battle of Bode Hill. He'd proven an invaluable asset to the overall mission thus far. Next to Bahr, he had the most combat experience in the group.

Anienam ignored their conversation and turned to Bahr. Their relationship was fragile at best and he needed to smooth over the creases before they returned to Delranan. Otherwise…. "Bahr, might I have a word with you in private?"

Suddenly wary, the Sea Wolf debated staying with the others. He had no secrets, at least not since it was discovered that Maleela was his niece and he was the true heir to Delranan's throne. That great weight slipped from around his neck, leaving him more content than he'd been in a very long time. He exhaled a sharp breath before nodding once.

They walked into the near cavernous hallway out of earshot and Bahr folded his arms across his chest. His dark green shirt crinkled under the pressure. His eyes were tired but strong. They searched the wizard's face for any clues as to what this impromptu meeting was about.

Anienam didn't wait. "You and I don't care for one another. I recognize this and accept it for what it is. We are both so set in our ways nothing will change. That being said I want to ensure the air between us is clear before we head back to Delranan. Too much is at stake for petty differences to get in the way."

"I agree, but don't see why you bring this up now," Bahr countered. They already expressed their grievances en route to Trennaron. Bahr, grieving the loss of his niece, was ready to cut his losses and run. His animosity shifted onto Anienam for reasons even he wasn't sure of. Yet the wizard's words were wise. The time for disagreements was past. The war was coming, barreling at them at full speed while the world burned around them. Anienam was the last in the distinguished line of Mages. Bahr needed his magic to get home and survive the long darkness.

Anienam rubbed his palms together. "In order to fully understand you must realize what is about to happen."

"I already know. We fail and the world is destroyed."

Anienam shook his head. "It goes far beyond that, Bahr. The dark gods are the very definition of evil. They will stop at nothing to get revenge on the ones responsible for imprisoning them so long ago. Bahr, *every* race played a part in that banishment. Should the Dae'shan succeed in opening the nexus between dimensions, all life on Malweir will wither and die under the torments of the dark gods. No one will be safe. Every life will suffer endlessly until their hearts expire and death mercifully claims them. If we fail, our suffering will be the greatest. Even Artiss Gran does not know the full extent of the horrors that will be visited."

"You once said all the nexuses were destroyed," Bahr countered.

"So I had thought, but my time here and during our journey south has led me to believe otherwise. Arlevon Gale is the final nexus. The one most scholars thought was destroyed centuries ago during a minor border war."

He paused as old memories rushed back, redirecting his train of thought. "My…father once glimpsed the dark gods. He led a group of heroes similar to ours to destroy the Silver Mage one thousand years ago. He was never the same again. Nightmares plagued him unto his death bed. It was sad affair. I don't want to go through this. I don't want any of us going through this. The only way to prevent it is by the two of us presenting a unified front and leading the others."

Bahr remained silent, casually contemplating his options. He doubted he'd ever care for the enigmatic wizard but knew he was going to need his magic before the end. A small part of him wanted to punch Anienam in the jaw and call it even but violence wasn't going to solve much, not at this stage. Reluctantly he agreed with what the wizard had said. They'd nearly come apart after the battle with the Gnaals, leaving them weak and ready to fall. The lament over finding Ionascu's murdered corpse and traces of Maleela being captured left a gaping hole inside. A hole he needed filled. Ionascu was one of Harnin's men, a twisted, bitter wreck of a man who deserved his fate. The only question was why his niece killed him.

Bahr responded quickly before his thoughts got sidetracked. "Very well. For the sake of the others I'll set aside any animosity towards you. You have my full support and cooperation until we end this."

"Thank you. You have mine as well," the wizard replied.

Bahr unfolded his arms. "Anienam, know this. Once we've stopped the dark gods, I don't ever want to see you again."

The wizard grinned and returned to the remnants of his breakfast.

THREE

The Chamber

Bags packed and a new wagon presented to haul their supplies and weapons, the small band of heroes assembled in the courtyard. Sunlight beamed down, warming their flesh in a way they wouldn't see again for months once they returned to the frozen north. Unexpected tension encompassed the group. Conversation faded to the bare minimum. Hands absently toyed with sword hilts or loose buttons on clothing. More than one of the group stared off into nothing as thoughts began centering on the fight of their lives.

They'd spent months on the road. First to rescue Princess Maleela from her captors in Rogscroft--a lie that was later discovered--and then on the journey to the far southern Jungles of Brodein to find the mythical Trennaron. Constant battles with impossible creatures, river men, and Harnin One Eye left them depleted on many levels. They were already at the ends of their physical limits, mentally worn down to the point where poor decisions might lead to accidents.

The few days spent in Trennaron did much to heal and replenish their strength but Bahr questioned if it was enough. A man could only endure so much before he broke. The Sea Wolf looked to each of his companions, people he'd known for only a few short months in most cases. He tried remembering a time before they'd met but his mind was consumed with the quest. Imagining life without any of them in it was difficult. He'd come to rely on their skills, judgments, and friendship, much like the crew of the *Dragon's Bane*.

He watched Boen slide his leather armor down over his barrel chest, stretching and wiggling to adjust it just right. Despite his penchant for absolute mayhem on the battlefield, the Gaimosian nearly always laughed and joked. At least he did now that Ironfoot was along. Bahr shook his head ruefully. Like minds and all that, he supposed. The big man was Bahr's best asset and longest friend. They'd shared journeys before, though none so dangerous as right now. He couldn't help but think how empty he'd feel if Boen got killed. Friends were hard for a man like Bahr to come by. Losing them was a sad fact of his lifestyle and only got harder as the years went by.

"Look at the old man," Dorl whispered out of the corner of his mouth.

Nothol Coll rolled his neck slowly and said, "He's just nervous. I don't blame him."

The younger sell sword was taller and stronger than Dorl but was the perfect complement to Dorl's worrisome nature. Lighthearted with dark hair and eyes, Nothol wandered through life trying to be a good man and make the best out of bad situations. He didn't bother looking to Bahr. There were enough conflicting emotions rumbling in his own mind to worry about someone else.

Dorl frowned tightly. "You should start thinking about more than yourself."

"Why? I have a hard enough time dealing with my own problems," Nothol answered tartly. It was an old argument.

"You might just live longer," Dorl accused with a pointed finger. "*I* might just live longer because of it."

"Now who's being selfish?" Nothol said and laughed. "Relax, Dorl. It's either going to work out or it's not. There's no point worrying over what we can't control."

The thought of being magically transported hundreds of leagues back to the kingdom where this affair began in the span of a few heartbeats left turmoil gnawing away at his stomach. He didn't trust Anienam as far as he could spit but was not confronted with having to rely on powers beyond his comprehension. Questions bothered him the longer he thought on it. He tried, failing miserably, to think of the power capable of moving a person across so much distance.

Even Anienam couldn't provide an answer; he merely mumbled confusing thoughts on space and time interchanging. Dorl had stopped listening early.

"You can't expect me to believe you're comfortable with what we're about to do," Dorl demanded as his anger level began to rise. After years of working together, Nothol knew exactly how to push his buttons.

Nothol shrugged lightly as he ensured his sword came out of the scabbard easily. "Dorl, you should relax. This is a once in a lifetime opportunity. Don't you want to be able to tell your children about what you did to save the world?"

"Somehow I doubt I'm going to live long enough to have kids," he replied flatly. "Nothol, we're all going to die."

Rekka finished strapping her pack down on her horse and glanced up sharply. The possibility of certain death wasn't new. Death was merely an unfortunate side effect she was prepared to deal with.

The sell sword paused. His mouth opened and closed as his mind cycled through the possible futures. There was never any real choice, not for a man like Nothol. He worked for the highest bidder and, in this instance, men he knew he could rely on. Bahr wasn't perfect, but he was good enough for Nothol.

"We've been hounded by Lord Death from the beginning," he said carefully. "How many times should we already have been killed? You've seen the darkness growing in Delranan and other parts of Malweir. Dorl, we have a chance to stop it. To end it all so our children won't have to endure the same trials." He held his hand up to keep Dorl silent. "I'm not trying to sound like a hero. You know me. But I think after all we've been through we owe it ourselves to see this thing through."

Dorl Theed had no comeback. No witty banter to lighten the situation. As much as he wanted to deny his friend, refute his claims, he couldn't. Deep inside he took pride in knowing his actions were going to matter. To make a difference for generations to come. How could anyone in their right mind argue against that sort of logic?

From atop the wagon bed Skuld listened to their exchange with rapt interest. Almost at the end of his teens, he was the least experienced one of the group. Childish dreams of grandeur made him stow away aboard the *Dragon's Bane* when Bahr sailed off to rescue Maleela. He'd come so far, seen so much that that youth was gone, replaced by a young, confused man burdened with more responsibility than he ever wanted.

He'd come to envy Dorl and Nothol's friendship. Growing up on the harsh streets of Chadra left him with little friends. The cutthroat world he endured for years made him hard, calloused in ways the others weren't. The one thing he ever wanted was a true friend. He hoped to find that before the end of this journey. Perhaps then he'd become a man. Skuld climbed off the wagon to inspect the wheels and undercarriage.

Ironfoot slapped Skuld on the shoulder and grumbled, "They bicker like an old married couple."

The youth didn't have any witty reply so he meekly nodded. His lifestyle hadn't allowed for family, brothers or sisters, leaving him with no frame of reference. Ironfoot noticed his awkwardness and walked off chuckling. Skuld watched the Dwarf, still unable to read him any better than he was Boen or Groge, the Giant.

Each step thundered across the courtyard as Groge, Blud Hamr strapped securely to his back, ambled over to stand beside Bahr. He wasn't a warrior and had no aspirations to become one. Violence was anathema to his clan. They secluded themselves away from the rest of the world, claiming the mountaintops to establish Venheim, the forge of the gods. Each day they labored to create the perfect tools. Legend said Giants had forged the Blud Hamr in response to the coming war between the gods of light and their dark brethren. Perhaps forge master Joden knew the truth of this, but at his advanced age it was near impossible for him to recall.

Surrounded by others who had no qualms with taking lives, Groge struggled to find his way in almost the same manner as Skuld. While he stood nearly seven feet taller than the boy, and was roughly a hundred years older, he found himself liking Skuld greatly. They'd spent countless hours discussing the small matters that revolved around youth of every race.

"Ah Groge, feel any different?" Bahr asked with a bright smile.

The Giant cocked his head as he tried to decipher Bahr's meaning. "I slept well last night, Captain."

Boen broke out with laughter. "He's talking about the hammer, lad. Does the hammer make you feel different?"

Cheeks reddening, Groge said, "No. It's heavy but I haven't felt any of the magic transferring into my body."

"Nor should you," Anienam added. "From what I've been able to discover, the hammer's magic won't become activated until it is near the Olagath Stone. You should be fine until then."

"What happens then?" Bahr asked.

Anienam didn't offer an answer.

Artiss Gran arrived in his fashion, silent and drifting a few inches off of the ground. He listened patiently as they dithered over minor, unchangeable details before making his presence known with a gentle cough. Not all the subtle nuances of mortal interaction had been lost to him. "The time has at last arrived, my friends. Captain Bahr, is your team prepared?"

"They are," Bahr answered without looking back.

Artiss nodded, the gesture almost faint beneath the gossamer hood. "Good. It is time to go into the chamber. I ask you all not to touch anything. The way is guarded by powers left behind when the gods of light departed Malweir. They will destroy you instantly. Follow me and all will be well."

Nothol gave Dorl a playful shove. "See, how bad can it be?"

Ignoring the barb, Dorl shifted the weight of armor and watched as Artiss Gran spread his long arms. Raw power danced between his fingertips, violent shades of green in stark contrast to the gentle smoothness of the alabaster walls. The ground trembled as a crack opened. Thin at first, it widened to reveal a wide slope going down. Dust began to settle. Rocks stopped rolling. Artiss slowly lowered his arms and bowed his head. "Follow me, please."

The Dae'shan effortlessly began to glide down. A rainbow of lights reflected sunlight back up to the surface, temporarily blinding the others. The passage down widened enough to allow both horses and wagon and deepened enough for Groge to walk comfortably. Bahr followed without hesitation. Better to get it over with. Delaying survived no purpose.

"Great, we're going back down," Dorl complained just loud enough to make Nothol laugh in reply.

Going down didn't prove as difficult as any of them imagined. Soon enough they stood on level ground scarcely one hundred meters below ground. Artiss strode to the center of the circular chamber and produced a thick rod of oak and steel the height of a man. Gesturing for the group to gather in front of him, he slammed the staff one time. Ringing echoes danced throughout the chamber as it came to life in seas of colors. Bahr looked around and noticed the entire chamber was made of glass. The effect was dizzying.

"What is done cannot be undone," Artiss said, his voice baritone, authoritative. "Once the light is summoned you will be taken across space and time to the kingdom of Delranan. Stay within the light until it fades completely or you will be lost, trapped in a dimension akin to the prison of the dark gods. Do you understand?"

Half nodded while the rest mumbled a quiet yes.

It was enough for Artiss Gran. He slammed the staff once again and brilliant white light bathed the chamber. Bahr and the others were forced to shield their eyes lest they were blinded. One by one they faded from reality. The journey back to Delranan had finally begun. Artiss stood alone in the cold chamber once the light faded. Exhausted, he leaned against the staff for support. Much of his strength bled away from the raw power the chamber demanded. He'd done all he could, for Bahr and for Malweir. The rest now lay in the hands of the eight individuals en route to the frozen north.

FOUR

The Army Moves West

The column of horses wound nearly a full league back to the east, to the city of Rogscroft. Bundled under thick cloaks from wolves and bears, the riders shivered under the cold steel of their body armor. Sharpened spears jutted from their sleeves attached to each saddle. Swords clanged and jangled with each bouncing step. Banners waved in the light breeze. What had been a sight reviled--the bloodstained wolf head on snow-colored background--was now celebrated in the small towns and hamlets as the Wolfsreik marched west towards the Murdes Mountains.

Just a few short months ago they'd come fighting and killing their way across Rogscroft to lay siege to the capital before conquering the kingdom. King Badron executed King Stelskor and claimed the kingdom in the name of Delranan. The victory, which should have gone down in history as one of the Wolfsreik's proudest moments, became tainted by the un-expected involvement of an army of Goblins. The Wolfsreik's commanding general, Rolnir, suspected foul coercions between his king and the Goblin commander. Worse, dark influences altered Badron, subtly at first but progressed to the point of brazen dementia. Rolnir did the only thing he could to keep his army intact. He rebelled.

Virtually all his army, those still combat effective to carry on, sided with him. Only a handful of units that were closest to Badron refused. Rolnir had nearly seven thousand soldiers ready to throw into the field. Another fifteen hundred were wounded, most not severe enough to stay out of the war. The rest were either dead or on their death beds. Seven tenths of his army remained intact and, combined with the survivors of Rogscroft and the mountain tribes of the Pell Darga, he found himself in command of nearly fifteen thousand soldiers. There was no greater military force in the north.

Commander Piper Joach looked back at the snake his command had transformed into with a mixed grin and grimace. Compared to what lie ahead, they'd already accomplished the easy part. Rogscroft had been secured from Badron's insanity and was already being rebuilt. Rolnir commanded the allied armies as they drove what remained of the enemy out. Most of the Goblin force was dead, ambushed by the Wolfsreik at the turn of the tide. All that remained was to drive them back into the Murdes Mountains and let the Pell deal with them.

Only that wasn't enough. The mountain passes were buried under feet of snow and all but impassable. Goblins and traitor soldiers alike would flounder and be caught or killed by Cuul Ol's odd fighters. They had orders to offer any captured Wolfsreik soldier the opportunity to return to the army, but Piper had a feeling none would make it that far. He'd seen the Pell Darga in action, fought against them personally, and the thought of them sent chills down his spine.

Far from handsome, Piper fit the role of second in command perfectly. He'd been the first to engage the Rogscroft defenders and, while he considered the battle a stinging defeat, opened the way for the main body of the army to invade. He bore scars from a dozen wounds, marring his stern facial features. Proud eyes watched all keenly beneath thin, brown eyebrows. Lightly muscled, he wore his armor like a second skin.

He was the perfect soldier. Everyone in the allied army knew his name and his exploits. He demurely shrugged aside any accolades while remaining focused on the mission. A mission he wasn't sure of the purpose any longer. The invasion of Rogscroft had been simple. Badron responded to the murder of his only son and attacked after following the evidence. Only when the Goblins became involved did Piper's notion of justice begin to muddle. Right and wrong mixed without jurisdiction. In the end he was forced to follow his commander, and his heart.

Cold winds blasted down from the north, driving under his cloak to the millimeters of space separating armor and clothes. Piper spent his entire life enduring the harsh conditions of Delranan. The north was no place for weakness. Men and women alike learned to grow hard from an early age. Punishing winters were offset by humid, blistering summers. The only respite came from fleeing south. The men of the north were among the toughest in all Malweir. That didn't mean Piper enjoyed freezing in the elements when he might have been sitting in front of a roaring fire with a mug of his favorite ale.

Dreams of that moment kept him going. A professional soldier, he forced aside his simple dreams of warmth to lead his men back to their homeland. He'd never be able to rest until they reclaimed Delranan from Badron and Harnin. Peace came with a price too few understood or were willing to pay. He'd already buried more friends than he ever wanted and was burdened with the knowledge that yet more would go to the ground before the campaign ended. Cut off from Delranan, neither he nor Rolnir knew what to expect upon their return. All reports suggested Harnin had systematically transformed Delranan into a living nightmare.

"Winter seems to be taking her sweet time moving on this year," General Vajna commented upon noticing the look of consternation pinching Piper's face. The Rogscroft man grimaced as another blast of wind slashed through.

Suppressing a shiver, Piper nodded. "It grows most tedious."

While neither considered the other a friend, both men had grown to respect the other. Once enemies, Piper and Vajna had tried their best to kill the other before Rolnir defected and changed the scheme of the war. Now they shared command of the massive vanguard as it slowly ground through mounds of heavy snow into the foothills of the Murdes Mountains.

"I hope the passes aren't too congested," Vajna continued. "Spending time in the mountains isn't my idea of fun. Nor the men's, I suspect."

Piper thought back to the beginning of the campaign when he'd led the Wolfsreik over the Murdes Mountains and down into Rogscroft and replied, "We were more concerned about the Pell than snow."

Nodding, Vajna said, "We've had more than our share of ill dealings with them in the past. Nasty fighters but good to have on your side. I'm glad Aurec managed to gain their trust over these last few years."

Otherwise they'd never be able to cross the mountains intact. The Pell Darga had been driven from their homes in the east long ago and settled in the heart of the mountain range separating Rogscroft and Delranan. Fiercely independent, they ignored the laws of most lowland kingdoms in favor of their own brand of justice. They'd spent generations fighting with the peoples of both kingdoms, earning a fierce reputation. Fact turned to fear and fear into legend. Eventually the Pell Darga became the creatures mothers warned their children of. Until Aurec made peace with their chieftain, Cuul Ol, no one had any reason to believe otherwise.

"They are among the fiercest warriors I've ever encountered," Piper added respectfully. He found it odd how allegiances shifted so casually. What had once been improbable only a few short months ago was now taken for granted. The war proceeded with unprecedented twists, making it difficult to follow, even for a seasoned veteran like Piper. In the end it came down to one simple conclusion: his sole purpose was to keep as many of his soldiers alive as possible until the end of the war. Nothing else mattered.

"We're less than a day away from the base of the mountains," Vajna explained, shifting the focus of the conversation before it devolved into past hatreds and rivalries. "The sun's going down. I suggest finding a bivouac site. There's no sense in trying to scout out the mountains in the night. Nor letting the men freeze while they wait."

Piper agreed. He couldn't wait to warm his frozen toes, even if for only a little while. "I'll lead a scouting patrol out and do the rounds. Badron may have already taken ship back to Delranan but there is still a strong Goblin force somewhere between us and the mountains." His gaze fell upon the distant mountain range. "Set up camp at the first suitable place and get the fires going. I don't want to lose anyone to the cold. This damned war's already taken enough from all us."

"Stay safe."

"As much as I can be," he replied.

Piper wouldn't feel safe until the Goblins were found and eradicated. Their filth was a blight on the world, one threatening to spread if Badron was suddenly in league with them. Technically subordinate by rank, both Piper and Vajna agreed that it would be best if he remained in command of the Wolfsreik regulars until the war's conclusion. Vajna had no qualms with that. He doubted his own men would find it easy to take orders from a man from another kingdom, much less one who'd been an enemy only months before.

The alliance was still extremely fragile. Petty fights and arguments broke out daily, resulting in several trips to the field hospitals, prisons, and more than one body being buried. Those guilty were punished according to their infractions, regardless of which army they had once served. Rolnir and King Aurec understood that the only way to forge a strong alliance was by enacting a singular set of rules for everyone. Balance must be maintained to facilitate the full assimilation of three different cultures. Failure here meant failure at the end.

The one hundred men in the scout company divided into two equal groups. Piper led the one that rode north while the other hurried south. They'd cross paths halfway around and meet back up at the starting point in a few hours, hopefully before the sun dipped over the distant horizon.

Daylight temperatures were tolerable, if just, but the combination of darkness and wind chill drove the cold deeper past freezing. Piper didn't relish the idea of moving through unfamiliar terrain while worrying about freezing a finger off.

Still, he had no other choice but to move slower than normal. Uneven snows left the terrain hazardous. They'd already lost several horses on the push west, each one further constricting their combat capabilities. He knew it was just the beginning. The soldiers, all of them, were tired. They'd been fighting for months. Mistakes stemmed from exhaustion. Mistakes got people killed. More soldiers died from accidents and diseases than enemy contact. Until the day came when that was no longer true, Piper was forced to make the difficult choices.

Soon the sounds of axes and hammers ringing across the snow-covered fields faded. The scouts had gone far enough away from Vajna's camp that they felt totally alone. Already shadows crawled across the world as the sun began to drop. Piper shivered as the temperature plunged more cruelly than any dagger ever could. His face was red, raw in places. His lips burned. His eyes were sore, tired, and on fire. Thoughts of going home didn't help, leaving him truly miserable for the first time in many years. He made a note to give Rolnir a piece of his mind when the main body joined back up with the vanguard.

"Rider coming in, sir!" the burly sergeant with flowing crimson hair announced and pointed.

Piper followed the direction and his heart leapt at seeing how fast the rider was approaching. Snow kicked up with each thundering step. Speed meant trouble. His horse pranced with nervous anticipation, causing Piper to pat its neck reassuringly. "I feel it too. We might be heading into a fight."

The sergeant shot him an interested look, his mind racing over pre-combat procedures in the event of a fight.

Too anxious for his own good, Piper gestured his sergeant to follow and rode forward to meet the flustered scout. The rider reined to a halt and tried to catch his breath.

"What's the word?" Piper asked.

"Commander, we ran into a small column of Goblins marching this way. Must be a few hundred of the bastards. Looked like they were dragging fresh kills. We saw smoke coming from the direction they're marching out of."

Piper frowned. The Goblins were still strong enough to be raiding villages successfully. He glanced back at his fifty men. They were light cavalry, not meant for heavy charges. Piper's force was specifically designed to engage the enemy fleetingly and keep them distracted until the heavy infantry arrived. They were never meant to fight a pitched battle against large numbers of infantry. Pikes and horses didn't mix well.

"How well armed are they?" he asked, the words coming out rushed.

The scout used a sleeve to wipe the sweat dripping down his face. "Enough to give us trouble. They got pikes and spears. Bevin saw a few axes, too. All of 'em carried swords and were heading this way.

"We have enough to keep them busy, but not destroy them, Commander," the sergeant offered thoughtfully.

Piper struggled with the urge to strike something. "We don't have a choice. A force that size can cause mayhem across the countryside. If what this man says is true they're fresh off of a kill. We have a chance to strike now and catch them with their guard down."

"We're going to need help."

"Dispatch three men back to General Vajna. He's to bring five hundred men as quickly as possible," Piper ordered.

An eyebrow rose. "You mean to attack them at night?"

"Is there a choice?" Piper didn't want to. Night attacks were hazardous for all parties. Goblins were creatures that lived without the sun. Darkness was their element. Fighting a numerically superior force at night and on unfamiliar ground was tantamount to suicide. A thought sprang to life, quickly growing from spark to flame. "Have the rest of the men gather as much kindling and torchwood as possible in the next few minutes. We'll have a nasty surprise waiting for those Goblin scum when they arrive."

Rolnir came upon the battlefield shortly after dawn, having ridden through the night to reach the vanguard. A regiment of heavy infantrymen panted behind him. They'd come expecting to dig their scouts out of a mess but were almost stopped in their tracks when the sun showed the full extent of the fight. Bodies littered the area for hundreds of meters. Most were the dark, grey bodies of Goblins but more than enough were Wolfsreik. Rolnir lamented the losses but saw them as manageable enough to call it a victory. Piper and Vajna were standing in the center of the field pouring over maps and captured documents.

Haggard, much as he normally looked these days, Piper looked up to his friend and commanding officer with exhaustion in his eyes. He was tired of fighting and it was beginning to show. Every soldier endured their own private struggle with how far they could go before the breaking point crept upon them and dragged them down. Piper was almost there. He threw up a hasty salute and waited while the red-haired general slid to the ground.

"Piper, Vajna. I wasn't expecting you to engage without heavy support," he said, keenly eyeing the battlefield. Delighted as he was to see so many Goblin bodies, he subconsciously counted his own losses.

Piper barely mustered a shrug. "They left us little choice."

"What happened?"

Watching from the side, Vajna saw Piper's reluctance to answer and decided to jump in. "The outriders spotted a small raiding party heading towards us. We only had a short amount of time to react. Commander Joach dispatched riders back to warn the main body while we prepared an ambush. The men strung wire across all likely avenues of approach and set traps. They weren't much but I've seen more than a few killed by them. We had a limited number of archers but used them to harry the Goblins into the areas where we'd be most effective."

Rolnir listened intently though his mind never strayed from the deep streaks of black circling the immediate area. "And these? What are they from?"

Vajna broke a grin. "Fire. We had collected a lot of scrub brush and fallen trees. Once the Goblins walked into the trap we set the whole damned area on fire. They panicked enough for us to hammer them from three sides. And a good thing too. If it hadn't been for that distraction we wouldn't have won."

Nodding his approval for Piper's innovative thinking, he asked, "Why did you engage? Light cavalry against heavy infantry isn't the ideal situation."

"We didn't have a choice," Vajna said flatly. "They moved faster than anticipated and very nearly caught us off guard. Most were drunk from their previous raid on a village not far from here. Runner came back and reported everyone there was murdered. The houses burned." His eyes blazed fiercely as he took in the nearest corpse. "These bastards got what was coming to them."

Rolnir had heard enough. "Gentlemen, very good work. That's two hundred less Goblins we need to worry about. Have your vanguard form up and return to the main body. I'll have another unit dispatched to cover the advance to the mountains. You did good today. All you. Get some hot chow and refit. The campaign is just beginning and I'm going to need you if we've any hope of succeeding."

Piper took offense at being relieved; memories of his first engagement in Rogscroft started replaying in his head. "General, we can continue the march. Give me an hour to bury the dead and collect their gear."

Rolnir's eyebrow rose sharply. He seriously doubted his second in command was in as good of shape as he insisted, but he didn't have any reason to pull him from the line. *Not until he makes a mistake and gets someone killed. Damnation, but being a commanding officer is hard. Retirement doesn't sound so bad right about now.* "Very well. I want your unit refitted by the time my infantry cleans up the battlefield. Piper, that's an order. I don't want to hear it."

"Yes sir," he replied meekly and went back to his soldiers.

Rolnir returned Vajna's salute and watched his best friend stumble back through the carnage, all the while thinking he was going to have to find a way to rest Piper before the end. Some lives were too valuable to waste in the preliminary campaign engagements.

FIVE

Delranan Burning

"Ever you have sought to be more than your ancestors allowed. Countless decades of servitude to others have left you bereft of dignity. What it means to truly be your own man. Did you find it difficult to carry on day after day as the world progressed while you stagnated?"

Harnin One Eye glared sharply at the coalescing shadows dancing across from him. He despised being mocked by anyone, much less one of the mysterious Dae'shan. Two facts prevented him from acting on those raw emotions. The dark creature, Pelthit Re, was infinitely more powerful than any mortal and he had facilitated Harnin's rise to power. If it hadn't been for Pelthit, Harnin might never have had the nerve to make a grab for the throne. Badron should have insisted he accompanied the army on campaign. Harnin snarled. *Look where that arrogance took you! Delranan is now mine.*

"I feel your hatred, One Eye. It consumes you in glorious pain, slowly devouring each piece of your conscience. Give in and become more than yourself," Pelthit cooed. It was an old game he enjoyed playing with his victims. Righteous men fell so quickly and easily. The Dae'shan preyed upon their strengths, casually turning them against themselves until only a bitter husk remained.

"You've given me enough of your gifts, demon," Harnin snapped. "I rule this kingdom and no longer need you."

Pelthit concealed his amusement. If only Harnin knew he could snap him with a thought, he wouldn't be so smug. "Do you? The rebellion you have failed to quash has found new life in the countryside. How many units have you lost over the past month? A dozen? More? This Ingrid has proven more than capable of stymieing your grand intellect.

Towns and villages are steadily abandoning your rule, choosing to become independent rather than live under your brand of tyranny."

"The rebellion is my problem to deal with, though I suspect you had a hand to play in their resurgence," he accused sharply. "I can take care of Ingrid's rebellion."

"Perhaps but there's the matter of King Badron's return you forget." He'd used the royal title purposefully, hoping to inspire Harnin to new levels of hatred and depravity.

"Badron's a non-factor. He's bogged down in Rogscroft and won't be able to return until after the spring rains melt the snow in the passes. I have time to deal with him," Harnin said, waving the concern off.

"Less time than you imagine, One Eye," Pelthit taunted. The air between them grew chill.

Harnin's face tightened, the mass of scar tissue twisting like a handful of earthworms pulled from the dirt. "What do you mean?"

"The Wolfsreik has abandoned him. Even now he is heading back to Delranan to reclaim *his* throne."

Harnin slammed his palm on the hard, wooden table. "The throne is *mine*! With no army he has no hope of stealing it back."

Shadows swirled, solidifying long enough for Harnin to make out the Dae'shan's harrowing face. Ice-cold eyes glared through the darkness. "That is where you're wrong, One Eye. I said the Wolfsreik betrayed him. He still has an army of Goblins at his side and another impossibly large army en route. You cannot win."

Goblins! In Delranan. They hadn't been seen this far west in countless generations. Harnin felt cold dread dance across his flesh. Fighting men was one matter, a nation of Goblins entirely another. His mind began calculating how best to approach this new dilemma while cursing Pelthit Re and his brethren for bringing his kingdom down to this point.

Despair threatened to consume him, robbing him of any sense of security he had been feeling.

He still clung to hope, if barely. Badron was weeks away, if not longer, giving him plenty of opportunity to finish constructing the defenses in the east while hunting down the rebellion in one final gesture. Harnin believed killing Ingrid would effectively end any resistance to his rule. Jarrik and Inaella were already in the field, wasting manpower as far as he was concerned. Their combined incompetence jeopardized all he'd struggled to build over the winter. The old Delranan was dead, burning away as the new order slowly crept into every corner of society. Harnin One Eye, the architect of this new madness, laughed gleefully as his world transformed.

Only now he felt it all spiraling away. His enemies were compounding while his own forces, meager by comparison, bogged down in a nasty, guerilla-style war. He needed to make a move now before the clock expired.

"I can win. All I need to do is eliminate Ingrid and her command staff and focus the bulk of my army along the line of redoubts I've ordered built in the east. Trapped between those forts and the mountains, Badron will grind his army down to the point I can attack." His twinkle had returned to his eyes as Harnin envisioned taking Badron's head in front of what remained of his army. The event would go down as one of the most renowned in Delranan's history.

Pelthit folded his arms across his transparent chest. The outcome was never truly in doubt. He played Harnin like an instrument while allowing the delusional man to think he was accomplishing some grandly designed purpose. It was an old game the Dae'shan played with mortals. Each generation had its share of degenerates more than willing to give in to depravity for their own selfish needs. Harnin had languished in Badron's shadows for years before garnering Pelthit's attention. His downfall was systematic and eventual. How he arrived to the dismal end was a matter of the Dae'shan's discretion.

"That is…plausible, but what happens when the Wolfsreik returns home? What then shall you do, I wonder?"

Harnin frowned. He hadn't thought of that.

Skaning entered the throne room with great trepidation. He'd never liked Harnin and was wary from their earliest days of knowing each other. The older One Eye was devious from the core. A man like that didn't stay at the right hand of a king for so long without taking care of the odds and ends behind the scenes. Skaning knew Harnin had personally killed over a score of men without Badron ever finding out. That was before the change. The rebellion and theft of Delranan changed matters drastically. Harnin was free to kill at will. Jarrik had already been banished, in all but name, to the west in a futile attempt at hunting down the rebellion and restoring order.

Given the rash of recent failures, Skaning tended to believe Harnin was about to drop the hammer. He was forbidden from wearing arms but managed to smuggle a short dagger under his tunic. Conspiracies ran rampant in Chadra Keep. Bodies swung from the ramparts daily, pecked apart by crows. Skaning had no desire to become the latest addition to the makeshift gallows.

"Come in already," Harnin snapped upon seeing Skaning's hesitation.

The younger lord, last of the council, entered and halted a respectful distance from the broken throne. "You summoned me."

Ignoring the impudence, Harnin drummed his fingertips on the carved armrest. His eye narrowed in what would have been a menacing glare if he'd had both eyes. Instead it merely made him appear to be squinting in the twinkling firelight. "Jarrik has failed me, again."

"The rebellion is spread out across the kingdom. Finding the head is not an easy task," Skaning replied, defending his friend.

"Truly. Perhaps you can explain how Jarrik managed to lose over a dozen supply trains while accumulating minimal results? Or how losses in personnel vastly outweigh enemy deaths? Don't preach to me about difficulties, Skaning. We have tactical and numerical superiority yet we can't defeat a militia comprised of peasants. Why?"

Because you command. Yet how could he explain that to Harnin without having his head taken from his neck? He already knew the answer and decided to redirect Harnin's accusations before becoming a victim. "We've successfully driven the rebels from all the major cities. They command a handful of minor villages and have less than a thousand capable fighters. Jarrik is driving them deeper into the wilds."

"He's being led deeper into the wilds," Harnin countered. "Taken away from the population centers where the army will be ineffective."

"The rebels will also be ineffective. They are scattered, incapable of coordinating a major attack," Skaning theorized. "We have the opportunity to cut them off and destroy them group by group."

Malevolence sparked in Harnin's eye. "I'm glad you and I agree on this, Skaning. You will take a small command of specialized soldiers and hunt down Ingrid and her leadership. Kill them all. Do you understand? Hunt them down to the man and do not return until the wilds are retaken. Only then can we focus solely on the east."

Turmoil sparked in his stomach. He'd expected something drastic and, thankfully, wasn't being ordered to kill Jarrik. At least not yet. Still, that didn't prevent him from wondering exactly what Harnin expected him to accomplish with a handful of men whereas Jarrik already had close to two thousand in the field. Life secure for the moment, he wasn't about to press. Instead he asked, "Is there word on Badron?"

Shadows swirled behind the throne, briefly yet enough to draw his attention. "Our beloved king is already making the return journey. I expect him to set foot in Delranan within the next few weeks."

Adding reason to your obsession with the rebellion. It begins to make sense. You can't move against Badron with an enemy force in your rear. How I don't envy you, One Eye. All your plots and schemes are boiling down into dismal failure before your very eyes. No wonder madness is your boon companion. "When do you want me to depart?"

"At the dawn. There is no time to waste," he ordered. "Do not fail me, Lord Skaning. I will have need of men I can count on when the dust of this war settles. Remember that as you conduct your business. Now leave me."

They made landfall in the middle of the night. Skiffs were launched to take the passengers to shore. Frigid water sloshed against the weather-worn boats, spilling over the rails already dangerously low in the water. Badron, King of Delranan and Lord of Rogscroft, clutched the rails with disdain to prevent from tipping into the sea. His disgust for water stemmed back to an early age. Perhaps having a famous brother who made a reputation sailing the seas aided in the rising jealousy, perhaps not. Regardless, Badron couldn't wait to be back on dry land again. He briefly contemplated ordering Grugnak's Goblins to kill the crews and have the boats burned but anticipated needing them again at some point, especially if his attempt at reclaiming Delranan went ill. A viable escape plan in his back pocket helped ease his troubled mind.

Each splash of the oar took them closer to the rocky shoreline of his kingdom. The men sitting beside and around him were just as eager to return to their homes, their families, their lives. Badron knew this through his dealings with Amar Kit'han and the other Dae'shan that whispered in his ear when no one was looking. He despised their involvement, secretly wishing he'd never made the deal with them in the first place. Grief over the loss of his only son and, he begrudgingly admitted, the kidnapping of his only daughter, drove him willingly into the Dae'shan's embrace. So far gone, Badron danced like a puppet on strings. *At least they have no qualms about letting me reclaim my own kingdom.*

Shadows of pine trees loomed, dark and ominous. They reminded him of the jaws of some great beast from legend, eager to swallow him and all who travelled with him. Ever since deploying the Wolfsreik to Rogscroft, Badron felt Lord Death barreling towards him. It was only a matter of time before events let them meet. He knew he lacked the strength to withstand any assault Lord Death chose to make and, oddly enough, he was ready to meet it. Life had never been kind to Badron, not even during his tenure as king. Watching his wife die in childbirth pushed him closer to the edge. Life lost its luster, turning to shades of grey and doom.

He'd placed all his hope in his son, who was so cruelly murdered one night at the end of autumn. Hatred for Maleela, his lone daughter and reason for his wife's death, spurred him to invade neighboring Rogscroft. The old king allowed Harnin to recruit Bahr and a crew of misfits to reclaim Maleela from her captors while he took the army to conquer the one kingdom he'd envied since rising to the throne. The nightmare campaign that followed was the result.

Now, months later, he'd lost his kingdom, his army, and what remained of his dignity. The few hundred men that remained loyal to his banner huddled together in the long boats as sea water splashed over them. Despite having so many familiar faces clinging to him, Badron found no comfort. They were the remnants of more than ten thousand soldiers and another thousand of his personal retinue. The Wolfsreik abandoned him almost to the man. That left him with a Goblin army not even he wanted.

Badron folded his arms, reluctantly, across his chest and frowned as his thoughts centered on Grugnak and his Goblins. They'd originally invaded Rogscroft under the direction of Amar Kit'han and the Dae'shan for purposes he wasn't made privilege to. The insult dug deep but Badron learned early on that his puppet masters never divulged more information than they wanted him to know. Killing and maiming their way across northern Malweir on their march from the Deadlands, the Goblins arrived in Rogscroft ready to fight.

He begrudgingly acknowledged their contributions in sacking the capital city and executing his rival, Stelskor. Everything went south after that. Somehow the young whelp Aurec got a hold of Rolnir and twisted his mind until he convinced the commanding general of the most powerful army in half of Malweir to turn traitor and take his army with him. That betrayal led to a near absolute slaughter of Goblins outside of Grunmarrow. Grugnak had been beside himself, much to Badron's chagrin. While the king of Delranan enjoyed seeing his longtime enemy destroyed, it left him with an exposed flaw. There wasn't a force strong enough to keep Rolnir from coming after him.

"Hold on, we're putting in," one of the crewmen said brusquely. Bald with a long moustache and tattoos covering his exposed forearms, he ignored Badron, treating him like nothing more than a common thief in the night.

Badron's stomach churned as the bottom of the boat ground across the gravel and sand. His ears burned at the sound. Forcing himself to stand, the king of Delranan steadied himself and prepared to take his first steps on his home soil in months. The time had finally come to reclaim what was stolen. Grugnak and his Goblins were behind in the other boats, well out of earshot but he kept his thoughts private just in case. Sound always traveled farther at night. The last thing he needed now was the complication of Grugnak overhearing his order to scuttle the other boats. Reluctantly he admitted he was going to need the Goblins to kill Harnin and reclaim his kingdom.

The decision to execute his longtime friend turned bitter rival wasn't easy to come to. Badron viewed decades of loyalty in great esteem. Every man was capable of moments of poor judgment. Harnin certainly suffered from his. The former first advisor in the council of lords seemed to abandon reason the moment Badron left for Rogscroft. Rumors said he'd turned Delranan into a nightmare beyond reckoning. Civilians were being massacred. Towns and villages burned to the ground as the survivors starved during the unusually cold winter. What his family spent generations trying to develop, Harnin ruined during a single season. There was no choice but to kill the man for his indiscretions.

"Captain says to wait here fer the rest of yer party," the same crewman ordered.

Badron turned on the swarthy man with a raised fist. "Mind your tongue, cur. You're addressing a king."

Tension filled the small boat until the crewman broke out laughing. "Not my king. I don't give a rat's ass who you think you are, mate. This is my boat. My rules. Now if you please, *yer Majesty*, get yer ass off my boat."

Badron quickly counted heads and saw he was outnumbered. Those few loyalists riding with him were the weakest of his group and would barely slow the pirates before he was skewered himself. Conversely, none of the pirates appeared meek. Each of them looked ready to kill for no reason. He didn't relish the thought of his body drifting out to sea as he bled out. Holding his tongue, he stepped onto the shore.

SIX

Darkness

Maleela drifted in and out of consciousness longer than she remembered. Her body was abused, scratched, and torn from the harsh treatment of the Harpies. Many long months on the road, first en route to Rogscroft under Aurec's care and then in the custody of her uncle, had taken their toll on her. She was mentally exhausted. Reality was fragmented as she struggled to put recent events together. Never had she expected to be torn from Bahr's protection and taken to…where? She had no way of knowing. Trapped in a semi-permanent dark room, Maleela could only guess they were back in the north. Cold wind gusts slashed into the room each time the door opened.

Her life was reduced to bouts of troubled sleep and poor meals of gruel and moldy bread. She might have been a princess but was never made accustomed to an easy life of luxury. She ate what those around her ate and lived in the same fashion. She'd been a prisoner before but this went far beyond the torments Harnin devised. Worse, she couldn't shake the feeling of being under constant surveillance.

Her skin crawled each time the door hushed open. She felt, more than saw, cold eyes scrutinizing her. As much as she felt the need to rise up and confront her captors, Maleela found she couldn't. She imagined they were drugging her food, trying to maintain complacency. How many days or nights she'd been trapped in her tiny cell she didn't know. Not a soul bothered to make itself known to her either, further compounding her building rage.

Maleela lacked the strength to stand so she crawled across the floor in an attempt at giving her prison definition. Unlike traditional cells, like the ones her father kept under Chadra Keep, this one was relatively clean. There was no decaying offal. No rats crawling through soiled straw. It lacked the smells associated with men condemned to never seeing the sun again. Maleela took small comfort in this, for it gave her a brief insight into her captors. If they wanted her tortured and killed they wouldn't have put so much effort in keeping her cage clean.

The door opened and closed suddenly before any light had the chance to slip in. Maleela cringed as the temperature dropped considerably. She wasn't alone.

"Princess, my apologies for keeping you like an animal," the wicked voice hissed with an oddly soothing tone. "I would give you better but it has been a long time since this place was last used. You are the first guest in generations. Welcome."

She tried to speak but only managed to croak from the lack of water. Her throat felt clammy. Her lips were chapped. So many accusations burned in her mind in a mental scream but failed to materialize. Frustrated, she huddled in the far corner and pulled her knees to her chest.

"Ah, your passion invigorates me. Long has it been since I've last felt such fire in a mortal soul," he cooed. "Turning you shall be…enjoyable."

Maleela coughed and spat a wad of phlegm on the floor. "Turn me into what?"

Her words were hoarse. Ill formed, they stumbled off her lips like a child learning to speak. Her tongue was swollen, slow to react. She resisted the urge to punch to cold ground, but what else could she do? Her body betrayed her.

"That is a conversation for another time. I leave you now with a final thought. All your long years spent languishing under your father's indifference have prevented you from becoming the woman you deserve. What punishments should be delivered upon a man who would neglect his own blood kin?"

"How dare you!" she tried to shout before her throat constricted and left her choking mildly as the door closed again. The second time she said it came out as barely a whisper. Feeling pathetic and helpless, Maleela collapsed in on herself and let darkness claim her.

She spent hours trying to think of a proper reply to her tormentor. Her mind bent around his words. Logic demanded he was trying to influence her thought patterns and change her preconceived notions of how life was meant to be. But to what ends? She was the current heir to the throne and would never sit upon it. Delranan would never accept a queen no matter how justly she attempted to rule. Superstitions and male-dominant dogma crippled their minds to the point where they, as a people, were intolerant of anything new. Maleela frowned, suddenly growing angry. She deserved better. Her kingdom deserved better. Perhaps it was time for a changing of the guard. Otherwise Delranan threatened to slide back into a darker, earlier age few remembered and even fewer wished to return to.

The thread of weakness that had prevented her from obtaining her full potential and becoming the proper heir to the throne finally frayed and snapped there in the impossible darkness of her cell. Events both past and present swirled like the waters of a great maelstrom, colliding into a bright and terrible future. The notion she could elevate to become a queen of dreams, of unbridled righteousness enticed her mind. She felt inspired. If only there were a way out of her prison and back into the throne room of her ancestors.

Memories of killing Ionascu suddenly burst to life. She closed her eyes to will the visions away, but all she saw was the slender blade punch into his crippled body and the confused look in his eyes as he died. Screaming, she opened her eyes and furiously rubbed her hands together in a desperate attempt at wiping the blood off. Guilt stained her soul much deeper than she imagined it ever could. Pain and nightmares mocked her from the distance. No matter how hard she tried to shove them away the memories returned time and again to clutch her, holding her in a lover's embrace as the future world burned around her.

Rage turned to sorrow. Maleela wasn't as strong as she wanted to believe. True, she'd killed a man in cold blood but the strength in her actions wasn't translated into her own blood. She was weak and knew it. Racked with conflicting emotions, she collapsed back on herself and cried herself to sleep.

The feeling of being watched returned the moment she opened her eyes. There was no telling how long she'd been asleep or how long her captor had been watching. She took small comfort in knowing he seemed to lack any urge of touching her.

"You must eat, princess of Delranan," he suggested smoothly. His words glistened in the dark like jewels waiting to be carved from mountain veins. "Strength is required if you are to ascend to your appointed place in the world."

She blindly kicked at the bowl somewhere near her feet, missing in the futile attempt.

He laughed. "Ever defiant. That is good. You will need that fire."

"What do you want from me?" she asked for the hundredth time since arriving here. Hope slowly bled away with each asking.

"To become more," he answered blankly. "What else is there?"

Maleela shook her head vehemently. "That's not an answer. You starve me. You torment me with endless questions and hollow promises. Why am I here?"

"Be careful who you accuse of what. It might not end well for you," he snapped. "You say we torment you, when in fact you are the one expounding an endless stream of questions with the vain attempt at discovering truths your mind is not prepared for. We feed you. Perhaps not the sort of food a princess is accustomed to, but enough to ensure your health. You have not been touched, nor shall you be. Tell me, what then have we done that prompts your insecurities?"

It was her turn to laugh. His redirection of guilt broke against her newfound rage. She clenched her fists defiantly. "I was taken from my uncle, my friends by force. Your pets cut and scraped me. They beat me on the way to wherever we are now. When my father learns of this, he...."

"Will do nothing! Your father is a pathetic waste of human flesh. Men like that better serve the gods as pack animals. They are meant to suffer and wallow like pigs while their betters rule. Spare me your false sincerity concerning your father. He has no more love for you than you for us. Oh yes, we know all about your broken relationship. The countless nights spent wallowing in self-pity as you struggle to know why you'll never be loved."

"There you are wrong," Maleela said between sobs. "I have all the love I'll ever need."

There was silence for a moment, as if her captor was taken off guard. When he spoke next his voice was softer, lacking the visceral edge. "You refer to your beloved Prince Aurec. Or perhaps I should say king, for the death of his father--at your father's hands--has left him the heir to a ruined kingdom."

"My father wouldn't have." Her protest sounded weak even as she said it.

"But he did. Badron relished murdering his way through Rogscroft. He personally took the head from King Stelskor and had the body strung up on the wall. I know. I was there. Your father killed all those people at my urging."

The revelation exploded through the corners of her mind. Maleela tried to push aside denial, refusing to believe her father capable of destroying so many lives. That's when she recalled an earlier conversation with Anienam Keiss where he'd explained the Dae'shan and their foul, manipulative ways. Logic directed her to the answers she desperately wanted.

"You're one of them," she said as her voice dropped to a whisper.

"Them?"

She could almost hear his head cock as he toyed with her. "One of the Dae'shan."

The hiss escaping his lips reminded her of a nest of snakes. "You are remarkably well informed. Perhaps we should have killed you outright rather than attempt to illuminate you."

"Your words drip poison. I know of your kind," she retorted. "Murderers and usurpers! You have been a bane on Malweir for generations."

Amar Kit'han snarled within the comforts of his hood. He underestimated her, a mistake he was unaccustomed to making. The leader of the Dae'shan regretted not having her killed long ago when he first arrived in Delranan. She was much stronger than any of her bloodline, save perhaps Bahr. But the Sea Wolf was a grizzled, old man soured on the idea of having anything to do with his kingdom. Badron had been weak, easily manipulated into doing his bidding. Amar Kit'han languished under fresh doubts on whether he'd be able to coerce Maleela enough in time.

"Humanity should never have been allowed to crawl from the muck. The gods played with life, manipulating evolution until you became the plague you are now," he hissed.

Maleela felt buoyed with an unexpected glimmer of hope. She saw a chance, just a sliver of hope of turning the tides on her captors. "Anienam told us you were once part of the very filth you now despise. You were once human."

"That was long ago. We abandoned those constraints in favor of ascending to a greater world. What could a mere child know of becoming more than yourself? Mind your tongue lest I forget what I need you for."

Frigid cold blasted through the cell and she was alone again. Maleela grinned, knowing she had just gotten the upper hand against a great evil. It was several moments longer before she tentatively stuck her hands out in search of her food. The Dae'shan was correct. She needed to eat to keep her strength. Time was fast approaching when she'd need it.

"She shows remarkable insight, misdirected as it may be," Kodan Bak said, reluctantly approving of Maleela's worth. His bone-thin arms were clasped behind his back. The blackness of his robes lightened and darkened with his thoughts. "This one will be dangerous if she is not properly broken."

Amar Kit'han stared down through the transparent floor watching Maleela hungrily devour her meal. As a special enticement they'd given her meat for the first time. The fact wasn't lost on her. She devoured it like a starving jungle cat. "We shall see. Time is fleeing us much faster than I admit being prepared for. The hour draws near and she has not yet been shown her true destiny."

"The girl is not necessary to our success," Kodan countered logically.

They'd prepared for this hour for centuries, culling humanity in efforts of finding the perfect genetic combination capable of releasing the power of the Olagath Stone and opening the portal between dimensions. Maleela and Badron were the results of all Amar's research and study. "A useful tool if nothing else. Is the Stone prepared?"

Kodan floated backwards a few feet before coming to a halt. "As much as can be without the chosen ones to finish the work. It has been a very long time since I felt the raw power of so much mortal suffering. The Stone has an intoxicating effect."

"As well it should. Thousands of souls have been bled into the Stone. The dark gods will be pleased with our efforts," Amar replied. His ice-colored eyes never left Maleela. Despite his willingness to use her as a tool he felt the odd tug of emotion deep inside. Could she be more than what he proclaimed her to be? He toyed with the idea of propping her up to be the wicked empress of the north. The idea was not without appeal.

Kodan Bak watched his superior with renewed hatred. Matters hadn't been the same since they came to Delranan. More and more his thoughts turned towards eliminating Amar and seizing power for his own selfish reasons. The dark gods would punish him endlessly if he displeased them. It was almost a risk he was willing to take. Almost. The time was not quite right for his rise to power.

"Ever you watch me with wicked intent, Kodan Bak," Amar accused. "You and I will have a reckoning. Soon. Until then I want you to continue trying to break her. She is decidedly more pliant than when the Hags brought her but not enough to be usable."

"As you command," Kodan Bak confirmed and faded away, leaving Amar Kit'han alone in his torment.

SEVEN

Return

Pain. Electricity surged through their flesh. Molecules were deconstructed and rebuilt in the blink of an eye. Time and space collided in a myriad of nightmares and pleasures. Sensation turned to nothingness. They watched the world being born, live out its life, and burn away into vast darkness. That same darkness robbed all thought and light, permeating reality until nothing remained but the cold ashes of what might have been.

The teleportation from Trennaron to Delranan took less than a heartbeat. Rays of blinding light exploded on the dawn, illuminating the far horizon in rainbows of color. Men and beasts collapsed within a ring of melted snow and ice. Their breaths came in ragged gasps. Steam burned off their flesh and clothes. More than a few vomited. One of the horses brayed in fright. It was all Boen could do in his weakened condition to snatch the reins and prevent it from running off. The others barely managed to regain their hands and knees.

White flames burned knee high in a ring surrounding the group. Slowly subsiding into the depths of the earth from whence they came, their absence allowed the brutality of winter in. Howling winds replaced the void the light created. Fresh snow slashed into them with unabated fury. Bahr shielded his face from the worst of it and looked around to ensure he had the correct number of bodies with him. *Living bodies. The Dae'shan will pay if anyone died from this.* He wasn't disappointed. They'd all arrived safely back in Delranan. Most were moving, at least a little, only the wizard lay curled up in the fetal position whimpering his pain away.

"I was beginning to forget how damned cold the winter was," Boen grumbled under his breath as he used the saddle to climb to his feet. He didn't particularly mind the cold, or the heat, but he figured it would give the others an opportunity to forget about the lances of pain reverberating through their bones.

Bahr cleared his throat with a deep sound and spit the residue onto the frozen rocks. "Try living here. You'd get all the snow you ever wanted. Funny thing is as children we couldn't wait for it to snow so we could go out and play in it."

"Keep your snow. I prefer the heat of the south," the Gaimosian argued and gave his horse a playful pat on the neck. "Looks like we all made it."

Bahr nodded agreement. *A little worse for wear, but we made it*. "See to the others. I'm going to help Anienam."

Boen looked around. "What about a perimeter? Do you think we were seen?"

"It's too early to tell. This close to dawn I'd think those lights were seen from leagues away. We need to get organized and move out before curious people start investigating. Find shelter first and then we can send out scouts to figure out exactly where we are."

The explanation was good enough for Boen and he eagerly began snatching the others off the ground. There'd be plenty of time in the future to lament their suffering, but not now. The true measure of courage came from the heart and each was in dire need of heart at the moment. He'd be lying if he denied the whispered urge to sit down and suffer through his pain. Age hadn't been kind to a man who spent six decades fighting and moving. His body ached. His mind betrayed his desire to keep going. Yet he pushed through the pain. There was more at stake than the private dilemma of an old man. They had a war to win.

"On your feet, lads! We've got to be away before the enemy knows we've returned," he barked. The sternness in his tone forced heads up, much like a general on the battlefield would. "Up, Skuld. There's no time for pain! Up and help with the horses. All you, up!"

One by one they reluctantly obeyed until only Anienam still lay on the ground. Bahr stumbled over, nearly falling twice, and knelt beside the ancient wizard. He placed a gentle hand on his shoulder and turned his body. "Anienam, we must be moving."

Anienam Keiss, last of the line of Mages and heir to the knowledge of Ipn Shal, turned his head so that Bahr could see his face. Tears of blood streamed down his cheeks. When he opened his eyes they were opaque. "Bahr, I can't see."

Bahr finished wrapping the dressing around Anienam's head, successfully covering what remained of his now useless eyes. Any hopes they might have held that the damage was temporary quickly vanished after a closer inspection. Anienam was permanently blind. The mood around the small camp darkened considerably.

Only the wizard found reason to chuckle.

"What can be so amusing?" Bahr asked. He didn't voice it, but they all were thinking the same thing. Anienam was their greatest asset and now he was blind. Hope began to fade.

Anienam's head swiveled to the sound of Bahr's voice. "Something my father once said. All magic comes with a price, especially the magic of the gods. It appears my vision is that price."

"Nice of Artiss Gran to mention this might happen," Dorl said glumly without taking his eyes off the small fire in the center of their camp. He'd never been a staunch advocate of the wizard but even he recognized they needed Anienam more than they needed him.

Anienam waved off the concern. "Nonsense. He's not to blame. I told you. Magic comes with a price. I have paid the price and there's no point in lamenting over it. My lack of vision changes nothing. The fate of Malweir rests in our hands. I don't need eyes to carry on."

"What about residual effects?" Bahr asked.

The wizard shrugged nonchalantly. "Time will tell. In the meantime I suggest you stop worrying over me. I can manage. After all, I'm just a passenger on the wagon."

True enough, but we rely on you more than I'm comfortable with. You being crippled dampens our plans considerably. This was a turn of events we didn't need. Bahr added another small branch to the fire and rocked back on his heels as he mulled over their next course of action. Their options were constricted, more so than before. He was the type of man who never liked relying on anyone other than himself, priding himself on his ability to be self-sustaining. All that changed when Anienam purposefully entered his life. Bahr dreaded facing the coming challenges without the wizard's eyesight.

He shook his head ruefully. "I just don't see how you can fend for yourself or use your magic well without your vision."

Anienam stiffened angrily. "I'm blind, not an invalid. I don't need vision to use magic, Bahr. We keep moving as if nothing's different. The dark gods and their spawn will not care one whit for my handicaps. Neither should you."

"It's not that easy."

He cocked his head. "How so?"

Bahr shrugged, not expecting to explain his reasoning. Each time he thought he found the thread leading down the correct path he paused and swallowed the words. None of them felt right. Frowning, he decided to stall. "You are the only one among us with magic and we're about to go up against not only a pantheon of gods but their magic using minions here on Malweir. How can we successfully counter whatever evils await us with you in a diminished state?"

Anienam began to understand more clearly. He'd been at odds with most of the group since the beginning of their quest, some dating back to the voyage to rescue Maleela from Rogscroft under false pretense. Only now did they realize he was more vital than they imagined. More than an enigmatic old man, Anienam possessed raw power and the wealth of knowledge capable of seeing them on to victory. They were scared, unsure of what the future held. If he wasn't quietly lamenting his own suffering he might have found time to chuckle at their newfound sympathy.

"Bahr, all you, can rest assured that I am more than capable of handling my end of this affair. Our way ahead is fraught with danger, more so than any we have encountered to date. I cannot promise any of you will survive, but I retain my full ability to wield magic. You do your parts and I will handle mine. Now please, can we change the subject? Or get a meal finished? My stomach is very upset with me at the moment."

Bahr gave in. There were times when even the soundest argument was trumped by hunger. He motioned for Skuld and Dorl to start cooking the brace of rabbits they'd caught after finding a suitable clearing. Boen rummaged through some of the supply sacks on the wagon and produced a handful of potatoes and a few carrots to add to the pot. He wasn't much for stews or soups, but was experienced enough to know when the heavy, gravy-like stew was good for a soldier in the field.

Handing the vegetables to Skuld he said, "Here, cut these up and toss them in. The heavier the stew the better on a night like this."

Skuld accepted them and went about his work. Long fingers of dark draped across the land like curtains of despair. Bahr looked up to the frozen fields long buried under snow and ice and wondered what would become of his homeland. Never caring for kingdom or crown, he was in the unique position to care for a land and people who didn't care for him. He doubted he'd be welcomed with open arms upon his return, especially after the debacle his brother had plunged Delranan into. His thoughts gradually turned to the two scout teams out patrolling the wilds, hoping they went unnoticed.

"Don't you get cold?" Ironfoot grumbled, pulling the collar of his bearskin cloak tighter around his shoulders. His battle axe nestled snugly on his back, easily drawn in the event of trouble. His eyes were nearly lost beneath a heavy forehead and thicker brows but they were sharp, missing nothing as he and Groge stalked across the land.

He wasn't the finest soldier in King Thord's retinue, nor the most professional. He'd been chosen for the sheer fact that he had not only captured Bahr and the others after they trespassed on Dwarven lands, but also led the raid in which Bahr and Boen performed the vital task of destroying the dark Dwarf cannons at Bode Hill. Ironfoot was deemed the most logical choice, though he didn't fail to notice how none of his peers volunteered for the task. He vowed to have words with his fellow captains upon his return.

Groge wanted to shrug indifference to Ironfoot's comment but felt awkward. His tribe had been locked away from the rest of the world for so long they knew next to nothing of modern Malweir. He struggled to adapt to the subtleties and nuances of the lowland races, lost within the knowledge that their ability to work with and understand each other before the inevitable final battle arrived. Thus far he'd only bonded, loosely, with Skuld, Boen and the stout Dwarven warrior.

"I seldom feel cold or hot," he replied. "Living on the roof of the world gives you thick skin, as does spending the majority of each day in the forges."

No stranger to iron work, the Dwarf admitted the logic of the statement. He'd done his time in the smiths deep under the mountains, crafting weapons and armor. Every Dwarf did. It was a rite of passage from youth to adult. That being said, Ironfoot had no desire to live or work high atop the mountain peaks without the comforts and heat he'd spent a lifetime taking for granted. Groge could keep his lofty home.

"Doesn't the wind tear through there?" he asked, more for conversational purposes than the need to know.

Groge nodded. "It does, but we aren't foolish enough to be caught in the open when it does. I prefer sitting in front of a warm fire with a tankard of ale than being outside."

They shared a brief laugh abruptly cut off by the sudden snap of a branch. Ironfoot had his axe in his hands in one swift movement as he immediately took cover behind the nearest tree. Not so conveniently sized, the young Giant froze in place and scanned the surrounding forest. Night had fallen, shrouding the area in the hazy world trapped between light and dark. Bushes could well be enemy soldiers drawing ever closer and Groge would be none the wiser. Never the warrior, he felt the pull of the Blud Hamr. It called to him, whispering the promises of power should he take it in his hand and use it against the enemy. Conflicted, Groge struggled with the newfound urge to commit violence.

"What do you see?" Ironfoot hissed. He crouched, ready to strike.

Groge continued looking in the direction the sound came from. He saw nothing. But something or someone had broken the branch. But who? What? His inability to find even the most remote trace of movement stilled his blood. His hand drifted towards the hammer. Another snap, crisp and loud in the night air, immediately drew his attention. His heart thumped louder, surely drawing attention from the perpetrator. Unused to tense situations, even after their harrowing flight from the Gnaals in the jungle, the Giant bordered on panic. He relaxed instantly when a female elk emerged from the dark, calmly going about her business. His sigh was audible.

"I must be getting old. Sent into a frenzy over an elk," Ironfoot snarled as he sheathed his axe. Crisis averted; the unlikely pair continued with their patrol. It was getting late and both were hungry.

Rekka Jel and Dorl Theed stalked through the undergrowth of the lightly wooded area to the south of the camp with the grace of experienced trackers. Neither spoke, knowing all too well the dangers Delranan posed. They'd already been run out of the kingdom once, harried practically the entire way by Harnin's forces. Rekka briefly thought of her confrontation with the Dae'shan in the woods of Rogscroft. She'd been taken off guard for the first time since Artiss Gran dispatched her to Delranan and vowed never to let that happen again. Their lives depended on her ability to perform her job. The momentary respite in Trennaron did nothing to remove or reduce the edge she'd spent countless years building. It was her greatest protection.

She was light enough to barely leave any tracks, a feat Dorl couldn't hope to match. He lumbered through the snow in comparison. Rekka found his attempts at stealth amusing, if not entirely hazardous. Eventually he'd make enough noise to rouse the suspicion of any eavesdroppers or spies in the area. She couldn't let that happen but neither did she feel the need to chastise him for something beyond his control. He was far heavier than she and not trained in the arts of stealth. Jungle life demanded she control her movements lest she get caught and killed by one of the great predators. The people of Delranan had no natural predators large enough to worry over. Bears were the only animal capable of killing a man and they were seldom seen outside of the mountains and deep forests. Or so she'd been told by Artiss Gran.

Rekka took little comfort in that knowledge. That now familiar, eerie feeling of being stalked crept through her muscles. Her eyes never stayed on one target long enough to be caught in a trap. A professional tracker, she was unhurried in her task. Her sword rested lightly in her small hands. The weapon was an extension of her being. She'd spent countless hours drilling and training with the weapon until it became part of her. Rekka often questioned the need for such excessive techniques, never fully understanding or appreciating their value until this quest. She whispered silent prayers to the gods of light and continued the patrol.

Any comfort Rekka might have felt did not translate over to Dorl. Born and raised in the north, he was accustomed to winter's harshness. That didn't mean he enjoyed the cold.

He hated it as much as he could hate anything. The deep, wild lands of Delranan weren't his choice place for operating. He much preferred the cities and larger towns to conduct his business. Worse, he didn't have Nothol with him to watch his back. The sell swords had worked together for so long they perfectly complemented each other. While his blossoming love with Rekka made him a better person, he still wasn't used to working with her in a tactical sense.

Frustrated after sinking knee deep into yet another snow drift, Dorl cursed under his breath. "This is pointless. No one is out here."

Rekka shut out his complaints. Her unyielding brown eyes focused intently on the dry creek bed that had become a game trail a few meters in front of them. She looked to both sides, ensuring nothing was near and knelt at the creek edge. She traced a hand over the snow, lightly enough not to disturb it.

Dorl finally managed to pull his leg free and stumbled beside her. "What is it? Do you see something?"

Rekka ignored him and hopped down the short drop into the creek. What she saw made her freeze. Her sword rose instinctively. Hundreds of horse tracks, mixed with military issue boot prints, filled the creek bed. She pointed. "We are not alone."

Dorl Theed gazed upon the seemingly endless stream of tracks and felt his world crumble. The tracks were less than a day old, if he was any judge. Not only were they not alone, but whoever else was here had a lot of strength. They needed to get back and warn the others.

EIGHT

Into the Wild

"We must back up and move, now," Rekka said as she reentered the small camp.

The glow of their fire, small as it was, could be seen from nearly a third of a league away, marking their position for any prying eyes. She smelled the smoke long before spotting the glow. Rekka was torn. They needed the fire. The chances of freezing this deep in the wilds was too great to ignore. Compounding matters was Anienam's malady. Whatever comforts Trennaron offered were quickly becoming distant memory. They were back in the north, where the weak perished without thought.

Bahr rose from beside Anienam. "What do you mean?"

She explained quickly, knowing time was expiring. Bahr listened as she told of the tracks and what it meant. He didn't feel the same concern as she but recognized the fact they couldn't stay where they were. Artiss Gran had given him a warning before they left Trennaron. The Blud Hamr was one of the most powerful magical talismans ever created. Evil would be drawn to it like moths to a flame. As much as he wanted to believe the tracks were nothing more than hunters he couldn't take the risk. Army issue boots meant only one thing: the enemy was moving through the area. They had to be more cautious than ever before.

He nodded his agreement. "Pack everything non-essential. We leave at first light."

"Will it be safe to travel in daylight?" Groge asked.

"More so than during the night," Bahr answered. "It's too risky to walk the horses in the dark and if our foes are nearby they will hear us or spot the lanterns long before we have the chance to flee. At least in sunlight we'll be on even ground. All you get some sleep now. I'll take first watch."

Dawn found the wagon trundling north. Bahr still wasn't sure exactly where they had been transported to or where the ruins of Arlevon Gale were but they had to move. Sitting stagnant wasn't productive and worse, time was steadily slipping through their fingers. The day Anienam Keiss long prophesied was almost upon them. The end of the world. Or the birth of a new one. Bahr still wasn't sure what was about to happen.

No one had seen any other sign suggesting enemy patrols were in the area, thankfully. Boen rode ahead, screening the area and guiding them closer to a small range of hills. The clouds broke and the sky turned bright blue. Sunlight, cold in the winter day, blinded them. Weapons out, the tiny band moved north.

"Does it hurt?" Skuld asked timidly. He couldn't imagine the world suddenly turning dark.

Anienam reached out and pat the back of Skuld's hand. "Not in a way you'd think. I feel no physical pain but my memories are burned into me. It is unlike anything I have ever experienced. Most interesting if you think about it."

Skuld didn't want to think about it. In fact, the longer the quest drug on the more he wanted to return to his old life and forget the rest of the world. Sneaking aboard the *Dragon's Bane* had been the biggest mistake of his young life. "Doesn't the darkness bother you?"

"That's where you are wrong. It's not dark. Not in this world. I can see swirling patterns of light. Impossible, one might say. I can no longer see shapes. My world is considerably restricted. My other senses are amplified. I can smell better, feel better, hear sounds the rest of you take for granted and ignore. I must admit that it will take me some time to deal with losing my vision. It is most difficult living this way. My heart grows heavy with the thought that I will never be able to gaze upon the familiar sights of Malweir." *Or that I won't be able to see what I'm doing once the final battle arrives.*

He left the thought there. Worrying over the unchangeable served no purpose. He was blind and must accept it if was going to be able to move forward and contribute his special skillset to the group. They might not realize just how important Anienam was to the overall success or failure of their quest. He tried to downplay his importance, but the point was coming where he wouldn't be able to hide it. War was a despicable act, among the worst in civilization's litany of grievances, and the one about to erupt was unlike any seen in ten thousand years.

Skuld secretly thought the old man was crazy but he'd never muster the strength, or stupidity, to mention it. Losing vision seemed nearly as bad as having a limb cut off or, he shuddered at the thought, losing his tongue. He'd long had nightmares of the sharp blade of a dagger slicing through his tongue. The very thought turned his stomach and filled him with dread. He stared at the wizard with newfound admiration. "Just let me know if you need anything. I will help you."

Anienam smiled warmly. "Thank you, my boy. It doesn't sit well with me to accept charity, but I'd be a damned old fool if I turned it down now. I'll be sure to get your attention if I need help. I do, however, think you should be driving this wagon. Wouldn't want to run into a ditch or a large boulder would we?"

They shared a nervous laugh and continued.

Bahr listened to their banter and took hope. He'd worried the old man might turn in on himself and become reclusive. He could discover the depths of despair from his ailment. But Bahr knew Anienam wasn't that sort of man. He'd gone through foul events over the course of his life few others could relate to. The tortured past of the order of Mages his legacy, Anienam made his way through life burdened by being the last of a long line. Bahr began to wonder if there was coincidence between the approaching final battle between the gods and the fact that Anienam was the last of his line. The idea certainly garnered attention.

He spurred his horse, deciding to catch up to Boen. Riding blindly with the wagon served no purpose and he needed to get his bearings. Nothing in the immediate area bore a hint of familiarity. Loath as he was to admit it, Bahr was lost in his own kingdom. A lesser man might suffer great embarrassment but Bahr never felt truly close with his homeland. The separation between brothers and the crown had much to do with that and, until recently, he harbored no regrets. His life was one of his choosing. Coming home after Harnin One Eye burned it all to the ground was disturbing.

Bahr found the Gaimosian riding slowly. There were no roads in this part of Delranan, telling Bahr they were well to the west of Chadra. Depending on where in the west they'd arrived, they had a great deal of travel east to find Arlevon Gale. The ruins were marked on every map as one of the few places to avoid at all costs. Dread things were said to haunt them. Rumors of those foolish enough to ignore the warnings only to disappear were spread throughout every village and hamlet in Delranan. Evil thrived where men seldom dared to dwell.

Hearing another rider approach, Boen reined in and turned. The look on his face was of satisfaction. He was back in his element. A Gaimosian's strength lay in working alone in hostile situations. He took pride in being able to cut through enemy soldiers without thought or effort. A born warrior, he found working closely with others distasteful at best. Being an integral part of the group changed his perspective, slightly. He'd always enjoyed Bahr's friendship, at least since their first adventure nearly thirty years ago. The battle with the Cave Trolls in the foothills of the Kergland Spine still brought its share of laughs and retellings.

His mind drifted as Bahr rode up to him. The Sea Wolf was in worse shape than Boen. It was a sad fact not unnoticed by the others. This quest was draining their lives, hollowing them out into crisped hulks. Boen was ready for it to be finished so that he might move on to warmer climates with less danger.

"It's damned cold," he grumbled. His eyes were just as col d as the freshly fallen snows and hard as the ice coating. "I was getting used to the jungle again."

Bahr eyed him queerly. How could anyone get used to the sweltering heat of a jungle, especially when they came from the north? He'd be just as pleased if he never saw Brodein again. "You get used to the cold. Besides, it won't last much longer. Winter is nearly done. The spring thaws aren't far off."

"Far enough if you ask me," Boen replied. "Shouldn't you be back with the wagon? The others will need you more than I do."

Bahr struggled not to find insult in the comment. "They talk too much. Have you seen anything?"

He shook his head. "Nothing but birds. This isn't a very habitable part of the kingdom. Not enough trees or rivers."

"I can't help that, at least it gives me a vague idea of where we are." He paused as a small wind devil whirled across the snow. He half expected Boen to ask the obvious. "Chadra is far to the east and the ruins even farther. I don't know exactly how far, but we've got a long way to go before Groge can use the hammer."

Boen crossed his wrists over the saddle's pommel and leaned forward, stretching the tensed muscles of his back. "This could be lovely country if not for all the snow."

"Have you seen any tracks?" Bahr shifted the conversation. They'd come too far to waste time with idle banter. Each knew the other's strength and weaknesses. Small talk wasn't for either man.

Boen shook his head. "Nothing human. There's plenty of game around but none of the heavy horse or infantry Rekka claims to have seen. Are we sure she was accurate?"

"I trust her more than some of the others," Bahr admitted. The jungle woman was standoffish to the point it was almost uncomfortable being around her but she had proven her worth several times over. "If she says she saw tracks I believe her."

He wished he didn't. This far out in the wilds there was no reason for an armed patrol. It didn't make sense. "Boen, we're missing some vital element to this mess."

"That being?" Boen asked without hesitation. He'd gone over their impossible scenario a hundred times and still hadn't come up with an answer.

Bahr stifled a yawn. "We know there's a rebellion against Harnin going on. Argis abandoned us to aid them. Without the proper infrastructure there's no reason for the enemy to be patrolling this far west, if we are as west as I think we are. Not even the rebels would be operating this far out."

"Unless they've been driven from the cities," Boen countered. "Rebellions seldom end well. Most are crushed by the reigning monarchs. The others manage to overthrow the throne but do so with extreme violence that betrays their own motives. Kingdoms have shattered under such. It's not hard to imagine the same happening in Delranan."

As much as he didn't want to admit it, Bahr held the same suspicions. The more he became invested in this quest the more he began to care for his kingdom. Frowning, he knew what he had to do, not only for himself but for the good of the people. "Perhaps Argis altered their direction and pulled Harnin out of Chadra. We can't assume the rebellion has failed or succeeded at this point. There's not enough information."

"We should focus on what we control," Boen offered. Thinking about the infinite number of futures they were heading towards served little purpose.

Reluctantly Bahr agreed. They needed to get their bearings ad set the proper course. Much as he enjoyed the quiet the countryside offered, he needed to get his group moving in the right direction. Each day they wandered aimlessly with the Blud Hamr threatened to bring more of their enemies closer. A giant target was painted on their backs and he needed to get rid of it before something bad claimed them.

"Once we reach those hills to the northwest I should be able to get a better notion as to where we are," he said.

"In the meantime?"

"Keep your eyes open. Let me know the moment you see anything, whether it's tracks or smoke from a chimney," Bahr paused. "We keep moving until then."

Boen unfolded his hands and picked up the reins. He clicked his horse forward as Bahr turned to leave. Snow burst upwards from a score of positions surrounding them. Men and women dressed in all white and armed with long spears, swords, and crossbows surrounded the pair. Bahr reached for his sword as his horse bucked from shock. Boen already had his out, the cold steel glimmering in the sunlight.

"Put your weapons down and raise your hands. Do as we say and no one needs to die," the stern voice commanding them echoed across the plain.

Bahr felt his heart sink. They'd been captured.

NINE

Chance Encounter

They were blindfolded and bound to their saddles. Brusque hands shoved them into compliance. Their captors balked at the sight of Groge, ready to break and run until one of the rougher ones put his blade to Bahr's throat and threatened to split him open. Groge complied willingly. The rest were put atop their horses and forced along an unfamiliar path. Bahr guessed they travelled for the rest of the day before halting for the night.

He was the first to de-horse. Hands tied behind his back, he was led into a stand of thick pines. The center had been cleared out. A handful of stumps dotted the ground with their trees lining the circle to form a protective barrier capable of hiding them from prying eyes. The warmth of a fire kissed his face and his heart sank. Harnin had captured them. The quest was over.

"Remove his blindfold," a woman's voice ordered.

Bahr stiffened. The last he knew there were no women in Harnin's army, nor was he keen on finding any. Rumor had it that Harnin was partial to finding satisfaction with other men. Bahr didn't know, nor did he care. The only thing that mattered was here, now. His blindfold was dragged off his head. Cold fingers scraped across his brow. Bahr blinked rapidly to get used to the light quicker and tried to take in his surroundings.

The clearing was as close to a field command area as his captors were going to get. A few cots were set up on the far side with packs and other bags stacked nearby. Tree branches arched, forming a natural dome. What little snow managed to drift in melted quickly. He heard sounds of movement outside the clearing, suggesting many men and women.

"Where am I?" he asked, deciding to sound firm. Each of his captors wore different clothes. They were either mercenaries or specialty commandos Harnin started using after Badron went on campaign.

The woman raised her hand sharply. "I'll ask the questions here, Bahr, brother of Badron. What are you doing out here?"

He suppressed a frown. How could she possibly know who he was? There was no better way to find out. "How do you know my name?"

She laughed in his face. "You didn't think the brother of the king could go unnoticed in his own kingdom, no matter how far west we are, did you? You are not the most welcome person in Delranan. Even if you have made it your business to avoid connection with Badron."

"I haven't been in Delranan for months," he protested, genuinely confused. "In fact, I only just returned. You have me mistaken."

"I think not. I've seen you several times, enough to recognize you no matter how grey your beard grows or the lines on your face deepen. This is not the same kingdom you once knew." She fell silent, questioning her next move. The relationship between brothers was well documented throughout the kingdom yet Bahr didn't seem interested in discussing it. Perhaps she was wrong?

"Tell me, Bahr, if you haven't been in Delranan, just where have you been? Don't lie. I have no problem ordering Orlek here to cut your throat," she told him.

Not feeling the threat she promised, Bahr did. He glossed over several key areas. Whoever this woman was didn't need to learn about the Blud Hamr or the quest to stop the dark gods. At least not until he discovered whether she was another of Harnin's agents or not. When he was done, he was exhausted and, near as he could tell, so was she. Mention of Boen set her back some. Clearly she hadn't been expecting to run across a Gaimosian, or a Dwarf and Giant for that matter. If she learned nothing else from his tale she learned Bahr traveled with dangerous companions.

"It appears I have been rude to you, Captain, but I needed to ensure you were not in league with that bastard One Eye," she said with measured tone. "My name is Ingrid and I am the leader of the rebellion. Welcome to our camp. I believe there is much for us to discuss."

The rebellion! How it came to be led by a woman was a mystery. The last he knew Lord Argis had returned to assume the leadership position. Had matters gone so drastically wrong in such a short period of time that he was no longer with them? Having been a prisoner in Harnin's dungeons himself it didn't take much thought before his mind wandered down foul paths best left forgotten.

"Thank you, Ingrid, but I can't sit here in comfort while the rest of my companions are out in the cold freezing," Bahr said.

"They will be taken care of, now that we recognize you as friend. Orlek, please see to his companions," Ingrid ordered.

Orlek, a swarthy-looking man in Bahr's opinion, gave him a withering glare and followed his instructions after a moment's hesitation. "Clearly he's not as convinced as you are."

Her gaze lingered an extra moment longer on her second in command before she turning back to her guest. "We have endured a great deal of turmoil in your absence, Bahr. Delranan is not the kingdom you were born in. Darkness rots the heart. Brother turns on brother without thought. Many hundreds have died this winter and, unfortunately, there is no end in sight. I fear for the future."

It gets worse and I'm not sure you can handle it. He contemplated telling her about the dark gods' influence and their urgent need to get to Arlevon Gale but wasn't convinced himself that she was who she claimed to be. Anyone in her position would almost have to consider turning him over to Harnin in exchange for a reduction in hostilities. He admitted he'd be hard pressed to ignore such a proposition if he were in the same position.

"As much as I'd like to help, I need to know more," he said.

Ingrid pursed her lips, debating how much to divulge. In the end she realized there was no actual choice. The only way to garner the brother of the king's aid was to appeal to his patriotism, if any remained. Bahr was notorious for having turned his back on Delranan in pursuit of his own interests.

"Harnin has roughly seven thousand men at arms. Most are the Wolfsreik reserves but enough of the citizens have sided with him to significantly bolster their forces. Rumors of Badron's return from the war have centralized his focus to the east where the main body of soldiers is busy constructing a series of redoubts and fortresses. He clearly intends on jam-ming up the Wolfsreik long enough to make it a war of attrition. I'm hoping he does."

Bahr frowned. The last he'd heard the army had abandoned his brother, at least according to Artiss Gran. The truth in that remained to be seen. "I don't see how that will help your rebellion. From what I gather you are either seriously understrength or spread too thin to be effective. Whatever battles are fought in the east will only delay the inevitable. Whoever wins will eventually turn their eye west, to you." *Not to mention I'll have to fight through two armies to reach the ruins. Can this get any more difficult?*

"Harnin is desperate to finish us off before the king returns. He can't and he knows it. We've estimated he's thrown close to two thousand men at us. We're hitting supply trains and small patrols every chance we can get and, while it's gone far in disrupting his warfighting capabilities, he still has enough in store to starve us out before spring." She shook her head fervently. "I can beat him. I know this, but I need more than what I have."

Bahr exhaled a careful breath. "We didn't come here to fight a war, Ingrid."

Anger flashed in her eyes. "It appears some things are incapable of changing. Aside from wasting my time, why have you returned to your birth kingdom?"

"That…is a tale for your ears only," he stated flatly.

"Why are we wasting our time with these people?" Ironfoot asked Boen. Naturally disgruntled, the Dwarf wasn't prone to sitting idle when important matters needed to be done. "We should be on our way east to finish this affair with the dark gods."

Boen casually stirred the long-handled wooden spoon in the stew pot. "Bahr knows what he's doing. Remember, he's the brother of the king." *A fact none of us knew until after we'd rescued Maleela. Interesting, the secrets we keep.*

Ironfoot tossed his meaty hands in the air. "I don't care if he's the bloody king of the world. We are losing valuable time. What's the point in dealing when we have a Giant among us? Groge could swat their people like insects."

"Calm down, Ironfoot. Your ire won't help our situation. We felt much the same way while your own king dithered over our intent. This is but another temporary setback."

Ironfoot's face shaded crimson. Planting his feet shoulder width apart, he folded his arms across his chest. "Setback? When did Gaimosian knights become known for their patience? I say we move. Now."

Boen shook his head, fondly recalling his own rash adolescence. There was a time when he wouldn't have waited to make a move. Sitting still like this offended him but he'd been among the others long enough to utilize his limited amount of patience. They would either get to the ruins in time or they wouldn't. Those were the only real options. All the pressure lay on Bahr's shoulders, not his. When the time came for him to get involved he would. Until then his focus was on dinner.

"You realize Groge isn't a warrior? Even with his immense size there's not much he can do. Even if he wanted to. Here, taste this. It's missing something but I don't know what." Boen chuckled under his breath as he raised the spoon for Ironfoot.

The Dwarf snorted and stormed off.

"He's a jolly sort," Rekka said as she took his place by the fire.

Boen nodded. "Dwarves are an odd breed, that's for sure. I'd rather have him on our side than against us. Give him a little time to settle down. Dwarves aren't known for their even temperament."

"The more I witness of this world the less I understand it. So many different races with so many different beliefs and ways. It is very confusing," she confessed. "Life was much simpler in the jungle."

She paused. Memories of the jungle and her village of Teng would never grow more than what they were now. Banished, wrongfully, for the death of Cashi Dam, Rekka could never go home again. Her heart twisted with guilt, but for reasons other than Cashi. His love for her was false, based on an empty premise from when she was a child. Now she was forced to sever all ties with the people she'd grown up with, abandon all her friendships and loyalties, and live a hollow life wandering like a Gaimosian. Unless Artiss Gran decided to keep her on.

"Malweir is a strange and wonderful place. That's part of the beauty of being Gaimosian," he said and paused. "Not that there's much, mind you. We have no kingdom, no place to call home. I've wandered from ocean to ocean and dealt with practically every race in the world. The wealth of experience alone is irreplaceable. I still haven't seen a dragont. That would be something to claim before I head for the ground. A dragon."

"The histories all say the dragons are either dead or have returned to their ancient homeland of the Crystal

Mountain. I do not think you will be able to achieve your dream."

"It is good to have dreams, even if they never come true," Boen countered. "What do the jungle folk dream of?"

Rekka found the question unsettling. She'd long held the belief that she knew without doubt which direction to take her life. Recent events shattered that carefully constructed world, leaving her trapped in unknown horizons. The notion was both unnerving and invigorating.

"Elves," she blurted out before realizing it.

Boen's eyebrow rose. "Elves?"

Slightly embarrassed, she nodded. "Yes, Elves. I've never seen one, at least none other than Faeldrin and his mercenaries."

"I've seen plenty. If you think Giants and Dwarves are strange wait until you run into a band of Elves. They're the happiest folk I've ever seen. Maybe they know something we don't, who knows? There's none in this half of Malweir, though. Most of them stay east of Averon," Boen said. "Those Aeldruin are strong fighters, but not representative of their people. Most won't lift a sword unless they have to. A damned better people than me to be able to do that."

She empathized. Secretly she longed for the day when she no longer needed weapons to get her point across. Malweir might not be the friendliest of places, but there had to come a time when violence failed to solve matters. Sadly, it was naught but a dream.

Her thoughts dissolved on her tongue at the sight of a warrior marching sternly towards them. Boen noticed her change in demeanor and glanced up. The man was one of the ones who captured them.

"I'm Orlek, I was ordered to provide you all with shelter and what little food we have to spare."

Boen nodded his appreciation and subtly unclenched his fist. "My thanks to you, though we don't need your food. We've enough of our own, for now."

Orlek was unimpressed. Whether they ate or not wasn't his concern. He'd done what Ingrid instructed. As far as he was concerned his task was complete. "That's your business. Ingrid doesn't want you to starve or freeze tonight. Looks to be a rough one. Bundle up and take shelter under the cover of the trees. That should protect you enough."

He glanced over Boen. Even without weapons the big man was a formidable opponent. He doubted there'd be much of a fight. Even with his knowledge of hand-to-hand combat, Orlek wouldn't last long. The idea was mildly enticing and might prove entertaining if the weather permitted, but now wasn't the time.

"Best get moving now, while there's still some daylight left," he added. He started walking away but stopped and turned. "Where are you from?"

Boen grinned savagely. "Nowhere."

A cold sensation ran through Orlek as he realized why the big man seemed dangerous. Awkwardly, he realized was staring down a Vengeance Knight.

The fire was warm, but the wind still managed to worm through the stacked trees at precisely the wrong moments. Orlek would have liked to have been in a nice tavern with no elements to deal with. Life as a soldier wasn't that kind. He grunted. Probably why he didn't last very long in the rank and file. Still, he couldn't complain about being part of the rebellion. Before Ingrid came along he was just another body with a sword. A part of the initial mission to raid the weapons locker on the docks, he'd worked with Joefke and Lord Argis. That had been a battle worthy of remembering. Nothing he'd done since fleeing from Chadra held much meaning, despite his elevation in rank. Nothing, that is, but his blooming love for Ingrid.

Thoughts of the tempered blond kept him warm on cold nights. She was a remarkable woman just beginning to come into her full potential. He hoped she survived this war. Delranan needed better people like her. Hells, he needed her.

She caught him staring fondly at her from across the fire and flashed a tender smile. It warmed his heart to know she might feel the same.

"What do you think?" she asked him.

Orlek rubbed a hand over the top of his head. "They're a dangerous bunch. The Giant alone could kill every one of us without breaking a sweat. A Giant, Ingrid! Who would have thought we'd have one in our camp? They're not supposed to exist."

"All legends are based on some form of reality," she said. "They do appear to be quite the eclectic group. A Giant, Dwarf, Gaimosian, and more. What do you make of the old man and that strange woman they travel with?"

Orlek's face turned serious. "I've heard whispers he's a wizard and she's his bodyguard."

Ingrid pa used. Bahr never mentioned a wizard being part of this. The last she knew, all the wizards and Mages had died out. Having one, if it were true, in her hands would drastically alter the balance in the war. She'd be able to drive Harnin from Chadra and assume the stewardship of Delranan until a rightful king was emplaced. Even the best-laid plans are filled with faults. This was no different. With Bahr returned, there was no chance for her to sit on the throne. Not that she wanted to rule. Quite the opposite, Ingrid merely wanted Delranan to be free again with a just ruler in place.

"We can use this to our advantage," she said, her mind already racing ahead.

Orlek wasn't convinced. Nothing about the group suggested they were interested in helping the rebellion. "I agree but don't see how. My guess is they are going to leave just as soon as the sun comes up and there's not much we can do to stop them. Not unless we get attacked by Harnin's forces first."

She briefly toyed with the idea before discarding it. Bringing Harnin down on them wouldn't solve anything. The latest reports from the field had Lord Jarrik and Inaella leading the two thousand man force hunting them down. She shuddered to think what the pockmarked woman would do if she ever got her hands around Ingrid's throat. As much as it pained her to admit it, the war was not going very well. Her fighters were tired, sorely trained, and running out of the desire to carry on. The initial boost they'd gotten when she took the fight into the countryside was fading. She needed to come up with a victory fast or risk losing it all out of sheer indifference.

"Bring me Bahr. I must try and convince him to help us. We are, after all, his people." The dominant glimmer in her eyes was one he'd seen too many times before. It thrilled him in different ways. Perhaps hope loomed on the horizon after all.

TEN

Aurec's Decisions

The last few battalions straggled into the night's encampment on weary legs. On the move since dawn, they were the rearguard and forced to endure endless leagues of stop-and-go movement. The elastic tendencies of an army on the move was well known to every infantrymen ever made, and none appreciated it. Stretching moments of standing still followed by having to hurry to catch up to the unit in front of the column drove many of the younger soldiers mad. Only the generals on their horses seemed unaffected.

Fires raged, having been set by the vanguard and logistics battalions Rolnir pushed to the head of the column. He believed in taking care of his men and that meant having warmth and hot food waiting for them when they reached the camp every day. As was his custom, he waited on foot for the very last man to pass before retiring for the night to a seemingly endless stream of meetings with his senior staff.

Normally the Wolfsreik operated alone in the field. He was the closest thing to a god the soldiers knew and that's how it should be. King Badron's decision to tag along with the main body during the Rogscroft invasion was frowned upon but he was the king. Rolnir was forced to shift tactics and endure what he considered pointless questioning from the king. The waste of man hours from standing in audience alone was infuriating. King Aurec was the opposite. Here was a man Rolnir could enjoy working with.

That easy-mannered work relationship didn't figure in to how he was going to explain to the freshly crowned king that the mountains were next to impassable. He smiled and waved at the last few ranks, reaching out to slap a few beleaguered men on their shoulders while shouting words of encouragement. Soldiers liked to feel appreciated. He had when he went up through the ranks. Every little thing to boost morale was being done. Most of these men were beyond sore, exhausted, and mentally fatigued. They only had so much left to give. Soldiers were hard men by necessity, but he felt he'd already asked for too much. Gloom cast over his face as he slowly headed towards the command tents. The Murdes Mountains loomed over them majestically in the background.

One minor problem lost amidst the horrors of war. What did I do to get myself in this situation? Life used to be so simple, now I'm mired in an unending nightmare from which there is no escape. At least the Pell are on our side. Fighting them once was bad enough. I do hope the young king can pull off what he's got in mind. Otherwise….

Lost in thought, Rolnir wormed through the army offering absentminded words of encouragement as weary men collapsed in front of fires, wolfed down their meals, or cleaned their weapons and gear. A life of marching was hard on any race. The slackers were long weeded out. All that remained were the resolute. The veterans. Muscles were hardened from overuse. Body fat was burned away from countless days of marching and fighting. Wars were not for the faint of heart. It takes a special breed of man to watch his friends die around him and still go willingly into battle. Empty places around the campfires haunted the survivors. Fond memories of those lost. Yet they carried on, for kingdom and each other. Rolnir could give them no less.

He ducked entering the command tent, returning the salutes of the pair of Rogscroft guards. Rolnir grinned ruefully. There was a time when the men at the door were staunch enemies. How fickle war was, he mused. Enemies become friends while allies turn their backs. The warmth from the fire hit him immediately, nearly making him forget the frigidness of the early night. A mass of bodies shuffled around. Most had parchments and evening reports from each small unit commander detailing the status of their soldiers and supply needs. The senior commanders would be along shortly for their nightly debriefing. Rolnir was in no mood to listen to the repetitive statistics, not tonight.

He felt lethargic, stale. Going home harbored mixed emotions he was only now coming to realize he wasn't prepared to deal with. They'd camped less than a day from the mountains yet close enough to remain enshrouded in the shadows for most of the day. Rolnir much preferred the open plains. There were too many places to hide in the mountains, making him uneasy.

Piper walked up and forced a mug of ale into his hands. "The last troops are tucked safely away in their bivouac I see."

Feigning a smile, Rolnir accepted the mug gratefully and drank deeply. "Do you remember a time before all this? I can't."

"This doesn't sound like you," Piper admonished. "I'm supposed to be the one down on his luck and all. What's wrong?"

Feeling trapped in his memories, Rolnir stood with downcast eyes for a moment. "Nothing," he finally answered. "Just tired is all. Is everyone here?"

A nod. "Our young king is busy in the back discussing matters with Vajna. The others are busy pouring over the maps."

Rolnir asked, "Why aren't you?"

Piper shrugged. "I can only look at a map for so long before my eyes begin to hurt. Besides, maps don't do much of anything. Especially when I have scouts."

Borderline arrogant, Piper was steadily, if too slowly, getting back to his old self. This war had taken an exhaustive toll on the second in command. He'd lost too much weight and bore an unnatural amount of guilt in his once-sharp eyes. Too much pain did that to a man, and Piper was just another soldier. He seldom utilized his position for anything other than to snag a mug of ale from time to time. A professional, he'd rather be out with the soldiers, living as they did. His men appreciated that, even if they never voiced it.

"You'd better not get us lost," Rolnir scolded.

"Where we are going? Not bloody likely," the thinner man said and almost laughed.

Enough said, the duo headed towards Aurec. Rolnir couldn't put the meeting off any longer without looking like a fool. Most conversation stopped with their arrival. Heads turned and nodded or bowed in acknowledgment. Rolnir greeted them all in kind. They'd become familiar faces by now. Not exactly treasured, but welcome enough that he'd regret losing any of them. The unifying endearing factor stemmed from most of them having prior military experience. He appreciated that aspect, knowing they'd tend to have more compassion for the army than a politician would.

King Aurec was the first to break the crowd and shake Rolnir's hand. "Ah, General Rolnir, now we can begin."

Aurec had developed, out of necessity, over the course of winter. He'd been a brash, impulsive young man when he stole into Chadra Keep to rescue his love from Badron's harsh grasp. The resulting war and beheading of his own father broke him and reforged him into a stronger, more mature man. Barely into his twenties, he was now monarch to a beleaguered kingdom.

Not feeling the need to explain his nightly actions, the Wolfsreik general marched over to take his place at the makeshift table occupying the rear tent. Vajna was already there, the older general looking haggard but in good spirits. Venten sat beside the king. His frost-white hair and face full of lines made him look older than he felt. A lifetime of being advisor to the king and a soldier before that had hardened him. Thorsson, now command sergeant major of the combined army, stood, as was the preference of most senior noncommissioned officers. They largely despised meetings, thinking of the myriad tasks they could be accomplishing at that same moment.

Raste and Mahn were the most unusual of the group. Scouts, the pair was mostly absent. They'd survived improbable situations over the course of the war and didn't really seem to get along. Yet they were among the most competent men Rolnir ever led. The Pell Darga chieftain, Cuul Ol, squatted beside the table. A man of the mountains, he was uncomfortable with lowland civilization and its faults. His dark, weather-stained skin stuck out from the rest of the pale-skinned warriors. If he noticed, he didn't care. They'd all grown to become equals over the course of the winter war.

"We are faced with a difficult decision, one I wish we could have delayed a little longer to let nature do the job for us," Aurec said evenly. His gaze swept over the council of leaders. "We're less than a day from the Murdes Mountains and still awaiting reports on whether the passes are clear or not. The way I see it we have three choices. First, we wait for the spring thaw, but with winter being more severe than in recent years, who can say how long that will take. Or we could spend countless man hours digging our way through. The men will be exhausted by the time we reach Delranan. Add the fact that we don't know what to expect once we arrive, we could well be slaughtered. The last option is to march south around the mountains. I don't need to tell any of you how many weeks this will add to our task, perhaps months. Gentlemen, my mind is torn. I want to hear what you think."

No one spoke. This was a moment they'd anticipated but long dreaded. The Murdes Mountains were harsh on a good day. In winter they were unforgivable. Hundreds of fools thinking to conquer the vast peaks were lost, their skeletons painful reminders to those who came after that the mountains would not be bested. Rogscroft and Delranan had each lost more men than could be easily counted. If Aurec had his way they wouldn't lose any more. They were going to need as many battle-ready soldiers as possible to crush the madness in Delranan and finally end the long war.

Cuul Ol was the first to speak his mind. As master of the Pell Darga, he alone knew the mountains best. If anyone was going to find a way through, it was him. "Mountains are never safe. Many places to fall and die. The snows are deep but there are secret ways. Ways no lowlander knows."

Hope sprang to life in the young king's eyes. This was the glimmer he'd been hoping for. "Cuul Ol, I know that never before have our tribes allied themselves. Your secrets are cherished as much as our own are to us, but will you consider showing us? I don't need to remind you that all our kingdoms are in grave peril should we fail to stop Badron and Harnin One Eye. Will you help us?"

The Pell chieftain gave a toothy grin that repulsed more than one at the council table. Broken, crooked teeth stained yellow and rare shades of brown almost leered at them. Mahn was positive he saw bits of chewed meat stuck between them. "The clan chiefs will not be pleased. Take much to make them agree."

"Are these paths wide enough to facilitate rapid troop movement?" Rolnir asked. He didn't care about the politics between Pell chiefs. Cuul was their leader as far as he was concerned and his word should be final. The rest boiled down to semantics. One way or another, the allied army was going across the mountains. Getting there was the trick.

Cuul scratched his lightly bearded jaw and nodded thoughtfully. "Maybe. We Pell have never had so many warriors. I must see the chiefs."

"What do you need from us?" Aurec asked. His eagerness bled through his voice. It had been so long since he'd held much hope, even after the successful recapture of his beloved home and unification with the Wolfsreik. Rogscroft remained in ruins and, despite their combined efforts to rebuild in the middle of winter, had so much farther to go. His people needed the victory over Badron to be complete before they could move on without the blanket of fear that had for so long permeated the air between them.

Cuul gestured towards the pair of scouts. "I take these two. They will witness what the chiefs say."

Raste looked sharply at the older Mahn who barely seemed phased. They were the natural choices as far as he was concerned. The first to contact the Pell, they had been captured on their way through the mountains after the raid to get Maleela. The younger Raste had been indignant, nearly getting them both killed before Mahn managed to calm him down. The longer the war dragged on, the calmer Raste became. He'd survived the siege of Rogscroft, watching several friends fall during the last few moments before Goblins swarmed the walls. Becoming an integral part of the new army was just what the young scout needed to mature and develop a stronger sense of responsibility.

Slowly, with deliberate intent, Mahn turned to his young counterpart with the faintest hint of a grin. Perhaps going back to the mountains with Cuul Ol was exactly what Raste needed to remind him of where they'd come from. No good came from having a misplaced sense of entitlement and that was certainly what tainted the young man now.

"We accept," Mahn answered for them. "It will be good to get back to doing our real jobs. We've sat too long in luxury. Scouts aren't accustomed to such."

Piper covered his broad smile so as not to offend Rolnir or Aurec. As the first man to enter Rogscroft, he knew too well how important it was for a scout to be in his element.

Aurec nestled back in his field chair. "Very well, it's settled. Cuul Ol will take Mahn and Raste back to the mountains. General Rolnir, how long will you need to order the army in line of march?"

"Not long. I generally advance in the order of battle I want to fight with. We can heavy load the infantry in the front with archer support directly behind. My only concern is with the cavalry. Depending on how deep the snows are and how wide the secret ways are, we might be without that heavy support for a while."

"Can't you load them in the front?" Vajna asked. An infantryman at heart, the versatility of the cavalry was a relatively new notion for him to consider. Rogscroft seldom had a large army and certainly no big units of horse.

Rolnir shook his head. "The horses would be useless without infantry support and, even if they managed to break through the snow, they'd outpace the rest of the army. If Harnin utilizes proper tactics he will have a line of defenses established along the mouths of the mountain passes. Redoubts and trenches dug to prevent a massed charge. This is a fight that will be done by the grunts, I'm afraid."

His mind was already tracking foreseen difficulties once they returned to Delranan. Harnin may only have the reserves, but they were all Wolfsreik, trained and proven on the battlefield. Once his full army was deployed on the lowlands, Rolnir didn't foresee many problems. The trick was getting the army deployed in battle mode. Harnin One Eye was bound to have nasty surprises in store.

Aurec had heard enough. Tired from marching up and down the line, amidst protests from his senior commanders, the young king was ready to collapse. He dismissed them with a salute and slipped into his heavy cloak for the short trek back to his own tent. Even though he had the same cot as the infantry, he'd never looked forward to a night's sleep more. One by one the council left until only Venten remained.

The aged advisor and former general folded his spindly arms and waited for Aurec to exhale and wave him forward.

"Are you sure this is wise?" Venten asked.

Aurec wanted to say no, he wasn't, but what was the use? The whole purpose of having a council was to get more than one opinion. Too many kings and generals failed for doing just the opposite. Wishful as it seemed, he wanted his rule to be long and fruitful.

Knowing his young king well enough, Venten proceeded. "Aurec, this is reckless. Cuul Ol has worked with us but his people remain an enigma. They are quality warriors who don't interact with our armies. What if he has some nefarious intent once we cross the mountains?"

As implausible as it sounded, Aurec couldn't take the chance to ignore the potential for disaster. The Pell Darga had ever been trouble for both kingdoms. It wasn't until Aurec's involvement that Cuul became *friendly*. Even that was cold most times. "Venten, I understand your point of view. I do. The fact of the matter is I can't afford to miss this opportunity. We are shaky allies at best. If Cuul can convince the other chiefs to assist us, we have the perfect chance of cementing relationships with the Pell Darga and unifying all three kingdoms. Can you imagine the trade possibilities? The peace? The strength that union might bring?"

"All true, but it is too early to think about that. We've still got a war to fight, much less win," Venten cautioned. "As much as I want to have faith in our new allies, I can't accept their sudden change of heart without grave reservations. Cuul Ol and his chiefs can still betray us all."

He left Aurec to ponder the what-might-be and what-ifs. His job as senior advisor was done for the day. Only the king could make up his mind, a decision that might well affect the future of a great many lives. Not happy with himself, Venten stepped into the open air. His breath caught in his throat as the sudden blast of cold struck. Unlike many of the others, he enjoyed winter the most. It was a time of rebirth, of purity unrivaled during any other time of the year. Clasping his hands behind his back, he whistled as he worked his way back to his tent, comfortable in the knowledge that Aurec would have many decisions yet to make.

ELEVEN

Of Dwarves and Goblins

"Are you sure about this?" Euorn asked, a thin eyebrow rising sharply.

Faeldrin debated which answer to give. A large part of him knew this was foolish at best, but that minor part of his mind screamed for action. Right or wrong, this needed to be done. "Have I ever been wrong?"

"More times than I can count," the Elf scout replied tersely.

Faeldrin suppressed his frown. "Fair enough, but we are all that stands in the way until Thord and his army can link up with the western armies."

Euorn nodded absently. The army heading towards them was among the largest ever fielded in Malweir. Goblins weren't exceptionally bright or industrialized, but what they lacked in intelligence they made up for in numbers. Fifty thousand enemy soldiers marched across the north toward what Faeldrin could only assume was Delranan. The Dwarves wanted to fight. Their depleted ranks would give the Goblins a good pounding but they weren't enough to stop the tide from rolling through.

It took an act of the gods, but Faeldrin managed to convince the Dwarf king to march west while leaving a small rearguard to cause havoc. The one-hundred Dwarf detachment tripled Faeldrin's strength and, combined with the pair of cannons graciously given, added immeasurable firepower. The Elf Lord intended to give the Goblin horde a shock once it gained the banks of the Fern River.

Euorn criticized his friend and commander silently. They'd served together for over one thousand years and undergone considerable dangerous situations. He still harbored a grudge against the quest to kill the dragon of the Deadlands. Normally Faeldrin led his Aeldruin mercenaries with implacable precision. Euorn was having a difficult time accepting the task set before him. He feared a great many Elven lives were about to be lost for no reason other than the vain quest for glory.

"The Dwarves smell bad," he finally said. Once Faeldrin made up his mind there was no changing it.

Faeldrin laughed, a cheerful noise dancing over the snow-covered fields. "Perhaps we can convince Master Scrum to get his soldiers to take a quick dip in the river before the Goblins arrive."

"Doubtful. They seem to enjoy their stench." *No doubt from living in the confinement of being underground all their lives.*

"To each his own, Euorn. Did you not notice the queer looks they gave us at breakfast? You'd think they've never eaten vegetables before. At any rate, inform me when Scrum has those cannons emplaced. They are terrible weapons of which I'm glad no other race has developed yet, but extremely effective in combat."

"No doubt they'll halt the Goblin advance for a good while," Euorn seconded, recalling the massive amount of devastation they caused during the civil war with the dark Dwarves. He'd grown accustomed to seeing twisted corpses rent or pierced on the battlefield but nothing in his long existence was comparable to seeing mangled body parts strewn amidst washes of blood. Worse was the smell. He'd retched violently after his first experience with the cannons. Sadly he recognized that civility, if any ever existed, had left warfare. It was only a matter of time before the other races developed that technology and employed it against their fellows. That, he regretfully admitted, would be a sad day for all Malweir.

"For a while, but not long enough. The enemy is too vast and our valiant Dwarves aren't supplied enough to wear the Goblins down to the point of being combat ineffective." Faeldrin's bright eyes darkened ever so slightly. Most Elves lacked the ability to see into the future, but a blind Elf could see that a great many lives were about to be lost on the banks of the Fern River in a few days. Friends and comrades, the Elf Lord readied his heart for the ache sure to come.

"Wait for it," Scrum growled quietly. The Dwarf commander crouched beside the number one cannon staring intently on the far riverbank. His rust-colored beard mirrored the late afternoon sunlight coming off the flowing waters.

The cannon crewmen waited anxiously for him to give the command. Veterans all, they lacked any of the nervousness a normal army might harbor. Hatred for the Goblins filled them with energy. Each Dwarf was chosen for his desire to make a name and leave a legacy behind. Bravery often met with death and each death was welcomed into their god's pantheon. Others feared to walk to the other side. Dwarves welcomed the opportunity.

"Steady, lads. I can smell 'em!" Scrum added. His savage grin matched the strength with which he grabbed his axe handle. "Another few moments and we'll show them how the Dwarves of Drimmen Delf fight."

More than one reached up to pat the cannon. Killing other Dwarves hurt deep inside, regardless of their allegiances, but killing Goblins was cause for merriment. Across the shore, the first ranks of the Goblin horde came into view. Sloppy, they loped along like children caught stealing. Any lack of tactical discipline they held, the Goblins more than made up for with lethality. Each was a capable warrior bred for the singular purpose of killing. That promise of bloodshed brought them from their kingdom of the Deadlands west towards Delranan and the rebirth of the dark gods.

Scrum didn't care why they were here or where they thought they were headed. His task was singular, simple. Stop them and turn the river red with their blood. A task he had no compunctions about fulfilling. The first scouts massed on the shore, debating where the most probable place to ford was. Their indecision worked in the Dwarves' favor. Each moment wasted in debate was one that brought the main body closer to the cannons. Scrum's grin widened as the first ranks of the main body lurched into sight.

Patience was never his strong suit, nor was it any Dwarf's. He preferred to attack immediately and seize the advantage while it lasted. Gunpowder changed that, slightly. Scrum clenched and unclenched his meaty fist. Time was almost up. More and yet more of the grey-skinned enemy came into view, unaware of what lay in wait.

Scrum glanced over at Faeldrin, the Elf nearly indistinguishable from the ground. All it took was the waggle of one finger. One finger that unleashed the fury of the hells.

"Fire!"

The grapeshot rounds from both cannons exploded amongst the Goblins before the blasts echoed across the water. Acrid smoke followed. Thousands of small balls of iron ripped and tore their way through hundreds of Goblins. Screams rose even as the Dwarves began reloading. Trained crews were capable of loading and firing in under a minute. Highly trained crews moved faster. The thunder of cannons roared again while the enemy was still disorganized. More screams. More mangled corpses. Body parts flew in all directions. The plop-plop of arms and legs splashing into the river was like music to Scrum's ears. He fruitlessly tried to wave the smoke from his vision as the crews rammed another round down the long barrels and prepped the fuses.

"Can you see, Elf?" he shouted.

Faeldrin, whose eyesight was far crisper than any other race, could only shake his head. The massive amount of smoke prevented him from seeing the battlefield, a handicap he failed to account for. He needed to get eyes up on the nearest hill and figure out a way to communicate effectively before the Goblins recovered and shifted their direction of movement.

"Aleor! Ride to the closest rise and give me a report on enemy movements," Faeldrin shouted above the roar of battle.

The younger Elf dashed back to his horse. His normally golden skin was paled, sickened from the sheer amount of violence unleashed this day. Never in his long life had he witnessed such devastation. And he never wished to again. Faeldrin watched him disappear into the haze before turning back to the river, desperate to see anything.

Scrum, to his credit, continued to fire. Each grapeshot canister delivered hundreds of small, iron balls that cut their way through flesh and wood at close range. The effects were horrifying psychologically. Unfortunately, the effectiveness diminished with range. The Dwarf captain had something else in store for those fortunate enemies out of grapeshot range: solid shot packed with large, round balls that exploded when they hit the ground were initially designed to fire against enemy cannon or siege machines. Nothing in Malweir, save perhaps a dragon, had such awesome effectiveness on the battlefield.

Scrum blinked as the fifth salvo blasted with smoke and fire from the cannons. He enjoyed the bitter smell almost as much as cleaving a Goblin with his favorite axe. No contrary orders, he continued to have the cannons fire into the enemy horde.

Faeldrin ripped his sword from his latest opponent. The thin rope of blood sprayed over the falling corpse and onto the snow. Hair disheveled, the Elf Lord was bordering exhaustion. Scrum's cannons successfully halted the Goblin horde for nearly an hour before the enemy started trying to find other places to ford the river. The body count was astounding. Corpses floated down river so thick the Elf could almost use them as a bridge. But the Dwarves only had limited quantities of ammunition. Each cannon now had but one shot remaining.

Aeldruin and Dwarves clashed with their hated foes north and south of the cannon positions. The initial assault was repulsed but the Goblins were most persistent. They kept coming in waves, hardly giving the defenders time to catch their breath. Several Elves had been killed and more wounded. Those able to ride were put upon horseback and sent west lest they perish for no reason. The fallen Dwarves were not so fortunate. They had clear orders from Thord. Defend to the last.

Their axes rang on shields as yet another Goblin push drove the defense tighter. It wouldn't be much longer before the horde would encircle them completely and crush them to death. Faeldrin and Scrum fought back to back. Axe and sword clove deep into Goblin flesh, yet for every one slain three more appeared. It was a battle the defenders couldn't win.

Scrum snagged the Elf Lord by his forearm and snarled, "Take your Aeldruin and flee. We'll handle this."

Faeldrin looked down into the fiery brown eyes, wanting to scream, *are you mad?* Suicide didn't serve any purpose, not even for a Dwarf. They were going to need every available sword and axe to stop the Goblin horde. Every life lost on the banks of the Fern River was avoidable. Sadly, there was no changing a Dwarf mind, especially not one willingly following orders. *Death in battle was a good death*. Regretfully, the Elf Lord nodded. "Let me take some of your wounded. We can heal them to fight another day."

Terms acceptable, Scrum nodded back. "We'll give you as much time as we can but, Elf Lord, it won't be much."

The slightest hint of fear lingered in his words, giving Faeldrin pause. He'd never heard a Dwarf speak of such and prayed never to again.

Scrum turned back to the battle. Less than forty Dwarves remained. All but a handful of the cannon crews were dead, but the Goblins had no idea how to use the terrible weapons so the heated iron barrels sat patiently awaiting their final roar. That time had come. Scrum gave Faeldrin a brief glance, enough to see most Elves and a handful of Dwarves fighting their way to safety. *Fare thee well, my friends. Look for us at Brek's table*!

He dashed over to the nearest cannon and lit the fuse. Goblins swarmed around him moments before the cannon exploded. Packed with as much gunpowder as they had remaining, both cannons were deliberately sabotaged by their owners. The resulting explosions killed scores of Goblins and more than a few Dwarves. Scrum's last sights were of fire and blood.

Crows and vultures flocked to the battlefield. Feathers drifted down while birds cawed and chased each other from the abundance of meat. The battle had lasted most of the day but was finally over. Eighty-seven Dwarves lay dead, their bodies hacked apart in a twisted ritual of hatred stemming back to the first Dwarf-Goblin war. Nine Elves were also among the litter of bodies, their near immortal flames snuffed by utter cruelty. As gruesome as those totals were, Goblin losses far exceeded any expectations. Close to eight hundred had been killed, most by the pair of cannons. Another seven hundred were wounded. Of those, at least two hundred wouldn't live through the night. While the losses were appalling, the Goblins weren't content with their victory. The true war lay in the west. Each moment of delay was one they couldn't afford.

Striding like a conqueror through the mass of bodies was a Goblin of immense proportions. Nearly five feet tall and well over two hundred pounds of honed muscle, the Goblin Lord Thrask surveyed all with great disdain. Smaller Goblins scraped and bowed to get out of his way. Elongated tusks dripped menacingly from his mouth. His face was a mass of scars. The right eye had gone dead long ago, after taking an Elf sword across it. He fondly recalled strangling the Elf in response. Long, jet black hair draped over his massive shoulders, falling halfway down his wide back. His armor was well used, unbefitting of a lord. But Thrask was a warrior first, lord second.

His piercing, black eyes, small and nestled under a thick brow, fell on the twisted metal of the cannons. So simple a thing to have caused such massive amounts of destruction. He stalked closer, overcoming his initial fear of the things. He reached a clawed hand out, tentatively touching the now cool metal. It was unlike anything he had ever encountered and, deep inside, ever wanted to again. Dwarves were known for their treachery. It was no surprise that the foul mountain dwellers would find new ways to slaughter his kind. Fresh waves of hatred pulsed from his dark heart. Thrask vowed not to stop until every last Dwarf was killed.

Growling his displeasure, the Goblin Lord turned to his retinue and ordered the advance. War was coming and he aimed to set the world on fire. The Goblin war machine lurched forward, leaving behind their dead and wounded. Weapons were shouldered. Ancient battle songs reached up to the heavens and the heavy stomp of hobnailed boots echoed across the frozen plains like the sound of impending doom.

TWELVE

Arlevon Gale

Malweir had not always been at war. Once, so long ago that none recalled, not even the long-lasting memories of the Elves, there had been peace. The gods ruled with utter surety. All matters of good and bad were metered out by their divine measure. Life developed slowly, almost casually. The gods maintained their presence throughout the course of several millennia. Entire species were created and discarded on whims during the exhaustive quest for perfection. The world expanded, heating and cooling in vast extremes.

No one could say from whence the gods came. Some speculated they originated in the distant stars and were making their way across space and time. Others argued they simply willed themselves into existence. The true power of the gods lay in belief. Without it they were nothing. Without it they died. The most prominent scholars among Elves and Dwarves agreed that this constant quest for perfection and the need for devotion was what led to the schism. The gods created obscene creatures for their own pleasures. A rift formed. Two sides emerged: light and dark. All who refused to take sides were destroyed without thought. There was no place in the new world for the unaligned.

The war of the gods consumed much of the world's population. Brother battled brother in the name of distant causes spurred by the gods. Malweir burned. Eventually entire races fell to darkness. Trolls and Goblins kept to the night, comfortable under the tutelage of their new, dark masters. Gnomes and dragons followed. Hope teetered on extinction. But all was not lost. Elves, Dwarves, Giants, and Men, always the upstart race, capable of either bringing great glory to all the world or plunging it down into total darkness.

Generations came and went under the conscriptions enforced by the gods. Generations lost on battlefields far and near. Mothers wept by hearths. The old languished under waves of guilt for not being able to stand with their kin on the line. Children grew up planning for the day when their names were called. A day every parent dreaded. Too few sons, brothers, and fathers returned from the war. Too few to rebuild their strength in sufficient numbers. Only the fell denizens of evil managed to break the code of immediate recreation. Goblins poured from the mountains in droves.

For a while, the balance threatened to shift towards darkness. Then the gods of light unleashed their most cherished creation: the knights of Gaimos. Bred to be the best fighters in the world, the Gaimosians dominated every battlefield they ever stepped foot on. Evil retreated on all fronts. The end was in sight. The forces of good surrounded their enemies and prepared for the final battle. A battle that never came.

Sensing their defeat, the dark gods sued for peace. They begged the gods of light to end the war, thus abandoning Malweir for their creations to rule as they saw fit. It was a scheme the gods of light failed to perceive. Already plans were in motion for the dark gods to return and claim total dominance over all life. Three nexuses were built, magical areas where the border between dimensions faded enough to allow passage. It was through these three hallowed places the dark gods attempted their return every thousand years. Trapped by the merits of their virtue, the gods of light were unable to return and prevent their fallen brothers from attempting their return. All their hopes rested on the shoulders of the Gaimosians. Only through their martial prowess were they able to prevent evil from ascending. Gifted with more than just military abilities, the Gaimosians became the fathers of the order of Mages. Such was the balance maintained until now.

The fall of Gaimos was a carefully orchestrated event. Manipulated by the Dae'shan and the dark gods, several kingdoms banded together to attack the fierce warriors with greed and jealousy. The annihilation was almost complete. Kingdomless, the survivors fled to the far corners of Malweir, ever searching for the return of their namesake. Prophecy stated that one day the realm of Gaimos would return and peace would follow. It was a prophecy the enemies of light struggled to be kept hidden from the rest of the world.

The war against evil continued for tens of thousands of years. Heroes and villains came and went, their legends passed down from father to son. Tokens of power were forged by master smiths. Timeless weapons that served their original intent with uncanny precision. Life and death took on new meaning. Without knowing it, the war centered around the nexuses. The first was destroyed by a band of Gaimosians recently displaced from fallen Gaimos. The war ended quickly and the surviving heroes marched eastward to found the castle of Ipn Shal and what would one day become the order of Mages.

Many thousands of years later the second nexus came under attack. Sidian, the Silver Mage, emboldened by the power of the dark gods, subsumed the land of Gren and raised a massive army with the intent of dominating the world. A small band of reluctant heroes assembled and marched into Gren while the war raged in western Averon. The dark gods nearly succeeded in returning to Malweir before a young boy from the village of Fel Darrins sacrificed his life to stop them. Rejected, the enemies of light retreated again.

Arlevon Gale was the last remaining nexus. Once a place of great prominence in northern Malweir, it was castle, trading post, and cultural center all in one. Folks of every race gathered to trade secrets and wealth, all blissfully unaware of the raw power threads lurking just beneath the earth. If only they had known Arlevon Gale was one of the three sacred places through which the dark gods could return, they might have ruled differently. As was the way of most civilizations, greed and avarice overwhelmed moral decency. People succumbed to their vices and madness took the land. Arlevon

Gale burned one night and didn't stop for a hundred years. Malweir had never seen the like.

Endless hours of torment and suffering pulsed into the atmosphere. Screams echoed for years before their pain finally wore out. Haunted, shunned by the rest of the world, Arlevon Gale fell into ruin and was almost forgotten. Only the Dae'shan dared occupy the once hallowed grounds. They twisted mortal flesh, creating new demons with which to wage their silent war on Malweir. They captured and manipulated the flesh, challenging genetic codes until the perfect combination of DNA was born. The bearers would be the ones to unlock the secrets of the Olagath Stone, a weapon of intense power that absorbed the torment of a hundred thousand souls. Souls that would force open the nexus and release the dark gods.

The Olagath Stone could only be unlocked by one of the proper blood. Amar Kit'han had originally believed that person to be Badron, king of Delranan. Breaking him had been easy, almost too easy. The challenge wasn't present, forcing the Dae'shan to reevaluate his previous observations. Badron was weak. His only son murdered at the hands of the prince of Rogscroft, an accident to be sure but a necessary one. That left Maleela. The unwanted princess. Her strength, passion, and resistance to evil made her the perfect choice. Breaking her wasn't going to be an easy chore, but Amar Kit'han was extremely experienced with torture.

He delighted in the mental torment constantly inflicted on the young woman. That she hadn't begun to crack was testament to the strength of her soul. When she did fall, it was going to be beyond the point of redemption. Amar Kit'han would forever claim her to be his proudest achievement.

Standing on the one-way glass roof, he watched as she greedily consumed the tepid water and semi-rotted loaf of dark bread. The princess of Delranan had abandoned all decorum, slowly giving in to animalistic urges. She didn't realize it but she was becoming less human. He needed her to be borderline aggressive, like the early races emerging from total night. Kodan Bak suggested drugging her with hallucinogens and mood enhancers, but Amar flatly refused. Mind altering chemicals were good for the common man, but he wanted Maleela to break on her own accord. She needed to understand what was changing inside on the basest level.

"You waste much time," Kodan hissed, materializing beside the elder Dae'shan. "She should already be a willing servant."

Amar contemplated ignoring his second. Their debate had become tiresome. He almost wished Kodan would make his move for power so that they could set it aside and carry on with the dark gods' will. "She already is, though she knows it not. The human mind is fragile, Kodan Bak, more so than you can recall. Her body remains hale while her mind slowly withers. Trapped inside this cell, and the husk that she is slowly turning into, Maleela will soon be ready to accept the blessing of the dark gods and fulfill her destiny."

"And the father? What of him?" Kodan asked.

Amar paused. He hadn't thought of Badron for many weeks now. The vagabond king was of no consequence. He'd played his part and committed the northern kingdoms to pure chaos. Whatever he became was no matter to the Dae'shan. "An unfortunate side effect. He served his purpose and is free to go where he will."

Kodan drifted closer, thoughts of murder entertaining him. "Perhaps you should know Badron has already returned to Delranan."

"With no army," Amar countered thoughtfully. "The Wolfsreik abandoned him and poor Grugnak's Goblin army is all but decimated. Whatever force remaining loyal to the deposed king is inconsequential. Our focus needs to be on Maleela."

"Using her to activate the Stone is a small matter. There is a war coming to this part of the world. Rogscroft is finished. It will take decades to rebuild. Goblins, Dwarves, and Men are about to clash on these very plains. Not even our power is sufficient to save our lives."

It was an interesting concept. Their lives were technically ended several thousand years ago when their mortal shells died. Their ascension to more left them without the complexities that restrained mortal beings. They were able to see oh so much more with the gifts bestowed upon them by the gods. Amar Kit'han didn't like being reminded of his past weakness. He'd risen to his rank through brutality and deception. Kodan Bak aimed to steal that from him. It was an old ploy the Dae'shan often succumbed to. Amar relished the opportunity to prove his dominance yet again. Until that moment arrived he needed to focus on the task at hand. Let Kodan deal with Badron if it concerned him so. Maleela was the true prize.

"What do you propose to do about it? We were never intended to fight wars, merely push them in the correct direction," he finally asked.

Kodan hesitated, suddenly caught off guard. He hadn't expected Amar to acquiesce so easily. The action made him wary. "Badron remains a power player. He will not stop until he either wins back his stolen crown or dies in the attempt."

"Perhaps you should facilitate that early demise," Amar suggested. Kodan's words bothered him on many levels. He despised being wrong, about anything, but there was no way of denying that Badron wasn't about to cause trouble. He knew too much of what the Dae'shan intended. It would only be a matter of time before he put enough pieces together and headed towards Arlevon Gale. That couldn't happen. On the other hand, Badron's interference was bound to further complicate matters developing around them. The distraction might prove beneficial as the hour of the dark gods' return approached. Amar was truly torn for the first time in recent memory.

Kodan Bak sensed his dilemma and pressed. "Could we not further use him to our advantage? Our enemies will still be hunting him. If he could reunite with the One Eye, Pelthit Re seems intent on toying with they could eliminate one another and draw focus far from here."

Interested, Amar asked, "What do you propose?"

THIRTEEN

New Allies

They stalked across the snow like wraiths. Footprints so light they barely left marks. Each of the three was focused. Their eyes never strayed from the target. Heartbeats thundered in their ears, unheard by the rest of the world. Stripped of armor, they were able to move quicker, cover more distance than being encumbered by the heavy cast iron and boiled leather that had saved their lives more times than any could count. That initial awkward feeling had passed. They felt lighter, quicker. More like scouts than heavy infantry, the trio was able to cover great distance in half the time.

The leader dropped to a knee and raised a fist, immediately halting the other two. Professionals all, they scanned left and right in hopes of spying their quarry. Bow strings were drawn tighter. One licked his lips in anticipation. Their leader leaned forward, examining the fresh layer of snow. He was rewarded with footprints and blood.

"Blood trail," he said, pointing at the already frozen, red spots on the snow. His gaze rose, following the trail. He took off without waiting for the others.

They loped after, always stalking. Half the day had passed. Half a day with the trio on the hunt with no other responsibility or worry. The sudden lack of doubts left them free in ways they had forgotten. Too many months on the quest burdened them considerably but all that was put behind them now.

A quarter of an hour later they halted again. The blood trail had grown thicker. The tracks more frenzied. They were close. Exhilaration pumped in their veins. They were close, so very close to ending this hunt and returning to camp. Unused muscles burned from exertion. They suffered from shortness of breath and mild cases of frostbite. It would all be worth it so long as they found their prey. Thinking of it as quarry didn't do them justice. They came out here looking to kill.

The bull elk was down on its knees, struggling to breathe, to keep fighting against the inevitable, slow crawl of death. The arrow sticking out of its chest prevented that. Plumes of hot breath came out in ragged clouds. The elk was dying.

The leader stopped and signaled for the others to stay back. Setting an arrow to string, he calmly drew back and aimed. His eyes closed briefly as he calmed his trembling nerves. It had been so long since he last did this simple task of mercy. Whispering a silent prayer that his shaft struck true, he loosed. The brush of feathers raked his cheek. The low-pitched hum of the arrow speeding across the distance between hunter and prey tingled his skin. The dull thwack as the arrow struck the elk just behind the shoulder to pierce its heart was like thunder rolling across the heavens. The elk groaned once and dropped over dead.

The leader got a pat on the back.

"Great shot, Nothol," Dorl Theed said, the appetite of his grin evident to all.

Nothol Coll slowly lowered his bow and rose. "I haven't done that since I was kid with my father. I'd almost forgotten what it feels like."

"It's going to feel like fresh meat going down our throats once we butcher and cook it," Dorl answered. The food of the Dwarves, Giants, and even of Trennaron was all well and fine, but there was nothing like freshly killed game from Delranan.

Rekka swept her gaze over the men, trying to understand their base ways better. The pair had been companions for many years and through many adventures. They knew each other better than she ever hoped to with another person. Her blossoming love with Dorl left her more content than she'd been in her short life, but she still felt like she was missing an important piece. What, she didn't know.

"We should offer our thanks for this blessing," she said once they'd finished their banter. Raised to believe one should only kill when necessary, Rekka appreciated the bounty the elk represented. It would feed them for many meals. Thankfully Groge wasn't partial to eating red meat. Otherwise the elk wouldn't last a night.

Dorl looked at Nothol and repressed the urge to shrug. Food was food. He'd never celebrated the life of any animal and, truthfully, didn't feel like starting now. Still, he wasn't willing to upset Rekka over so simple a task. "Sure, but we need to drain it, skin it, and dress it before it starts getting dark. I don't want to be caught out here after nightfall."

Ignoring him, Rekka skipped over and knelt beside the corpse. She gingerly touched it above the eye and raised her hands to the skies, offering half mumbled words of praise to the gods of light for providing such bounty. Dorl and Nothol watched, mesmerized by the simple perfection of the moment. Such times were rare in this new world. Finished, Rekka drew her dagger and slit the great bull's throat to drain the blood while she split it down the belly and began dressing it out so they could quarter and pack it for transport back to camp.

Sunlight turned the snows frosted shades of gold. A small flock of snow geese honked as they drifted past. Dorl almost relaxed enough to enjoy the moment. Almost, before he spied movement across the plains. His heart clenched with that old fear that had accompanied him since first leaving Delranan. Moments later that familiar sound drifted to them. It was the sound of armor rattling.

He reached out and slapped Nothol on the arm without looking. "Soldiers."

Nothol raised his eyes, following Dorl's pointed finger. "Soldiers" was the simplistic form. What he saw was a lot of soldiers, enough to run through Ingrid's paltry band of rebels without breaking a sweat. They were in trouble. No amount of experience was enough to prevent panic from springing to life. The odd chance of death was ever present, a permanent companion for men in their line of work, but he wasn't ready for death to come today.

"Have they seen us?" he asked in a whisper.

Dorl didn't think so but they couldn't take the chance. "Get down. There's no way we can outrun them. Our best bet is to take cover and hope they pass us by."

Nothol frowned. "What if they have dogs? They'll smell the blood and come running."

Resisting the urge to smack his best friend from mucking things up further, Dorl hurried over to Rekka and explained the situation. The warrior woman from Teng drew her sword and huddled down over the elk's corpse.

"They are too many to fight," she said while counting heads.

As they trudged closer, Dorl was able to make out the colors and insignia of Wolfsreik reservists. A heavy foot patrol meant one thing: they were too close to the enemy base of operations for this area. Any thought of salvaging the meat dissolved. Dorl knew what needed to be done, though he doubted he had the courage to do it. Bahr and Ingrid needed to be warned. He started low crawling back towards Nothol and the small stand of holly bushes. The red berries seemed almost obscene combined with the unending fields of snow stretching for as far as the eye could see.

Nothol looked worried. "Do you run?"

"Go ahead. You go left and I'll wait for you to draw them off," Dorl chided. Contrary to popular belief, there was such a thing as a stupid question. If it came to a fight it was going to be nasty and end unfavorably for the sell swords. Dorl didn't fancy dying in the middle of nowhere, with no one to recall his last deeds. Abandoned by the rest of the world, he'd wither and turn to dust without anyone ever knowing where he met his end. Not a particularly deep thinker, Dorl Theed eagerly began imagining ways to survive the day.

Sunlight glinted off spear tips. The patrol, close to fifty men, or half a company, marched dangerously close to their position. They looked forward, always towards where that next foot would step and hoping to catch a glimpse of their destination. Scouts and flankers were meant to search the general area while the main body marched. Ideally the scouts would spy the enemy and give warning, allowing the infantry to form up in battle ranks and either attack or defend based on enemy troop strengths.

If the Wolfsreik was using scouts, Dorl and the others were already dead. Their horses were back at camp. Abandoned by the rest of their companions, the trio couldn't head back to Bahr without risking giving away their position and bringing the entire enemy army down on their heads. Dorl doubted capture was in their mandate. At this point in the war neither side must be willing to take many prisoners. *It always circles back to death. Like an ill guest I can't avoid. Maybe I need to retire and move south.*

He was able to exhale in relief a short while later as the enemy patrol marched off to the north. Whatever they were about, it had nothing to do with fruitlessly searching the empty fields and small groves of pines peppering the landscape. They were on a mission, but what continued to bother the sell sword almost to the point where he considered following just to find out. Disregarding the notion as foolish, with more than a few stern words of admonishment for himself, Dorl finally rose and sheathed his sword.

"We're safe now," he said needlessly.

Nothol threw a snowball at him. "We haven't been safe since joining Bahr last autumn. Good thing they didn't have dogs. I like them too much to kill one."

"Not even to save me?" Dorl asked.

Nothol scoffed and helped Rekka finish quartering the elk. Waste not.

"Are you positive?" Bahr asked. His face was drawn, lips pursed in thought. The redness in his cheeks seemed almost permanent again and his eyes carried red strings of stress.

Ingrid passed Orlek a worried glance. The rebellion was fluid, thankfully, but it would take time for her to pack everything up and move out to their next position. Time they apparently didn't have.

Dorl nodded too eagerly. "Yes. They were heavily armed and armored and not worried about running in to anything they couldn't handle. Whatever they were about, they were moving with a purpose."

"But to where? We can't move without knowing their destination," Orlek jumped in. His natural soldier instincts were jump-started. It had been nearly a week since their last engagement at the old farmhouse.

Dorl shot him an incredulous glare. "You can go after them all you want. I didn't sign on to fight a war."

He calmed, slightly, after Bahr silenced him with a curt wave. "The question isn't where they are going so much as why. Heavy patrols serve no purpose this far out in the wilds. Unfortunately for my party, the enemy is too active for us to slip through unnoticed."

"Meaning what exactly?" the sell sword pressed. He didn't like the notion of being pirated by his own employer. He jumped after Nothol slapped the back of his head. "What was that for?"

"For being stupid," Nothol answered squarely. "Bahr hasn't led us wrong since this whole blasted affair began. Sure, we keep running into situations beyond our control but he's brought each and every one of us back from the beginning. Well, all save Ionascu and he wasn't a big loss."

"Ionascu? Harnin's worm?" Orlek asked, prompting Ingrid to again question just what her second in command had once been.

Bahr grunted. "The same. Delranan needn't worry about him again. His body is rotting in the Jungles of Brodein."

"Good riddance." Dorl scowled at the foul memories of being around the broken man. Even before Harnin's torturers mangled his arms and legs, Ionascu had been a pain for the expedition. Losing him was more blessing than bane.

Placing his hands on his hips, Orlek looked to Ingrid and said, "It seems our *guests* haven't told us everything yet."

"Nor should they. We all have secrets, Orlek," Ingrid said softly. "If Bahr were our enemy these three would have sold us out to the Wolfsreik already. I think we have a unique opportunity here. A chance to finally turn the tide in the rebellion and crush our enemies without them even knowing it."

"How so?" Bahr asked hesitantly. He didn't like the idea of being corralled in to fighting yet another war. There were only so many battles he and his group could fight before their luck, and time, ran out. How much remained to be seen.

"The rebellion isn't as strong as it might have been. The plague wiped out most of our able-bodied fighters. Those few who remained fled to the countryside and are now scattered, at my discretion of course. We can fight. Can even steal victories from Harnin's slacking forces. But we lack the heavy punch to crush our enemy for good. Your name alone will draw more fighters, more support to our cause. Even if you don't participate, which I am not asking you to, I can utilize your name and presence for the betterment of the kingdom."

Her request unanticipated, Bahr cracked his knuckles and began to pace around the fire. Deep inside he loved his kingdom, though whether enough to halt everything for it remained to be seen. The fate of a single kingdom was insignificant compared to the entire world unknowingly counting on his actions. He felt torn for the first time in decades. Both choices presented unique challenges that robbed from the other. Could he forsake one for the other? Which weighed more? The lives of a few thousand or all Malweir? The answer was obvious. He had sworn his life to accomplishing the task set before him by Artiss Gran and even Anienam Keiss. His internal debate quickly faded away. In the end there never was a choice.

"I can't tell you what we're committed to doing," he began slowly, taking time to pick and choose his words. Ingrid was ensorcelled by her rebellion and restoring order to Delranan. She didn't need to bear the weight of his problems moving forward. "But know that our actions, whether we fail or succeed, will determine the fate of all life on Malweir. None of us asked for this task, but we've come too far and done too much to quit now. We must continue east, back towards the Murdes Mountains will all possible dispatch."

"Your travel companions alone merit your hesitance in aiding us," she replied. "Giants, Dwarves, Gaimosians, and a wizard. Who could possibly travel with such friends in times like this? I won't pretend that I'm not disappointed by your answer. We need all the help we can get. What we have now is barely enough to keep holding on and winter doesn't seem to want to end any time soon. Perhaps there is a temporary solution to both of our problems."

He halted. "I'm listening."

Her heart skipped with joy. "You have an army of at least two thousand spread out in front of you. Going around is out of the question as you are on a strict timeline. Fighting through isn't an option either due to the risk you and your companions face."

Bahr nodded. As much as he'd like to fight for his kingdom he simply couldn't. The Dae'shan said they all needed to arrive at Arlevon Gale to have any possibility of success.

"I suggest we discover what interests the Wolfsreik so much and make a coordinated strike." She held up her hand to stop his expected protests. "If we force Jarrik to concentrate his forces and meet us, on our terms, we'll draw their attention away from the rest of the kingdom, thus giving you a clear avenue to the east. What happens after that is beyond my control, however. What do you say?"

Dorl Theed hung his head. The prospect of another battle soured his stomach. *Always back to death.*

After long, deliberate moments of contemplation, Bahr reached his hand out. "I think it sounds like a viable option. You have a deal, Ingrid."

The two sealed their agreement with a firm handshake. Dorl whimpered quietly.

FOURTEEN

The Heroes Go East

Ironfoot strapped his boiled leather armor down on the sides, adjusting the right so it fit snug but still loose enough for him to swing his axe without losing breath. He'd combed his beard out for the first time since leaving Drimmen Delf. The prospect of battle enthused him in ways the others thought mad. Not that he cared. He was a warrior. Dying in battle was the ultimate honor for any Dwarf to attain. Only Boen understood, for he too felt the irresistible pull towards combat. Whistling, he thumped his chest twice. Satisfied with his work, he headed back to the wagon to finish oiling his helm.

"He said it just like that?" Skuld asked, eyes wide with shock. The young man couldn't believe how easily Bahr had turned a potentially dangerous situation into one where they were able to continue to Arlevon Gale.

Dorl waved him off, not troubling to be bothered with insignificant questioning. "I tell you, Anienam, we're all going to die before we get to where we're going."

"How are we supposed to get there if we die before we do?" Nothol asked in jest.

"You shut your mouth. You had a chance to speak up and tell the old man what needs to happen but you chose not to," Dorl growled.

Nothol's face brightened with mirth. "I chose to keep my head on my shoulders. This isn't a game, you damned fool. I'm starting to think you are too focused about dying than trying to see this through to the end. We've got our opportunity to escape Harnin's men without getting killed in the process."

"Not if they find us before we can slip through their lines," Dorl countered too quickly. "Old Anienam can't see the enemy to fight them if we get stopped. Groge still doesn't want to fight, and I'll not be the one who tries to get him to change his mind. One swat from him and I'd be paste on the rocks."

"What rocks? Everywhere you look is snow!" Nothol all but shouted.

Dorl grinned sheepishly. Finally, he was beginning to make the other sell sword lose his patience. A rare turn of events indeed.

"Gentlemen, you worry over naught," Anienam interrupted. Being referred to as merely the "old, blind man" was wearing thin. He thought about a small demonstration to reaffirm their faith but decided it would only succeed in bringing attention to their whereabouts. "Bahr is entirely capable of seeing to our best needs. Keep faith, young sell sword. It would be a shame if I boiled your tongue in your mouth just to keep you quiet."

Dorl's hand flew to his mouth and he walked off, grumbling to himself lest the wizard overhear and take action.

Skuld leaned close to Anienam and whispered, "Can you really do that?"

Patting his arm gently, Anienam replied, "Probably, but I don't really know."

Chuckling softly, the former street urchin of Chadra went back to double checking the supplies on the back of the wagon were secure. Their journey promised to be difficult, more so due to them not being able to use the roads from fear of being captured. Groge had volunteered to take point and trample a suitable path for horse, rider, and wagon. His massive stride could clear meters of snow without much effort, thus saving them the trouble of digging through the larger drifts.

He didn't mind. Walking suited him, giving the Giant the time he needed to get his mind right. It also alleviated the need for pointless conversation. He'd come to enjoy the company of the others but they weren't Giants. He was surprised to find a longing in his heart to return home.

To be among the heat of the forges, even the criticisms of Blekling and the others so content with keeping change from Venheim. Change was coming, Groge mused. Change that none of them had the power or authority to withstand. He wondered if home would remain the home of his youth for much longer.

Boen watched the Giant lumber away, one hand gently rubbing the stubble on his chin. The Gaimosian knew what it felt like to be conflicted with internal debate. He'd undergone more than his share in his youth. Being a kingdomless knight was one thing, learning to accept that you would never have a home, a land, no lord to call king, or a place to raise a family among others of your own kind was disheartening. It had taken Boen several years to come to terms with his lot in life. Once embraced, however, he never looked back.

"He'll be fine," Ironfoot grunted from a nearby stump. He made slow circles with an oiled rag over the top of his battle helm.

Boen looked down and said, "I'm not worried about the Giant. Will he discover he has what it takes to make the hard choices when the time comes? His role is not for the weak of heart."

"I suppose not," the Dwarf replied. Part of a strong clan, he found the concept of being a singular warrior oddly frightening. Warriors needed to band together. There was strength in numbers. Weakness dominated those who lacked someone to watch their backs when times grew dark. Ironfoot reluctantly viewed his companions as fellow warriors who, in theory, had his back.

Boen nodded, his mind already thinking ahead. "Trust me, I know. Groge is a good lad. He'll be there for us when we need him. Too bad we're trying not to run in to the enemy. We're due for a good fight. It's been too long."

"Agreed. We haven't had a proper battle since the river men," Ironfoot said. Those memories continued to fade rapidly as each subsequent trial broadened their nightmares.

Boen frowned. A deep foreboding suggested they were about to come to a crossroads where neither of them would ever want to fight again or risk being lost to the iron. He let the thought fade and went back to his own preparations. The time for talk was ending. War was upon them.

"I don't expect many of you to understand why we make this agreement," Ingrid told her assembled rebels. "Bahr's name alone will change the course of our struggle, but he cannot, nor will I expect him to, stay for longer than his will. We both are sworn to sacred oaths. Today I have sent riders out to the other companies. We will consolidate and engage Lord Jarrik and his Wolfsreik murderers on our terms. Today we begin the quest to reclaim Delranan for ourselves. No longer will the tyranny of a few dominate the lives of all! We were born free and, by the gods, I will see to it that we all meet our ends as free men and women. Today we take the first steps in toppling Harnin One Eye!"

Cheers erupted. The rebellion had suffered many and varying shames over the course of the war. It was past time for that course to reverse. Even if it meant burning Chadra Keep to the ground around Harnin's head.

Ingrid reveled in their support. For a time, a much longer time than she'd anticipated, she felt lost, felt the rebellion was on its last legs and about to die. The passion of her assembled fighters changed all that. Holding up her hands for silence, she continued, "I do not command you to follow me. No, for I am no tyrant. Those of you who wish to return to your families may do so at any time. No one person has the right to expect others to lay down their lives for a cause they aren't committed to. Go now without shame or the burden of failure. You have served your kingdom and your people honorably and will be treated so."

She paused, nervous about the results. Long moments stretched on yet no one moved. Her heart relaxed.

Slightly. They were all with her. *Only to what end I cannot promise. I fear I may be leading you all to slaughter.* "Through your actions will our lands be free again! From your courage and sacrifice will Delranan rise from the ashes of this nightmare Harnin One Eye has created. You are the future and it fills my heart with great joy to see that each and every one of you is as committed to the cause as I am. Thank you, my friends. Thank you all."

She stepped away as the crowd roared their approval. Seldom were times calm enough to leave her feeling good about the path she'd chosen. The longer the rebellion stretched on the more she lost little pieces of herself. She longed for the days before the war, before her husband was killed. That moment burned in her mind, a blinding candle incapable of being extinguished. Her husband had been one of Piper Joach's captains during their first engagement with the soldiers of Rogscroft. While the report was intentionally vague about the manner of his demise, it did mention he was struck down saving a pair of fallen troopers. He had done his duty for Delranan. She could do no less.

"That was inspiring," Bahr told her once she exited the public view. "It's been a long time since the people of this kingdom had any reason to hope. My brother was never one for fancy speeches, especially not ones meant to inspire hope. I think you are the right woman for this position, Ingrid."

The admission did not come without a measure of guilt. Rebel leaders often found their heads trapped in a noose. He secretly suspected she and the others would meet much the same. Harnin had too many trained soldiers, too much experience, and a nasty streak unlike any Bahr had ever encountered. Artiss Gran cautioned the One Eye was under the sway of his fellow Dae'shan, prompting Bahr to question what could be worse than adhering to the will of demons.

Catching the sadness in his voice, Ingrid said, "Somehow I doubt whether or not any of that will matter when this is said and done. Harnin has no mercy for those outside of his favor."

Bahr nodded. A prisoner himself, he and the others escaped through blind luck and the treason of Lord Argis. The traitor lord of Delranan paid for his indiscretions with his life, as Ingrid explained shortly after her initial interrogation. *A shame. He was a good man. One this kingdom is going to need. There is much to be said for quality of character.*

"I've spent a few nights in Chadra's dungeons," he admitted. "Not the sort of place for a lady. Harnin will kill everyone he thinks gets in his way."

"You're still alive," she countered.

He barked a laugh. "Only because we escaped. Otherwise my head would be on the walls with all the others."

He felt silently abruptly, knowing the loss of Argis was still too real for Ingrid. She'd come to respect him in many ways and continued to feel his loss. Knowing better than to speak ill of the dead, he changed the subject. "We still have a problem. We need to know where these heavy infantry patrols are headed and in what kind of numbers. Until then there's no way we can risk moving."

"I agree. I've sent scouts out, but we could always use a little help," she hinted.

Bahr scratched the back of his hand. "I might be able to arrange that. Boen is itching to get back into the field. It might do him some good to stretch his legs."

"Can you trust a Gaimosian to avoid a fight?" she asked, suddenly rethinking her proposition.

Bahr hadn't considered that. "Who knows? He's focused on our task, but that doesn't mean his sword won't find its way into a belly or two along the way. No one enjoys battle like a Gaimosian. Still, I think he'll use his discretion, though it might kill him inside."

She hoped so. The alternative wasn't pleasant.

Boen rode into the darkness. His armor and helmet were stored back on the wagon, leaving him swathed in furs and heavy riding cloaks. His only weapon was his great broadsword. He didn't need anything else. Killing a man was just as easy with his bare hands as with a sword. Reluctantly, he forced himself to recognize that it wasn't about the act of killing. It was about being better than his opponent and avoiding death. Therein lay the true skill. So many warriors, of all races, failed to understand that simple concept.

The Vengeance Knight stalked through the night in search of the trail Dorl had run across earlier. It felt nice to be away from the incessant conversation and bickering. They'd been together for so long they were at the point where nerves frayed easily. Patience gradually wore away alongside the endless path of leagues stretching across half of Malweir. Rather than arguing with them, Boen jumped at the opportunity to get back into his natural element.

His breath came in plumes. Pervasive chills crept down his spine each time the wind grew too strong. His eyes bore that constant burn from being tired and cold. Every stumble his horse made jarred maddeningly through his body. Yet for each discomfort he found another pleasure to take his mind away. The call a great owl. The howl of a wolf. A snowshoe rabbit sitting immobile under a small bush as he rode by, hoping against being seen. The world was as fascinating as it was dangerous and he enjoyed living through each new experience.

Time meant nothing in the wild. There was no future or past. There was only now. Boen's mind casually drifted back to echoes of decades past. A young knight, he set out for Paedwyn, capital of the mighty kingdom of Averon. The world, it was said, revolved around what the king of Averon decreed. Minor border wars broke out from time to time and, rather than waste his own soldiers, the king often hired mercenaries and his favorite Gaimosians to break the backs of his enemy. Boen was hardly a tested warrior when he jumped at the chance to prove his worth.

A war party of Goblins had come down from hiding in the Gren Mountains to raid and burn a string of small villages along the banks of the Thorn River. Incensed, the king deployed his largest field force to crush the Goblins for good. Ever since the fall the Silver Mage and the destruction of Gren had they clung to the shadows, hiding deep in the mountain caverns while biding their time. Their defeat on the Nveden Plains remained a painful reminder of their failings against men. It spurred their hatred and drove them ever on in a pointless war of attrition they seemed destined to lose. While their kin could be seen as thriving in the Deadlands far to the northwest, the Goblins of Gren struggled just to exist.

Boen helped them ease that burden. He and a contingent of Gaimosians, Elves from Elvanara, and heavy horse from Harlegor disobeyed the orders of the king and went in search of the enemy base of operations. The quest didn't take as long as many feared and battle was met on the mountain slopes. Boen himself met the Goblin King in battle and took his head in a duel so engaging the rest of the battle stopped to watch. Disheartened in seeing their king's head roll down the blackened slope, the Goblins broke and ran. And were hunted down to the very last.

He'd heard rumors of a band of cutthroats braving the caverns to kill the Goblin women and children though he had no proof. A man was nothing without proof. Deeds meant little without witness. Boen took the Goblin King's baldric for a trophy and rode away. His task was complete. There was nothing else to prove in Averon. Only the king didn't view matters the same. He grew enraged over the disobedience of his orders and decreed those responsible were to be hunted down and brought to justice. Outlawed, Boen fled Averon.

His reputation had already spread. Word reached Paedwyn of how a lone Gaimosian struck the Goblin King down and turned the battle into a rout. The king of Averon, while ever grateful for the act, thought long and hard on whether to pardon the Gaimosian or not. Boen didn't wait to learn the decision. His fame brought wealth and no few assassination attempts by zealots eager to curry favor with the king. Boen killed all those foolish enough to cross his path and continued into new adventures. To this day he still didn't know whether the old king had ever rescinded the order to kill all involved.

Nor did he care. His life abounded with wealth and glory. His legend continued to grow with each new battle. Every quest went beyond the previous. Boen snorted. It seemed fitting that this last quest would not only change the course of all life on Malweir but determine the very fate of the world. One last quest before he packed his weapons and tried to find peace in what little time he had left.

The very idea of no longer fighting his way through life frightened him in ways nothing else could. Never one to languish under family constraints, Boen didn't know what to do with himself. He'd lived a warrior's life from an early age. He didn't know anything else. Combat was his legacy. It was all his people had left to them. Families and normalcy were anathema to Gaimosians. Still, the prospect of engaging in an entirely new facet of life offered great promise. Or so he told himself.

Half of the night was already gone by the time he crossed the heavily worn track. So many boots had marched through he could no longer distinguish individual prints. Boen nodded. It was the sign he'd been looking for. Wheeling down the trail, Boen rode north in pursuit of what the enemy seemed intent on concealing. To the best of his knowledge, no other scout had returned with so much as a scrap of actionable intelligence. The leadership needed to know the enemy's intent. That left only Boen. A Gaimosian could succeed where ordinary men failed.

He rode for another hour when he spied the first glimmers of torches. His smile spread. The urge to ride ahead and meet Harnin's forces head on nearly proved too much. Killing a handful would be self-gratifying but nonproductive in the grand scheme of the war. Seasoned, he knew better than to make rookie mistakes. There'd come a time for vengeance to boil over and for the blood to flow, but it was not now. The sound of hammers and saws working through the night enticed him. Dismounting, Boen tied his horse to the nearest tree and crept forward.

His size was a nonfactor. Bigger than most men, Boen was still able to walk with extreme stealth. Stealth he needed in order not to get caught. Bahr's words echoed as he walked. *Whatever you do, don't get caught. We can't afford a fight yet.* Frowning, Boen reluctantly agreed despite being forced to abandon his greatest asset. Making no more noise than a deer, he crept close enough to get a better view. What he saw confirmed his fears.

Walls were being erected, complete with murder holes for archers and deep, wide pits ringing the perimeter to prevent direct assaults. Four towers were in various stages of completion. Boen counted close to two hundred men working through the night. No doubt more tried to find some respite from the forced labor. Hard work left tired soldiers. Judging from the amount of construction already started, they were nearly finished. Harnin One Eye had just built his first redoubt in western Delranan.

FIFTEEN

A Sheep in Wolf's Clothing

"I'm going to piss," Maik said as he dropped his work axe and headed off without waiting for a reply.

Tired from being worked to the bone, Maik was normally a guard in a merchant's warehouse in Stouds. Harnin's call up of the Wolfsreik reserves forced him to abandon his life's work for, he wasn't exactly sure of what any longer. He participated in the near total destruction of Chadra and marched countless leagues into the middle of nowhere to hunt down what remained of the rebellion. Maik still hadn't seen an actual rebel yet, despite his commander's insistence otherwise. For the last seven days and nights he'd been building a small fort in the middle of nowhere. The reasoning why was well above his pay level.

Leaving his weapons behind--after all, what could possibly attack him this far away from all traces of civilization? --Maik trudged through the snows. He tried thinking about better times, like those summer days by the lake where he and his father used to go fishing. Three feet of snow and below freezing temperatures didn't allow for it, though. Everywhere he turned was another reminder of just how harsh life in the north could be. Unbuckling his trousers, he never saw the giant pair of hands reaching out from the night to grab his skull and twist.

The armor was a little too snug, reminding him that he was not in the shape he had been in. Frowning, Boen tried, and failed, to adjust the leather straps on the sides. No matter what he did he had to admit he was just too large for the armor. Hopefully he didn't stand out among the others. *At least the helmet fits. Now I only hope this man didn't have many friends.*

Boen glanced down at Maik's corpse one last time before heading towards the redoubt. Bahr would be furious if he found out, but the Gaimosian had an intuitive feeling that he had to know more before heading back to the rebel camp. Building a fortress in an endless field of snow made little sense, unless Harnin had information regarding the precise where-abouts of the rebel force. Boen couldn't shake the thought. Spies were common enough in Delranan these days. It certainly wasn't much of a stretch of the imagination to think Ingrid's ranks were riddled with infiltrators. He hoped to discover the truth tonight and possibly a name or two.

No one questioned him or bothered looking twice as he slipped through the lines and into the construction zone. *So far so good. Now I just need to find someone with a little rank and beat a confession out of them.* The last thought put a smile on his face. Bashing in the brains of an enemy without them realizing what was happening almost made him laugh, but laughter would have been a dead giveaway to him pretending to be one of them. No one in the redoubt had a smile or seemed the least bit happy with their lot in life. Another good omen. Soldiers didn't mind fighting but had nothing but complaints when it came to anything else.

He knew from personal experience that work details were the worst. Some genius with a little rank on his collar decided that the only way for him to gain acceptance from the soldiers was by having them undertake a seemingly mindless project. Idle soldiers were a waste, or so the military frame of mind went. Little did most new commanders realize was that their over eagerness to gain respect often turned sour and did exactly the opposite. Boen learned early on that the best commanders were the ones with shovels in their hands digging holes beside their soldiers. Respect was earned, never given, regardless of the luxuries of rank or privilege.

Fighting men were simple. They always complain, even under ideal conditions, and give their all for the soldiers to their left and right. Those few commanders who stay alive long enough to figure that out went on to become some of the best generals and lords in all Malweir. The rest were ground underfoot until nothing but powder remained of their bones. He'd seen it play out a thousand times over the course of his six decades. Boen, like all Gaimosians, learned quickly and had naturally ingrained martial abilities. That didn't take away from the learning curve that could only come from raw experience. A quick look around the redoubt showed him there were few enough walking around with that kind of experience.

He knew better than to let down his guard, however. The only thing Boen had going for him was the fact that it was the middle of the night and freezing. No one wanted to be working the night shift, nor the day for that matter. Frigid temperatures left the men feeling more tired than usual and wholly disgruntled with their lives. None of that would matter should one mistake him for the man he'd just killed. *Or find the body for that matter. Combine that with this damned idiot not carrying his weapon and I had to leave my sword behind.*

Going virtually unarmed into an enemy position was beyond foolish and he needed to make every effort to blend in. Camouflage was his best defense for what he had in mind.

Others accused or chided him of lacking the finesse to pull off working behind enemy lines. This was his chance to prove them wrong and quash all doubt while simultaneously producing sorely needed intelligence on enemy troop strength and movements, disposition, and operational status. All he had to do was slip away through the cracks and make his escape without being noticed well before the dawn sun broke the horizon.

He couldn't count on his size and demeanor to get him out of working. The idea of going on sick call briefly entered his mind but, knowing what he did about the inner functions of an army, he'd be degraded and sent back to the line, accused of sloth more than actual sickness. No, Boen needed to find another way to move freely about the encampment.

Lacking any frame of reference for what part of the labor lines the dead man came from, Boen headed towards the largest knot of soldiers struggling to move wagon loads of freshly cut logs to construct a wooden palisade on the southern perimeter. Stones were being set on the east and north. They were giant, squared stones polished smooth and near impregnable by any weapon in the Delrananian arsenal. He mused of the miraculous Dwarven cannons shattering the defenses under a hail of smoke, shrapnel, and thunder. Having seen their full destructive force in action, he knew they'd make quick work of this redoubt, not to mention the already waning morale of the soldiers huddled within.

"Hey, give me a hand with this."

Boen concealed his grin. *Finally*. He looked up at the man calling for him. Slightly smaller than the Gaimosian, the Wolfsreik soldier beckoned with one hand while his other rested on a log Boen guessed weighed around three hundred pounds. Between them both it was more than manageable. He rolled his shoulders to get the knots of a long day's ride out as he walked over. He'd had the presence of mind to keep his gloves on, otherwise his hands would be ragged slivers of flesh by the end of the night.

Wrapping his muscular arms around the near end of the log, Boen and his partner lifted. It weighed considerably more than his best guess. Grunting, they struggled over to the wall where engineers directed them. Another party relieved them and began emplacing it.

"But damn that was heavy," the other man exclaimed.

"Too many more of those and I'll be done for," Boen agreed without making any of it up. It had been too long since he last exerted himself like that.

Nodding, the trooper continued, "Don't think this place will ever finish up. We keep building and building, chopping and cutting, and it looks almost like it did before we arrived. Been the longest three weeks of my life."

Three weeks? How is it possible this has been going on for so long without Ingrid sniffing it out? A blind man would have heard the construction and come to investigate. The only logical explanation is someone's been bought off. We'll be heading into a trap. I have to get back and warn the others.

"Hey, you there?"

Jerked out of thought, Boen brushed it off. "Yeah, just didn't want to think about how much longer we got to go before we can get to the fighting."

Sizing him up, the other man said, "Big man like you seems like he'd want to fight." He shrugged haphazardly. "Dunno though. I'd rather be back home in my bakery. This soldier's life ain't for me. I figure if I can make it through this ambush we got coming up I might have a chance at getting home alive. Wife and little ones should be happy about that."

"Home's a powerful attraction," Boen said, knowing he lacked any sort of empathy for fighting men away from their own beds. Gaimosians were largely immune to such simplistic notions. "I been at it for a while now. No pension for me. Figure I'll either get run through or just die of old age when it happens."

"Not me. I got no plans of dying. Not for that damned One Eye nor any other man. Sure, I'll kill who needs killing but I ain't a savage. Been a baker all my life. That's where it's at, not out in this cold and snow. Man ought to know better than to act up this time of year."

If you only knew what was coming. I could kill you without effort and end your misery here. The only factor preventing that was Boen found the other man almost likable. And their conversation was beginning to make his stomach growl.

"You heard anything about when it's going to happen?" Boen asked despite knowing better. That sort of question would either deliver vital information or mark him for what he was. It was a risk he had to take.

The pause was almost unnatural, making Boen's hand drift towards the dagger secreted under his torso armor. "Officers are saying within the next few days. A week at most. Good thing too. I'm ready to go home."

"You two stop right there," a stern voice commanded.

Boen's heart jumped and he nearly gave himself away. Both men turned, reluctantly for different reasons. Boen feared being caught; his newfound partner didn't want to get placed on another work detail. The stiff-backed major marching towards them remained indifferent to their inner turmoil. His look was meaner than necessary, telling Boen he hadn't been compromised, yet.

"Both of you come with me," the major ordered.

Boen cast a glance at his counterpart before replying, "Yes sir."

They wormed through half of the construction area without another word. Boen tried to take in as much as possible, making mental notes of important positions and emplacements, but with so much to see he quickly forgot most of it. Discouraged, the Gaimosian fell in alongside the baker and waited for his orders.

He didn't wait long. Stopping in front of a series of massive tents, obviously for whoever commanded this detachment, the major wheeled on them. "Wait here. Lord Jarrik needs his trunks moved into the tents. Take extra care with them. Should any item drop or touch the ground I'll have your flesh stripped from your backs. Do you understand?"

"Yes sir," they answered in unison.

He left them in silence, both knowing better than to voice their opinions while he was still within earshot. The wait was blissfully short. Reappearing a moment later with a young lieutenant in tow, the major directed them to where they needed to go and what to move. He didn't wait for a salute before heading off on his next task.

Good riddance as far as Boen was concerned. One part of army life that didn't agree with him was the overabundance of extra officers lurking in the shadows with menial tasks. The younger officer lacked any composure when dealing with what were clearly veterans. He avoided eye contact with Boen entirely, fearing to anger the giant of a man. Utilizing as little actual verbal communication as possible, he directed the pair to the wagon bed of crates.

Boen immediately guessed they were all the pertinent maps and whatnot of the area the Wolfsreik needed to execute the campaign. Not to mention all Jarrik's personal belongings. The thought of ruining the enemy lord's belongings brought a smile to both men. Only one feared the repercussions. This miniscule dilemma brought Boen to a dark place. He was much deeper in the enemy camp than he wanted to be, raising his chances of being caught. He needed to find a quick exit before his carefully crafted plan disintegrated and he found his head separated from his shoulders.

They were down to the final few boxes when a man that could only have been Jarrik rode up. Guards saluted. Soldiers stopped what they were doing and went to attention. Boen's eyes narrowed as he took in his new foe. That's when the dark-haired woman with horrible pocks scarring her face emerged. His knowledge of the current Delrananian political system wasn't what it should be, considering this was the final kingdom in a long journey, but he had gleaned enough from Ingrid and Bahr's conversations to know she could be none other than Inaella, former leader of the rebellion.

Killing both was certainly achievable. They'd be bleeding out on the trampled snow before any of the guards could react. He'd effectively cut the head from his enemy in the west and, hopefully, give Ingrid and Bahr enough time to accomplish their missions. Sacrifice wasn't a new concept for Gaimosians. Many had given their lives for the greater good. He wasn't adverse to the idea though it wouldn't accomplish much. Artiss Gran said they all needed to arrive at Arlevon Gale if Malweir had even a remote chance of stopping the dark gods' return. Try as he might, Boen couldn't figure another way. The idea died as quickly as it had sparked to life. Worse, night was dragging to a close, leaving him with little time to make good his escape.

Boen and the baker finished unloading the last crate and, after he painstakingly took the effort to steal one of Jarrik's sigils, readied to return to their original work details.

"Wait."

Boen tensed. He'd been discovered!

Jarrik dismounted and walked up to them. Pulling his riding gloves off, the lord of Delranan extended a hand to each man. "Thank you for taking time to deliver the command tent. I know each of you is exhausted, though the work is far from finished. Know that our time is almost upon us. We'll soon be taking the fight to the enemy. All your dedication and hard work will come to fruition soon enough. Good night, gentlemen."

Well, I'll be. A leader in this miserable kingdom with half a heart. It's that woman that unnerves me. Not natural for one to be so marked. Her eyes are about as evil as I've ever seen. All that hatred will eat her up inside. Smiling, Boen and the baker headed off. There was still much work to be done before the Wolfsreik was ready to take the battle to the rebellion.

Halfway back to the palisade the baker halted and turned on Boen. "This is where we part ways, my big friend. Been a pleasure working with you. Stay safe out there. We need men like you once this foolishness is over."

Boen shook his hand but emotions choked him up. As much as he found himself liking his new friend, he knew that sooner or later one of them was going to wind up dead. He much preferred it was baker. Finally, he managed, "You as well. Good night, baker."

He stood and watched the baker go, briefly wondering where the war was going to take him. Domestic men like that didn't belong in war. Boen decided it was time to take his leave. He headed towards the perimeter with the excuse of relieving himself. Thoughts of shedding his uncomfortable, stolen armor enticed him to move faster.

SIXTEEN

Change of Command

"Damn it!" Jarrik cursed loudly as his arrow failed to hit the target, again.

Half a dozen shafts stuck up from the snow, leaving the center of his target untouched. He'd never claimed to be an archer. His lack of skill of any sort left no room for doubt in that matter. Jarrik preferred a sword in his hands and to meet the end face to face. Killing from a distance, while effective, wasn't honorable. Not that there was much honor to go around his beleaguered kingdom of late.

Delranan had fallen into disrepair. A kingless land content on devouring itself from the inside. Jarrik didn't pretend to understand any longer. His onetime admiration for Harnin dissolved a little more daily. Darkness surrounded the One Eye, so foul Jarrik considered severing ties. The longer the rebellion dragged on the worse Harnin became. Any aspirations of ruling Delranan in his stead slowly bled away.

Hammers clanged in the background. Axes chopped. Saw ground a near perpetual buzzing noise. He thought of trying to blame his archery woes on the construction going on around him but Inaella would see through the ruse with little effort. Discretion the better deed, he kept his complaints private. She'd already grown too desperate since leaving Chadra. There was an illness in her. Residue from the plague perhaps, he wasn't positive. All he knew was that she was steadily turning into the nightmarish presence Harnin was. *What evils can change people so easily? Am I next?*

"I would think a lord of Delranan highly capable in all manners of military tactics and weapons," Inaella's voice rasped over the cold ground.

Oh how he grew to despise her. The rot devouring his beloved kingdom threatened to consume them all. Abandoning Harnin and Chadra Keep enticed him more as days went by. Loosening his draw, Jarrik turned on the scarred woman. "Feel free to prove yourself my better. I'm in no mood to bandy words with you this morning, Inaella."

Wordlessly, she closed the distance between them as quickly as a great predator and took the bow from his hands. Her demeanor changed immediately. What grace she possessed was replaced by the poise of a cold-blooded killer. The arrows were longer than her relatively short arms were accustomed to. The bow larger. That didn't matter. Setting arrow to string, Inaella drew and took aim. A slight breeze wafted through without her so much as blinking. Exhaling slowly, she loosed.

Jarrik sucked his breath in as the shaft sped true, striking the center of the pristine bullseye. Smugly, Inaella turned back to him and gently handed back the bow. "Archery was a hobby the war. Choose your insults more wisely next time, Lord Jarrik. Or take the time to do a little research before opening your mouth."

His teeth audibly ground. "Were it not for Harnin's orders I would have you quartered before the entire force. Or perhaps you'd enjoy spending the rest of your days servicing the men on the eve of battle?"

His threats were empty and she knew it. Harnin despised both but recognized the need for each if he was going to end the rebellion and focus on the returning ten-thousand-man Wolfsreik coming from the east. Inaella had grown bolder as the days went by. Leaving Chadra gave her new life. Sense of purpose was restored. Each step into the wild brought her closer to the much-anticipated reunion with Ingrid the Usurper. The pain and suffering she had in mind for her former student went beyond anything even the Dae'shan concocted.

She stood defiantly before him, feet planted shoulder width apart, arms folded across her chest. "Enough childish banter. Did you notice anything peculiar about those men who helped download the wagon last night?"

What is she playing at now? "No, why?"

"The bigger one didn't have a Delrananian accent. Strange, considering we are deep in alleged enemy territory." The way her lips twisted downward when she pursed them sickened him enough that he looked away.

"What of it? Plenty of mercenaries have come to help fight. Harnin's coin is as good as any other kingdoms." His mind drifted back to their briefing meeting hours ago but, he hesitantly confessed, he'd been much too exhausted to remember much. He vaguely recalled shaking their hands and being wholly impressed with how large the one had been. Men like that were uncommon, easily standing out amongst their peers.

Frowning, Inaella pushed further by adding, "He was no mercenary. The smaller one had the sound and feel of a man from Chadra. The other, the more dangerous looking one, was a true warrior. Not some mercenary scum or part-time reservist."

As much as he thought she was grasping for a scapegoat to punish, Jarrik couldn't risk her being right and not doing anything about it. "Very well. I'll have the camp scoured and both brought to me. We'll get to the bottom of your paranoia soon enough."

"I doubt you'll find the one I am most interested in. He'll no doubt be long gone from here by now. The other headed towards the wagons by the palisade."

She wanted to say more. To issue commands to double the watch. To have commanders on all levels physically verify the identities of everyone in camp. But Jarrik bore the boneheaded stubbornness most men in power suffered from. He'd done things so long in the same fashion that thinking differently was anathema. Kingdoms rotted under such unwillingness to change. No doubt that was among the core causes of the discontent miring her beloved kingdom now.

Having spoken her mind, partially, Inaella excused herself and retired to her tent. She'd had enough of Jarrik's macho attitudes to last the rest of the campaign. The time had come to begin distancing herself from Jarrik, Harnin, and the entire sordid mess. Her only problem stemmed from not having anywhere else to turn to. She lacked personnel, resources, and the physical presence to change the hearts and minds of the kingdom. Alone, friendless and bitter, Inaella collapsed in on herself daily while secretly looking for a way out, a way to end the abject suffering she was forced to endure from the unending aftereffects of the plague. Life could be most cruel at times. Most cruel indeed.

Yet no matter how she tried to figure out the course to a better future, her thoughts returned to the dire nature of reality. The sands of her personal hourglass were bleeding through her slender fingers much too quickly for her liking. Logically she should have already died. The strange combination of plague and betrayal certainly left her dead inside. It was only a matter of time before her mortal shell followed.

Inaella snuck a quick glance back at Jarrik, who busied himself with refilling his quiver. Jarrik wasn't a bad man, she reluctantly decided. The conclusion shocked her. Much of her former life was spent idolizing those in power. She'd dressed in pretty gowns, attended glamorous parties in the name of the king, and traveled across the northern kingdoms carelessly tossing money away. Those days were naught but fading memory. The madness of the kings of Delranan continually strived to strip their subjects of humanity.

Feral instincts were becoming commonplace among the population. Neighbor turned on neighbor in a ruthless game of survival. Families were torn asunder by fears and rampant paranoia. Several of her kin had been killed. Some thanks to the plague, the others from violence. Inaella had a unique opportunity right at this moment, one drawing to a close with each passing breath. She could pack what scarce belongings were still in her possession and flee south or stay behind to rot alongside the rest of the kingdom. Neither choice enticed her enough to act on. Resigned to whatever inglorious destiny Fate decree, Inaella closed the tent flap.

Jarrik caught the brief flutter of movement from her tent and scowled. The woman was more trouble than she was worth. Her knowledge of the rebellion had proven invaluable during the cleansing of Chadra, but that usefulness eroded the further away from civilization they went. She'd become an increasing liability, one threatening to lead his neck to the hangman's noose. Jarrik feared the longer the campaign wore on the more Harnin was ready to exterminate their entire command.

Once an ardent supporter of the usurper lord, Jarrik now failed to find any value in his allegiance. The war seemed endless. His holdings in Chadra were gone. The houses of the lords had been among the first targets in the rebellion's sights. Little by little his wealth bled dry as he was forced to fund his campaign. Jarrik wasn't particularly brave, despite once having aspirations of attaching himself to Harnin's coattails in the vain hopes of achieving glory and, very distantly, a chance at the crown.

Delranan continually crumbled around his best efforts. Jarrik took some time before arriving at the only possible conclusion. Harnin One Eye was busily and actively trying to destroy the previous way of life and bring the entire kingdom to ruin. Stopping him was a most grievous waste of time. The fate of the kingdom was decided. It was merely a matter of time before the end came. Jarrik feared for those unable to defend themselves or find safe passage south. Their corpses would fertilize forgotten fields for years without ever being discovered.

His ruminations were disturbed by the commotion coming from the eastern flank. Horns bellowed, announcing the arrival of a figure of importance. Jarrik almost came to regret developing the signal system his army used. It had been more bane than the boon he initially intended. Setting aside his bow and quiver, Jarrik slid back into his bearskin cloak and headed towards the eastern gate. Calloused hands smoothed over his clothing. He was, after all, still a lord of Delranan.

What he saw emboldened him while silently crushing his spirit. Skaning's black hair stretched down his back, blowing wildly in the light wind. His menacing eyes were narrow, fixed from beneath his war helm. The newly arrived lord rode stiffly, as if he'd come with dire intent. Jarrik's world gently shattered. There could be but one reason for the unexpected visit. He was being relieved.

"Greetings, Skaning," he announced without betraying his emotion. "Your arrival is most unexpected. I would have prepared a tent for you had I known."

"That won't be necessary, Jarrik. Lord Harnin has sent me with haste."

There it is. The dagger in my spine. Will you have the nerve to finish me in public or take the coward's way out with poison? "We've received no word. Our preparations demand most, if not all, of our time."

Clearing his throat, Skaning offered the slightest hesitation Jarrik took as a good omen. "He feels you are not performing your duties properly. Where is Lady Inaella? She needs to be present for me to continue."

Jarrik looked behind his onetime friend. A double column of cavalry stretched back onto the snow fields. None of them bore the look of reservists. Each wore a hard face suggesting the disciplined lives of mercenaries or worse. *Perhaps I was too much the fool to trust to hope.* "She's retired to her tent for the moment. Shall I summon her?"

Skaning shook his head. "No. What I have to say needs to be done in private."

Dismounting, he followed Jarrik.

"Those are my orders," Skaning finished. He'd languished through days of doubt, never quite knowing how he was going to explain Harnin's desires or even what he was going to do about them. Plotting and imagining while locked in the solitude of his mind on the road west was one matter. Doing it before his old friend was another entirely.

"So this is it? A knife in the back while we sleep?" Jarrik accused.

Skaning held up his hands weakly. "It's not like that."

Inaella rasped, "We should kill him now before the others are aware. Harnin will have to come here himself if he wants me dead."

"Calm down, Lady. No one is killing anyone this day, or so I hope," Skaning replied quickly, suggesting his lack of faith in Harnin's ideals.

"For what other purpose would you have ridden all this way if not to obey the One Eye's orders?" Inaella pushed. She'd fallen victim to betrayal once before and it nearly cost her life. Doing so again was not in her best interests.

Taking the offered mug of water, Skaning blew out the tension building. *Days of travel and I still am not sure of what I should do. Would that I was a better man, or lesser. This would not be so damned difficult.* "I'd have been a fool to remain in Chadra. You've been gone for too long to understand. Bodies line the walls. Death and madness rule with stern surety. Our kingdom is already dead, Jarrik."

"We know all this. What else have you to offer before I summon my guards to kill your men?" Jarrik asked boldly. His words lacked the conviction they were meant with.

Skaning smiled sadly. "They won't. My men have orders to burn this camp to the ground and kill everyone if I don't reappear after a while."

"Traitor!"

"Which of us?" Skaning fired back. "We both betrayed the king to follow Harnin's fool dreams of conquest, thinking this was our best opportunity to finally advance our lots in life. What fools we were! Harnin doesn't care for Delranan any more than King Stelskor. We are alone, Jarrik."

"What can we do outnumbered thus?" Jarrik failed to find a scenario where he didn't lose. All the suffering of previous generations broke against the shore as Harnin continued to plunder his own kingdom. There was no way out.

Skaning considered the statement briefly. True, Harnin commanded the better part of five thousand soldiers and had a pool of roughly ten thousand more to draw from. Those would be civilians, most too old or young to make any other difference than being warm bodies plugging holes in the infantry lines, and of little tactical use. The two thousand soldiers in the west were largely oblivious to the power struggle going on and, both men agreed, they needed to remain that way. His private force of two hundred was considered among the best, most ruthless fighters in the north but even they would be ground under such overwhelming force.

Truthfully, Skaning had nothing to gain from betraying Harnin. His legacy would be tarnished and his corpse would hang beside Jarrik's, food for crows and buzzards while the madman laughed away in his wooden tower. Killing Jarrik presented more problems than it was worth. Friends for years, the pair won great reputation and glory during a series of border wars. Badron counted them among his greatest military minds. Skaning wasn't so sure about that claim. Rolnir and Wolfsreik officers devised and executed every tactical maneuver in the campaign while the young lords were given credit.

"I stand trapped at the crossroads," Skaning carefully said. His tone and words were measured for the best effect.

The scrape-hiss of Inaella's slender blade being drawn sounded as thunder in the confines of the tent. Murder danced in her pained eyes. "You should decide quickly if you expect to leave this tent alive."

Skaning looked to Jarrik who stood tensed, but with the faintest glimmer of mirth on his face. He was amused by this sudden turn of events. The board was set. He'd done all he could to buy a little more time. His fate now rested in Skaning's hands. Doubt gnawed away as swift as the minutes.

SEVENTEEN

Land of the Pell Darga

"This is a bad idea, Mahn," Raste half whispered as they rode higher into the forbidding Murdes Mountains. "They'd just as soon kill us as take care of us."

Mahn tried, and failed, to ignore the young, headstrong scout. He'd hoped that the string of adventures and mishaps they'd experienced over the course of the autumn and winter would build Raste's character, make him a better, wiser man. Those hopes were dashed the moment Raste opened his mouth. Not even surviving the fall of Rogscroft or being appointed to the fledgling council of King Aurec seemed to have made much impact.

King Aurec. Mahn still wasn't certain how he felt about that unexpected turn of events. Stelskor had been one of the finest men, and greatest leaders, Mahn had the pleasure of knowing. Working closely with his son was both privilege and honor. Now that son was king, the world changed drastically. Rogscroft was largely destroyed from the occupation. It would be years before the kingdom found any semblance of its former self. Compounding matters was the sudden alliance with the very men responsible for bringing his beloved home to ruin.

The Wolfsreik were fearsome warriors, an army without equal in the realms of men. They tore through Aurec's meager defenses in a matter of weeks and brought a king to his knees. No other fighting force in Malweir was capable of such. Or so he'd thought. The wave of Goblins coming from the Deadlands changed his mind quickly. They killed without reason or discretion. Hundreds of innocent men, women, and children lay buried under the snows, dismembered or worse.

The longer the war continued the worse the crimes became. Aurec's last, desperate gambit lay in the lands of the

Pell Darga. Only Cuul Ol and his secretive tribe of mountain dwellers could deliver the allied army back to Delranan where they intended on bringing the war to a close. Win or lose. Mahn looked at Raste and sighed. He greatly wanted the young man to be there at his side on that last day of the last battle. The cold reality was it probably wasn't going to happen unless he changed his ways.

"They just might as long as they can hear you plotting it out for them."

Raste's cheeks might have reddened if not for the severe cold they already suffered from. "You know what I mean. The Pell aren't exactly our friends, now are they?"

"Nor are they enemies," he scolded. "You and I have both been in their camps and set free under the provision we don't discuss what we saw. Aurec needs us to execute this task in order to keep the war from stagnating."

Raste cringed at Mahn's choice of words. "Execute" was the last comment he needed to hear given where they were headed. The Pell Darga, if they could hear, chose to ignore the bickering scouts. To be fair, neither party was enthused about the interesting turn of events leading the lowlanders up into the mountain passes.

"All I am saying is there must be another way," Raste continued. His nose began to run from the combination of their rising altitude and extreme cold, reminding him just how much he despised winter's kiss.

"What way would you have? It would take too long to go around the mountains and Rogscroft has never had the sort of sea power capable of transporting nearly twenty thousand soldiers. This is the only path ahead, Raste."

"Certain doom? I'd rather take my chances with the Goblins," he snorted derisively.

Mahn resisted the urge to reach over and slap his younger friend senseless. "Doom is a matter we all must face when the time comes. What we represent, to all the kingdoms and tribes involved, is the chance to right wrongs. To end a pointless struggle inspired by the greed and jealousy of a single man. If that calls for traveling deep into the Murdes Mountains to meet with people we aren't on sure footing with, then so be it. Don't you want to be on the side of history?"

"I'm not concerned with history, Mahn. I just want to survive the war and find a small cottage somewhere out of the way where I can try and find a different life." He paused. "I'm sick of war. If I never see another corpse or take another life I won't shed a tear."

He'd never admit it, macho pride demanded it that way, but Raste felt he was losing tiny parts of himself with each new engagement. The gods hadn't made him a killer. Life decided to make that detour for him. Dramatic twists ended whatever dreams he once had, leaving him adrift in unfamiliar waters. The war dragged on, dragging him down roads best left untraveled. Raste killed when he had to. He fled when necessary. Yet each day drowned his spirits further. It was a winless proposition.

Mahn eyed him carefully. To deny they'd been through a lot was foolish. Whereas Raste felt continually ground down, Mahn simply felt old. The years hadn't been overly kind. Life as a scout pushed him beyond the borders of what normal men would endure. His body was constantly sore. His mind worn down. Yet no manner of distress or personal misery was enough to keep him from performing his job.

"This war won't last forever," he tried consoling. "You'll have your chance at a decent life once we accomplish the king's purpose."

Only, I don't know what that purpose is. I don't think Aurec knows either. There must be a point to it all. We've taken back Rogscroft. Driven our enemies from our borders. Badron has lost his strength. What else remains before we can finally send our men home to their families? To the lives they've nearly forgotten over the course of this long winter?

Raste refused to look at Mahn. They'd ridden together since the young scout first enlisted, forming bonds few outside of military life experienced. He knew he was disappointing his mentor and friend, but there was no denying how tired his heart was. Too many friends had fallen, most during the siege of the capital. Each time he closed his eyes he saw faces that no longer sat at the same table. Empty chairs where the old and familiar once sat. He hoped, for all their sakes, that Mahn was indeed right. That the war wouldn't last forever.

"That doesn't change the fact that we are heading back into the mountains with a tribe of people who wanted to kill us the last time," he finally said.

Mahn couldn't ignore the logic in that statement. The Pell Darga were venomous warriors with fierce tempers. Secluded from the rest of the world, they avoided other forms of life whenever possible. Generations had been hunted down for sport, diluting the race until the few that remained left their grassland homes and took refuge in the mountains. The Murdes Mountains were the latest in the story of their evolution. Once they'd had a thriving community in the kingdom of Thrae. The war with the Goblins and the dragon Ramulus drove them west where they struggled to merely survive under the harshest conditions. With each passing winter freeze, their hearts grew colder.

"They didn't kill us, though. I have no reason to suspect they will now," Mahn said.

Cuul Ol and the other Pell chieftains were eager to help Aurec fight against the Wolfsreik and Goblins. They ruthlessly attacked supply convoys and rear echelon support troops while suffering few casualties. Aurec admitted he never would have been able to force General Rolnir and the Wolfsreik to switch sides without the help of the Pell. It was that same aid he was counting on now.

Knowing such didn't alleviate the doubt now growing in the pit of Mahn's stomach. As much as he wanted to curse Raste from bringing the subject up, he couldn't. Doubt was a natural thing for soldiers to feel, from time to time. Placing complete faith in the actions or concepts of others wasn't easy for most, but Mahn had grown to accept such from an early age. He prayed his king had the temerity to trust the Pell. Otherwise the war was going to come to an end much sooner than any anticipated.

Raste seemed more dazed now, as if his mind had been stunned with some irreverent fact made prominent by the severity of their situation. They rode in silence. Neither wanted to dwell on what fate might await them once they reached the secret meeting place of the Pell. Only time would tell if death hid in the shadows.

Winter's chill was driven back by the warmth of their fire. Cloistered in a deep cave, those assembled spoke softly in small groups. Mahn and Raste watched and ate a meager few bites of the smoked meat the Pell chieftains offered without much interest. Following the broken, almost guttural speech of the Pell was virtually pointless. They largely ignored their guests, although the scouts received an occasional menacing glare or thoughtful stare.

Raste's nerves were getting the best of him. The cave was larger than he imagined, coming from the lowlands. A domed ceiling more than half again as tall as a man was stained with soot and smoke. A fetid stench clung to the air. Not the smell of death but of rot and worse. Warriors came and went as the chieftains talked. Whatever was being discussed was no business of theirs. Curiously, Raste didn't see any women or children. Surely they existed, for how else would the tribes have so many warriors with which to fight? The near perpetual crawl of darkness spreading and shrinking with the glow of the fires left him feeling claustrophobic. He wanted to be back under the open sky. Breathe the fresh air even if it was so cold his nose hairs froze almost instantly.

"Relax," Mahn soothed. "I can't imagine this taking long. The Pell we've dealt with are of the immediate decision sort. Not ones for taking excessive amounts of time getting to the point. I wish some of our leaders were more like that."

He winced, knowing that last bit should have remained unsaid. Aurec and the others were doing their best to piece the kingdom back together but the resurgence of politics was inevitable. Already the young king was forced to remove a vaunted councilor of the old king, Paneolus. That sort of cancerous need for consolidated power was what drove Badron mad in the first place and led to an invasion. A conquered man should know better.

Raste tried to stretch, desperate to shake the feeling gnawing its way down his spine. "We could have done this outside."

"In below-freezing weather? Now who's mad? We have food, heat, and shelter. What more could we ask of our hosts?" Mahn countered.

The young scout offered a baleful look and bit his lip. Enough of the Pell spoke the common tongue to get him in trouble if he dared voice the thoughts dancing around in his head. Instead he reached for another piece of the smoked meat--mountain bear he guessed, though he'd never eaten it--and took a bite. The meat was tough with a gamey taste. While filling, he almost would rather stick with field rations. The life of hunter-gatherers was more difficult than anything he'd been forced to endure during his childhood or early adolescence.

Mahn forced out a sigh. "Look, Raste, there's no point in giving in to your emotions. We're here representing our king, our kingdom. Any tantrum will only make Rogscroft look weaker than we already are. These Pell are good warriors and, I'm daring to guess, a good people. We'll be fine as long as you remain calm."

"That's just it. The longer I stay here, in this cave, the more I feel like going mad." Raste looked away lest Mahn see the raw emotion burning his face. "It…it reminds me of the siege."

Mahn paused. They'd served side by side during the siege of the capital. Each day the battle lasted drew the noose tighter around their necks. More friends fell. Enemy numbers swelled with reinforcements. It was only a matter of time before the inevitable conclusion arrived. Rogscroft had to fall. There simply weren't enough defenders to prevent the thousands of Goblins and Wolfsreik from storming in.

Those final moments when the decision to fight or flee was instant were among the most harrowing of his old life. He could still smell the blood and he could still see the bodies when he closed his eyes and dared to let his thoughts drift back. Watching friends cut down ingloriously as the dark tide of Goblins murdered their way through his beloved city left gaping holes in his heart. He too had lost during the siege. Raste didn't own the market on suffering.

"Those days are over," Mahn said, staring into the fire. "We survived, and so did plenty of other good men. Be proud of what you accomplished there, Raste. Very few in the entire kingdom can say they lived through that experience. Use the anger and the fear welling inside to your advantage. We've cleansed most of the kingdom of enemy. King Aurec seeks to take the war back to Delranan to finish this sad, sordid mess. I don't imagine he's apt to kill the entire population like Badron tried with us, but I have no doubt there won't be any threat once we finish our business. History remembers the deeds of the great. I doubt you or I will be named in those pages. Our stories will go largely unknown to scholars and future generations, but we go to the earth knowing it was through our actions that Rogscroft was rebuilt. Pride, Raste. Always take pride in what you do."

After several tense moments of silence Raste finally said, "You should be one of the old, grey-bearded scholars at the academy. Scout life doesn't agree with you any longer."

Mahn chuckled absently. The boy had a point. His merriment was disturbed by Cuul Ol summoning them to the chieftain fire. Hesitant, Mahn obeyed. The scouts were unceremoniously invited to sit alongside the chiefs, war-hardened men of distinction among the clans. No fop made it through the trials to assume leadership of a clan. Each eyed the scouts with the strange combination of admiration and mistrust.

"You being here again is most unusual," Cuul began.

Gol Mad, the Pell warrior initially sent to Aurec with news of the Pell's decision to help with the war, seemed almost upset, thus living up to his name. "You should not be here. This is sacred to Pell."

Mahn held out his hands, palms up. "We come with the greatest respect for the people of the Pell Darga. It is not our intent to spy upon you."

He cursed silently, wishing Aurec would have sent a proper statesman. But Cuul Ol had insisted on the scouts. Perhaps there was something to be said for familiarity. Mahn wasn't the sort born with a golden tongue. He handled his own when it came to verbal duels in the barracks. Most soldiers were low on wit but dealing as an ambassador for his entire people was almost too much for him to handle. Almost. Reservations aside, he intended on making the most of the situation. After all, his life hung in the balance.

Sint Ap had been opposed to aiding the lowlanders from the beginning. His pinched face and narrow eyes looked upon the scouts with obvious distaste. "Your wars are not our problem. We live here. Not on lowlands. Keep your wars to yourselves."

"You have to see this war affects us all. How many Pell have died since the Wolf soldiers invaded Rogscroft?"

"Too many," Cuul Ol replied sadly.

"Should Badron or Harnin One Eye succeed, your entire race will burn. Their hatred knows no moral constraint. Their soldiers, and Goblins, will march into the mountains and hunt you down to the last child for what you've done to help King Aurec. No one is safe." Mahn rocked back on his cushion, hoping his words bore enough weight to persuade the secretive mountain people.

"Pell will fight!" Gol Mad shouted as he slammed his spear butt into the compact ground.

"Not against what is coming," Mahn countered, growing tiresome. "No one can withstand the power of this evil if we do not band together. All we ask is that you grant us passage through your secret paths so that we may take the war back to Delranan where it was spawned. King Aurec does not ask you to fight with us."

The Pell bickered amongst themselves, deepening Mahn's worry. He'd seen what they were capable of on the battlefield. The Goblin slaughter was some of the fiercest combat he could imagine and the Pell handled it without hesitation. How anyone could willingly undertake such savageness was beyond Mahn. Like his young counterpart, he only killed when necessary. Everything else was a waste of life.

Unsure where to turn next, he offered Raste a false smile and waited. What else was there? The Pell would either agree or not. He'd spoken his piece as compellingly as he could. Men were fickle beings, capable of immense violence or creations of grandeur rivaling the gods. He'd seen the best and worst over the course of his life and now prayed that the best would return. Too many sleepless nights of strife tortured him. It was time for change.

Cuul Ol at last broke away from the conversation and looked Mahn in the eyes. There was wildness Mahn had seldom seen lurking behind the dark brown. "We will show you secret ways. And we will fight!"

EIGHTEEN

Decision Factors

Swords clashed. Spears were leveled, shields raised. Horses cried out in bloodless screams. The roar of thousands of soldiers crashing together echoed across the frozen lands. Arrows hissed across the sky and struck their targets with deafening thwacks. Men roared as the two lines collided. The sound was as thunder rumbling through the heavens.

General Rolnir and King Aurec stood atop a small knoll watching with active interest. Fists clenched, the freshly crowned king of Rogscroft felt his blood boil. Not a true warrior, the young king received a forced education over the course of winter. The worst thing he had ever done was watch his soldiers die while executing his orders. The pain in such knowledge was irreversible. How was he supposed to go to the families of the deceased and express condolences when their deaths were his fault? *How my father managed for so many years is beyond me. But then again, we weren't in a war like this.*

Tamed by a lifetime of preparing for combat, Rolnir was the exact opposite. Where Aurec saw savage movements and loss of life, Rolnir looked for errors, tactical judgments of field commanders. A consummate professional, the general of the Wolfsreik lived for his soldiers and the thrill of the hunt. Each battle presented unique challenges and circumstances that were virtually impossible to duplicate. He enjoyed the thrill of the challenge. Matching wits with the enemy commander was the ultimate game. There was no other feeling quite like it.

"The men are rusty," he offered. His tone was callous, measured.

Aurec didn't agree. "They seem fine to me. I've never been in such a frenzied battle."

"Your Highness, take my word for it, the lack of recent fighting has left these soldiers rusty. A few more training drills and they'll be ready for a real fight."

As a prince growing up in the castle, he was privileged enough to watch his father's soldiers and royal guards go through endless training exercises. All of his childhood amazements and wonder inspired countless dreams and mock battles with sticks plucked from the gardens. The commanders humored him, offering miniscule classes on how to fight or defend himself. Aurec was adopted as a sort of mascot but his presence only detracted from training.

"I wish I had more to offer, but I'll trust you, General," he said. Admitting he wasn't the supreme authority on everything was good for his ego from time to time. Too many leaders simply assumed they knew everything. He refused to fall into that trap. "How long will it take for them to be ready to attack Harnin?"

Rolnir scratched his jaw. "We could attack the moment the first infantry battalions arrive on the lowlands. That's not the issue. Arriving piecemeal into whatever his defenses are will grind us to dust. We need to attack in force. I imagine even a poorly trained army of this size could sweep through him in a single day. Our largest problem is getting three armies' worth of soldiers to set aside their training in order to incorporate one united training method. Which brings me, or rather you, to an important crossroad."

"That being?" Aurec asked. He tensed, dreading further criticism.

Fixing him with a stern look, Rolnir said, "You need to establish definitions for victory. Going there to fight is well and fine but the army needs to know what the overall objectives are."

Not the conversation I wanted this morning but one that can't be put off any longer. Not if I want our army to survive the coming fight. Father, I wish you were here to guide me. Sometimes I feel so lost without you. He had

Venten and a host of others with more than enough experience. Reluctantly, he turned from the mock fighting just before the two lines of opposing cavalry crossed.

"Summon the council and tell them it's going to be a long day," he said and sighed. There were times when being in charge had more downfalls than pleasantries. Today was going to be one.

Command Sergeant Major Thorsson loathed going back inside the command group tents. While being in a warm environment away from the elements was fine, he felt the longer he was in his current position the more he missed being around the soldiers. Stagnation crept in around his naturally rough demeanor and he didn't like it. Some soldiers were meant to fight, others to lead. He preferred fighting.

"You can't delay for too long."

Frowning, he turned to see Venten marching towards him. Already aged enough to retire, and then some, the former advisor to the king and mentor to Aurec turned brevet general, walked with a pronounced limp. Physically he wasn't half the man he'd once been, but his mind was sharp as a whip. He also understood how a man like Thorsson wasn't prone to sitting through pointless meetings where those who didn't fight theorized.

"That's easy for you to say," Thorsson replied. "How do you manage?"

Venten chuckled. "I've been doing it for so long I know when to pay attention and when to avoid falling asleep."

"I feel like stabbing my eyes out listening to them drone on," Thorsson admitted. "I never thought it was going to be harder than actual combat."

"You've seen nothing yet. Wait until Aurec establishes his court in Rogscroft. You'll put in for retirement faster than you agreed to accept this position," Venten said with a playful slap on the back.

"That's not encouraging," Thorsson scowled.

Together they entered the main command tent. Thorsson was relieved that no one else had arrived. He didn't like it when they all stared at him for being a few moments late. And, this way, he got to pick his seat. His brief stint in the command world left him with the distinct impression that sergeants were frowned upon by senior leadership, despite the fact they were the backbone of the army. *Guess it's always been like that. The men who do the fighting go unremembered while the genius who thinks up the plans gets the fame and glory. Not that I ever wanted to be famous, but there comes a point when a little recognition is due. If not for me at least for the troops.*

Sensing his turmoil, Venten poured two mugs of coffee and handed Thorsson one. "You realize they value your insights?"

"I wonder at times," he replied. The coffee burned his lips but instantly warmed him.

"Understandable. I was once much lower than you, if that helps. Performing menial tasks that I felt certain the people in power didn't appreciate or even know about. For the most part I was right. Those in power don't tend to think about the results of their orders. Aurec is different. He always has been."

"In what ways?" Thorsson asked. His interaction with royalty had been severely nonexistent until the siege. He'd seen Stelskor and Aurec but never had the pleasure of speaking to either. His life revolved around soldiers. Being in the thick of things gave him purpose, a sense of direction. The sergeant major stumbled through his current position, often reverting to his simple sergeant days when he wasn't accountable to anyone but his own soldiers.

Venten swallowed a mouthful of the slightly burnt coffee. He was amazed that after all his years of experience he still hadn't tasted anything worth calling coffee. "You bring dimension to the group. Generals and field commanders are all well and fine but the king needs to hear the voice of the common soldier. We can sit here all day long theorizing this tactic or that, but it's the soldiers who are going to execute our orders. Small-unit commanders and sergeants are vital in the war effort. The king is busy incorporating a new academy system to develop the lower ranks. So far as I know there is no other kingdom attempting such."

Thorsson saw the raw potential a leader development system offered. An army that didn't rely on generals or nobles! He found excitement in the concept. Soldiers would fight harder for their direct supervisors. These were the men on the line right beside the soldiers. Death was just as likely to strike the low-level leader as it was the new soldier. He imagined there might be loyalty or discipline issues, but the benefits would heavily outweigh the detractors.

"We'd be unmatched," he whispered.

Venten cocked his head. "As long as it works. We'd still have to contend with powerful armies in the future. Who's to say how long the Wolfsreik will remain our allies? Politics change so rapidly there's no point in predicting."

The tent opened, allowing Aurec, Vajna, Rolnir, and Piper Joach to file in and take up their seats.

Aurec visibly brightened when his gaze fell on Venten. Now more than ever he felt the need to console his inner turmoil with his old friend and mentor. Leading a kingdom was far more difficult than he imagined, much less trying to rebuild the ruins of one while prosecuting a war simultaneously.

"Good, you're both here," he said as he acknowledged both Venten and Thorsson. The newly minted command sergeant major seemed different, more attentive perhaps. Aurec shook it off and began, "Gentlemen, I've summoned this impromptu meeting because General Rolnir has brought up valid points I, up until this point, hadn't considered. For simplicity's sake, we need to know what our objectives are for winning this war. Thoughts?"

Venten couldn't keep the grin from his face. *Young Aurec is learning quickly what it means to be king and a true leader. Rogscroft will be in good hands for many years, so long as he doesn't get killed before the end of this war.* "We've already accomplished our primary task: driving Badron and his Goblin filth out of Rogscroft. The kingdom is largely secure and we are in the reconstruction phase. If we go by those parameters we have already achieved victory."

"While I agree with most of what you say, I'd argue your victory is temporary at best," Rolnir countered immediately. Arms folded across his chest, the Wolfsreik general was working through multiple scenarios in his head. "Once Badron returns to Delranan, his focus will be on Harnin One Eye. Should he find victory, he'll be back."

"With what army?" Vajna asked. "The strength of Delranan is now allied with us. For which I am eternally grateful, by the way. Even if he managed to raise an army he'd still have to cross the Murdes Mountains and deal with the wrath of the Pell Darga."

"Vajna brings forth a good point. Where would Badron find a fighting force capable of mounting an invasion?" Venten asked.

Rolnir offered a deadpan look. "Goblins."

"We defeated them already. What remains are ghosts of their former strength," Aurec said.

Shaking his head, Rolnir continued, "We destroyed *this* army. Goblins breed faster than any other race in Malweir. It is not inconceivable for them to have another, larger force en route to offer support for the first army."

"Rogscroft has no proper defense to stop another invasion," Vajna said. His face had gone ashen with the thought of another Goblin invasion.

"Not with the war in the west under way," Rolnir confirmed.

Aurec, feeling the conversation was heading in the wrong direction for what he wanted, interrupted, "Bringing us back to my original point. What constitutes victory in the west? If there is even the remotest possibility of another Goblin army marching on us, we need to conduct our campaign quickly and return home. I have no aspirations of occupying Delranan."

"Then victory would fall on capturing or killing Badron and Harnin and emplacing a proper monarchy," Venten added. Decades of political experience made him take the leap quickly.

"The royal family is no more," Piper cut in. "Badron's only son was murdered. His daughter has disappeared, more than likely dead. His brother is no better than a pirate, seldom home to mind his own kingdom. Who would we place upon the throne?"

Aurec's face darkened at the mention of Maleela. His heart bled for his love. Not knowing whether she lived or not all but crippled him on those lonely nights when life grew too difficult to bear. Still, he couldn't let that detract from what needed to be done.

Surprisingly, Rolnir spoke next. "Perhaps it is time for new leadership. Badron's family has held the throne for generations. Delranan has collapsed under their rule. A man like Venten would bring us out of the darkness."

"There is no one in the entire kingdom worthy of that title," Piper snapped. The shadows under his eyes suggested a dearth of sleep, making him edgy.

"What do you say, Venten? Care to become a regent?" Aurec asked, half-playfully.

The older Venten had nothing to say.

Aurec continued, "So, we finish Badron and Harnin. I suggest disbanding whatever military and police forces are currently in place. I have no intentions of leaving an occupying force once we cut the head from the snake. Who we leave in command is as important as ending this campaign quickly but I think it's too early to begin serious discussion on the matter."

"It seems our dilemma is solved," Rolnir said thoughtfully. "Victory means the immediate and irreversible removal of both Badron and Harnin and the disbandment of all uniformed services. Naturally the Wolfsreik will need to deploy around the kingdom to maintain peace and stability. We're not exactly trained for support and stability operations but our time here in Rogscroft has helped."

"Under the circumstances I would have to agree. We've yet to encounter any citizens in the towns or villages who have anything negative to say about your soldiers," Venten complimented. It was a minor mercy for which he was eternally grateful. Too many armies carried out campaigns that left the conquered kingdom pillaged of resources and life. That Rolnir managed to prevent the same from happening to Rogscroft was both a wonder and a blessing.

Rolnir nodded his appreciation. "They'd best not. Discipline has always been one of our strongest principles. I expect my soldiers to live under the same code of honor I do."

"A matter I want you to instill in the rest of the army. Combining three kingdoms' worth of traditions, doctrine, and standards isn't an easy task. I certainly don't envy you but I wouldn't think of having another in your place." Aurec panned the room. "We have the chance to make history. Through our actions, the blood of our soldiers, and the courage of those we intend to liberate, we can achieve a feat that has seldom been accomplished. The north will be free from this dark malaise and our two kingdoms will finally know peace and prosperity."

Strong words. I wonder if he is the one to forge an empire from the ashes of what's left over? Rolnir ran his fingers through his red beard while he continued to think of what tomorrow might look like. Lesser men might not grasp the full effect of events building now. Historians might misjudge the people responsible for creating a vastly different future, one with unlimited potential of trade or equality. Rolnir suspected the people sitting around him in the command tent would be made into mythical, demi-god figures by the survivors of Delranan and Rogscroft.

One fact he knew for certain was the world was changing. The old ways were slowly eroding out of complacency and the complete lack of relevance. A new age was rising. He felt it in his bones. Futuristic visions of tomorrow haunted his dreams. He didn't know which way the tide was turning, but the air of change was undeniable. Being a part of such a momentous event left him with mixed emotions. Perhaps one day he'd be able to look fondly back on this moment and realize it was the singular point in time when his life finally changed for the better.

"All that remains is for Mahn and Raste to return with word from our Pell allies," Aurec said.

His tone soured slightly, allowing his doubts to bleed out. As much as he enjoyed having Cuul Ol and the Pell Darga for allies he wasn't wholly sure he could trust them. The Shadow People of the Murdes Mountains were elusive and confrontational. They'd enjoyed countless decades of anonymity, ever apart from the rest of the world. What nightmares did they endure to force them into seclusion? History not being his subject, Aurec could only guess at the events that forced the Pell up into their mountain isolation, knowing his own people were close to following the same pattern. The young king of Rogscroft closed his eyes and hoped against all hope that he wouldn't share the same twisted fate.

NINETEEN

Battle in the West

Night was busy crawling across the land. It was that murky period after light and before dark. Visibility was difficult. One couldn't see with clarity much further than a few meters. It was the perfect time for an attack. Modern armies almost never fought at night. Too much could go wrong. Fratricide was commonplace under poor conditions. In order to combat that sad fact, Ingrid had her rebels each marked with red bands of cloth on their arms. The majority of Jarrik's forces would be in proper Wolfsreik uniforms but, according to Boen, there were enough mercenaries within the partially constructed redoubt to lend pause.

Hundreds of rebel fighters had converged on this position to execute a loosely coordinated assault. Much to Orlek's disappointment, Bahr and his crew decided to stay out of the way. They hadn't come all the way back to Delranan just to fight a rebellion. Getting to the ruins of Arlevon Gale was the only priority Bahr had. Everything else simply stood in the way. They watched the rebels pack out for the raid and slip quietly away. Only Boen volunteered to lead them, for he alone had been within the vast defensive structure. Bahr reluctantly agreed, though he knew the Gaimosian well enough to know he wasn't going to try very hard to stay out of the fight. *Damned thickheaded Vengeance Knights. Who in their right minds decided toppling Gaimos was a good idea in the first place? They all but cursed the rest of the world!*

Ingrid stalked along beside the big Gaimosian-- whether from pride, arrogance, or the need to see this matter through remained in doubt. She was one of the strongest women Bahr had ever met. Knowing she led the fight to restore normalcy, the sense of righteousness to a broken people, left him with hope for the future. Her dyed white cloak and leggings blended perfectly with the snow-covered world.

Determination twisted her face. She felt the sense of urgency that only a commander on the battlefield could. Many of her friends, her fighters, would fall this night, but it was a blood price they had to pay if Delranan was to be free from the tyrannical hands of Harnin One Eye. Orlek and Boen trotted at her sides. One insisted he wasn't here to fight. The other vowed to risk his life to keep her alive.

She didn't particularly enjoy that feeling. Orlek was a fine warrior and was becoming a good friend. His rugged demeanor and roguish charm marked him for a dangerous man, but she couldn't help feel a certain closeness to him. Love was a word she felt uncomfortable using since her husband was killed. Love was the curse of the world. Fools spent their lives in pursuit of a mythical emotion that resulted in hopeless despair more times than not. Love was singularly responsible for more death and hardship than any other emotion. Yet no matter how hard she tried to steel her heart against letting love back into her grieving soul, after all she'd dedicated her work in the rebellion to compensate losing her husband, Ingrid couldn't deny the raw feelings building within.

Cursing, Ingrid shoved the thoughts from her mind and tried to concentrate on the mission. Boen offered detail schematics for the redoubt, including major weaknesses. With a little luck she'd be able to funnel the main body of her assault through the gaps and gut the redoubt while skirmishers and archers kept the defenders occupied on the walls. Firing the parapet was her first priority. Once the wooden wall began burning she'd have the distraction the rebellion needed.

Hope struggled to overwhelm the rest of her emotions. She'd been beaten down for so long it felt strange to have a glimpse at true victory. All the skirmishes and ambushes conducted up to this point were mere bumps in prelude to the rebellion's first major victory. Killing or capturing Jarrik and Inaella certainly brought anticipation. Lord Argis betrayed the king and his one-eyed advisor in the attempt of reclaiming Delranan for the people. His death came at the hands of people like Jarrik and the bitter, broken Inaella.

Clearly Harnin decided to concentrate his efforts in the west here, in this centralized location. Ingrid stumbled upon it by sheer coincidence. Her forces were scattered in small groups to facilitate widespread chaos against the Wolfsreik oppression. Never did she dare to dream her tactical dispersion would result in being in such a ready position for assault. With a little luck and a quick strike they'd burn the redoubt to the ground and kill most of the garrison.

Harlan and the other elements of the rebellion converged on the redoubt over the past few days, bulking the forces at her disposal close to fifteen hundred fighters. It was the largest force she'd wielded in combat to date and very nearly numerically even with what Jarrik had. They weren't the best fighters in Delranan, nor the best armed, but they were all she had. Each had endured many months of nonstop warfare. They'd lost friends and made new ones. Each had the same passion as Ingrid, a fact she sought to capitalize on tonight. Victory often came through zealotry. She prayed that was the case.

Boen raised his fist and the rebels halted, crouching down to reduce their silhouette against the fading light. He looked Ingrid in the eye and motioned her forward with a hooked finger.

"What is it?"

Pointing through a small stand of trees, Boen replied, "The main avenue is just beyond these trees. While there weren't any guards posted the other night I'd advise sending a few people ahead to be sure. We're close enough to the redoubt for Jarrik to mount a serious counterassault on limited notice."

Ingrid's heart nearly seized. All her carefully articulated hope, dreams, and well wishes for a future kingdom felt as if they'd been dashed against the rocks, shattered beyond repair. If Jarrik remotely suspected the rebellion was about to strike, her losses would effectively end the rebellion for good. There'd be no rebuilding from such a massacre.

The first signs of an attack came from the small blanket of arrows peppering the guards on the walls. Successive waves of shafts struck wood and flesh, effectively keeping the defenders from getting a good look at their attackers. A few were killed, more wounded. Orlek didn't expect many to die from the attack. Effective in select hands, bows were more for rapid rates of fire and shock value than actual casualty producing. They did however, keep heads down.

Fire arrows came next. Cowering against the walls from unseen shafts streaking down in the night was one thing, facing waves of flames arcing towards them completely another. Smoke soon drifted into the early night sky. A bell began clanging. Soldiers rushed from tents, chow lines, and work details to man positions on the walls. Light cavalry hurried to the long barns to saddle and ready their war horses. Amidst the confusion, Orlek began the assault.

Hundreds of camouflaged infantry dashed across the exposed area leading up to the walls, an area that normally would have been the perfect killing ground but was rendered ineffective because of the time of night. Ingrid had chosen wisely. Rebels hit the gap in the wooden palisade, cutting down those defenders who were able to man the wall in time. Standing at the opening, blood dripping from his chest armor, Orlek bellowed and led his fighters in.

They killed everyone they could find. Disorganized by the now roaring flames on the western wall, Jarrik's reserves valiantly attempted to defend the redoubt. Men ran screaming from wounds. Others died where they fell, steam pulsing from their cooling bodies. Orlek managed to breech halfway through the interior before he realized there weren't nearly as many defenders as there were supposed to be.

A lone horn blew baleful tunes across the battlefield. The sounds of battle slowed. Men stopped running, looking around for the source. Orlek briefly closed his eyes. It was a trap. Jarrik had lured the rebels into thinking they had the upper hand. He had to move quickly if any of the rebels were going to survive the night.

"Out! All you! Fall back to the rendezvous point!" he roared and began shoving those closest to him back towards the gap.

Those closest to him panicked. Some dropped their weapons as they turned to flee. Others, still trying to get into the redoubt, continued forcing their way inside. The jam quickly turned ugly, making it next to impossible to escape. Orlek had only one option, though he was loath to do it. Collecting as many fighters as he could, the grizzled veteran led them towards what had to be the command structure. If, just if, he could break in and seize the Wolfsreik commanding officer, he might be able to negotiate an escape. If not, they were all going to die.

A pair of guards flanked the doors to the partially finished building in the center of the redoubt. Sprinting to close the gap, Orlek leapt over a freshly slain body and brought his sword down diagonally. Too slow, the guard cried out as blood fountained from the wide line arcing down from his shoulder to his navel. Entrails spilled onto the mud, followed closely by the rapidly dying guard. Distracted, Orlek yelled as the second guard's sword plunged into his thigh. Rebels charged in to cut the guard down before he had the chance of killing Orlek. Once dead, the rebels paused to help their leader.

"Go on! Keep moving. Take the building!" Orlek insisted.

Those closest were reluctant to leave him behind. Orlek was their leader, the driving force behind the assault. They'd be lost without him at their front. Another horn note blasted over the area, this time much closer. Whatever trickery Jarrik had planned was getting closer to revealing itself. Desperation set in. Orlek looked out over the courtyard and was dismayed to see many of his fighters on the ground in pools of their blood. Wolfsreik infantry were pouring from the barracks now, evening the odds in moments. Momentum was at the point of shifting completely. He had to move now or die with his men.

Orlek snatched the rag torn from a dead guard's tunic and pulled it tightly three inches above the wound to stop the blood flow. The tourniquet was meant to save his life, though he'd probably lose the leg once the battle was finished. He snorted. Who was he kidding? He didn't think he was going to need to worry about it. Leaning on a rebel for support, Orlek limped into the command center.

Harlan couldn't help but grin tersely as flight after flight of fire arrows sped towards the redoubt. Watching flames stretch up over the tops of the walls enthused him in ways much failed to do of late. Once a self-defined playboy, Harlan had wandered Delranan and the rest of the north in search of pointless love and adventure. He'd chosen the worst possible moment for his return. The war broke out shortly after, leaving him trapped in a land intent on devouring itself from the inside. Siding with the rebellion was the only logical choice.

Excited tension filled him, making it difficult to stand still. No hero, he wanted to be storming the walls with Orlek; it was the only time he'd ever been jealous of his swarthy companion. Instead Ingrid posted him to the flanks with what he considered a menial assignment. Guarding against fleeing soldiers seemed to lack any distinguishing characteristic of glory. And glory was the one factor he needed to cement his name in the future kingdom. A few defenders panicked and tried to escape over the walls. Their bodies decorated the ground.

It wasn't enough. According to Boen, the redoubt was filled with hundreds of enemy soldiers. While Harlan recognized the odds were almost even, nothing the rebels had in their arsenal or tactical knowledge base was enough to contend with even the Wolfsreik reserves in a head-to-head fight. Harlan was the biggest proponent for their guerilla-style war, thinking Ingrid mad to brazenly conduct this raid. Still, he couldn't help but admire her tenacity. Should she pull it off, the raid would go down as one of the greatest military maneuvers in the kingdom's storied history. He'd finally get his chance to play the hero.

The first sign things weren't going according to schedule was the lack of bodies trying to escape. Best-case scenario had Orlek's fighters hacking them down in their beds. Harlan wasn't an idealist by any measure. The horn blast coming from the frozen plains to his north confirmed those darkest fears he didn't want to admit. Ingrid had been duped. They all had.

"What was that?" a nervous young lady with bright, blond hair asked.

Thankful it was finally dark, Harlan spit his displeasure. "Keep firing but be prepared to fall back on my signal. If that horn is what I think it is this fight is about to turn nasty. I'll be right back."

Clearly not liking the answer, she strung another arrow and fired.

Harlan stalked off, moving as quickly as he thought safe. Night presented different challenges, some he hoped the enemy suffered from as well. They'd already salted the roads leading into the redoubt with homemade caltrops of sharpened wood. The spiked weapons would cripple any horse stepping on them and cause confusion to the remainder of the force. Harlan had seen them used effectively in the east. Implementing them here was too easy. Ingrid needed every advantage she could muster just to hold on.

The caltrops were highly effective, but only so long as the enemy stayed on the main roads. Once they realized what was happening any good commander worth his salt would divide his forces and come around the road. Harlan hoped the reserve commanders followed doctrine. He had a surprise for that as well. He dropped behind a row of holly bushes, the thorny leaves pricking his exposed hands as he slid.

Night had grown dark and cold. He strained to make out any attacking force. Trees and boulders became Giants crawling across the world. His mind played tricks on him. Each time he blinked he imagined he spotted the fleeting images of soldiers stealthily marching his way. The end of the world crept nigh. He blinked. Rubbed his eyes. Finally, the glow of torches rewarded his diligence. A lot of torches from what he could guess.

"Sneaky bastards," he whispered to no one. Close to two hundred cavalry was barreling towards the redoubt and Harlan's rebels. Two hundred heavily armed and angry, professional soldiers. Harlan didn't stand a chance. Yet if he left he'd abandon Ingrid and Orlek to a fate worse than death. *Seems my timing is never right. My mother always told me not to try to be a hero. If she could only see me now.*

Knowing he couldn't abandon his only true friends to the horrors of Harnin One Eye, Harlan hurried back to his line of archers. The time had come to shift focus and execute the second phase of his defense. He only prayed it worked enough to give those within the enemy fort enough time to escape.

"All you, follow me quickly. Just as we rehearsed." The urgency in his voice made them move faster.

Every third archer shifted and hurried to their alternate positions. He briefly contemplated bringing more but the attackers needed all the aid they could get. Harlan dashed to the front of the column and began placing archers where he thought they had the best chance of creating massive havoc. A quick glance confirmed the enemy cavalry was much closer and in great numbers. *There are times I wish I was wrong. This is one of them.*

Withholding the order to fire was among the hardest things he'd ever done but firing now would only give away their position and prevent maximum damage. He only had one shot at halting the cavalry advance. One chance to help Orlek and Ingrid escape before the raid turned completely sour. He could hear the horses breathing. Smell their sweat. Each step closer made their riders more discernible. So close he could almost make out faces.

His heart began to pound. A series of hand signals made his archers nock and draw. Harlan struggled to keep his nerves from taking control. If just one should slip their hold and fire, the ambush would fail. Cavalry would divide and run the archers down without any casualties. With the burning walls of the redoubt in plain view, the cavalry broke into a charge. Hooves thundered over the fields. The clanging of armor jarred his bones. Harlan could feel tension building. They were so close.

Please don't loose. Please don't loose. He could hear the battle raging behind him, though in whose favor remained to be seen. Harlan couldn't concern himself over elements beyond his control. All he could do was wait helplessly until the cavalry struck the caltrop field. And strike they did. Horse and rider barreled unwittingly into the field. The lead ranks were crippled before pain registered fully. Panicking, several riders pulled their reins too hard and their mounts tipped.

The noise was deafening. Razor-sharp, wooden spikes dug into the horses and exposed sides of the riders. Men shouted desperate warnings to those following. Orders rang over the chaos for a halt. Soldiers milled about, suddenly unsure what to do. Many of their comrades were down and in grave pain. Horses struggled to rise. Harlan watched in mute dread. He'd never seen the like and, now that he had, never wanted to again. Reluctance didn't prevent him from doing what needed to be done.

"Fire!" he roared.

Horses and men screamed as arrows drove deep into flesh. Dead men dropped from their saddles. Horses fell, blocking the road. Two hundred enemy soldiers were effectively stymied. Harlan ordered his archers to empty their quivers, knowing they didn't have enough ammunition to kill all the riders. It was a chance he had no choice but to take. The enemy commander wasn't as slow to react as Harlan hoped.

The majority of cavalry began backing their mounts away to reform beyond arrow range. A tenth of their strength lay dead or wounded. Impressive for the lack of marksmanship among the rebels, Harlan led his people away while the enemy was still in disarray. His small band of rebels did the best they could do given their inexperience and lack of proper equipment. They'd given Orlek and the others the only chance they were going to get. It was with heavy heart he gave the order to retreat.

Inaella watched as a handful of rebels fought their way into the command building, clearly aiming to decapitate the Wolfsreik leadership. *More the fools*. Little did they know Jarrik was already dead. The coward swallowed a vial of poison after discovering Harnin's plan for removing him from command. While she couldn't agree with his actions, she recognized Harnin's devious intent by sending Skaning. The younger lord's ruthlessness was matched only by his lust for power. Men like that were dangerous. Too dangerous to trust. Yet as much as she wanted time to dedicate plotting his removal, Inaella knew she'd never get it.

Survival instincts kicked in. The redoubt was lost, though it was never meant to be permanent. She and Jarrik built it for the sole purpose of luring the rebellion in and crushing them. Too many soldiers had already been killed for her liking but soldiers were expendable assets. She wanted revenge. No amount of bloodshed was enough to compensate for her losses. The indignity suffered went far beyond emotional or physical scarring.

Firelight danced in her eyes. More soldiers and rebels fought and died as she watched. Inaella made no efforts to help. Instead she waited for her chance to flee back into the night. With a little good fortune the majority of rebel fighters would perish before dawn. She only hoped Ingrid managed to survive. That was the only person she truly wanted to watch the life flicker and fade from. Everyone else could burn.

Inaella slid out of her cloak and stole a weather-worn jacket from a dead rebel. The material was old and of poor quality. She began itching the moment she slid it on. Survival being more important than comfort, she ducked back into the darkness, what little remained, and hurried to get in the mass of people fleeing the redoubt. It was only after she blended in that she realized she lacked a weapon. The press of bodies forced her through the gap in the palisades before she had the opportunity to rectify her problem.

Away from the fires, the night was especially cold. Less than one hundred pounds, Inaella shivered uncontrollably. The plague ravaged her body, leaving her mere fragments of her former self. Whereas her body struggled to keep going day after day, her mind was sharp as a sword. It was her most important, and effective, weapon. She managed to escape with the others. Together they escaped to fight another day. Inaella used her inner hatred of Ingrid to keep her legs moving.

Boen snatched Ingrid roughly by the collar and forced her away from the engagement area. He still wasn't sure what went wrong. Why the rebels were fleeing back into the night. The professional warrior in him recognized the ambush and found it a sound tactic. The rebellion had been using guerilla-style ambushes effectively since being forced from the capital city. Boen judged they'd met their match here.

The Gaimosian couldn't help but feel at least partially responsible for the failure. He'd been the one to infiltrate enemy ranks. The one who provided the last raw, up-to-date intelligence of the situation before Ingrid made her decision. Unable to fight, Boen had but one option left. He was forced to watch and listen to the sounds of brave men and women fighting for their kingdom and their lives. Only when it appeared the end had come did he grab Ingrid and retreat.

She sputtered, protesting how she needed to be with her fighters. Share the same fate. He'd heard it a hundred times from those who view military failure as something personal. They all believed they needed to die beside their soldiers. He never understood that passion. No commander worth his salt would willingly lie down and die while he still had forces in the field. Forces that relied on him to carry them through the dismal aftermath just as the rebellion needed Ingrid. He resisted the urge to punch her between the eyes, settling for forcibly removing her from the field. Only when they were more than a kilometer away did he slow.

"Why did you do that?" Ingrid raged. Anger flushed her features. Her body trembled from the pent-up frustration threatening to break free.

Boen raised an eyebrow. "Do what? Save your life? What would getting killed now accomplish?"

"That's not the point! This was my idea. My attack. I should have stayed with…."

"You did exactly as you should have done by allowing me to drag you away," Boen snapped back. "What do you think Orlek would say if he found you ignorantly trying to break into the kill zone while he was busy trying to save as many lives as possible? Are you mad?"

"Furious more like it," she retorted.

Boen almost laughed. He admired her tenacity but such attitudes could easily be used against her. Ingrid was one of the toughest women he'd ever met, from any race, and might have made a good Gaimosian. The thought might have been inspiring if he wasn't at least three decades older.

He grabbed her softly by the shoulders and pulled her close enough to see her face clearly. "Ingrid, listen to me. Whatever comes out of this raid, the rebellion is going to need you more than ever. There will be survivors, enough to keep up the fight. There will be losses as well. More than you are ready to reconcile with. Use this night to steel your resolve and keep up the war."

"What for?" She gestured futilely back towards the redoubt. "We've lost."

He shook his head. "No. The enemy may have ambushed us but we tore a mighty chunk out of their combat power. Harnin can't keep funneling troops and resources into this rebellion, not with Badron rumored to be en route. You might have been stung but he is also at the breaking point. This is not the hour to wallow in lament."

Reluctantly she agreed. They made their way back to the rendezvous point without another word. Boen's thoughts were already beyond the ambush. He'd told Bahr to ride ahead, promising to meet up with them once he'd fulfilled his obligations to Ingrid. Satisfied he'd done all within his power, Boen mounted his horse and rode east with a final farewell. Ingrid and a handful of others watched him disappear into the night.

TWENTY

Aftermath

Bodies continued to trickle in over the course of the following day. Ingrid took heart with each small cluster of survivors. Some offered weary smiles. They bore no ill will. The veterans who understood war knew there was no way for any commander of troops to plan for every contingency or anticipate how a battle will develop. Ingrid already planned on utilizing the veterans to buoy spirits and refocus the rebellion. She dreaded to think of the alternative.

Ingrid waited at the makeshift perimeter from dawn to dusk. She refused to leave for meals and only reluctantly to relieve herself. Her silent vow to remain until all her people were accounted for gave her warmth as the day began to fade. All day and not a sign of anyone from Orlek's command. She began to worry. Orlek had commanded five hundred rebels. Surely there was no legitimate way all had been butchered. Neither Jarrik nor Inaella were that cruel. Or so Ingrid hoped. With the massive levels of carnage she'd already witnessed in Delranan she'd be a fool to put it past them.

Many of the faces passing by were familiar though most weren't. Regardless, she put on a brave show and offered encouraging words she didn't particularly feel. Spirits had all but dissolved. The will to fight was soundly beaten from most of the eyes brave enough to look back at her. *It wasn't this bad when we abandoned Chadra. I don't know if I can carry on much longer. Each new challenge devours another part of my soul. How much more have I to give before I am nothing?*

Her first good news came halfway through the afternoon. Riders came in bearing messages from Harlan. He'd suffered relatively few casualties and had been able to withdraw his command back to his camp without incident.

The messenger went on to detail the engagement with the cavalry and Harlan's discretionary retreat, making it clear that such acts weren't even considered until the situation became too dire to stay in place. Ingrid might easily have blamed him for Orlek's death. She didn't. Harlan performed as any good field commander should and saved nearly all his command. *They'll provide the bulk of our combat power from here on. Perhaps I should cede control to him and fade away?*

Ingrid accepted the victory for what it was. Every warm body she had remaining to carry on the fight was a benefit she felt most grateful for. The rebellion, while suffering an indefinable defeat for the moment, was far from over. She hadn't been foolish enough to commit all her strength to the raid. Hundreds of able-bodied men and women waited in their predetermined positions for further orders. Her only fear came from what those fighters would do once word of the failed assault reached them. *No doubt Harnin's forces are already spreading propaganda about our defeat. If only I had the strength as he.*

She thanked the messenger and, after giving him ample time to recover and eat, sent him back with a message of her own. Harlan needed to know that she was immobile until she had positive accountability of all her fighters. Until then he was to continue executing small raids and ambushes to the north, if for no other reason than to draw Harnin's eye away from the main base. If, and only if, Harlan deemed it safe, he was to send scouts back to the redoubt to gather fresh intelligence. The messenger saluted and rode off.

Alone again, Ingrid maintained her watch until well after dark. She only left after practically being forced away by guards claiming it wasn't safe for her to be outside of the perimeter with so many enemy soldiers about. She reluctantly agreed and was escorted back to her quarters. Yet much troubled her mind and she found it difficult to take comfort in the rest. Frustrated, Ingrid gathered her cloak about her and headed towards the healing station. Wounded lay about small fires. Most had already been seen to and were trying to find some small measure of comfort in the warmth.

Her heart cried upon seeing so many friends hurt. Those who succumbed to their wounds were taken out of sight of the rest of the camp, to be buried when the snows melted and the ground thawed. The psychological trauma of sitting beside the corpse of a familiar face was well known to be demotivational amongst fighting forces. Ingrid pushed those dark thoughts from her mind, at least as far as she could, which wasn't very, considering all she'd seen and done over the course of the last day, and tried making small talk with the wounded.

Many surprised her by being amiable to conversation. They laughed and joked, eager to be taken away from the pain they suffered. Others were morose, choosing to roll over rather than speak with her. Through it all Ingrid kept reminding herself it was nothing personal. They'd suffered extreme trauma and needed time to work through their emotions. She needed to believe that, if for no other reason than to remain convinced she was on the path of the righteous.

"Pardon, ma'am, but you're needed at the perimeter," a young rebel politely interrupted.

Ingrid looked up from the wounded woman she was speaking with. She had no desire to confront any new challenges or issues this night, but a leader's work is never done. Excusing herself, she followed the rebel back to the camp entrance. Several guards were on duty. Others patrolled the perimeter at random intervals.

Greeting returning knots of fighters was proving tiresome but each new group buoyed her optimism. Each new face was one less the enemy managed to kill or capture, leading her to believe the disaster wasn't nearly as complete as her mind imagined. She wanted to talk with the young man who'd come to escort her but lacked the words. He was doing his job, she hers. The farther she walked the more she couldn't shake the feeling he was up to something. The youth struggled to keep amusement from tainting his stern features. She sighed. Perhaps she was just too tired to think clearly. Either way, they reached the main entrance point to the camp. Her escort slowly dropped back, leaving Ingrid alone for the moment.

"I never thought the smell of sweat would make me feel welcome."

Ingrid's eye widened. Shock rippled through her body. There, standing before her, was the one man she'd been desperate to find. "Orlek!"

Ingrid ignored all vestiges of protocol and rushed forward. Her slender arms encircled his waist and she tipped her head back to kiss him fully on the lips with months of pent-up passion. Several fighters coughed or turned away to avoid embarrassment as Orlek slowly responded. Several long moments later they broke apart, slightly out of breath and flushed in face and heart.

"I worried you'd been killed," she whispered.

He could only shrug, though parts of a sheepish grin escaped. "For a while so did I."

Ingrid noticed the thick blood staining his leg and the bandages swathed over it. More than one had lost limbs this night, enough she immediately feared the worst.

Catching the look in her eyes, Orlek said, "It's not as bad as it seems. Cut me good but I'm not going to lose the leg. At least that's what my surgeon's been able to deduce while we traveled back."

So many emotions she'd repressed flooded through her. Love. Yes, finally love won through all the rage, hate, and despair. Pieces began to fall into place. Holes were filled. Her life took on new meaning. She had something worth fighting for once again. Determination warmed her nearly as much as her admitted love for Orlek. The war would continue. Victories and losses edging each other in a mad dash to the final battle. The war could wait for one night. Tonight she intended on taking Orlek back to her tent and doing what she denied wanting for so long. Tomorrow was another matter.

"Dead?"

Ingrid couldn't believe the news. Jarrik had been one of Harnin's staunchest supporters, even before Badron left for the east. She couldn't imagine one of the senior ranking nobles in Delranan willingly killing himself, especially not with victory still a very real outcome. Events must have taken a considerable turn for the worse.

"Yes, but we didn't do it. He was already that way when we found him," Orlek continued his recounting. "After I got stabbed I managed to drag myself inside the command building. I must tell you, most of it was just a frame. The walls were incomplete and there were no furnishings except in his office. Some of the lads had already broken through the interior guards and were breaking down the door by the time I arrived. We charged in, hoping to take him alive so we had a bargaining chip once the rest of the Wolfsreik finished mopping up outside."

She winced at his callousness. Relegating so many lives into bare statistics seemed cruel. She felt it was much too soon to be leaders.

Orlek cleared his throat, a mild attempt at easing any perceived tension. "Jarrik was sitting at his desk. His head was tilted back. Foam and spittle ran down his chin. His eyes were glazed over. The body was already cooling by the time I checked for a pulse. Didn't have a wound on it."

Ingrid hung her head as she tried deciphering the riddle. Clearly he'd taken poison, but why? "What you say doesn't make any sense. Jarrik was one of the few nobles remaining with allegiance to Harnin. He wouldn't knowingly take his own life."

"Not unless he had a damned good reason to," Orlek added. "I don't think all is well in our enemy's camp, Ingrid. Cracks are forming."

"Yet we're not in a position to take advantage of it," she replied. "I ordered Harlan to send scouts back to the redoubt to give us a better idea of how much damage was done. With any luck they'll be able to sneak in and out without being seen."

"I don't think that will be much of a problem," Orlek answered. "From what I saw the majority of Wolfsreik abandoned what remained shortly after we managed to escape. The body count is high on both sides, though there's no accurate way to assess enemy casualties. I'd estimate our losses at close to two hundred dead. Maybe twice that wounded."

Five hundred! So many and for what? The Wolfsreik remained in control of the area, regardless of whatever losses they suffered. I've led my people to slaughter. We can't sustain another battle of that magnitude.

"It would have been more if not for Harlan's quick thinking. I can't say for certain what he did, but he managed to keep the bulk of their cavalry from striking us when we were most vulnerable," Orlek said upon seeing dejection in her face. "They bloodied our nose but we took out a healthy chunk of flesh as well. This battle wasn't as lopsided as you seem to think."

"Perhaps you should have led with that?"

His grinned defused her rising tension. "I thought that kiss was a perfect opening."

"Don't get used to it," she snapped. "At least not in front of the men."

His laughter was soft, contradictory to his rough exterior. Orlek wasn't an easygoing man. Life had been hard from an early age, continuing to worsen as the years fled. He'd loved and lost. Suffered and celebrated. Through it all he followed one mantra: live for now. Tomorrow might not come. Until now it seemed like the only way. Ingrid's warmth thawed him in ways he never imagined possible.

"We're not in front of the men now," he said.

Ingrid looked around coyly. "No. No we're not."

He leaned in for another kiss.

Ash drifted down like troubled rain. Fires still burned throughout the redoubt, or rather what remained. Most of the interior structures were char-blackened shells of their intended purpose. Bodies littered the courtyard. Most wore Wolfsreik uniforms but there were enough rebels to satisfy Skaning. The dark-haired lord of Delranan strode through his new command with the arrogance of one who'd never been in a heated battle before.

He found the term amusing given the waves of intense heat choking the area. Soldiers and mercenaries moved about. Most carried bodies to the mass grave being established within what had been the stables. The smell of cooked horse flesh choked him. Skaning wrapped an old scarf around his nose and mouth. Several soldiers tried, and failed, to conceal their looks of disdain as he passed by. They'd been fighting the rebellion for months. Most had seen friends die and were well versed in the art of death. A tragedy for ones still so youthful.

Skaning ignored them. He didn't care what they thought of him. He was a lord of Delranan, answerable only to Harnin One Eye. The rest of the world could burn for all he cared. His boots, once polished immaculately for life in Chadra Keep, were soot stained. Bits of gore and blood clung to them like parasites. He'd only killed one last night: a woman unfortunate enough to get trampled by his horse before he stabbed her to death. The death invigorated him in ways he'd nearly forgotten. Killing in duels and through the subterfuge gripping the capital city was another matter altogether.

"Lord Skaning, its Jarrik," one of the scar-faced mercenaries told him without flourish.

Irritated by being disturbed, Skaning asked, "What of him?"

He couldn't believe his former friend had stayed. Jarrik was given a way out. He could have disappeared into the south, never to be seen or cared about again. Life wouldn't have been as kind to him as in the courts of Delranan but it was still life. A man could make anything out of nothing if he put his mind to it. Jarrik had been given a new start. So why hadn't he taken it?

"Dead," the mercenary answered. The scruff of his beard was salt and pepper, blending in with the background. An indifferent look seemed to pass between all the mercenaries.

Skaning couldn't believe it. "Dead how?"

The mercenary shrugged his indifference. "I don't care. Dead is dead."

"Where's the body?"

Gesturing behind him, he answered, "Back in his office. Want us to throw him in the pit?"

Skaning paused. The urge to strike the mercenary down for his callous indifference to a noble was inexcusable, even though Harnin hired them for exactly that reason. Instead of wasting time bickering with the man, Skaning brushed by and made his way into what remained of the command center. Blood stained those parts of the building that weren't burned. Dark spots spread from where the bodies still lay. Skaning stepped over a corpse, partially frozen with an intense look of despair twisting its face and entered Jarrik's office. *Though I suppose this is technically my office. A shame I had to let the rebels burn it to the ground. I could have used the redoubt to solidify my presence in the west.* Wars call for sacrifice, however, and Skaning had done the prudent deed.

He found Jarrik's corpse where the man had died. His skin bore a bluish tint. Glazed-over eyes stared up to the ceiling. Crippled hands curled on the desk. A crow managed to find its way inside, pecking at the steadily freezing flesh with impunity. Skaning looked down upon the man who had once been his friend. He didn't know what to feel. On one hand, Jarrik's death meant Skaning had completed his task. One of Harnin's perceived enemies was dead, leaving room for Skaning to assume uncontested control of the west. Yet Jarrik was a friend. His loss would take time to sink in, but it would eventually return to haunt the younger Skaning.

"Poison's a bad way to go."

Skaning frowned at the mercenary without turning. "Prepare his body for transport back to Chadra Keep. I think Lord Harnin needs to see this for himself."

"Just so long as I get paid for it."

A pair of mercenaries walked by to collect the body.

TWENTY-ONE

Dorl's Doubt

They rode as fast as possible, which wasn't very, considering how deep the snow was in some places. Groge managed to outpace them all thanks to his massive height and stride. The Giant wasn't accustomed to snow accumulation but seemed not to mind. Each new adventure was a step into a world he'd grown up only hearing about. Giant elders banned the young from venturing out of Venheim for fear of reprisals by the lowland races. Groge didn't find pleasure in his dealings below the mountaintops, but the wealth of knowledge gained was more than all the acquired past for the fabled Giant clans.

The youthful Giant strode merrily through the snow, managing to forget, temporarily, the trauma of the war in Delranan or the curious weight of bearing the Blud Hamr. Walking through the pristine wilderness presented fresh perspective on life. Years had gone by under the inglorious teachings of forge master Joden. While Groge was eternally grateful for the privilege of learning from such an esteemed master, he chafed at being held behind.

Being chosen to accompany the wizard and Bahr far surpassed his dreams of one day visiting the lower world. Their adventures ranged over half of the continent, giving him new insights into previously stale histories. Groge understood the elders' reasoning for keeping the Giant clans away from the rest of the world, but their self-imposed exile only resulted in the Giants becoming largely obsolete. Malweir didn't need Giants any longer. In fact, it had been so long since any were last seen roaming the world that most citizens stopped believing. Reality turned to myth, myth to legend.

Humans weren't nearly as bad as Blekling and the others portrayed them to be. Groge had entered this agreement with trepidations. After all, a lifetime of mistrust couldn't be erased in the span of a few days. The ensuing weeks solidified his views. While he didn't consider any of them friends yet, Groge was smart enough to know they were well down that path. His greatest concerns were in not letting them down and living up to what the wizard Anienam Keiss seemed to think he was. All doubts would be tested once they arrived at Arlevon Gale.

Bahr watched the innocence in the young Giant and wondered if the youth was on to some incredible secret the others weren't. No matter what implausible scenario they were thrust into, Groge handled it with surprising acceptance despite never having encountered anything of the sort back in Venheim. *How many others would willingly undergo such stress without so much as a single complaint? Hells, I'm not sure I could.*

He reined back his horse and turned towards the rear of the column. Most of the others bore haunted looks. He knew they'd wanted to help the rebellion. He did as well, but their task was far more important than an internal power struggle for the throne of a single kingdom. Even a kingdom where he technically had the only right to contest Harnin's rule. That they overcame their internal deliberations to continue to follow Bahr towards the ancient ruins spoke volumes. Bahr couldn't have asked for a better group of people to try and stop the dark gods.

Only one was missing. Since agreeing with Ingrid's plan, Bahr couldn't shake the dreaded feeling harbored deep within his spine. Boen was their most important military asset. The Gaimosian was the very definition of what a warrior was meant to be. If he chose to ignore his orders of not getting engaged and wound up being killed or captured, the entire quest would shatter. Artiss Gran said that all were needed to complete their task successfully. Boen was a risk taker, often finding it near impossible to resist the urge for combat.

Boen was the closest Bahr had to a true friend. They'd shared more adventures than either recalled, spilling blood and drink together. Such companionship was rare in these times. Bahr appreciated the Gaimosian without understanding him. Should any ill befall Boen now when Bahr needed him the most…he let the thought drop. There was no time for self-pity. The world depended on the actions of the select few in Bahr's care. Who was he to ignore such needs?

"He will come," Anienam said as Bahr rode past.

The Sea Wolf glanced up at the blind wizard, wondering how a man with no vision could know who was near. A quick look at Skuld's surprised face confirmed the boy hadn't told Anienam.

Rather than waste time with asking the obvious, Bahr said, "He's been gone a long time. I'm debating whether I should send someone back to fetch him."

Anienam shrugged. "You could, though I doubt it would do much good for your peace of mind. Instead of fretting over one you'd be consumed with two or three. Boen is highly capable, Bahr. He will return and the quest will continue."

"How can you be so positive?"

The wizard flashed a smile. "I'm blind, not ignorant. What this quest needs is positivity. As much as we can get, too. Time is steadily winding down and we still have much to do before Groge can wield the hammer and end this nightmare forever."

"Forever? That's optimistic."

Anienam shrugged. "What else am I going to do with all this time on my hands? The gods of light saw fit to take my vision yet I retain all my other faculties. My knowledge is vital. Perhaps I am the victim of a private joke."

"Sounds more like the butt of one to me," Bahr replied. "Anienam, what are we going to find once we arrive at the ruins?"

A pause. Weeks of theories and speculation boiled down to an educated guess. One the wizard wasn't comfortable making, especially not with his loss of eyesight. "Honestly? I don't know, Bahr. All I can say is expect the worst evil can throw at us. The Dae'shan will undoubtedly be there, as well as whatever armies or forces they've mustered to their cause. Gnaals. Harpies. Goblins even if any are to be found this far west."

"Men." Bahr's voice was barely a whisper.

Anienam nodded sadly. "Yes. Man has ever been among the weakest of races. Human will is notoriously weak yet simultaneously strong. We have the capacity for great achievement yet the majority squanders that gift with petty desires and base sins. I'm beginning to think the gods abandoned the world to teach us all a lesson."

"What lesson would that be?" Bahr asked.

"That no matter what, we must endure, no matter how much adversity life throws at us, we must remain true to our origins. All life needs a deity, even if there is only base belief. It is the quest to live up to the expectations of our religion that makes us who, what we are. Anything less is in disservice to the entire race."

Bahr gestured towards the Giant and Dwarf. "What of them? The Giants believe in a single god whereas Dwarves worship warrior gods of steel and blood. How does either compare to what awaits? Gods of light versus gods of evil. No wonder most men have turned their backs. To them we are naught but playthings for their amusement."

Anienam couldn't argue that point. He'd endured his own crisis of faith many years ago and came out a better person when cold realization finally struck. Faith was a cornerstone of individual development. The entire purpose of life was to continually grow, nurture, and develop future generations. To become more than all your forbearers and to leave the world in a better condition than when it was handed to you. Anything less was merely wasted.

How do I explain that to a man jaded by his experiences? Anienam decided to change the subject, slightly. "How are the others holding up?"

Bahr was secretly grateful for the change. His mind was tired, sore from having to endure endless, deep conversations designed to prompt deep thinking. "Exhausted. We've been on the road for months now and, even though the end is in sight, we're borderline fatigued. There's only so much we can endure before the time comes to sit fast and rest."

"I would like to say there'll be time to rest once this is finished, but even I'm not going to be so naïve. I truly believe the gods selected each of us for specific purposes and that we are the only ones, collectively, capable of finishing this task. This is a war unlike any other the races of Malweir have seen or fought. More will be expected of us, Bahr. So much more than I am willing to fathom."

"Tired men get people killed, Anienam. Our brief stay at Trennaron was well and fine, but it wasn't enough. We're going to need serious downtime to take on what you think awaits us in Arlevon Gale."

Bahr shook his head. His salt-and-pepper beard scratched his neck and chin. He longed for the day when he'd finally be able to bathe and shave again properly. While a naturally gruff man, Bahr still managed time to return to his villa and indulge in self-pampering. He despised being filthy and he was well beyond that state now. They all were. Thankfully they rode the open plains where he didn't have to smell the others, very much.

"I make no promises, Bahr, but there is still time before the final dawn. We may yet find a moment to rest," Anienam soothed, hoping it was enough. He would never admit it, but the combination of his age and disabilities rendered him practically ineffective. There was no going home, not for him. He left the ruins of Ipn Shal fully knowing that this would be his final quest. He'd spent a lifetime defending Malweir against the dark gods and their ilk. If, just if, Bahr and the others were successful in destroying the nexus and the dark gods, Anienam would finally be able to rest. The thought left him oddly satisfied. Mortality had its virtues. It was time to move on to the next world.

"Every little bit helps. These people have been pushed beyond the breaking point. Any good field commander would find the time for them to recover, at least partially." Bahr knew he was wasting his breath trying to change Anienam's mind. Their timeline was set in stone, incapable of changing simply because their tiny band didn't know if it could carry on, but it felt good to vent.

Anienam nodded morosely and added, "We shall see. We shall see."

Nothol and Dorl forged ahead of the others. Both were eager to be away from the group. Tension continued to build, threatening to tear them apart long before reaching Arlevon Gale. Dorl could care less. He'd done what he was contracted to do as far as he was concerned. The only thing keeping him with Bahr was the fact he still hadn't been paid. To be sure, there were other, more important reasons that he'd never voice aloud. Some matters needed to remain private for them to retain meaning.

"It feels good to be back on our own," Nothol commented in an attempt at thawing the casual chill growing between them recently.

Dorl continued looking ahead. "So to speak. We're still not far from Bahr or the rest. This quest has taken so long I don't rightly remember a time when it was just the two of us."

"Those days will come again. You'll have to ask your wife if you can come out and ride with the adults," Nothol chided. Hands folded over the pommel, he let his horse guide them down the snow-covered road.

Dorl might have fumed, but it was hard to tell with their continually reddened faces. "There will never come a time when I need to ask a woman if I can go do something!

You'll see! I am my own man, Nothol Coll. Not some caged beast in need of primping or grooming."

Nothol burst into laughter. "I don't recall the last time you seemed interested in grooming. You stink worse than your horse half the time."

"Only because there's no lady present!"

Nothol pretended to look over his shoulder. "I wouldn't let Rekka hear you say that. She might not take kindly to being referred to as anything less than a lady. Especially one with a very sharp sword and better skill set than you possess."

Unable to think of a witty comeback, Dorl merely clenched a fist and ground his teeth to Nothol's laughter. Some battles weren't worth fighting. Despite the lightheartedness of their banter, Dorl couldn't help but shake the intense feeling that he wasn't going to live long enough to enjoy a lifetime with Rekka bossing him around. He tried concealing his emotions but he and Nothol had been around each other for far too long. His best friend easily picked up on the deception and decided to use their time alone to confront it.

"What gives? You haven't been yourself since we reached Trennaron." *Farther back than that if I'm any judge of character. This quest has you spooked and I need to know why if I'm going to continue trusting you with my life.*

Eyebrows furrowed, Dorl tried to keep his mouth shut. They'd been through this argument before and walked away with negative results. He wished Nothol would respect his privacy and give him space. Dorl wasn't ready to go in depth. Not until he knew for certain one way or the other what his fate was going to be. Reluctantly, he couldn't avoid his internal deliberations of entrusting his best friend with complete faith.

"Nothol, I'm scared."

The finality of that statement left them in total silence. Nothol never expected such admission; he wasn't capable of doing the same, regardless of the situation. They were in a business where any form of weakness meant nearly instant death. Even when they felt fear they weren't foolish enough to admit it openly. Their very lives depended on the secrecy of their feelings. For Dorl to come right out and admit his fear could only have grave implications on the future.

"Scared of what? Look at all we've been through and survived. How much worse can there be to throw at us?" Nothol asked slowly, choosing his words carefully.

Dorl reined his horse in. "Have you ever had the feeling that Lord Death is lurking right behind you? That he's ready to reach out and claim you when you least expect it? That's what I've been living with since we escaped from Harnin's dungeons. Lord Death is riding for me. Of that I am certain. There's only so much time remaining before I fall and am lost."

"What nonsense is this? We're all going to die, Dorl. It's a fact of life. Don't go giving me that sad tale of Lord Death barreling through time to tear you away from all you love long before your time. I've heard it before and think its rubbish. We're fighters, Dorl, and fighters don't succumb to petty weaknesses."

"Easy for you to say! You don't know what I'm talking about. You haven't suffered from the nausea of imaginary fingers curling around my throat when I sleep," Dorl added quickly.

"Are you sure that wasn't Rekka feeling frisky?"

Dorl jabbed a finger at his friend. "Leave her out of this!"

"How can I? You've been acting like a man with his balls cut off since the two of you became involved, as if you've lost your will to fight out of fear of living without her. Or vice versa. I need my old partner back, not the eunuch you're becoming."

"What in the hells are you talking about? Eunuch? I'm expressing a feeling no sane man would and you reduce it to mockery!" Dorl fumed.

Holding his hands up, Nothol said, "All right, calm down. I didn't mean anything by it. But you must admit, you haven't been the same since we left Delranan and that frightens me more than I'm comfortable with."

"You and me both."

Dorl slowly lowered his hand, ashamed at being so harsh with his best, and until recently, only friend. They'd gone through so much over the last few years he couldn't imagine facing any sort of danger without Nothol at his side. True friends seldom entered one's life and were to be treasured when they did. Dorl wasn't a particularly attractive or witty man. He got by on natural charm and the tenacity of a pit fighter. Life wasn't especially kind to a man like Dorl Theed so he took what he could, when he could.

"I'm not thinking clearly I suppose," he broke down and admitted, hoping to get Nothol off his back. "We tend to say crazy thoughts when we're tired. Don't mind me."

"I have no choice but to mind you, Dorl. We've come far, but there's still more to this messed-up journey. Chances are we're all going to die when we get to the part with the gods and Dae'shan and whatnot, but that ending hasn't been written yet. There's still more fighting for you and I. Don't dwell on what we can't change."

"Keep your sword sharp and your privates protected," Dorl finished their traditional pre-battle mantra. That finally brought a small grin to his weathered face, though not enough to keep Nothol from worrying further.

Nothol turned around, facing west. "Can you see the wagon?"

"No. We rode out of sight awhile back. Think we should turn around?"

"Bahr wanted us ahead of the main body in case we ran into the enemy. I don't think he'd want us to come back without good reason. Especially not with Boen still gone," Nothol answered.

Dorl cocked his head. "He might have come back. The Gaimosian's not prone to following any traditional protocol in the field. He could come and go without so much as bothering to make sure one of us noticed him leave."

"Still, can't hurt to have a Gaimosian along to keep order," Nothol said.

"Not at all. We're much stronger with him along. Which means he needs to be riding scout, not us," Dorl said. "We're much better in defined bad situations."

"Agreed. I worked better when those skeletons attacked us under Chadra. Not that I enjoyed it, mind you, but there was no anticipation of what was coming. The skeletons showed up and we fought."

Dorl recalled the battle in the underground temple and how they'd nearly been killed by the dead, or undead. He still wasn't sure what the skeletons were supposed to be. There'd been so many of them their small group almost didn't last. It was only through the late Lord Argis' contributions they managed to slay the last skeleton and escape back to the surface. Considering all that, most of rest of the events on their quest seemed too common. He purposefully ignored any memories of the battle with the Gnaals in the jungle. Some things needed to remain in the past.

"Nothol, I believe it's time we went back to what we used to make a living with," Dorl told him. "Odd jobs here and there. The intensity level on this quest is too much for me."

"I agree but there's a lack of nobility in Delranan at the moment. We might need to start looking south."

"The weather's bound to be better at any rate. I'd almost forgotten how cold winter is." Dorl's mind drifted towards roaming the world with Rekka and Nothol at his side. There was little left in the frozen north keeping his interests. Perhaps what he needed was a complete change of scenery.

Nothol shrugged nonchalantly. "I wasn't overly fond of the humidity in the jungle. It made my skin itch."

"Worse than the freezing up here?" Dorl couldn't believe it. The humidity, from what he'd learned from Rekka and Anienam, often broke materials down at an incredible rate. *That explains why the villagers of Teng didn't seem too concerned over clothing or material possessions. I wouldn't either if they were only going to rot away shortly after getting them. There must be some happy medium where we can settle down and find fat purses.* "What about Averon?"

"Don't you think there's enough of our sort already down there? I can't imagine the self-proclaimed high king enjoying having to put up with the two of us for long," Nothol said and grinned.

He'd only been to Averon once. The splendor of the central kingdom went unmatched by the rest of the world. Gold-capped towers poked high into the sky, pennants waving in the breeze. Vast armies maintained the peace, extending far beyond their own borders. Not since the war with Gren had there been a large struggle on the plains. The people of Averon enjoyed wealth, freedom, and peace for the durations of their lives. It was a dream for those born in the bitter reality of the northern kingdoms.

Now more than ever, the peoples of the north wanted an escape. So many had already fallen--from many kingdoms--that the continuation of their race was in doubt. A war that had originally begun as a feud between kings quickly spread to consume numerous races. They'd witnessed the effects all the way in Drimmen Delf. Anienam theorized the Dwarf civil war was the result of Dae'shan manipulations. Dwarves, Elves, Pell Darga, Goblins, and Men were all involved now.

"People are people," Dorl replied. "Life has to be easy away from all this. I'm tired, Nothol. I've had enough of our life in Delranan."

Nothol regarded him quietly. How could he tell Dorl he was struggling with the same emotions, the same feelings of dissatisfaction tugging at his conscience? "We're all tired. Bahr's pushing us harder than we've ever been pushed before. It's almost over, Dorl. We'll be at the ruins soon enough and once Groge smashes whatever he needs to with that hammer we'll be free to head on to a better life."

"If any of us are still alive to do so," Dorl added softly.

He turned his horse and headed back on the trail.

TWENTY-TWO

The Army Moves West

The longer Mahn and Raste remained in the mountains the more anxious King Aurec became. His trusted scouts, men who'd led his beleaguered forces into and out of more terrible situations than any other since the war began, had been gone for far too long for the young king's liking. Worse, Aurec felt continually restrained as time went by. He'd always known the crown of Rogscroft was meant to be his. Attaining it at such a young age wasn't in the bargain, but King Badron left him no alternative. The brutal murder of Aurec's father changed how life would forever be in his tiny kingdom.

Until the siege of the capital city Aurec had been free to come and go as he pleased. Most of his time was spent trying to find new ways to stymie the invading Wolfsreik. He was only answerable to his own soldiers. Their lives came before his, at least in his estimation. Others would argue differently. A king's first duty was to survive. It was a fact Aurec wasn't willing to accept.

Since being crowned in the tiny celebration in Grunmarrow Aurec had been strategically kept from the field. His council of advisors and those who automatically assumed they knew best managed to successfully divert his focus from grabbing a horse and riding to the front where he felt most comfortable. Instead of leading troops in the field he was mired with bureaucratic items which devoured his time. Refugees pouring into the capital city. Minor skirmishes with remaining Goblin forces strewn across western Rogscroft. Supply issues. Armory issues. Horses. Wagons. Weapons. Houses. Fresh water. Food. It was so much he wanted to resign. To give his crown, the legacy of his family, to a random passerby. Aurec had just learned a valuable lesson: there was no freedom in royalty.

He stood at the western edge of the main camp as he had every dawn after sending his favorite scouts into the mountains with Cuul Ol. His black bear cloak immediately marked him to everyone within the army camp. None were so foolish as to approach him during these private moments, which was a small grace he was immeasurably grateful for. Running a broken kingdom and conducting one of the largest wars in recent history was taxing beyond belief. The young boy forced into becoming a man was reaching his breaking point.

Five days came and went without sight or sound of Mahn and Raste. Without them, the army was trapped in place. Rolnir and Vajna organized a steady series of drills and training exercises to reinforce a new standard discipline throughout the army. Soldiers being soldiers, there was much grumbling throughout the ranks as they struggled to learn new ways of doing the same old business. It was all coming together nicely, despite varying degrees of difficulty. Aurec couldn't complain. They had the time to spare, after all.

Sounds of early morning training drills echoed across the open plain, losing itself deep into the mountains. Aurec once enjoyed the sounds of steel clashing. Now he cringed with visions of men being slaughtered for reasons they didn't understand. War was neither glamorous nor to be celebrated. War, in his humble opinion, was one of the worst acts any race could partake in. Some of the best and brightest from each generation ignorantly gave up their lives so that others might live. He didn't find any value in that. All lives should be considered equally important. Any ruler who thought otherwise didn't deserve to wear their crown.

"Training is proceeding as well as can be expected," he told Rolnir at the sound of his boots crunching the fresh layer of frost covering the snow.

Rolnir, nearly twice as old as the king, grinned ruefully. He admired Aurec's inherent sharpness. It was a good quality for any man planning to sit on a throne for more than a few years. "I don't have many complaints, though I've heard plenty from the men."

"I'd be worried if they weren't complaining," Rolnir replied. "My experience has been that soldiers' griping is a surefire sign things are going according to plan."

"Based on that we should be more than prepared for whatever the One Eye has in store for us," Aurec joked.

The Wolfsreik general couldn't have agreed more. "Any sign?"

"None. I'm starting to question if sending them back with Cuul Ol was a wise decision."

Rolnir studied the young king briefly. Fresh lines had formed in the corners of his bright eyes. His hair was shaggier, more unkempt than usual. Aurec had lost weight, they all had. "Don't waste your time with second guessing. The Pell are worthy allies. While I once viewed them as enemies, they've proven themselves time and again."

"That doesn't negate the possibility of them having an ulterior motivation for coming to my aid. Cuul Ol is an honorable man, though there are others with strong voices less so. You have no idea how difficult it was to convince them to allow my group to pass into and back from Delranan unmolested." Aurec paused. There was an unspoken tension between Delranan and Rogscroft allies concerning the raid that resulted in the death of Badron's son. That singular deed sparked the war.

Rolnir ignored the unspoken intent. What was done was done. There was no point in lamenting moments in time that were unchangeable. The only way to maintain any semblance of sanity was by continuing to look ahead. Tomorrow was a new dawn filled with unlimited potential. Thinking anything less was a disservice.

"What's the first thing you're going to do once this horrible war is over?" the general asked softly. Too much time wasted on deep thoughts helped to break a man.

"I need to find Maleela. My heart tells me she yet lives. I'm nothing without her, Rolnir. She and I were supposed to be married." Sadness tainted his voice.

Rolnir reached out to lay a rough hand on Aurec's forearm. "I give you my word that I will assist you. She may be the love of your life, but she is my princess. What sort of man would I be if I didn't at least try?"

"Thank you," Aurec said with tears welling.

Rolnir smiled briefly before his eyes fell on a pair of figures riding back from the Murdes Mountains. "It appears our scouts have returned."

"No tricks? The Pell will help?" Aurec asked.

Mahn ran a weathered hand through his thinning hair and swallowed another mouthful of water. "Yes, Sire. There was resistance but Cuul was finally able to sway the others."

"You paused. What else concerns you?" Rolnir asked sharply.

Mahn appreciated Rolnir's ability to catch minor details. He had indeed been reluctant to offer the other piece of information. Aurec needed all the positive news he could get. Mahn felt guilty for bringing even a sliver of bad news back. "Sire, I believe we need to move quickly. Cuul Ol still controls the main vote among the elders but his support is weakening. Many of the other chieftains are of the mind to leave us to our worries. Something about having been through this all before in another land. I honestly don't think we can continue to trust the Pell Darga in the same manner as we have."

Aurec was no fool. Inexperienced yes, but never a fool. His father taught him better than that. Aurec always felt his alliance with the Pell Darga was based on mutual benefit. From what he could tell, Cuul Ol had no benefit in allowing the lowland armies to cross the Murdes Mountains at will. How much longer would it be before they decided the Pell were a nuisance and seek to either turn on their former allies or turn their backs entirely? Alliances were only as good as either party needed them.

"We've enjoyed a healthy relationship with Cuul Ol over the last half year," Aurec said, choosing his words carefully. "Should the Pell chieftains decide to sever our alliance we will naturally abide. Good relations are necessary if we're to rebuild both Rogscroft and Delranan."

"Relations that might need to take into account alternate routes between our kingdoms," Rolnir countered. "The mountain passes will be useless should the Pell choose to betray us."

"I don't get the feeling that Cuul will allow for any betrayal so long as he remains in control," Mahn said, shaking his head. "He's still very powerful."

Aurec nodded. "Those in power are apt to lose it quickly. If the other chieftains are as insistent on changing command as you suggest, Cuul might find a short spear wedged between his shoulders."

There was no denying the logic in his statement. If any of the chieftains wanted control, they wouldn't hesitate to reach out and claim it. The internal problems the Pell suffered weren't his concern at the moment. He needed to get twenty thousand soldiers with full equipment and supplies across one of the deadliest mountain ranges in Malweir and have them arrive in fighting shape for what promised to be a long campaign that would test loyalties and strain allies.

Rolnir paused to clear his thoughts. He didn't relish the idea of having to fight the Pell on their terrain again. The first time bore near-disastrous results for the Wolfsreik. It certainly ground the offensive to a crawl as supply trains were all but obliterated in the passes. The general theorized marching past burned wagons and frozen corpses of half-forgotten friends wouldn't sit well with many of the army. Maintaining discipline was going to be even more important on the return trip.

"I'll order the infantry to double their watch just in case," he said.

Aurec fixed him with a curious stare. "You don't seem to have much faith in our allies."

"Faith is something earned, not given. Once we get the army down on the flatlands in Delranan safely and begin the next stage of our campaign will the Pell have retained my confidence." Rolnir was ever the pragmatic man.

The king nodded. "Fair enough. Mahn, when will the Pell be ready to guide us through?"

"Now. Cuul Ol and several others have emplaced at the foot of the mountains to begin guiding us through," the scout replied quickly. "They claim we should be nearly finished with the crossing in only a matter of days."

"Days? To move an army this size?" General Vajna asked, not believing a word.

Mahn nodded quickly. "Yes, sir."

"Did you get to see these passes?" Piper Joach asked from his stool beside the fire. He'd avoided most of the conversation out of principle. All he needed were orders and the ability to shift laterally as he saw fit. The rest could be accomplished without his interference.

"We did not, but I have them marked on the map," the scout said. Seeing where the line of questioning was headed, he preempted the next obvious question. "I have no reason to believe we are being led into a trap. Cuul Ol himself will be awaiting us. I think the Pell, for the most part, understand the necessity of this war and want to help in any way possible. It's only a few rabble rousers keeping the fires of dissent from burning out."

Rolnir, satisfied by the answer, asked, "Will they continue to honor their military commitments? We've got a tough campaign ahead of us and, frankly, I'm not overly keen on using the Wolfsreik to subdue my own population. Badron may have been a world-class lunatic without regard for personal life but the people of Delranan aren't like that. We sorely need the Pell to take out the first line of defenses Harnin has established."

Piper glanced up again. "You need to remember we don't know if he is expecting us or Badron. Could be he's only waiting for the king so that he can separate his head from those hunched shoulders."

"Piper, either way the Wolfsreik will be returning home. Whether still allied with the king or as we are now, we don't know. Harnin has no choice but to prepare for a full defense. That means forts, trenches, and traps. The roads will be watched. He'll have ambushes established at critical choke points along the route of march. Make no mistake: this is going to be one nasty fight. At least at first. Once we break through the defense, all Delranan will be wide open for us to occupy. I said this before, but I want to end our conflict with minimal loss of civilian life."

The others said nothing, choosing instead to let that final thought sink in.

Piper gazed out over his prized vanguard. These were men who'd fought and bled with him from the moment the Wolfsreik entered Rogscroft. They'd struggled through losing friends and comrade, working alongside the vile Goblins, and helped turned the tide of battle against their fallen king. These were the very best Delranan had to offer. Men who willingly sacrificed everything they had, including their lives, for the greater good of family and kingdom. He couldn't have been prouder to stand alongside them, especially now, as they readied to return to their homes.

Home. Piper found the thought oddly disturbing. It was the one guiding light in his course since being deployed but now he felt it lacked the promise it once held. Home wasn't what he'd left behind. Home went wherever the army went. His family was these men around him, looking to him for leadership and guidance. Each of them steeled themselves for what they might find upon stepping back into Delranan.

He drew a deep breath. Cleared his throat. Too many individual thoughts rattled around in his mind, only occasionally colliding to create the inspiration of brilliance. Piper was no great orator. He led with sword and sharp wit. Speaking to hundreds, even thousands who'd followed him unquestioningly from the beginning, seemed almost daunting. There was nothing for it. Words must be spoken. Speeches needed to be given.

"Today…today marks the beginning of the end," he began unsteadily. "You've all come so far. I ask only that you carry on at my side. The storm passes and we ride the wave towards our final destination. None of us asked to be put in this situation. None of us wanted to travel across the Murdes Mountains in the middle of winter under the false promise of glory and conquest. We did all that our kingdom asked of us, and more.

"We lost brothers, fathers, and friends. Somewhere along the way we managed to lose a part of ourselves. Each of us has left a little piece on a frozen battlefield. We've changed. Adapted through struggle and the forging on war can accomplish. I've never been prouder of any group of soldiers." He paused, taking a moment to look across the sea of faces staring up at him. Hope inspired them. The promise of looking upon their own kingdom again after so long. "I wish I could tell you job well done, but not yet. Much remains to be done. Our beloved kingdom, the very same one that we travelled hundreds of leagues to defend, has been usurped by Harnin One Eye."

Murmurs rippled through the vanguard. Oaths of vengeance mixed with gasps of disbelief from those who hadn't listened to the rumors yet.

Piper continued, "The One Eye has stolen everything good about our homes and transformed Delranan into a mockery of its former grandeur. We came to Rogscroft to conquer but found unexpected allies in the ranks of our foes. Rogscroft is no longer in danger. Through your efforts we've helped to find a new beginning out of the ashes of what we helped destroy. I know many of you are confused by this sudden turn in events. I confess I was as well. But wars are fluid beasts. They change with the wind at times. So the winds now blow back to Delranan."

He was forced to pause again as shouts of encouragement and vows of redemption rose from the men. A good omen if ever that was one.

He continued when they finally burned out. "We don't know what we're going to find when we cross the mountains. We speculate Harnin has been waging a war for the very soul of Delranan. Any opposed to him would be hunted down and killed. Rumors of a rebellion engulfing the land have reached us. Supposedly hundreds of civilians have already been killed. All for a madman's glory! To each of you I stand and say no more! The hour of despots has come to an end. This is our time. Our glory! We march on our ancient homeland with fire in our hearts. Our people suffer under totalitarian rule while winter continues to ravage. We are the last hope for what remains. We are the future of Delranan. Who will step forth and claim destiny as his own?"

They surged to their feet. Fists rose to the sky. Cheers erupted across the formation. Piper's heart swelled with pride. Sweat beaded across his brow. He didn't think he had that sort of speech in him, but now that he'd delivered to rousing ovation, he felt he could conquer the world. Being a leader was both difficult and consuming, but it was also intimately rewarding. He drew his sword and raised it high to the sky. "For Delranan!"

The vanguard echoed, "For Delranan!"

The vanguard slowly rolled out of the encampment before dawn of the following day. Piper and Vajna rode side by side. The Rogscroft general found companionship in the enigmatic, and slightly standoffish, Wolfsreik commander. Despite cultural differences they were the same. Soldiers' lives meant more than ground taken. They fought alongside their men, even taking places among the ranks from time to time. Both bore respect for the other, making them a lethal combination to confront on the field. Vajna learned to enjoy riding with Piper, if for no other reason than it helped him escape being in charge for a while.

"I hope this works," Aurec told Rolnir as they watched rank after rank of horsemen plod by. "We're taking an awful chance."

Rolnir mused over the king's words. Only a day ago their opinions had been opposite. "I thought I was the one that was supposed to be in doubt? Piper and Vajna are very good at what they do. I wouldn't trust this mission with anyone else. They'll link up with the Pell and either find their way into Delranan or get into one nasty fight along the way."

"General Rolnir, I believe you are finally back in your proper element," Aurec said with sly grin.

Rolnir folded his arms across his chest. *I certainly hope so, young Aurec. I certainly hope so.* The vanguard continued to march.

TWENTY-THREE

Hatred's Heart

She stabbed again and again. Ropes of blood whipped off the blade each time it ripped from the flesh. Anger, hatred, and pure malevolence dripped from her soul. She felt empowered each time she stabbed the helpless body pinned against the wall thorns before her. Pain echoed deep in those eyes, the wounding of the soul beyond compare. It inspired her. Drove her deeper into fits of delicious agony that only pain could satisfy. She continued to stab until the body hung limp. Blood pooled at her feet. With a last gasp, a gentle rattle, the body found peace through death.

It wasn't good enough. Maleela stabbed harder. Faster. Her intensity picked up as she expunged years of mistreatment. Years of neglect that had anchored deep within the wells of her heart. She became vengeance. She became hatred. Only when her strength faded did she drop the now dull dagger and look upon her work. Hundreds of deep stab wounds scarred the corpse. She reveled in delivering such damage.

Maleela looked upon the glossed-over eyes of her victim: her father. He'd gotten what he deserved. The same as all those ever snubbed her or ignored her when she needed attention the most deserved. A cold, painful death stretching for hours. Reaching out, she gently touched her father's mangled face and laughed. Vengeance was finally hers!

She awoke with a startled scream. Bad images choked her. Violence immobilized her. Maleela tried to comprehend what the act of murdering her father meant. For more years than she cared to count the princess of Delranan managed to keep her true feelings private. Her father hated her, and she likewise. But a good daughter and worthy member of the royal family would never let it show. It was the worst kept secret in the kingdom.

Maleela drew her legs up and rested her chin on her knees. Her only thoughts were of ending this nightmare and trying to find some semblance of peace. Days stretched into one long experience of sheer torment. Hours of endless waiting in near perfect darkness mixed with moments of inspired terror when her captors visited. She'd been lost at first. Her mind refused to accept what her body was going through. Slowly, oh so slowly, Maleela began to suspect she was prisoner of the Dae'shan. Everything about her situation suggested it.

Despair took root. Past conversations between the wizard and Rekka Jel played through her mind over and again. What little they knew of the eternal enemies inspired stark fear. Their quest to stop the Dae'shan led them down dark, twisted roads best left untraveled. She'd left pieces of herself along the way, culminating with the murder of Ionascu. Perhaps he deserved it. Perhaps not. She stole that decision away by brutally ending his life in the jungle while the others were trying to fend off a pair of Gnaals.

More impossible creatures never meant to exist. How cruel this world is. To live with the promise of hope only to have it ripped away when you least expect it. She wondered if Bahr still lived.

Maleela found it odd that she missed her uncle so much. Bahr had never been there for her during her youth, save for the occasional visit delivering gifts from distant lands. His choice to abandon Delranan diminished her respect for him. That respect begrudgingly returned the longer the quest lasted as he'd proved himself time and again. He was, realistically, the only family she had left. Closing her exhausted eyes, Maleela wept herself back to sleep.

"She continues to show remarkable resilience to your wiles," Kodan Bak teased. His distaste of Amar Kit'han's devolving leadership was evident in each syllable.

Amar kept his eyes on the sleeping princess. "Can you not feel it? Her spirit is breaking. Each new torment drives her closer to my arms. Soon she will awaken to find a new world. One filled with wretched possibilities. She is breaking, Kodan Bak."

"Too slowly. The time is approaching faster than she is changing. We must either break her now or find another."

"There is no other. Badron proved most wasteful. His greed and avarice transformed him into something much darker than our needs require. He is a most unpleasant creature bent on revenge rather than opening the nexus." Amar shifted slightly to get a better view of his subordinate. Thoughts of killing Kodan Bak once again entertained him.

"A creature you created through poor manipulation," Kodan said and frowned. He felt as if they'd been locked in the same stagnant conversation for months, neither point of view garnering any support from the other. A stalemate that needed breaking. "He will become a problem for us. You know Badron is already back in Delranan attempting to reclaim his throne. Should he and the One Eye rejoin sides and take the fight to us...."

"Why would that happen? Logic dictates the deposed monarch will do everything in his power to remove Harnin by force. There is no love lost between them. Pelthit Re has seen to that. Harnin won't bother with speaking to his former liege. He and Badron will make war, thus distracting them to the point where they won't notice an army of Goblins marching in from the south to seize control while you and I use the young princess to open the Olagath Stone and release the dark gods." He licked his lower lip. "All is proceeding as foretold. We are on the precipice of accomplishing our purpose."

"You place too much faith in those undeserving of it," Kodan countered. "The first Goblin army failed miserably. Their corpses burn even now in Rogscroft. What can this new army hope to accomplish with not only the Wolfsreik standing against them, but Rogscroft and the Pell Darga as well? Whispers have reached my ears of the Dwarves preparing to march west, with Faeldrin at their head and his Elf spawn Aeldruin. Our enemies are banding together and you insist on focusing on this wretched girl. She is not the one."

"She is all we have!" Amar roared. He began collecting power in his hands, tempted to lash out and destroy Kodan. Patience calmed him, if barely. "Perhaps you are right, Kodan Bak. Perhaps there are too many loose strings still in play."

Kodan glanced down at the electricity dancing across Amar's knuckles. "They will need to be cut before the time arrives."

"Indeed. I believe we should begin in Delranan. The impending battle between Harnin and Badron might prove too costly for us. I don't want the upstart king of Rogscroft marching into Delranan unopposed. It might be time for us to draw to a close the war between usurper and usurped.

Summon Pelthit Re. The time has finally come for him to uphold his end of our arrangement."

"As you wish," Kodan replied casually. He briefly dwelled on Amar striking him while his back was turned. A coward's way but one Amar Kit'han had no qualms of using.

Amar Kit'han watched him dissolve into the nether and turned his thoughts towards other endeavors. The world was changing much too rapidly for him to keep track of it all. Grugnak's army proved most disappointing, though Amar never took into account the possible betrayal by the Wolfsreik. Their combat power would have changed matters entirely. He and the other Dae'shan wouldn't be in this situation if not for Rolnir's decision to side with his kingdom over his king. Amar had a special torment designed for the rogue general.

Aurec was no major issue. He was simply the newly crowned king of Rogscroft--a kingdom that technically didn't exist any longer and had little resources to spare for a prolonged campaign in the west. His army would facilitate the return of the Wolfsreik and fade back to their broken lands.

The Goblins had been successful in one aspect: they burned and killed their way across Rogscroft until it was but a shell of its former glory. He placed a lot of faith in this new Goblin army arriving in time, though he doubted they would. Already the troublesome Dwarves managed to delay their march by an entire day, killing or wounding an incredible amount in the process.

He thought. It would take some doing and no small amount of power but Amar might be able to open a portal long enough to bridge the space between Rogscroft and Delranan, eliminating the time it would take to march the distance. Fifty thousand snarling savages from the Deadlands would hamper any reconstruction plans Rolnir or Aurec held and finally push the Olagath Stone past being filled. Such delightful torments would allow for the return of his masters.

For now it was merely pleasant thought. He was going to have to ask Kodan Bak to aid him in opening the portal.

Amar didn't appreciate not being able to accomplish difficult tasks on his own. However, the possibility of the most minor operation going wrong presented him with all sorts of amusing thoughts. Perhaps he could finally arrange for Kodan Bak's untimely demise and be done with the sordid mess. Amused, the Dae'shan resumed his vigil over the gradually declining princess of Delranan. He'd only just begun.

TWENTY-FOUR

A Rat Drawn Out

Harnin stared at the corpse blocking the main entrance to Chadra Keep with obvious disgust. He'd once viewed Jarrik as a rival to the crown. This was before the man began to change, grow more sympathetic to the rebellion. Seeing his nearly frozen body in such deliberate suffering brought only minor satisfaction. Harnin had wanted Skaning to handle the matter personally, not allow Jarrik the option of suicide. Yet another episode of incompetence to add to a growing list.

Most of the old council of nobles was dead. Skaning struggled to maintain Wolfsreik presence in the west. Heimdol hadn't been seen since the rebellion began, leading Harnin to suspect the fat redhead was either a traitor or dead. Not that it was much of a loss. Heimdol hadn't accomplished much over the last few years, certainly nothing to warrant looking into the situation. Harnin's most concern stemmed from Ulfdane. While the youth had been instrumental in flushing Argis out, he'd been laying low since.

He debated sending the youth out to the eastern defenses just to get him out from underfoot. Each day that sped by brought the Wolfsreik closer to returning. While Harnin hadn't been out to the arranged defenses he suddenly found it difficult to place faith in his commanders. Perhaps the time had come for him to visit the front. He'd always been the kind of man who needed to see matters for himself, seldom relying on the whims of others. Disappointed by the failure of so many he'd claimed to have once trusted, Harnin contemplated replacing the council of nobles with stronger men of his choosing.

Delranan was weak, gutted by the rebellion and the vast amount of support personnel following the army east. Harnin lacked the resources and manpower to establish a firm grasp on his kingdom. Standing atop the wall Chadra Keep, he gazed down upon the ruins of the capital city. The refugee columns were mostly gone. Those few choosing to remain struggled to stay alive as winter continued to ravage the north.

The fools. They should have run when they had the chance. Harnin wanted to view the survivors with admiration but could only find disdain. As far as he was concerned, the entire population needed to be put to death for aiding and abetting the rebellion. He was certain many of those who stayed had been allied against him. Killing them served no other purpose than instant gratification. His hands were permanently stained with the blood of civilians. What difference did a few hundred more make?

Inspiration struck suddenly. Pillars of smoke drifted up from hovels patched together. Storm clouds edged closer to Chadra, threatening rain. Harnin shivered. The stubborn survivors in the city might be able to aid in the war effort after all. He needed bodies to fill in the gaps in the lines on the eastern defenses. Whether they wanted to fight or not, he aimed to conscript the entire population of Chadra for the coming fight. Snorting, he decided to use the children as shields to stop the Wolfsreik. No professional soldier wanted to kill women or children. That natural reluctance might prove beneficial for Harnin's plans.

"Usurper."

Harnin stiffened. His one eye narrowed sharply at the sudden sound of his most-hated foe's voice.

Succumbing to the Dae'shan had been simplistic at the time. Their promises of wealth and power enticed him to abandon all the principles with which he'd lived his life. Greed propagated his desire to become more than history intended. Now he was all but a slave to his desires. Harnin slowly felt life slipping through his fingers, like sand being washed out to sea. His only problem lay in not being able to find a way out of the situation.

"I don't recall summoning you, demon," he replied weakly.

Pelthit Re hissed wicked laughter. "As if a mere mortal had the indulgences to summon one of the Dae'shan. I could take your other eye for that insolence."

Harnin turned to face the monster who laid claim to so much of his life. "If you wanted me dead I would already be swinging from the gibbets. Why have you come this time?"

Pelthit drifted closer. Harnin found it most disturbing how he never seemed to touch the ground. The otherworldly factor in that act alone twisted his stomach. Cold, clear eyes the color of a dying sun glared at the One Eye from beneath the foreboding black cowl always concealing the Dae'shan's true nature.

"War is coming, One Eye."

"I've been fighting a war for the last few months," Harnin snapped, reminded of his inability to crush his enemies.

"This is not a civil war, or fruitless rebellion you ignorantly waste your attentions on. Great forces are allying against Delranan. Forces your limited mortal mind cannot comprehend. I would see you come through this new challenge. There is a place for you in our new world order."

More lies aimed at enticing me further into chains. How much more weight can I bear before I give out and collapse? Will my soul find its way to the halls of my ancestors or will I be damned to walk the face of the world for all time while all I know wilts and fades?

"I'm tired of empty promises. You come to me with sweet words better meant to entice a woman to your bed. What glory is there for a man such as me to blindly obey your whims? I've seen much of this world, demon, but I've never heard of one like you. Will you make me a king? An emperor perhaps? More likely I will be slaughtered along the way and left to rot in a forgotten corner of Delranan." Harnin shook his head as resolutely as possible. "I want no part of your schemes. Not anymore."

"These are not schemes, Usurper. The end of the world is nigh. The dark gods are returning. Where will you stand when they come to claim their heritage? Death is but the least of your concerns," the Dae'shan soothed. His initial reaction was to reach out and crush the life from Harnin's throat. Amar Kit'han would be most displeased, for the one eye still had a part to play in the coming war. Reluctantly, Pelthit Re calmed his rising anger. He hadn't come back to Delranan to kill Harnin, but instead to coerce him into the proper direction. "If you should wish it, I will be more than willing to end your life the moment this war is ended. I will tear your soul from your bones so that you may watch as your brittle form withers and crumbles to dust. Your agony will rival a dying god's, echoing down through eternity. Should you choose it."

Harnin paled. His bluff called, he bowed meekly. "What do you wish of me?"

Pelthit grinned within the shadows. Breaking Harnin hadn't proved much of a challenge. In fact, he found it sorely disappointing. Still, Harnin was expendable. Some people were meant to die. "The Wolfsreik approaches with alarming speed and cohesion. Their numbers are swollen thanks to the remnants of Rogscroft and the Pell Darga. You do not have enough resources to withstand the approaching storm."

Immense sorrow awoke deep within him. Harnin felt his strings steadily ripping from him. Nothing in Delranan could withstand such a massive, armed force.

"Your situation worsens, Usurper. Badron returns. Even now he seeks to garner enough support to sack your northernmost fortress. Should the first one fall, the others will collapse far more quickly than it took to build them."

Harnin raged. Helpless. Harmless. "What more can I do? Argis' rebellion is taxing what little strength I have left. The man is long dead yet I continue to struggle. Continued incompetence by my commanders leaves the rebels ripe to attack us."

"Worry not over the rebellion. Their fire will burn and fade before long. The one who leads them is strong, but she lacks faith in her cause. Instead you must focus on Badron. He will take back the crown and your head with it. Take what forces you have in Chadra and ride out to the eastern defenses. Meet Badron head-on before he has the opportunity to make an impact. This is the only way."

"Ride? To the front lines with a massive army heading towards me? Are you mad?"

He couldn't believe what was being asked. The Dae'shan might be immensely powerful and immortal, but those traits certainly didn't pass down to Harnin. Already partially crippled and steadily being driven mad, the One Eye wouldn't accomplish much away from his seat of power in Chadra Keep. He'd become cloistered within the wooden halls without realizing it. Delranan's seat of power became his tomb.

"No madder than you, hiding within these pathetic, wooden walls. Do you truly believe this Keep can last forever? How long will the empty ramparts hold back the tide of the Wolfsreik before it crashes over the top and into the halls? Do not be so naïve as to place faith in mortal constructs. Even the mightiest fortress falls."

Pelthit Re grew tired of this game. He'd undertaken twisting Harnin as a pet project while Amar and Kodan dithered with Badron. Their attentions were fixed on the king of Delranan; Pelthit was able to almost completely transform Harnin into much less than a man. It had been centuries since he last attempted such prolific and irreversible changes, and he found the ordeal less than satisfying. Harnin had been too willing of a subject. If it weren't for Amar Kit'han's insistence that Harnin live to confront Badron, he would already be dead.

"You spend your days like a rat trapped within the walls, frightened the rat catchers are awaiting the moment you show your face. This is no kind of life for a man destined for greatness. The dark gods are forgiving, Usurper. They reward those who distinguish themselves in the dark cause." Pelthit dug deeper, hoping to inspire that last fragment of fear residing deep within Harnin. "Delranan needs strength in the coming days. Total darkness is set to consume Malweir. Entire races will be ground from existence. I would like to see your kingdom rise above the tide and rebuild to greater glory. All it takes is for you to ride out and meet your nemesis before he can do the same to you."

"Does Badron have even a sliver of a chance of success?" Harnin asked meekly. The anger and fear had bled from his voice. Defeated, he resigned to follow the Dae'shan's instructions. At this point he'd do anything to retain control of his kingdom.

"He does, but only if you wallow away within these walls," Pelthit chided. "Conscript the survivors and ride out to meet him. Break him in the wilds and parade his body throughout the kingdom. Only then you will finally attain the strength to undergo the coming struggle."

Harnin nodded slowly. "I can best Badron. He lacks any support. I can beat him and finally stop looking over my shoulder. But what of the Wolfsreik?"

"One item at a time. Find and kill Badron and the rest will be taken care of. You have my word." His last few words dissolved along with him, leaving Harnin standing in the echoes of the past.

"How much further? I grow weary of this skulking," Grugnak growled to the wizened, old man guiding them.

The deposed king of Delranan took a small force of handpicked warriors into the nearest fishing village upon putting in to shore and abducted one who claimed to know the land intimately. Through sputtered protests and more than one attempt at escape, their guide was finally subdued under threat of having his family murdered before his eyes. Badron still didn't trust him.

Grugnak slathered at his side, eager to slay the fisherman and move on. His hatred for men worsened the longer the Goblin commander was trapped alongside them. His pitiful hundreds were a pale shadow of their former strength. Ten thousand Goblins had marched from the Deadlands under the promise of plundering one of the finer kingdoms of men. Their initial conquests were drowned under the heels of Wolfsreik boots. He'd stood upon battlefields where his forces were overrun by their former allies. Thousands of his best lay dead, forgotten by all but time. That travesty needed to be avenged.

Badron scowled at the smaller Goblin. "Patience, Grugnak. This gentleman is going to lead us unerringly to the first redoubt. You may kill him later if he doesn't."

The old man's knees trembled, threatening to buckle. He closed his eyes and prayed this nightmare ended soon. "Please, milord. I got a family. Mouths to feed."

"So did I," Badron growled menacingly. "Life seldom asks us what we want. Instead it takes from us, ripping and twisting away all those things that once made life special. Any endearing quality I once possessed lay dead in the halls of my own Keep while a usurper sits upon the throne. Do not think for an instant I won't allow my Goblin companion to rip your body to shreds just so that he might have fresh meat for supper."

Throwing his hands up to protect his face, the old man begged, "Please. I wasn't part of no rebellion. We didn't know of what happened in Chadra until just recent. I swear."

Badron's eyes narrowed warily. "What happened in Chadra?"

He'd known about Harnin's betrayal and the construction of the defensive positions for some time. Amar Kit'han took pleasure in detailing how the rebellion further stripped away the strength of his kingdom while Harnin struggled just to maintain the semblance of power.

"You…you don't know?" the old man asked, eyes now wide in shock. "Why, a terrible plague ran through the major towns. More than half the population was wiped out by it, or so we heard. But we're all the way on the coast and don't have much interaction with the interior folks. We only just found out when a trader caravan rode through. Said the capital is all but burned to the ground and no more."

No more? My beloved city burned to the ground under the disease of plague! My beloved kingdom ruined beyond repair! What have I allowed to happen? Harnin will pay for what he's done. I swear it upon my ancestors. I will strike that one-eyed bastard's head from his shoulders and feed his body to the wolves.

When he at last found his voice, it was shaky, unstable. "Has this plague burned itself out yet? I can't risk marching into Chadra only to take ill."

The old man was more than willing to deliver any information the mad king required. Anything to keep his life at least a little longer. "So far as we was told, aye. Trader said those still well enough were fleeing into the countryside before the One Eye accused them of being traitors."

Badron scoffed. As if Harnin had the authority to accuse anyone else of his own crimes. "You're not a rebel are you? I suddenly find myself growing suspicious of your desire to help me. I don't need another traitor in my midst."

"Never been no rebellion out this way. We keep to ourselves as much as possible. This ain't our war."

"But it is. This is a war for the very soul of Delranan. How could anyone who calls himself a patriot stand idle and watch it burn around him? I'm beginning not to like your tone, fisherman."

Hanging his head, certain death was able to snatch him from the mortal world, the fisherman struggled to find a way to buy a few more precious moments. "Milord! Folks in our village have always been loyal to the crown. My own father served in the Wolfsreik when I was but a pup. Delranan is our heart and blood. T'would never seek to turn against you."

"We shall see. Now, lead us to the redoubt quickly," Badron demanded. "I have no qualms with putting your head upon a spike to use as my banner."

Whimpering, the fisherman led them deeper into Delranan and Badron's appointment with destiny.

The former king of Delranan brooded as he stalked through the light forest. His thoughts centered on Harnin One Eye, former friend and confidant. A man who might have become the interim heir to the throne. One who certainly rose higher upon the death of Badron's only son. Now a mortal enemy, Harnin continued to drive a wedge between king and kingdom.

New thoughts entered his mind. Wandering in solitude was a dangerous thing. Badron began to wonder if Harnin had had a hand in killing the heir to throne to get closer to power. It wouldn't have been the first time in Delranan's history. Badron fumed. His son had been his life, the promise of a better future to ensure his kingdom's prosperity. Those dreams died on the polished, wooden floors of Chadra Keep in pools of blood and compounding misery.

The very concept that Harnin helped orchestrate the break-in and murder of so many guards the night Maleela was abducted hardened his heart. Badron conceded the One Eye often dreamed of power. It was only natural for one in his position. Badron managed to keep him in check, but that sense of control went out of his hands the moment he ill-advisedly went on campaign with the army. *The bastard even cautioned me against going, as if he'd planned it all out ahead of time. I should have killed him when I had the chance.*

Remnants of the Goblin army marched at his heels. They plodded through the undergrowth with the grace of Ogres devouring cattle. Badron winced each time a small tree was knocked down. Snarls and wicked laughing drifted on the wind. The Goblins clearly weren't interested in being obscure. Grugnak had increasing difficulty keeping them from lashing out at Badron's remaining soldiers. Their allegiance slipped further apart daily. Not that Badron cared. The Goblins were merely a means to an end. Should they all die attempting to sack the redoubt, he wouldn't mind. Their filth needed to be expunged from Malweir entirely. The deposed king of Delranan continued, following a weak fisherman whose loyalty remained questionable. Soon, very soon, his time was coming. Delranan would be his once again and the world would burn for it. Hatred raged in his cold, dark eyes.

TWENTY-FIVE

No Forest Safe

"I'm tired of freezing. We've been cold for too long."

Nothol rolled his eyes. A few days had passed since they parted ways with the rebellion and, while there'd been no sign of enemy activity, none of them could shake the feeling that they were being hunted. Nerves stood on end, worsening the longer they spent on the road.

One of the horses had gone lame the morning before. Bahr was forced to put it down. Just to make matters worse it was one of the wagon horses. The Sea Wolf reluctantly gave up his horse for a replacement and the exhausted band carried on. They'd gained the border of a small forest whose name escaped them and pushed in. All were eager to get out of the elements and find warmth with a fire and freshly roasted meat.

"Do you get tired of complaining? You're looking at the wrong side of the situation, Dorl. Each day we spend out in this lovely wilderness is one closer to reaching our objective and finally being able to go about our business. Don't worry so much about the cold as what might happen when we get to the ruins."

"You're the reason I drink. I hope you know that," Dorl replied tersely.

Nothol shrugged. "I suppose we all need a reason. You're welcome."

"Not funny. How much further did Bahr want us to scout today? I can feel the sun going down." He shivered gently beneath his furs. It had become almost comforting since returning to Delranan. The constant motion served as a reminder of his misery.

Nothol reached back to grab his canteen. "I don't know. All these trees look the same to me. We're not doing much good out here. Even if we get captured or killed they're too far behind to know about it until it's way too late."

Dorl's eyes narrowed. "Why'd you go and bring that up? I'm not trying to think about death, you daft bastard. A warm fire and a belly full of cooked food, hot, cooked food, is all I need to get my mind right again. Bring up death again and we're going to fight."

"Ha! You couldn't beat yourself up right now," Nothol chided. "I guess we should start looking for a suitable campsite. A fire does sound pretty good right now."

They kept riding, bickering back and forth. Neither noticed the three sets of eyes watching their every movement from within the shadows of a nearby stand of holly bushes.

The wagon ground to a halt not long after Dorl rode back with news of a suitable position. Words of praise and relief were passed to the sell sword. Everyone was tired of travelling and ready to take advantage of those precious few hours when they weren't heading towards the inevitable confrontation between good and evil. Ironfoot and Groge headed off to chop down pine branches to use as protection from the wind, and to reduce the fire's visibility to prying eyes when it got dark.

The Dwarf and Giant were perhaps the most unlikely pair working in tandem at any point on Malweir. Groge, despite being taller and much larger, was a relative novice compared to the experienced, disgruntled Ironfoot. The Dwarf stalked his way through the underbrush like a warrior on the hunt. Martial prowess was ingrained in every Dwarf, and these skills translated into every action they performed, regardless of intensity or relevance. Groge, conversely, was the exact opposite. Giants weren't the warriors of old. He stumbled and plodded his way through the forest like an inexperienced child.

"You need more training," Ironfoot grunted as he chopped through a thick pine bough.

Groge did the same, though from much higher up. "Training for what?"

"For being a soldier. It takes skill to move through terrain unseen, unheard. No Dwarf would have ever allowed himself to be heard approaching through this scrub," Ironfoot half scolded. He found it difficult to remember Groge was older, but barely considered an adult among his people. The Dwarf simply didn't understand some of the other races.

Thoughts like that made him miss Drimmen Delf. He ached to be back in the mighty caverns, in front of roaring fires trading stories of exaggerated battlefield heroism. Ironfoot had earned his place among the greatest tales from his experience in the raid on the dark Dwarves' cannon batteries. King Thord sent him off with Bahr before he got the opportunity. The Dwarf captain relished his chance to stand before his peers with tales of his adventures in lands far from the Dwarf kingdom. His place of honor as grand story master was secured for generations, provided he made it home alive.

Groge offered a child-like grin that was lost between the branches. "Ironfoot, you know I am no warrior. I am just an apprentice to a forge master. Wars are not what I was created for. I am a craftsman."

Shaking his head, Ironfoot grumbled, "Indeed. This isn't Venheim, Groge. We are alone in a savage world. Everyone we meet seems inclined to kill us. You're the biggest of our group and could be a terrible force once you learn how to use your natural skills. I'd go so far as to think even Boen would respect you."

He embellished slightly. Boen was Gaimosian. He didn't respect anyone, regardless of their race, unless they were Gaimosian. That made Groge's quest more difficult, if not impossible. Ironfoot decided not to bother explaining that last part. What the youth didn't know wasn't going to hurt him any. His lack of experience just might, however.

Ironfoot set his axe down. "Groge, I need you to understand this." He paused for the young Giant to kneel.

Damnation. Even kneeling he's still more than twice as tall as I am. "This is war. I know Bahr has tried to steer us clear of actual fighting, but this is war. Not all our merry little group is going to survive to see it through. We've already lost two before reaching Trennaron."

"I understand, Ironfoot. I do."

"No, I don't think you really do. Ionascu was a waste of life. It was only a matter of time before Lord Death claimed him. I won't pretend to lie to you. We are better off without him. He was cancerous. Maleela's loss hurts worse."

"But we don't know if she's dead," Groge protested.

"Does it matter? She might as well be. The emptiness of her place among us fills many with grief. Can you honestly say that won't affect them once the final battle begins?"

Groge shook his head. "Why does this matter?"

"It matters because we all need to be at our very best if we're going to survive. That means I need you to take an interest in weapons and fighting, even if for the sake of saving some of the rest of us." Ironfoot slapped him on the kneecap. "Besides, if you can't use that hammer for anything you can always step on people."

They shared a brief laugh. Groge wiped his eyes clear before saying, "Very well. I will do my best to learn just enough to keep us all alive. I'll do it for you, Ironfoot."

"No lad, do it for yourself."

The brigands struck the camp while most of the defenders were gathering firewood or water from a nearby stream. Only Anienam and his warder, Skuld, remained behind. They were quickly overwhelmed and held at sword point as the score of brigands rummaged through sacks and personal belongings in search of a quick reward. The street thief wanted to retaliate, despite knowing he'd be run through long before reaching the brigand guarding him.

"These people have shit! I say we kill the old man, take the boy to sell him to the slave traders in the desert, and burn the wagon," a tall man with a pencil-thin, black moustache snapped.

Several heads nodded agreement.

One other stepped forward. Heavily muscled, or perhaps just bundled nicely against the cold, he bore the look of an ex-soldier. Skuld had seen his sort before. Thinking they were better than everyone else, they shoved others aside and took what they wanted from ones unwilling to stand up for their rights. Skuld had fought against men like this his entire life. The perception that any one man was greater than the next offended him. He may have been raised in the streets of Chadra, but his worth was unquestionable.

He'd never be able to live with himself if he didn't at least try to stop the brigands. "You'll never get away with this."

He was rewarded by a swift backhand across the face and a chorus of laughter.

"Pipe down, boy. The world's not going to miss one old man and a gutter trash boy," the moustache said.

Anienam remained quiet, though he could hear Skuld struggling to understand why. The last wizard on Malweir should be more assertive. Magic should already be rendering these common thieves into ash. Alas, his magic didn't work that way. Anienam was vowed to preserving life, not exploring new ways to destroy it. Besides, he couldn't tell Skuld that it was all going to be fine. Not without the brigands hearing.

"Leave him be. We don't want our property damaged. Nobody will buy a boy with marks on his face," their leader laughed.

Glaring, the moustache slammed a fist hard into Skuld's stomach, doubling him over.

Between tears and the sudden urge to vomit, Skuld struggled to rise and show his defiance. "You... shouldn't ... have done ...that."

The moustache looked up at the rest of his group with mock surprise. "The boy's a comedian! I haven't laughed so hard in years."

"Maybe we should keep him around as a jester. Every court needs a fool," the leader said.

"Dress him in a costume and make him dance!"

"Parade him around. We need a good laugh!"

"The old man can be his keeper!"

Laughter sang across the campsite. The brigands went about their work, steadily growing more agitated that the wagon held practically nothing of importance.

Finally the leader could take no more. Hands held high, he marched to the center and faced his men. "Let's put it to a vote, lads. Keep 'em or kill 'em!"

The man standing directly in front of him suddenly pitched forward with a gargled cry and a spray of hot blood bursting from his back. The ensuing roar took everyone by surprise. Stunned faces turned to see Ironfoot barreling out of the trees. The Dwarf ripped his axe from the dead brigand and dove into full attack. His first blow disemboweled the nearest brigand. The second took a head from the shoulders. By then the others recovered enough to defend themselves. It wasn't enough.

No one anticipated the Giant breaking through trees. Still unsure of weapons, Groge kicked the nearest man. The body flew hard and fast through the trees, striking a large poplar with a bone-breaking crunch. He quickly reached down to snatch another by the neck, throttling him before he could get his hands up in a futile attempt at stopping the Giant.

"RUN!" the leader bellowed. Fighting a lone Dwarf was one thing, but a Dwarf and a Giant were an entirely different matter. The situation had become untenable. They were all going to die unless they fled back to their cave deep in the forest.

They never had the chance to run. Boen and the others arrived moments later, sealing the brigands in what devolved into a slaughter. Not a one was left alive. Some managed to put up a fight before being ground under sword and axe. The moustache man faced off against Rekka, a small woman who should know better than to play with swords. Grinning savagely, he lunged hard and fast. Rekka sidestepped and tore his throat open with a lightning fast strike. He died with the most confused look etched on his face.

The last survivor, their leader, dropped his weapons and raised his hands in surrender. "Please! I'm unarmed! You can't kill an unarmed man."

Boen jerked his sword free from the stomach of his last opponent and stalked towards the leader. Without a word he plunged his sword into the leader's chest so hard three inches burst from his back. The last brigand dead, the battle was over. Fuming, the Gaimosian ripped his blade free and paused to wipe the blood and gore on the dead man's chest before sheathing it. His menacing glare kept the others at bay, though Bahr stared him down from across the small battlefield.

They'd all seen, and some had done, harsh acts of violence before. Most were done through necessity, but what Boen just finished went beyond comprehension. He'd been calm the entire journey, save for his continual tirades and need to get into a fight. Killing an unarmed man who had already surrendered was murder. Gaimosians didn't murder unless there was no other way around it.

Daring any of them to comment, Boen swiveled his gaze to each before stalking back to his horse. His chest rose and fell rapidly. Steam poured off of his head and hands. His breath nearly froze the moment it touched the open air. He could feel their eyes on him as he walked away, and he could care less. None of them noticed the pain hidden behind his eyes or the way he just wanted to leave this life behind. Boen, for all his faults and strengths, was tired.

TWENTY-SIX

The Quest Continues

Warming his hands over the fire, Bahr had finally had enough. The uncomfortable silence mocked him with indecision. The time had come to confront Boen and get this matter aired out before they continued and it caused problems when the quest needed to be cohesive. He spit roughly to the side and fixed Boen with his sternest look.

Boen gradually lifted his head, catching the look from the tops of his eyes. "Go on."

Slightly taken off guard, Bahr recoiled and said, "What was all that about? I've known you for decades and never have I seen you commit blatant murder."

"Murder?" Boen asked sharply. "He would have killed us all if I didn't do what I did. That man was a cold-blooded killer. I saw it in his eyes."

"He was an unarmed prisoner," Bahr countered.

"So you think. The moment one of us would have reached for him he would have taken their weapon and killed quicker than the rest of us could react."

"You don't know that."

Boen's laugh was pure mockery. "Don't I? That one was clearly their leader. Don't you find it odd how quickly he decided to surrender once the rest of his thugs were dead or wounded?"

Bahr shook his head sadly. "He was a coward and did the prudent thing. Would you have gone down swinging?"

He'd never asked a more pointless question. Of course he would. Gaimosians may be the world's premier warriors, but their stubborn adherence to their rules of combat resulted in so many futile deaths. How many had died since the fall Gaimos that didn't need to? And for what?

Names and deeds are recorded in history but no one actually remembers.

Boen glowered but held his tongue. At last he reached out to the fire and dangled his fingers just inches away from the lapping flames. "I know in my gut that man was going to try something. Beating him to it was my only recourse."

"There is no proof," Bahr argued, weaker than before.

"Let it go, Bahr."

"I can't. What you did wasn't right. We're supposed to be better than that. We're the heroes in this tale."

"Heroes?" Boen asked. "I don't recall asking to be a hero. The only reason I am part of this sordid affair is because I had the bad fortune of being in Delranan when this old man came calling. If it weren't for that I'd be far away going about my business with no knowledge of your deeds. I didn't ask to be a hero."

"No one does," Anienam said from across the fire. His blind eyes, wrapped under folds of cloth, seemed to glare at the Gaimosian. "None of us were asked to be a part of this quest. Yet for reasons we'll never know each of us was fated to be in Delranan at precisely the right moment. Our opinions weren't required."

"You stay out of this," Boen growled, pointing an accusing finger before realizing the act was foolish. "I've gone through more foul experiences at your side than a lifetime of wandering Malweir could ever prepare me for. This is between Bahr and me."

"But it's not. Your actions with the brigands affects us all," the blind wizard countered.

Bahr added, "He's right. No one is arguing you acted inappropriately according to how you read the situation."

"Then what?"

A pause. "The morality of your deed. Killing is one thing. I'd argue it's a natural state for mortal men to engage in, but what you did was murder. Ethically it's wrong, Boen."

Throwing his hands up in exasperation, the Gaimosian rose. "Ethically? Who gives a damn about ethics here, now? We're struggling just to stay alive. Friends are being wounded, even killed while our enemies continue to strengthen around us. Your very niece was stolen while we battled against creatures that simply shouldn't exist. What difference do ethics make in the middle of this whole, impossible ordeal? I'm prepared to answer for my actions when I move on to the next world. Are you?"

He stalked off. Grooming his horse helped take his edge off. There was a calming effect from running the brush over his friend. Silence would lower his rage. Being alone would help him remember his roots. He knew without a doubt their supposed prisoner had ill intent in his mind. Killing him was Boen's only option. Already pushed to the extreme, their band didn't have the capacity to ward over prisoners. At some point during the haphazard incarceration their prisoner would have made his move. Blood would have been spilled and more bodies laid to rest in the cold snow. He'd done the others a favor by killing the brigand. Why couldn't they understand it?

Sighing, Boen reflected on his monotonous past. He'd been born into a warrior's life. How many hundreds of lives were ended by his blade, he didn't know. All that mattered was adhering to the Gaimosian code. He lived and breathed for the security of others. Seldom did he manage to find the time to put his own desires first. He was a Vengeance Knight. People feared his name. Feared the very idea of his race. More often than not his kind was shunned. Doors were slammed and locked. Windows shuttered.

His was a legacy of bloodshed. Intense moments of extreme violence. But was it enough? He'd never questioned his lot in life until now. None but Gaimosians understood, for they worked towards a unified goal. Each sought revenge against the men and women of the kingdoms who foolishly banded to destroy Gaimos. Kings and nobles were murdered in battle. Armies were destroyed under Gaimosian leadership. When revenge was finally achieved, the survivors of Gaimos would reunite and carve out a new kingdom. All Malweir would tremble. Boen doubted he'd live long enough to see those days of glory renewed. It was a fanciful dream. Sighing, he set brush to horse and began brushing.

Dawn broke behind heavy, angry clouds. The quest packed up and continued. Arlevon Gale was still many days away and the ride became increasingly perilous. Their circuitous route took them too close to Chadra, though Bahr argued that it was the one place Harnin wouldn't seek to look for discontent. Truthfully, the One Eye didn't know Bahr had returned or for what reason. Conversely, they didn't know he'd already taken off to the eastern front for his confrontation with the returning Badron. Only a handful of rebels knew of the king's brother. Potential implications for the future were staggering, yet deceptively hidden behind the fog of war.

Bahr intended to use this lack of knowledge to his advantage. His decision to push the quest faster, harder, left many grumbling displeasure, but it was the right move. Each step brought them closer to Chadra and the heart of his enemy's command. Bahr wanted to depose the usurper and reclaim the throne en route to their date with destiny. Anienam cautioned otherwise. Time was not in their favor.

It was a tired song. Time had been their enemy for months now and they were still standing. How many more enemies did they need to battle before their well-deserved rest? Bahr harbored no illusions towards their survival. He fully expected them all to die in the final battle. Well, all except Anienam. The old wizard was wily beyond need and the only one capable of escaping the very worst the dark gods had to throw at them. The thought left a sour taste in the Sea Wolf's mouth.

He glanced over at the blind man, trying to keep his dissatisfaction from showing. They'd had their differences along the way, certainly more bad times than good, but Bahr held a deep respect for the wizard. Naturally he'd never admit it. Pride often led to a man's downfall. Bahr tried his best to keep pride from overwhelming his common sense. That tactic didn't always work, but at least he tried.

"You're brooding," Anienam remarked with a wry grin. The wagon plodded on.

Bahr checked his initial reaction, deciding not to get into another heated argument. "Aren't I allowed to?"

Anienam shrugged. "From time to time. I don't see what purpose it serves now, though. As Boen said, what's done is done."

Boen. As much as I agree with his actions I can't condone the abrupt murder of an unarmed man, no matter how devious his real intent was. Bahr shook his head. *I wish I had the answers we all need. The longer this quest goes on the more I get the feeling that I'm leading us all to our deaths.*

"That doesn't make what he did right," was all Bahr managed.

"What constitutes right or wrong? That brigand intended on killing us all and taking our belongings. He ordered his men to abduct Skuld and myself and was busy robbing us when you all returned. Did they put down their weapons? Did they turn and flee back into the forest? No. They acted according to their natures. Boen did the same. Can you condemn a man for following a lifetime of training?"

"You know it's not that easy, Anienam."

"Isn't it?" the wizard asked innocently enough.

Slightly exasperated, Bahr turned to him and replied, "No. We've all killed during this quest. Yourself included. I don't hold any particular reservations towards taking a life, especially when it comes down to them or one of my friends. But I have an issue with murder. The absence of morality bothers me more than I want to admit."

"The mark of a good man. Very few in this day and age have the moral compass that you do. I feel confident that you're in charge when I think on that fact. Very confident indeed." Anienam fell silent, having said all he needed to.

Bahr stayed quiet for a while. The scenery remained unchanged. An endless sea of pristine white intermingled with spears of faded green and brown. The occasional hawk or snow eagle circled overhead. Most complained of the extreme cold, but Bahr found comfort in being alone in such wild conditions. He enjoyed the company of his thoughts. The only sounds were the wagon wheels creaking and groaning. These moments didn't last. They rarely did. Inevitably someone had to speak. If not for the stigma of being a hermit, Bahr might have already wandered off into the unexplored wilderness of Malweir, never to be seen again.

His mind felt calmer after the short period of quiet. Refreshed for reasons beyond his comprehension, Bahr turned to Anienam and said, "Thank you."

Anienam reached out and pat Bahr's leg. "You have no reason to doubt yourself. There is no other being I would entrust our lives to. No one."

Comforted by the wizard's admission, Bahr flicked the reins and looked forward. Arlevon Gale was drawing closer.

Skaning slammed his fist onto the charred desk. "Why am I just now hearing of this?"

The young reserve sergeant swallowed his rising fear. "Sir, we've only just discovered their involvement in the assault. Chances are their group was far away by the time the battle was finished."

"That's not good enough, sergeant. How am I supposed to explain to Lord Harnin that the king's brother was here and escaped without us even knowing of it?"

Secretly the sergeant was thankful that task didn't fall on his shoulders. Coming to see Skaning was bad enough. He couldn't imagine standing before the dreaded One Eye.

Not and living to see the next dawn. Thankfully, Skaning continued his tirade, preventing the sergeant from replying.

"This is unacceptable! We had the rebellion *and* Bahr within our grasps only to let them slip away unmolested. Bring me my commanders. I want the Sea Wolf caught. Perhaps then Harnin will forgive our failures."

Saluting briskly, the sergeant dashed off before Skaning had the chance to change his mind. Less than an hour later all Skaning's and Jarrik's former commanders stood before the young lord, shifting nervously from foot to foot. Eyes cast in corners, hoping to find that same nervousness in their peers. These were troubling times in the kingdom. Jarrik's apparent suicide followed by Inaella's disappearing into the wilderness left many loyalists unsure of where they stood. Skaning marched to the redoubt with orders to kill the leadership and assume command. The few that managed to survive the rebellion assault anxiously awaited their fates.

Skaning didn't care for any of that. His sole focus rested on catching Bahr and producing a trophy worthy of keeping his head attached when Harnin learned of the battle's events. He drew a deep breath and narrowed his gaze. "The battle against the rebels did not go accordingly. You all are responsible for the deaths of too many loyal soldiers. Soldiers that are sorely needed on the eastern front."

More shifting. A nervous gulp. Eyes growing large.

"What concerns me most is the Sea Wolf was nearby and none of you knew it. Finding him is our first priority. I want Bahr's head on this desk as soon as possible. Do I make myself understood?" His hardened gaze swept the room.

Heads nodded. A few murmured consent. Whether Skaning's or Jarrik's, these men were all his now. His fate would be theirs.

"Now go. Bring me Bahr's head."

TWENTY-SEVEN

Hunted

The battle with the brigands ended almost as quickly as it developed. Ill-advised battles often did. Bahr ordered the bodies buried not far from the campsite. This far away from civilization there was scant chance of them being discovered any time soon. He didn't recall hearing about bandits this far west and wondered what foulness drove them so far away from the rest of the kingdom they risked death from the elements. There was but one answer. Harnin One Eye. Delranan must have fallen far for criminals to take such dire measures.

Bahr had little time to spare on random thoughts. They were dead and buried, already forgotten by the rest of the world. His concern lay on pushing the quest ahead. They packed up shortly after dawn and headed east on the nearest road winding through the forest. Snow dropped from overladen branches, crashing down in the unseen distance. Horses jumped at the sound. Riders soothed them accordingly while keeping a clear eye out for more brigands.

The sun rose without being witnessed. Storm clouds darkened the horizon. Bahr took it as an ill omen. Even after a long, uneventful night he still couldn't shake the feeling of being watched and hunted. Rather than expose his concerns and potentially needlessly worry the others, Bahr kept quiet as he guided the wagon. His eyes never stopped roving, however, for being caught unawares like the prior night might spell disaster.

A lethargic air surrounding the quest. Few of them managed to sit erect in their saddles any longer. Ground down by constant travel and a seemingly unending string of small engagements with various enemies, the group struggled just to get up in the mornings. Only Rekka seemed unaffected by their ordeal. The diminutive woman from the

Jungles of Brodein carried on as if she'd been born into it. Bahr had to admire her. Without even knowing it she was the glue that kept them all together when times grew too dark.

He paused to consider her blossoming relationship with Dorl. It was the worst kept secret among the group. The only one who didn't know was dead back in the jungle, but Ionascu never cared much for any of them. His loss was more of a blessing, liberating them from the burden of having to care and worry over an invalid. Ionascu's treachery brought him to a well-deserved end, but Bahr took little comfort in his loss. Something must have gone extremely wrong for Maleela to snap and take his life. Compounding Bahr's misery, his niece was missing and there was nothing he could do for her.

Life seldom asks what we think or want. It takes and gives as it sees fit. Bahr rode on, trying to abandon thoughts of his niece and refocusing back on Dorl and Rekka Jel. Awkward as it seemed, their relationship suited them. Bahr once longed for the same, until he realized life wasn't meant to be that simple for him. Turning his back on Delranan had been more than difficult, it was downright intolerable. He knew that he was going to die without producing an heir. Without knowing a woman's love. A true woman, not a midnight dalliance with a nameless lass he didn't intend on seeing more than once or twice. The weight of that sacrifice drove him down.

That two entirely opposite people could find love in the middle of what might well be the end of the world astounded him. A skeptic might think otherwise. That it was impossible for anyone to find love under the constant threat of death. Bahr knew better. The simple looks they gave each other confirmed it. The way they held hands when they thought no one was looking warmed his heart. Oddly, he felt embarrassed when one of them caught his stares.

Broaching the subject with any of the others was pointless. They'd mock him for spying and play it off for him being overly sentimental in his twilight years. Suddenly foolish, Bahr knew he wouldn't be able to defend his position. He was the rock. Their anchor in the storm. The slightest hint of supposed weakness would crack their increasingly desperate, fragile shell beyond the point of repair. Bahr, of all people, needed to remain strong. He was a pillar beckoning them to the very end, whatever that may be.

He never wanted the weight of that responsibility. It was one of the reasons he turned his back on family and left Delranan in search of his own name. Bahr was remarkably strong. His will was iron, unbreakable. What he lacked was the desire to be a leader. Greatness comes for a man in its own time. Bahr was subsumed by the desires of many far beyond his reckoning. Delranan would live or burn away in the fires of agony all at his discretion. Such choices should never be made by a single being.

Anienam tried to condition the Sea Wolf from the moment he turned up on Bahr's doorstep all those months ago. Barely a season had gone by, but the days dragged endlessly. The burden of decades heaped upon their shoulders. Questions formed. Impossible to answer, they furrowed brows in confusion and the slightest hint of despair. How many more battles could they endure before all hope abandoned them? Who would live to see the end, if any? Did glory await them under the premise of salvation or was it a hole in the cold earth? Bahr internalized all these issues before arriving at one inescapable conclusion: he didn't know.

The wagon plodded forward as he lost himself deep in seemingly irreverent thought. So engrossed was he, he failed to notice Anienam Keiss slowly turn his head towards him. Judgment was being reserved.

"Why do you keep spooking?"

Dorl glanced at Nothol. "We're being hunted, Nothol. I can feel it."

"You're being paranoid. I doubt there's another soul within twenty leagues."

Nothol's carefree attitude didn't translate this time. Dorl tried, unsuccessfully, to abandon his feelings of dread only to find them infinitely stronger as time progressed. This unbidden fear affected every aspect of his life and it trembled his knees. He wasn't a man prone to giving in to his emotions. Life was hard. Hiding from it made little sense to the sell sword. A fighter by trade, Dorl Theed was suddenly faced with the nearly overwhelming desire to turn and run. The shame was almost unbearable.

He fixed Nothol with a baleful glare. "Just like those bandits we ran into, right? Nothol, we've been hounded from the moment we broke out of Harnin's dungeons. I think Skuld is the only one of us who hasn't been wounded."

"Lucky bastard," Nothol agreed wistfully.

Dorl paused to nod. He had his share of scars crisscrossing his body but the boy proved remarkably fortunate thus far. "Every time we think we're finally in the clear something else pops up to block our way. Mark my words, we're being hunted."

Nothol made a show of looking around. "By whom? You might not have noticed, but we're in the ass end of the world."

"Agreed but we don't seem to have an issue with running into people. The rebellion found us easily enough. Then there was that mishap with the assault on Harnin's new fort. The bandits, need I continue?"

Observantly recognizing he wasn't going to win, Nothol caved, slightly. "Fine. You think we're being hunted. I ask by whom? I've got your back no matter what, my friend, but I need to have an idea what's coming up against us. Otherwise I'll just be sitting here aloof like certain others among our illustrious party."

His voice lowered ominously at the last sentence, lending the ruffled sell sword a nefarious appeal. A small part of him enjoyed the conspiratorial aspect of it all. Twisting

Dorl's words against him wasn't as challenging as it had once been, but it still offered a measure of friendly maliciousness. He regarded his friend for a few moments longer in hopes of getting a rise, looking away only when Dorl refused to play by the rules.

"Dorl, who's coming for us?" he asked in all seriousness.

For once, Dorl Theed didn't have any answers. He gave Nothol a mournful look before resuming his watch on the surrounding forest. Scratching branches reminded him of wicked fingers raking frozen glass. All the evil he'd seen during this quest inspired fresh terrors he'd never thought possible. Visions of the Gnaal left him scarred emotionally. Their nightmarish forms were beyond mortal comprehension. Such creatures weren't meant to exist. So why had the Mages created them in the first place? He failed to imagine the depths of depravity necessary to envision such a monster.

He liked to think he was a simple man. Dorl lived by a lone code. Take care of your friends and they'll take care of you. Hopefully. He and Nothol had stuck by each other through numerous adventures, though more adequately categorized as mishaps, making them uniquely qualified to undertake this quest.

Perhaps Anienam had known all along. The old man was enigmatic if nothing else. When he spoke, it was in riddles. Infuriating, to be sure, but Dorl thought it necessary given the severity of what they were about to endure. To struggle through centuries of an endless war in the hopes, slim as they might be, of finally defeating the eternal enemy must be frightening. Friendless, the last wizard scoured the lands in search of those handpicked by the gods. The very thought left Dorl weak.

Neither wealthy nor particularly brave, Dorl Theed was content with just being a good man. He stumbled through life making the best of bad situations, which was a lesson he'd do well to remember out in the forest. Chosen by the gods? Now that the thought took shape he couldn't get past it. What did it mean? Why was he, of all people, chosen to step forward and defend, defend what exactly? He still wasn't sure. Assuming it would be far too presumptuous to second guess the gods, Dorl went along for the ride. Living or dying didn't mean much until Rekka became involved.

Rekka Jel. Dorl reluctantly admitted that she was largely, though inadvertently, to blame for his sudden hesitancy towards fighting. Did he want to live more than before? Was she the sole reason he held life in higher regard? He'd never known love before. The thought that it might happen to him was preposterous. He was a sell sword, prone to drinking, whoring, and taking fat purses for minimal work. The prospect of dying, now that he'd fallen deeper in love than he was willing to admit, left him rattled.

Crazy as it sounded, Rekka had become his world. He'd willingly lay down his life for her, knowing in his heart she'd do the same without question. There was only one other in all Malweir he felt confident enough in to do the same. Nothol Coll. Blessed to have such friends, Dorl started to rethink his inability to relax. If they were being hunted, not for the first time since leaving Delranan, there was absolutely nothing he could do to change it. Mind locked deep in conflict, Dorl was left with one conclusion.

"Let the bastards come," he mumbled under his breath.

Nothol eyed him strangely but kept his lips shut.

Luck abandoned them a few hours later when they stumbled upon a trail of freshly crisscrossing horse tracks. Nothol peered down, knowing instinctively that the depth of the prints meant heavily armed and armored riders. Wolfsreik. He didn't recall any of the rebels wearing decent armor and, to the best of his knowledge, they hadn't ranged this far east yet. He was about to tell Dorl when a horn blast rattled nearby tree branches.

"Dorl, ride back to the wagon and tell Bahr to push the pace. We're going to have company soon," he ordered. Panic danced in his tone. The prospect of confronting a heavily armed force of semi-professional soldiers blanched the experienced sell sword. He'd listened to Boen's recounting of the assault and had seen the real Wolfsreik in action during various raids and police actions. Even with a Gaimosian and slightly demented wizard in their company, Nothol knew they just didn't have enough to withstand a serious assault.

Dorl instantly recognized the spark of fear in his best friend's eyes and wheeled his horse about wordlessly. Heels dug in and horse and rider took off at a sprint. Time slipped through their fingers as he desperately attempted to salvage their quest before the snows ran red with blood. A second horn blast sent chills through him. Dorl didn't dare look back. Couldn't think of his friend alone against the tide. Visions of battles yet to come, battles turned violently into slaughter, haunted every stride. He not only rode for his life, but for the very life of the world. It was a daunting task for anyone, much less a smalltime sell sword on the verge of losing his nerve entirely. Dorl rode harder.

The thunder of hooves sounded angrily across the late afternoon sky. Snow kicked up with each hoof as the leagues raced by. Wolf skin cloaks trailed behind the riders, all mercenaries under Skaning's personal command. Their faces were grim and nearly frozen. Normally chalky skin was bright red. Ice crystals formed in eyebrows, moustaches, and beards. They gripped their reins with murderous intent. Each was eager to be the one to claim Bahr, brother of Badron, for his own. What better trophy could there be than the head of the brother of the deposed king?

Broken down into twenty-man units, the mercenaries spread out in a wide semi-circle meant to force Bahr back towards Chadra. Skaning already sent riders ahead to wait for word while he concentrated the rest of his two-thousand-man force for the final push to destroy the rebellion. Capturing Bahr became a secondary objective. He admitted it always had been. His only purpose in executing the task was to achieve greater glory in Harnin's eyes and cement his place in the new Delranan.

His true intent was to seek out and thoroughly destroy the rebellion to the point where there'd be no regeneration. Ingrid's days were numbered. Her forces had taken a beating during the botched assault. They'd claim Jarrik's death as their own, parading the information across Delranan in a blistering propaganda campaign designed to inspire false hope in the people. Skaning scoffed. It would all be for naught. Jarrik's suicide had nothing to do with Ingrid or her petty force. He died because Harnin wanted it.

Maps covered the burned walls and charcoal table. Skaning knew more about this portion of Delranan than Jarrik had, but that knowledge was tainted by childhood memories hazed over time. His father often took Skaning and his three brothers into the west on hunting expeditions in deep winter, claiming the adverse conditions toughened the boys up. He was a man who couldn't stomach having weak children. Skaning grew up under his father's totalitarian hand, shaping and forming his life on the harshness of necessity. Ascending to Badron's court was only natural given the brutality with which he'd grown from.

Skaning closed his eyes and remembered the lessons his father strove to instill while in the deep winter. Shelter became the priority. Once adequate shelter was established they could set out for a fresh water source. Snow wouldn't do. Even melted it would lower body temperatures too much too fast. Hypothermia would set in and then death. Only once those two were established would his father lead the boys out on the hunt.

Opening his eyes, Skaning looked at the maps for suitable places to hide a large body of soldiers. Options were limited. A few forests sprouted up not far away. Judging from the rebels' speed of attack and their ease of retreat, Skaning reckoned them to be much closer than any of his commanders were bothering to look. What better way to remain hidden than by doing it in plain view? Skaning suppressed a grin. The rebels had to be squirreled away somewhere nearby.

He slid over to the appropriate map. A long finger traced invisible lines to the nearest forests large enough to house well over a thousand people. Many of the forests in this area were too thin to support concealed camps. Ingrid was no fool. She'd have taken her role seriously. The damage to Jarrik's redoubt was proof enough of that. Not wanting to risk easy detection, the rebel leader would have driven her people as deep into the trees as possible and have plenty of escape routes. There was no way she was going to repeat events in Chadra.

Skaning appreciated a cunning foe. The youngest of the original cadre of Delranan lords, he'd never been in actual combat before the other day. Taking a life proved exhilarating. He unexpectedly reveled in watching his victim writhe in pain as death slowly spread through her body. The experience already behind him, Skaning looked forward to doing the same with Ingrid. She deserved no less.

Distracted, he frowned and went back to the map. Western Delranan had an abundance of adequate hiding places, though most were small enough to force Ingrid to break up her rebellion into small, easily manageable units. All he needed to do was find them and bring the full weight of his field force down. Speed was the key. Only a lightning quick response to their daring raid would drive his point home. No fool, Skaning knew that there was little chance of catching and killing all the rebels. But if he should kill enough, the survivors would flee to their homes and do their best to erase all traces of their involvement. Skaning had plenty of time to hunt down the survivors after the war was won. The thought of breaking into homes to carry away collaborators warmed the darkness growing in his heart.

At last his eyes drifted to the largest forest in the general area. Nameless, the forest was ancient and sprinkled with intermittent areas of dense foliage and wide-open clearings. Skaning's heart jumped. There could be plenty of other hiding spots, and this was surely the most logical to avoid, but his opponent was wily. Skaning grinned fiercely. The hour of his ascension approached. Countless days and nights skulking in the shadows doing Harnin's dirty work were about to pay off. He'd done his time lurking in Chadra while others went forth to achieve individual glory. Blooded at last, Skaning was about to crush the rebellion in one final, swift stroke and change the course of destiny. Visions of usurping Harnin entertained him as he continued to glare at the map.

I've found you. Enjoy these last few days, for they will be your last.

"Captain! Summon my commanders. I want the army ready to move within the hour."

TWENTY-EIGHT

Through the Mountains

Shadows crawled wickedly across the ground, driving down temperatures as the vanguard began winding through the long-forgotten mountain passes. The Murdes Mountains, coined the Mountains of Death by travelers over generations of rising mishaps and disappearances, were ancient, formed when the world was young. The rock was bitter, stained with cruelty and jagged. Winter bathed them in new colors of despair. Winds howled like screaming demons from the pits of Hell come to ravage the world with violent intent.

Piper Joach hated the mountains. He always had. *Perhaps that's why I feel so put off now. Could these heartless stone facades know my vehemence?* Reflection brought him to an unsteady conclusion. His life was much like the cold, stone walls towering over him. Hardened by years of rigid military discipline and the unnatural lifestyle associated with countless campaigns and fallen friends, he had become stone. The campaign in Rogscroft changed him fundamentally. Where once stood a bright, effervescent officer now was a bitter shell.

Losing friends didn't bother him so much as the lack of cause. Badron's will turned to dementia, making each death an exercise in futility. There was no justification for the fallen. Their lifeless bodies lay buried beneath mounds of snow when unrecovered or were scattered ashes on the wind. Piper spent more time than was healthy each day contemplating the reasons for their deaths. To this moment he still hadn't reached a conclusion. The wounding in his heart whispered echoes of the truth, however. His friends had died for no other reason than the madness of a broken king.

Conflicting emotions tormented him as his thoughts turned towards finally going home. A soldier's life was no easy task. Many young and foolish who thought they had what it took were swept aside effortlessly. Likewise the slackers and shirkers. War demanded the very best and very worst in people. The weak were weeded out quickly, most falling prey to sword and spear. Only the veterans remained. Those strong enough, perhaps just lucky, carried on while their lesser comrades fell behind on nameless fields forgotten by all but those who'd shed their blood and tears.

"I don't like feeling closed in," Piper idly told Vajna, who rode beside him.

The elder Rogscroft general felt increasingly claustrophobic the deeper they traveled into the long-forgotten places of the mountains. A natural cavalryman, he much preferred the open steppe with clear view of the terrain. All manner of dark thoughts mocked him now. Vajna glanced up against his better judgment. Paranoia swelled. It didn't take much to imagine being locked in the jaws of an ancient beast hungering for flesh.

The old general agreed. "Nor do I. Aurec seems convinced this is the best course of action, however, and when a king speaks...."

"His army marches," Piper finished. "Still, they might have picked a more scenic route. I can't help but feel the mountains are against us. Almost as if the very stone will come alive and swallow us whole."

Vajna cast a sidelong glare, disturbed with the vivid imagery Piper aroused. Old wives' tales resurfaced after their brief meeting with Cuul Ol. He warned of creatures lurking in the deepest recesses. Creatures so foul there were no recorded images or descriptions. Vajna outwardly scoffed at the notion, downplaying it to little more than childhood superstitions gone awry.

"Local villagers claim there are ghosts in the passes," he ventured, unsure where the thought came from.

Piper scowled. A soldier should know better than to allow his mind to devolve with base superstitions. "Ghosts? I should think the prospect of childhood bogeymen were beneath a general of the army. We've come too far to revert to primitive understandings. There are no such things as ghosts."

Vajna stared back blankly, mildly shrugging his shoulders with indifference. "I remember tales my mother used to keep me in line when I was small. Soul-robbing creatures that oozed from the face of the stone. One look and you'd be lost in a dark, brooding world." He paused to laugh. A brittle, twisted sound. "I never put much credence into them until seeing the walls close in around us."

The Wolfsreik commander seconded Vajna's personal fears. Nothing in the Murdes Mountains was natural. Imposing, their jagged teeth stretched far into the skies, reminding both men of an ancient beast rising from the depths of the world to devour. The possibility of mythical creatures lurking in the deepest recesses wasn't remote, not in this forgotten part of Malweir. Piper thought back to the myths and legacies of his own kingdom. Even now strange creatures were said to be seen wandering the forests and wilds. He'd never seen one personally, and generally frowned upon those with wild claims. Too often people wanted to make their mark by falsifying sightings. They proved to be tremendous wastes of resources. Any proven lying were imprisoned under Badron's rule.

His sharp eyes looked around at the rocks. Shadows, moss, and an odd slime formed random patterns, some vaguely bipedal, that could easily inspire the imaginations of lesser men. Since entering the Pell Darga's secret pass he hadn't seen real any signs of life. The lack thereof was disheartening to a man who'd spent his life in the wilds. Used to seeing shades of green and brown interspersed with the drab white and grey of winter often kept him centered. Kept him in the proper frame of mind to carry on when exhaustion and fatigue demanded otherwise. Piper Joach needed the break in scenery for peace of mind if nothing else.

"You don't suppose the Pell have any truth in their warnings?" he asked, wishing Vajna never brought the subject up. His unease growing, Piper found his eyes roaming over every inch of nearby rock face.

Vajna suppressed a grin. "Perhaps. They're a cagey folk, that's for sure."

"That's what worries me. I don't want to get caught on our backs if Cuul Ol's warnings bear merit. Raise the guard and have word passed back to the following units to be prepared for," he said and paused, unsure what they needed to be prepared for. "Just have them ready to engage any potential enemy that might surface."

Vajna was a man unused to taking orders from any but the king, but his growing relationship with Piper left him unoffended. They shared responsibility as well as command. Either was capable of issuing orders soldiers from all three armies were expected to obey unquestioningly. If forced to express the truth he felt inside, Vajna appreciated not having to give orders. Enough of his men had fallen during the Wolfsreik invasion and subsequent campaign across

Rogscroft to leave an inconsolable guilt in his heart. His orders resulted in so many deaths sleep often was long in coming. Letting Piper make the difficult decisions might have seemed like an easy way out, especially considering how Piper's own guilt hounded his actions, but Vajna felt he'd earned at least a minor respite.

"Where are you going?" he asked.

Piper gestured down the pass with his chin. "To link up with Cuul Ol. I want to find out a little more about the dangers he seems to think are tracking us."

"Alone?" Vajna's eyebrows rose, barely visible above the fur-lined rim of his helmet.

Piper caught the mild look of surprise and matched it. "What's the worst that can happen? I'll be fine, Vajna."

The older, more seasoned general stretched his jaw left and then right. As much as he wanted to mess with Piper's rattled state of mind, he couldn't think of any comeback so he merely nodded and wheeled back towards the long, winding column of the combined army.

They parted without another word. Piper didn't look back for fear of knowing he might lose his nerve and return to the safety of his army. Yet there were moments when a commander needed to be seen leading by example. Piper recognized this was one such moment. Tension filled the pass. His soldiers felt the same apprehensions as their leader, making this expedition potentially dangerous. One panicked man could incite a hundred others to lose their discipline. He forced thoughts of what might happen from his mind. There'd be time enough for reverse speculation once the war ended.

Well out of sight of his lead scouts, Piper found the quietness of the mountains disturbing. Howling winds drove down from the snow-capped peaks with angry song their entire trek through the mountains, yet this stretch of perpetually abandoned pass was oddly still. Nothing moved. No wind echoed down from high above. Piper did his best to ignore the imposing feeling crawling over his flesh. A supernatural air clung to the rock. He felt marked.

The sudden flash nearly threw him from the saddle. His horse cried out. Piper's gloved hand reached for his sword as sulfurous clouds of smoke choked the way ahead. Stones and broken bits of rock showered down from unseen heights. The smoke was noxious, choking Piper. He tried, futilely, to wave it away.

"You are the soldier of the Wolf."

Piper froze, gently lowering his hand from his face. Peering through the smoke he could barely make out a small figure perched upon the rock. Leathery wings curled up and behind the lizard-like body. Long legs ending in three-clawed toes curled into the stone and were encircled by a rapier, thin tail. Short, powerful arms hung to the creature's waist. Impossibly large eyes dominated the smallish face. Piper was reminded of ancient horrors conjured by hedge wizards and mothers eager to see their rambunctious sons calm down.

When at last he found his voice it was strained. Cracked. "What are you?"

The lizard cocked its head, debating how much to tell. "I am one of the zha'foral."

Piper bolted upright. Fingers tightened around the worn, familiar leather straps of his sword. "A demon."

"Mortals always have such limited concepts of what exists around them. Demon? There haven't been demons in Malweir since the world was young."

An age of impossibilities challenged Piper's reality. He'd witnessed the dark powers surrounding Badron. Seen armies of the once mythic Pell Darga sweep across snow-covered fields. Fought against an army of Goblins intent on the absolute destruction of all humanity. What was one more seemingly insignificant creature taunting him in the depths of the Murdes Mountains?

"If you're no demon what are you?" he demanded.

"A summoning. There are powers greater than man's imagination at play in the north. I am the messenger come to deliver words of my benevolent master. Your soldiers march to a war they cannot hope to win. Always through blind eyes do we try to see tomorrow."

"Speak plainly, summoning. I am in no mood for mind games," Piper said harshly. His eyes flit left and right, suddenly wary of a lurking ambush.

The zha'foral cocked its head and hissed. "Man is by far the most infuriating creature I've encountered. How you've managed to dominate the world is beyond the scope of my imagination. Better races lay scattered in shallow graves. Very well, *man*, I shall tell you what I know. Your army marches towards certain, gruesome death. What you think will be a glorious return will end in rivers of blood. The north will never recover and all life on Malweir will grow corrupt and decay."

Piper felt his breakfast rise in his throat. *Could this creature whisper of what afflicts Badron and Harnin? If so, what foul game have we stumbled upon? Clearly this war is not from the minds of man.* "What awaits us in Delranan?"

"Death."

The finality of a singular word haunted Piper. He'd already had apprehensions towards attacking and fighting his own people. If what this creature said bore any semblance to truth the campaign was going to be much worse than even General Rolnir imagined. Death had been a boon companion since the first units left Delranan at the end of autumn, snatching one or two at a time until the thirst for life grew so great a wash of misery dropped on them. Piper lacked any fear for himself, always figuring he'd die with a sword in his hand or one in his back. Professional soldiers rarely lived long enough to know the insecurities of retirement.

His eyes narrowed on the zha'foral. "I can't go back to the others with wild speculations from a creature that shouldn't exist."

"Shouldn't exist?" the zha'foral sputtered indignantly. "I roamed this world long before your ancestors crawled from the mud. All you see before you was once my domain. When you are naught but dust I will remain!"

Piper's horse snorted, clearly unimpressed with the tiny temper tantrum. Piper leaned forward to pat its neck. "My apologies, but this conversation is an impossibility. You come unbidden, whispering hints of disaster without concrete information I can use. What purpose do you truly serve? Who is your master?"

The impish zha'foral twisted its head to the opposite side as it debated the consequences of telling Piper his master. Names held power. To ignorantly give a name without understanding the repercussions often meant the difference between life and death for creatures such as he. In the end there was no real choice. He'd been sent with specific instructions to find the leaders of the Wolf soldiers. They needed to be warned.

"My master is the lord of the house of the gods," he finally said.

Piper sighed frustration. "House of the gods? No such place exists in Malweir."

The zha'foral sighed disgustedly. "Ah yes. You mortals tend to stop believing in higher powers. Do not be so blind as to think that simply because you no longer believe in the gods they do not exist."

"We have no use for gods in Delranan. Men built our kingdom, not ethereal beings too aloof to become involved," Piper countered.

"Yet your legends are riddled with such tales. What does that make you, exactly, having abandoned all vestiges of whence you came?" The zha'foral crooked his head skyward and hissed a wicked laugh.

Piper was growing agitated. This cat and mouse game needed to end, quickly, if he was going to have enough time to hash out his differences with the Pell leaders in time before reaching the end of the pass. Still, he couldn't help but adhere to at least a measure of caution. Nagging suspicions lurked just beyond consciousness, enough to give the second in command of the Wolfsreik pause. Most of the soldiers scoffed at the notion of being controlled by some defunct higher power. Unless it could be seen, the concept of gods was intangible.

"What warnings would you have me pass along? A faceless monster awaits, eager to consume us the moment we set foot upon our home soil?" Piper snapped. Rationalizing was getting him nowhere and each moment delayed was one lost.

The zha'foral grinned sheepishly. "Ever the favored sons. What the gods saw in your species I'll never understand. My master issues warnings that higher powers are in play. The dark gods are at work in Delranan. The kingdom of the Wolf will burn to ash."

Clearly as agitated as Piper had grown, the zha'foral blinked and disappeared in a second cloud of ash and smoke. The stench of burnt hair clung to Piper's cloak, twisting his stomach. Alone again, he had no choice but to internalize what just happened and push ahead. The prospect of being strung out overnight in the confines of the mountains bothered him as a tactician. Should the Pell choose to betray their alliance, it wouldn't take much to rain down a hail of spears and arrows, slaughtering hundreds.

Spooked by the unexpected encounter with the zha'foral, Piper rode on. He tried to reorient his mind on tactics and the problems inherent with deploying a twenty-thousand-strong army through such a narrow gap without sustaining heavy casualties. Harnin wasn't going to make the transition easy. The one-eyed bastard no doubt had traps and ambushes established from the foothills all the way back to Chadra Keep. Fortunately for the allied army, Harnin didn't know of the secret Pell ways. If he did, he'd be able to keep the army bottlenecked for months, all but forcing Rolnir to retreat and circle south around the mountains. The war would drag on well into the following year and who knew how many casualties each side would sustain.

Mood darkened by too many complications, Piper Joach listened to the crisp sound of hooves striking the hard granite of the mountain floor. Of his many duties in the military, he despised trying to convince leaders of any faction to bend to the will of the Wolfsreik. The Pell Darga were his most-feared competition. Once feral enemies, the shadow people remained ready to turn at a moment's notice. Piper scowled. *Thank you, General Rolnir. I don't know what I'd do without this added responsibility.* His thoughts were disturbed as Cuul Ol came into view. The Pell chieftain leaned heavily on an ash walking stick. He grinned, flashing missing teeth as Piper rode near.

TWENTY-NINE

Drimmen Delf Goes to War

Cold winds lashed into their faces, bitter with winter's kiss. The Dwarves laughed it off. Their thick skin and heavy beards buffeted most of the harshness the elements offered. Most in the four-thousand-strong army were haggard veterans all but immune to the worst of weather conditions. Their heavy boots stamped a thunderous sound across the rolling hills and gentle valleys west of the Kergland Spine. The grind of wheels echoed in stark contrast. Files of cannons were pulled by oxen. Wagons filled with ammunition and gunpowder followed at a safe distance should an unfortunate accident occur and destroy most of the army.

Thord marched at their helm. His thick beard was decorated with jewels and polished, silver trinkets woven into the hair. His round belly strained under armor he last recalled fitting slightly looser. The Dwarf Lord barked rich laughter when confronted by his peers and advisors. Dwarves weren't known for their sense of humor and were more apt to challenge a battle of axes, yet Thord knew he needed to set an example for the others. If what Faeldrin cautioned was even partially true this was going to be a war unlike any other. He relished the opportunity to test his people's mettle against dark gods and their ilk. Time had come when Dwarves would return to prominence.

He stepped off the lane to watch the first battalions march by. These were his elite: battle-hardened veterans individually chosen for feats of valor on the field. Five hundred of Drimmen Delf's best would lead the tide of Dwarves into battle in the western kingdom of Delranan. None knew what to expect, yet each was willing to sacrifice his own life to win the battle for the glory of their kingdom.

Sunlight reflected off their silver armor. Dwarves enjoyed inspiring fear in their opponents. They marched into battle with resplendent armor worthy of a king's collection. Spear and axe sang with fresh polish. Only the very best weapons were good enough for the elite. Fierce helmets covered the upper portions of their faces, only the lower jaw exposed. Dwarves were fearless, warriors of the highest caliber. Thord's heart swelled with pride. These were *his* Dwarves. *His* army. All Malweir would tremble at the sound of their guns.

Never before, so far as he knew and the Elf Lord Faeldrin confirmed, had any army successfully used gunpowder weapons on a massive scale. Many, the Elves included, found them largely disturbing. Such destruction wasn't meant for the hands of mortals. Images of fields strewn with severed body parts, grass, and snow painted in blood haunted many of the survivors. Secure within the observation post on Bode Hill, Thord watched in abject disgust. Amazed by the ingenuity of his smiths and war masters, the Dwarf Lord could only stand with puckered lips.

His was a warrior's life. How many victims had fallen to his axe over the course of his long, decorated life? Numbers weren't easily counted. Foes and rivals alike dropped in defeat. Some cooled on the hard ground. Others were subsumed into Drimmen Delf's culture. A select few rose to become fast allies whose voices counted equal in his war councils. Those were the ones he felt most comfortable around. They were Dwarves who knew the value of strength in leadership.

Halfway through the day he received ill-welcomed news. The Aeldruin had returned and were riding to the head of the column. Whispers arrived ahead of them. Whispers of the horrors of the battle along the Fern River. Curiously, as if to hammer the truth in, none of the one-hundred-Dwarf element marched alongside. Thord ordered a brief rest while waiting for the Elves to deliver their report. Ill news needed to be prepared for lest it overwhelm the receiver.

He removed his winged helmet and wiped his knotted brow with a thick palm. Calluses from a lifetime of iron work gnarled his hands into weapons of their own. His eyes squinted in the midday sunlight. The color of flint, they lost some of their earlier luster. Pride of history was one matter, dealing with the loss of such an important battle commander another. Snatching a canteen from his adjutant, a position he insisted didn't need to be filled, the Dwarf Lord drank deeply. Faeldrin would have sent riders ahead if they'd found victory. Thord prepared for the worst news. News he already knew in his heart. He'd sent one hundred of his bravest to their deaths without second thought. Being a king certainly had drawbacks.

"Greetings, Thord, Lord of Drimmen Delf," Faeldrin announced less than an hour later as he slid from the saddle of an exhausted mount.

Thord didn't understand horses or the attraction to them. Being able to traverse countless leagues in a day-- tripling what a Dwarf could walk--meant little in the grand scheme of his life. There was naught but disconnect with the earth when mounted, even on a pony. Thord, and practically every Dwarf, greatly preferred their own boots to carry them where they needed to go. He looked up at the lean, almost lanky Elf Lord and offered a curt bow.

"Faeldrin. How fares the east?"

The distant stare mirrored in the depths of the Elf's eyes was answer enough, yet Faeldrin began a thorough recounting of the heroism involved. His shoulder slumped as he finished. "I have never seen a host so vast. Not in all my many millennia of roaming Malweir."

"Tens of thousands?" Thord nearly balked. Goblins were reclusive by nature, choosing to thieve and murder under the cover of darkness or the light of a pale moon. For so many to move across open expanses of land in the middle of the day was a feat unheard of.

"Many times that," the Elf corrected. "I believe the world will never be the same again."

Even with the amount of casualties the Goblins suffered on the riverbank, they still had enough to sack every kingdom between Drimmen Delf and the western shore. Thord's meager force, by comparison, would be swept under without putting a dent in the Goblins' weight. The warrior in him wanted to test that theory, to put Dwarven steel against Goblin savagery. His blood surged with fire.

Faeldrin recognized that cagey look and intervened. "You wouldn't be enough to break them. Their numbers are too much, even for mighty Drimmen Delf."

Thord offered mock ignorance. "I didn't say a word, despite what those pointy ears of yours might have heard. Though now that you mention it I think my Dwarves would carve a bloody path straight through the heart of those foul bastards."

"No doubt. Goblins may be fierce and have numbers but they lack the natural martial instinct of Dwarves. Thousands would fall. Perhaps even a third of their force, but your loss would be complete. Are the lives of four thousand Dwarves so casually discarded?"

Muscles tensed under the heavy chainmail. "You know better. Dwarves have always answered the call the old allegiances. How many battles have you and I stood side by side? Once more the ground will tremble at the sound of Elves and Dwarves going to war."

"I have no doubts of your courage or veracity. Only the number of our enemies coming for us. We held the banks for almost a day before they crossed in such numbers I had no choice but to withdraw."

"At least it wasn't a total loss," Thord countered, desperate to salvage at least a small measure of dignity.

Faeldrin suppressed the sadness threatening to overwhelm him. He'd thought he'd been able to internalize his grief during the long ride back to the main army but giving an account of the battle reopened those wounds. He felt each death again and again as the events played out in his mind's eye. Elf or Dwarf. It didn't matter. Each life was precious to him. Many Elves disagreed with his lifestyle. They remained cloistered in the great forests, heedless of the developments between kingdoms and races. Faeldrin viewed that as the great failing of the Elves. They'd grown so frightened by the prospect of dying that their lives were wasted under a blanket of fear.

The Aeldruin were considered the finest mercenary force in all Malweir. Never numbering more than a hundred, Faeldrin and his Elves ignored the claustrophobic pleas of their people to strike out in the effort to do good in the world. They lived like no other Elf and, as a direct result, thoroughly enjoyed life. Losing a single one might be considered travesty by the general population, but Faeldrin knew they died fully appreciating what life had to offer.

He gazed down on the Dwarf and smiled sadly. "No, there were survivors. We managed to bring back a handful of your wounded. They are already with the healers and should recover to fight again."

Thord, brooding, grunted approval. "Strong blood runs through our veins. Did the others die well?"

What a difficult question to answer. How does one define a quality death? By the number of enemies heaped at his feet? Or by the amount of lives one saves in the act? I've searched long for these answers without ever discovering the truth. All life is precious, but to give one's life in the pursuit of doing what one loves might be considered worthy of praise. "Yes, Dwarf Lord, they died with axe in hand and enemies at their feet."

Thord accepted this cold truth and ran thick fingers through his beard. His eyes swept back over his army, yearning to set sight on those survivors. Regret would betray them. They'd all gone to the river knowing death awaited. To be removed from the field while their comrades fell shamed them. Thord felt their misery, for it also laid in his heart. There'd come another time, soon, when those brave warriors were given the opportunity to die for their kingdom. He prayed to Kruk, the Dwarf god of war, that their internal torment be short and their axes reap a terrible price on the Goblins. No other vindication would suffice.

"How much time do we have before the enemy arrives?" Thord asked brusquely.

Faeldrin couldn't shake the feeling the Dwarves planned on wheeling about to meet the Goblins head-on despite his warnings. "Not before we arrive in Delranan."

Both leaders knew Drimmen Delf lay in the Goblins' path. Should the foul creatures decide to lay siege, Thord would see the end of his line. Dwarf women were stout, capable fighters, but they lacked numbers. Goblins would sack the mighty Dwarven kingdom and leave the mountain a burning wreckage of corpses. The token defense force left in place wouldn't do much more than hold the Goblins for a day before the unending wave of darkness swelled into the tunnels and caverns.

"Thord, the west needs our aid. Anienam Keiss and I spoke at length. Whatever this culminating event is, it will occur in Delranan. We must arrive in time to do our part. The world of Men is not strong enough to withstand the dark tide alone," the Elf pressed.

A fierce glare was his only response.

League after league ground away under the heavy clomp of Dwarven boots. Dwarves came up lame. Wagons broke down. Wheels on cannons snapped from traversing rough terrain. Yet the army moved on. They sang ancient songs to the gods. They sang of glory in battle and the coming age where Dwarven life might would be celebrated by all. They sang for those who were about to die. Hearts buoyed with song, the mighty army of Drimmen Delf pushed out of the foothills and into the far eastern fringes of Rogscroft.

Faeldrin and the Aeldruin ranged ahead, scouting the best possible path of march for the large army. Elvish horses danced across the snow, so light in their step. It didn't take long before signs of the war overwhelmed them. Faeldrin buckled under the sheer amount of havoc caused by the first Goblin army. Entire villages lay burnt to the ground. Skeletons lay in awkward poses where they'd been murdered. The sudden prospect of facing a potentially equal-sized Goblin force ahead of the Dwarves paled him.

"This is madness," Euorn cautioned as he rode past skeletons of three butchered horses. "We should not be here."

"If not here, where?" Faeldrin asked. "You saw how large the first army was. We have no choice but to continue pushing westward."

The lord of the Aeldruin frowned. It was an old argument, stretching back to when Euorn was first recruited.

"You risk forcing the Dwarves into a confrontation they can't possibly win should the Goblin army responsible for all this lie in wait," the Elf scout replied.

Faeldrin conceded the point. "We risk even more by keeping out of this. You heard what the wizard told me. This is a battle for the soul of Malweir. Should we fail, all life will wither and die under the tyranny of the dark gods' return. Are you willing to ride home to Elvanara in shame and wait for the end?"

Euorn stiffened, visibly disturbed by the conjured images. "You know better, Faeldrin. I've ridden alongside you for more years than I care to recount. We've fought countless battles and I've remained singularly constant in my caution. Not even the time we slew the dragon Ramulus were matters this dire."

Killing a dragon was no small accomplishment, yet the Elves managed, along with the help of Anienam's father and a tribe of Pell Darga hunters. Faeldrin's memories had turned to fondness, one that didn't relate to what lay in store for them now: tens of thousands of Goblins, the Dae'shan, and the return of evil so vast there was no counter measure.

Euorn continued, "You're not taking into account the war that has clearly struck Rogscroft. If the Goblins were even a quarter of the size marching west behind us, this kingdom might already have fallen. Do we take the chance of marching too close to the capital while being pursued?"

Every instinct demanded the Elves march ahead to the cities offering aid when available. Doing so increased the risk of being discovered by the current Goblin force potentially occupying the Rogscroft countryside. Faeldrin wanted to help the men of this kingdom but in doing so would damn the Dwarven army.

"We can't risk it," he reluctantly exhaled. "Our task is to get the Dwarves to Delranan in fighting condition before the appointed time. Anienam seemed convinced we can break the enemy before they unleash the dark gods. The people of Rogscroft must be the price for our success."

"Faeldrin, I feel your pain, for it lies in my heart as well, but we can't stop this evil from returning if we pause at every village and town along the way. Skirmishes with shadow forces of Goblins won't win this war. We need to follow the wizard's directions and attack with concentrated power. Only then can we turn our sights on setting the rest of the north to rights."

The mercenary gave a long look at the field of bodies littering his line of sight. Imagining the horror these villagers must have felt upon seeing waves of Goblin warriors marching into their homes with sword and torch left his stomach in turmoil. Confronting death with a sword in hand was vastly different than awakening in the middle of the night. Residual screams must have echoed long into the next day. He sighed.

"These people must be avenged."

Euorn nodded. "They will be, but not now. It's time to ride, Faeldrin. Let me take Aleor and two others so we can range a league ahead. We'll find a way around this Goblin nightmare, more than likely south. I'm not too familiar with this part of Malweir."

They'd both poured over what maps Thord's people had in their vast library. Major land features and characteristics were studied until eyes burned. Formidable mountain ranges peppered the area, growing more imposing the farther west the army marched. A full, and impossibly harsh, winter's worth of snow threatened to make the fields and plains too dangerous to move over. That left what travel infrastructure Rogscroft had remaining. Faeldrin conceded it wasn't much, given the severity of the Goblin campaign.

In the end the Elves were left with no real choice. The army must turn south and march around the Murdes Mountains. This course of action offered the least amount of resistance while giving the army maximum speed. Time being of the essence, Faeldrin allowed Euorn to ride. Just getting to Delranan on time and in fighting condition was going to prove challenging enough. As loath as he was to accept it, the Elf Lord knew that stopping to help along the way was a lofty impediment to victory. He whistled sharply and watched as four Elves blazed away into the setting sun.

Golden sunlight warmed Artiss Gran's withered face. The longer he stayed away from the rest of the Dae'shan the more human he felt. He'd already taken on mortal characteristics. He felt tired, old. His body was stretched too thin. The sensations were delicious after centuries of being insubstantial. Enjoying these long-forgotten conditions, Artiss knew his end was fast approaching. Any loss of power meant death stalked ever closer.

Winds blew the surrounding trees gently. A flock of ibis burst from the verdant leaves, their white feathers in stark contrast to the earthy tones of the surrounding jungle. Trennaron remained peaceful throughout the seasons. Winter's kiss didn't reach this far, nor did summer's brutal gaze penetrate the residual magic smothering the temple of the gods of light. It was the most serene place on Malweir, and it was doomed.

Artiss Gran reluctantly turned from the view he'd enjoyed each morning for two thousand years. His time was nearly expired. Ages of waiting, planning, and enduring the pain of abandonment were wrapping up. He felt it in the air. Deep in his bones. He'd told Anienam Keiss that leaving Trennaron would kill him and allow the temple to fall into ruin. Death was coming for him regardless. Should the quest to destroy the dark gods succeed, he and the other Dae'shan would perish. There were very few certainties in life. He'd taken much for granted during his supposed immortality. The sobering reality of what came next weakened his conviction.

Planning for the hour of death was one matter. Waiting for it to finally occur distinctly different. His shoulders sagged some. He stood smaller than normal. The conviction of his principles kept him steady. He was of singular purpose. Nothing mattered aside from stopping his errant brothers from opening the nexus. Artiss hoped he'd prepared Bahr and his group enough to deal with the nightmares awaiting them. The Blud Hamr was a powerful tool, but only if used properly. Groge the Giant was young, inexperienced. Artiss doubted whether the Giant had the necessary strength to destroy the Olagath Stone.

If by chance he did, Groge would seal the dimensional paths forever. The threat of the dark gods would be ended, allowing the races of Malweir to deal with their own affairs unencumbered by the promise of doom. Artiss partially wished he'd be around to see how man, Elf, and Dwarf would learn to cope with their sudden abandonment. Sadly, he wouldn't. His fate was determined. His death foretold.

Giving the sunrise one final glance, Artiss Gran headed down the alabaster stairs, passing gargoyles with leering faces and judgmental eyes. He reached out to caress the cold stone. The ever present protectors of Trennaron, the gargoyles remained impassive as their master walked by. Artiss silently wondered what was to become of this most special place. Trennaron was unlike any other structure. It held the promise of all races, should they ever learn to set aside differences and grow for the good of all life. The former Dae'shan recalled the dismal failure of the first grand experiment: the Mages. *Perhaps their sad tale will help guide new generations to succeed where so many others failed. Perhaps, but I fear life is doomed to repeat this mindless cycle of violence.*

Artiss Gran, last of the true Dae'shan, mouthed a last mournful sigh and passed under the main arch for what promised to be the final time. His intent remained private. Not that there was anyone else to talk to. Most of the servants and staff were still asleep. He preferred it that way. They'd been given their instructions for once he'd gone. Artiss wished he didn't need to leave, but the nagging feeling in the back of his mind left him without doubts concerning the Giant. Such an important task couldn't be left to chance.

Whistling an old--ancient, he reckoned--tune, Artiss made his way to the chamber that would transport him to his destination. He had a war to wage.

THIRTY

A Last Parting

"At this rate it will take the rest of the week to get the army through the mountains."

Venten glanced at his king with pursed lips. The impatience of youth struggled to regain control. It was unbecoming but expected in one Venten agreed wasn't prepared for the responsibilities of the crown. Each diadem bore hefty weight, Aurec's most of all. Losing a father so violently would change anyone. Venten decided his fledgling monarch's rash of immaturity stemmed from the nearly intolerable wait they'd been forced to endure.

"Moving so many soldiers and equipment takes time. You'd do well to focus your attentions on less stressful matters," he cautioned.

Aurec visibly snarled but his words lacked venom. "Venten, we're wasting time. Our enemies have more chances to prepare than we have to reach Delranan. Each delay will cost lives. Lives none of us can afford to spare."

"There's more to this than pre-battle jitters," Venten concluded. "What troubles you, Aurec? I've seldom heard you talk this way."

Suddenly bashful, the young king wiped his face with both palms. *Where do I begin? How can I tell you that I know in my heart we are marching to a desperate, hopeless battle from which the majority won't return? Oh, Venten, how can I tell you I'm afraid you and I won't be around much longer? The world conspires against us and we blindly march into whatever traps awaits us. This will not end well.*

"Nothing. It's just a feeling I have. A premonition of sorts," he finally admitted without giving away too much.

Venten frowned. "Premonitions? You speak of witchcraft."

"Don't be foolish, old friend. There are no witches in this part of Malweir. Well, none we know of at least. My great grandfather's campaigns saw to that, as I believe you instructed me one summer night." He paused to smile. "I can't explain why I feel the way I do, Venten. All I can say is that we are heading into a dark time. I'd be lying if I denied being scared."

"A king should know fear. To be without leads down paths men like Badron accept. I'd be more than willing to lay you flat with my pommel if you insist," the former general admonished smoothly. "Quality of character is not easy to come by. Your father prepared you for this day as best he could. I've done all I know to ensure you find success, even in the direst of circumstances. None of that means a thing if you refuse to exercise a measure of patience. Vajna is a capable man. He will lead us safely through the mountains. Combined with Piper Joach, I wouldn't want to put any unit up against their prowess."

"What if their concerns over the Pell's loyalty are founded?" Aurec asked. His eyes hardened at the thought of betrayal. The only reason the Pell Darga became involved in the war in the first place was through his insistence. Now all his hard-won battles stood on the precipice of ruin.

Venten shrugged, a nonchalant move vague in meaning. "We've gone decades without their support. I can't see how their abandonment will matter much now. Not with the Wolfsreik on our side."

Aurec wasn't so sure. Rolnir and the Wolfsreik were certainly unexpected allies, but how long would that last? Shifting allegiances remained the bane of leadership. Rolnir and his ten-thousand-strong army flipped sides in the span of a night. Nothing prevented them from doing so again once the army returned to Delranan. Aurec and his meager force would be overwhelmed and destroyed before they could flee back into the mountains.

The loss of life would be catastrophic for Rogscroft's population. Leaderless and lacking military strength, the civilians desperately trying to rebuild would be ripe for invasion and worse. Aurec's legacy would be written in shame and defeat. Rogscroft would cease to exist. It had happened before. Kingdoms with names like Gaimos and Gren were thoroughly transformed or removed from existence entirely. That fear crept into Aurec's mind and refused to let go.

"We're going to need all the help we can get if Rogscroft is going to recover," the young king said, expressing his latent fear.

"Keep your mind focused on the task at hand," Venten reminded. "We've got more than twenty thousand soldiers to deploy in enemy territory. Rogscroft hasn't invaded another kingdom in generations. Unused to being the aggressor, we must remain grounded in our principles. Remember why we march on Delranan: not only to avenge your father and our fallen, but to remove a hideous stain on humanity."

"Is self-proclaimed righteousness enough of an excuse to lead yet more to their deaths?" Aurec countered.

Venten eyed the boy approvingly. No leader worthy of the title marched to war without extreme caution. Life was precious. There were many who'd either forgotten that lesson or were never concerned with it to begin with. Aurec had great potential to be the ruler his people needed, possibly surpassing his father. All he needed to do was stay focused. Venten was a firm believer that all matters worked themselves out with time. A little nudging didn't hurt either.

"Righteousness has nothing to do with what we're about. I would argue revenge is the underlying factor to this movement. Revenge for both you and Rolnir. Wrongs have been committed yet we are not the designated defenders of justice. You seek to end a threat to Rogscroft. Once that threat is removed we will be able to go back to our homes and rebuild in earnest. Don't be so fast to pass harsh judgment on your actions, young king. There will come a time for grief and doubt. Let them come on their own accord."

"Venten, I wish you were younger," Aurec said after many long moments staring off into the looming Murdes Mountains.

The elder statesman's eyebrow peaked. "Why is that?"

"So that I'd have the benefit of your council long into my twilight years."

Rolnir tossed down the overused charcoal pencil and leaned back in his field chair. His cramped hands roamed through his full head of hair before dropping down over his face. He traced the deep groves and lines carved into his skin through time and emotions with blistered fingertips. Raw exhaustion left him sluggish. Muscles conditioned through years of campaigning and the daily rigors of military life were sore beyond belief. His body ached with each movement. A headache pounded behind his temples. He couldn't recall the last time he'd felt this miserable. Compounding his misery were a stuffy nose and sore throat. *Damned bad time for me to catch a cold.*

Every healer and medic in the combined army insisted he needed to drink plenty of fluids and rest but, as general of the army, what choice did he have? The army needed strong leadership, now more than ever. With Piper and Vajna already deep within the mountain passes, that left Rolnir as the singular leader in place. He needed to be seen trooping the line, offering words of encouragement to the army. Morale was already slipping. He felt it ebb daily.

Nerves stood on edge. Especially for the Wolfsreik. There was no escaping the cold fact that the soldiers of the Wolf were about to attack their own kingdom, own people. It sat ill with many. Armies were designed to protect their population, not destroy them. The soldiers of the Wolfsreik would do their duty, though with mild reservation. Of that Rolnir had no doubts. But he couldn't shake the feeling that many of his soldiers would either desert or refuse to fight if they came across family. Best-case scenario left him with enough strength to crush Harnin's defenses and retake Chadra quickly and with minimal loss of life.

Of course there were too many outlying factors beyond his scope of control. The Pell Darga bothered him greatly. They'd been uncanny opponents and brutal allies. Capable of shifting their allegiances without notice, the mountain tribe presented too many problems. Cuul Ol wore an uneasy mantle while dealing with the young king. Rolnir couldn't shake the feeling he was walking into a trap.

Nothing for it, he turned his attention to the Rogscroft army, or rather what remained of it. They were brave, capable fighters but they were also at the end of their ropes. He couldn't blame them. Any army who'd gone through as much as the soldiers of Rogscroft over the past six months deserved to be sent home to their loved ones. Rolnir would have cut them loose without second thought but they came because of Aurec. The last defenders of Rogscroft followed the boy king out of respect and love.

Rolnir admired that. Admirable qualities were rare these days. Loyalties notwithstanding, the soldiers needed adequate downtime. They were more exhausted than he was and tired soldiers made mistakes. As much as he wanted to order a stand down for a week or more, Rolnir couldn't. He needed to get them through the mountains and in battle order before tomorrow's end. Their haste would serve to bring down Harnin's regime, hopefully, before Badron managed to worm his way back into Delranan.

Blinking away his exhaustion, Rolnir rose and slid into his heavy winter cloak. The day was getting on and less than a quarter of the army was deployed into the passes. Campfires were being lit. Meals prepared. Rolnir had originally argued to keep moving throughout the night. His advisors said otherwise. Armies were incapable of moving or fighting at night. The dangers far outweighed the rewards and, given the restrictive terrain of the mountains, Rolnir expected numerous accidents over the course of the night. Casualties he could ill afford.

The cold blast of wind lashed him as he exited his tent. Winter was in the latter stages yet refused to relinquish claims on the land. He didn't mind the snow and wind so much as the endless hours trapped in the cold. Guards snapped to attention and saluted as he passed. Soldiers from all three armies looked up, acknowledging his presence. The general had become well known over the last few weeks. He treated them all with equal consideration. Old loyalties dissolved as the newly formed army adjusted to new roles. Rolnir and Aurec decided to maintain most of the unit integrity, building specialized units of all three armies to bridge the gaps. Some of those units were already deep in the mountains.

Even Rolnir was amazed at the ease with which three distinct styles and types of leadership combined to form a cohesive fighting force. They'd been blooded against the Goblin army. The old ways remained strong but were subsumed by this new concept. Aurec's soldiers felt rejuvenated now that the threat to their kingdom was removed. Rolnir's soldiers now suffered from the lethargy they'd encountered upon entering the ruined capital city. Their nerves were frayed. Apprehensions unsteadied many. Their greatest trials were upcoming. He hoped the ingrained professionalism of the Wolfsreik would stay strong, using the strength of the Rogscroft army to buoy them during the dark times.

"Evening, General."

"Sir."

Heads nodded. Waves rose up from the crowds of soldiers trying to find a little warmth in the dying day. Despite the underlying feelings working through each soldier, they greeted him with real enthusiasm. Rolnir took hope in their faces. He returned the waves with genuine gladness. Their strength built upon his own. Stifling a cough, he wormed through camp en route to Aurec's tent.

He paused at his commanders' fire. Their roles in the campaign were greatly diminished since the alliance yet they remained the brain trust of the army. Rolnir needed each to perform to his utmost capabilities to achieve the lightning quick strike he intended. Being around his old friends again rejuvenated him, albeit slightly.

"General Rolnir," Colonel Herger, commander of the cavalry, greeted him with a cup of hot coffee and a smile. "I didn't think to see you slumming with the rest of us."

Rolnir smiled back, choosing to ignore the rib. "Nonsense. Too much time dancing politics with the king and his council leave me stagnant. I need to find you rogues to keep me grounded. Wouldn't do for a general to suffer from delusions of grandeur."

Chuckles spread through his commanders.

Ulaf, seated on a blackened tree stump, looked up at his general and asked, "Any word from the front? My lads are aching to take a crack at Harnin's defenses."

Rolnir's chief of engineers was a likeable enough man but lacking in proper military decorum. An accomplished veteran, Ulaf offered unique pragmatic views to complicated scenarios stymieing more traditional leaders.

"Piper and the van are pushing as fast as possible. The weather and the mountains are against us," Rolnir answered flatly. He found it difficult to present his most-senior commanders with false bravado. The truth was no one knew what to expect upon arriving in Delranan and that worried Rolnir to the core.

"All the more reason to include a company of sappers in the front. Harnin could have built walls to seal off the passes for all we know," Ulf added.

Rolnir held up a hand, gesturing his chief engineer to stop. "Ulf, there are some matters we can't change. If Harnin is that prepared, we're in for a nasty fight. Having a company of your sappers in the front would only get in the way while the infantry try to break free. I know what you're going to say. We've been through all this before. There is no other way. Your boys will have their chances soon enough. I doubt this campaign is going to go as smoothly as our councils believe. We're in for a fight."

"It's about time. I'm tired of sitting here babysitting the infantry," Herger chided.

His remark drew a scowl from the normally taciturn Colonel Krueger. The infantryman bore a long scar down the side of his neck, bleached white by the cold, and a natural bitterness born from a lifetime of heavy fighting. His voice was gruff, reminding Rolnir of steel scraping stone. "Remember that when you need my grunts to bail your pretty horses out."

Herger laughed and tossed a winter apple core at his friend.

"We'd all do well to remember that when the time comes," Rolnir added. "I want you to ensure all your men get as much downtime as possible. It'll be at least another day before the last units get into the passes. I'm expecting a fight as soon as we get on the ground in Delranan. Harnin's a crafty one. We can't leave anything to chance."

"We'll be ready, General," Krueger said. His large arms were folded across his broad chest. The long-stem pipe jutting from the corner of his mouth puffed grey-white smoke.

Rolnir nodded. He hoped his army was a match for the tenacity of its leaders. He reached out to slap the joyful Herger on the back. "See to your men. Hot food, water, and clean socks. As much as possible. The march continues at dawn."

They saluted and watched him stroll through the ranks, pausing here and there at random to speak with privates and captains alike. Only the smaller Pell warriors avoided him. They stuck together in small packs, reminding Rolnir of feral beasts waiting to attack. *Hard allies*. Speaking in their native tongue, the Pell warriors huddled around their fires. Many sharpened their wickedly short spears. Others busied putting a keen edge on swords and daggers. Few laughed. A sad fact which struck Rolnir odd.

It was another hour before the redheaded general made it to King Aurec's tents. The sun had already dipped below the horizon, releasing its hold and bringing bitter cold sweeping in behind it. Rolnir frowned as he thought of the long walk back to his tent. Thankfully there were plenty of fires between stops.

"General, I'd expected you to be in the passes with the vanguard," Aurec said without looking up from his map table.

Quick lad. Are you trying to get rid of me or merely overstating your confidence in my abilities? "Piper made it abundantly clear I'd only be in the way. He's one of the few I trust. He led the army into Rogscroft and established a head for the rest of us. I have no reason to think he can't do it in Delranan."

Some things didn't need to be said. Rolnir left it at that. Venten chose that moment to poke his head from the back chamber. Chewing quickly to swallow the bite of hard tack, the elder statesman sauntered up to them. Rolnir didn't think anyone could appear with a more haggard appearance yet somehow Venten managed it. This campaign needed to end quickly so they could get back to their lives.

"Venten, Rolnir and I were discussing Piper Joach's tactical capability," Aurec said with only the faintest hint of irony. He'd not forgotten what the Wolfsreik's second did to his forces in the opening days of the war. Their battles were worthy of training sergeants' lessons.

Venten blanched but was experienced enough to let bygones remain such. "I've seen few equal to his zest for perfection. If Rolnir says he can handle it, you should have no reason to doubt."

Aurec scowled before going back to his maps. "Rolnir, I admit that my experience is coming to an end. What little I know of Delranan isn't going to be of much use."

"Understood. Piper and I know every trail and road in our kingdom blindfolded. We'll get your army all the way to Chadra Keep and back," Rolnir affirmed.

"I hope so, Rolnir. I really do."

Aurec looked upon the light forests and harsh foothills in the shadows of the Murdes Mountains with an aching heart. Twenty-one years seemed but a blink as he absorbed as much of his beloved kingdom as possible. Memories of this moment would sustain him during the coming darkness. Memories of playing in these fields. Memories of kissing his one true love under these trees. Aurec relied on memories to keep him grounded in his frailty. He was a king, but only with the backing of a powerful army.

Sensing the young king's rising melancholy, Venten laid a gentle hand on his forearm. "It's time. We can't delay any longer."

"I know, Venten, but it doesn't get easier. I fear this will be the last time I look upon Rogscroft," Aurec said sadly.

"Perhaps, but that is not for you to decide," Venten scolded. "All you need to do is ensure this army arrives in fighting order and does what it was meant to do. Nothing else matters until Badron and Harnin are both accounted for. This is the hour of our retribution, Aurec. Today marks the beginning of the end of this long, twisted nightmare. Finish what your father wanted. End this war and bring your people home."

Spurned into action, Aurec foolishly wiped the tears clinging to the corners of his eyes and nodded sharply. "To victory, Venten."

"For your father."

Satisfied, the king of Rogscroft nudged his mount forward into the mountain pass. The combined army was at last going back to war.

THIRTY-ONE

A Long-Awaited Confrontation

Less than a year had passed since Badron last set foot on his home soil. Less than a year in which Delranan was fundamentally transformed into a land of wicked nightmares. Everything he'd witnessed upon his return suggested the end had been nothing but violent. Broken bodies peppered villages. Victims of a rumored plague. While Badron couldn't conceive how such a plague managed to wipe out nearly half of his population, it didn't stop him from pushing deeper inland.

He turned to the half-broken fisherman guiding them through the northern stretch of wilderness. The threat of a murdered family kept the old man in line for the moment. At some point Badron was convinced he'd try to either lead them into a trap or sneak off in the night. The deposed king had a plan in place to deal with treachery, perceived or real.

"How much further?" Badron hissed. He reached down to dig some of the hard snow from the inside of his boot.

The fisherman trembled, but whether from the cold or fear remained to be seen. "Not far, milord. You'll see. The fortress is not far now."

Grugnak stormed up behind the smaller man, blade barred. "Kill him now. Blood needs to be spilled."

"Patience, Goblin," Badron snarled. *Blood will be spilled and soon. Only no matter who lives, I promise your corpse will be food for the crows.* "There will be killing enough for your bloodthirsty Goblins once we arrive at the fortress." He turned back to the fisherman. "I won't be able to prevent his rage much longer, peasant. Get me to the fortress and our accord is ended."

The fisherman nodded profusely and loped back down the trail. Badron's gaze lingered on Grugnak a moment longer before following.

"It's only half complete," Badron's highest-ranking sergeant said between gasps. "I don't think the garrison is more than a few hundred. We can sneak in and kill their leadership under cover of darkness. The rank and file should capitulate easy enough."

Badron closed his eyes lightly and allowed himself a brief moment of delusion.

"There's more, Sire," the sergeant proceeded.

Badron's eyes reluctantly opened.

"*He's* there."

Impossible. Delranan was a large kingdom. Harnin could be anywhere, though logic suggested the One Eye remained holed up in Chadra Keep far from the battlefields. *Has the rat been drawn out? Will this be the day I exact my vengeance and set this kingdom to rights? You should have stayed hidden from me. You'll pay for that arrogance.*

"Are you certain?" he asked more timidly than he wanted.

The sergeant nodded enthusiastically. "Yes, Sire. One of my men spotted him walking the parapet. The One Eye has been drawn out."

At long last. Vengeance is mine. "Take me there now. This ends tonight."

"But Sire," the sergeant protested. A veteran, he knew too well the folly of fighting at night. Fratricide came too easily.

Badron wouldn't be swayed. "Follow your orders." Turning to his newest adjutant, he ordered, "Rouse everyone. We march in full strength. Harnin dies tonight."

The sounds of weapons and armor jostling in the night filled the tiny clearing. At long last the humiliation of being betrayed by their kingdom was coming to a satisfying conclusion. Badron's remaining loyalist, numbering in the few hundreds and combined with a Goblin remainder of less than a hundred, moved as one towards the fortress. Retribution was coming.

Smoke choked the defenders. The unexpected assault in the middle of the night took them of guard. A handful of guards were slain by the initial salvo of arrows. Several more were lightly wounded. Chaos ensued. Alarms bells rung, followed by scores of soldiers swarmed out of their barracks. Sergeants and captains bellowed orders, trying to reduce confusion and restore order. Streaks of flame rocketed over the snow-capped, wooden walls. Roofs burned.

Harnin, wrapped in a thick bearskin robe, burst from his quarters with murderous intent twisting his face. "Who's in command here?"

Soldiers ran by en route to their battle positions. The abject terror in their eyes suggested this was more than a mere harassment. The redoubt was being assaulted in force. Harnin's mind reeled. How had Badron returned with numbers without his scouts' warning? The odds of their first attack conducted on Harnin's position were minimal at best. The current steward of Delranan thought quickly. The Dae'shan's warning mocked him from the back of his mind.

If Badron's army was indeed here they'd have arrived with sufficient numbers to reduce this position to ash and kill all the defenders. Harnin had but one chance at salvaging this night before the vengeance of ten thousand soldiers crashed against the walls. His first priority was laying his hands on a weapon. A pair of arrows thudded into the ground near his feet.

Ulfdane emerged from the fog of battle. His tarnished helmet was dented. His armor burnished and worn. Sweat ran down his weathered face. Shoulders bunched from the strain of climbing the two-story walls under armor, the young lord cut a path through the ranks to greet Harnin. His sword was yet to be drawn.

"Lord Harnin, we are beset on all four sides by what I believe to be a slightly larger force. Some of the soldiers have witnessed strange, dark figures moving among the attackers," he informed Harnin between breaths. His calm demeanor failed to spread to the soldiers of the Wolfsreik reserves.

Harnin halted in midstride and wheeled on the younger Ulfdane. "I had thought only Badron had arrived."

"I can't be certain, but I believe they are Goblins," Ulfdane admitted. Strands of blond hair poked from beneath his helm.

"There haven't been Goblins in this part of the world for generations," Harnin snapped back. Still, he couldn't leave that to chance. If Goblins had returned ... "Get me a sword. We must discover the truth and repulse this assault quickly. Badron can't be far off. Winter won't halt their return."

"What of the Goblins?" Ulfdane persisted.

Harnin took the proffered sword. "Kill them all."

Half of the southern palisade was reduced to charred ruin. Flames fanned by sudden winds blowing in from the north spread quickly, threatening to engulf the entire construct. The defense struggled to keep the flames in check while fighting off successive infantry feints. A handful of bodies littered the area on both sides of the wall. Most belonged to Harnin's defenders. Only one was a Goblin warrior.

Harnin's worst fears were confirmed. Goblins had returned to the west but in what numbers remained to be seen. Should they outnumber his meager forces, all Delranan would be swept under their boots in a tide of blood and steel unlike any in modern history. Ditching his robes for armor and helmet, the one-eyed lord of Delranan made his stand. A roar broke from the nearby tree line. He braced for yet another attack. Instead of a score of fighters, Harnin looked upon massed ranks of close to a hundred.

"On me!" he roared above the fires and drew his sword.

Men charged across the open ground lest they get killed by archers seeking an easy target. They bellowed cries of rage, pent-up frustration. Murderous intent reflected in their cold eyes. Harnin felt awed by their desire to kill every single defender. Loping at the back of the pack was a score of more Goblins. *What strange deeds are these where men and Goblin fight alongside each other? Have the end times arrived at last?*

Ulfdane was unimpressed with the assault. Man or Goblin, each could be killed. "Shield wall! Form ranks!"

His voice bellowed richly across the redoubt. Drawing his sword, Ulfdane stepped to the burnt remains of the palisade. Ranks formed on either side. Shields interlocked moments before a salvo of spears slammed into the wood and lightly hammered iron. Men buckled but held. They braced for the clash of bodies, inevitable as the spring rain. Ulfdane risked a look above the shields and grew dismayed. The front ranks parted, allowing the Goblins to continue their reckless charge.

Their squat, powerful figures slammed into the shield wall, driving it back several feet. Defenders tripped and fell. Spear and sword stabbed. Blood fountained from a host of wounds. Cries of agony sang a miserable choir. Ulfdane pushed back, desperately trying to gain enough ground to use his sword. Goblins' hot breath blasted his face. Pushing with his left shoulder, he stabbed through the gap to his right and was rewarded with a howl of pain. A Goblin dropped back. Dark blood painted Ulfdane's sword. He stabbed again.

The man to his left fell, half his neck severed by a throwing axe. Hot blood washed across Ulfdane's cheek. Without a replacement, the gap in the line threatened to expand. His situation was quickly becoming untenable. Ulfdane roared and slammed his shield into a charging Goblin. Off balance, the beast left his chest exposed for

Ulfdane's sword to puncture above the heart. Grinning savagely, Ulfdane leapt forward, ripping his sword free before plunging it back through the Goblin's mouth.

The young lord of Delranan twisted his sword to pull it loose but the Goblin's dying move had been to clamp down. The sword ripped out of his hands leaving Ulfdane exposed. A black, shafted arrow stole his breath. He staggered as the pressure of the tip pierced armor and muscle. Knees threatening to give out, Ulfdane grasped the arrow shaft. A second took him in the heart, killing him instantly.

The shield wall broke and fled. Their leader's death disheartened them more than the physical presence of a Goblin host ever could. The attackers forced their way into the gap. A few stout defenders remained in place, ignorantly sacrificing their lives while their comrades tried to flee.

Harnin One Eye stood in the center of the courtyard surrounded by a handful of guards. Pride demanded he hold his position, even if that meant dying ingloriously. He watched as the defense crumbled. Some threw down their weapons, pleading for their lives. They died quickly. Others stood and fell, abandoned by their fellows. Harnin's dreams for the future Delranan bled out on the snow with what remained of his army.

Instincts screamed for him to get on his horse and flee south to another fort. The rest of his defensive line needed to be warned. The expected assault from the Murdes Mountains wouldn't matter if Badron's force rolled down the line from the north. None of that mattered. He was trapped within a burning position as his soldiers died in greater numbers.

Goblins surged through the gaps in the wall. Their swords hacked and slashed. Men screamed. Goblins died. Harnin watched an elderly man split down the middle. His blood drenched the Goblin. A young boy, no more than twenty summers, desperately tried to keep his guts from spilling out of the gaping wound across his stomach. Two Goblins ran into a squad of axe wielders who were determined not to die without reaping a terrible count. Limbs hacked off, followed by their heads. Any victory the defenders might have enjoyed washed away with the arrival of ten more Goblins. The battle raged in earnest.

And suddenly, quiet. Those few scores of defenders left standing dragged into the perimeter around Harnin. All were wounded. Panting. Thirsty and caged. Their war was finished. Goblin and Man alike ceased hostilities. They stood atop the walls, leering at the meager force. They lounged against the buildings still standing. Harnin couldn't help but feel he was being toyed with.

Shoving aside his protective ring, One Eye clutched his sword as if for the final time. Age and fate conspired against him. Not only had the Dae'shan enticed him from the security of Chadra Keep, Harnin assumed the half-creature meant for him to die. If Lord Death wished to rip him from his body there wasn't anything he could do to change that, but he'd be comfortable in the presence of many foes.

"Who leads you?" he demanded. His voice was hoarse, ragged. His heart hammered suddenly. "No. It can't be."

Murmurs rose from the defenders. They'd seen a ghost. No one expected the return of King Badron. They'd been assured of his demise in far off Rogscroft. Betrayed, they stood frozen in place as the true lord of Delranan emerged from the ranks of his ragged army. Hatred rarely took physical shape, yet Badron was consumed by it. His massive body trembled as he struggled to keep control. Fingers bled white around the handle of his bitten battle axe. Slowly, as if to emphasize the drama of the moment, he raised and pointed it at Harnin.

"Your reign is at its climax, usurper."

Harnin struggled to find the words. The Dae'shan had been correct after all. Any thought of reconciliation died on his tongue. He'd gone too far to turn back. Delranan was plunged into and endless cycle of torment, suffering from his visions of the future. Ravaged by plague and war, Harnin doubted there'd ever come a day when his kingdom returned to the glory of yesteryear. The past lay dead alongside the dreams of a fallen generation. Empires rose and fell on the whims of a select few with the tenacity to make change. Harnin was given his chance. He failed terribly.

"I was warned of your return," Harnin said. His voice lacked emotion. *It was only through my own ignorance I chose to ignore those warnings. Perhaps you've lost a step and I can slip my blade between your ribs before you kill me. Perhaps.*

Badron suffered no doubts. His rage was justice. Memories of betrayal flooded unbidden to the forefront of his mind. The overpowering desire to carve his once closest advisor to pieces propelled him forward.

"Enough banter. Come and meet your destiny, worm," Badron growled and leapt into an attack.

Harnin blocked the savage, overhand blow, barely. The unleashed power nearly drove him to his knees. Staggering back, he fended off three quick, successive blows aimed at hacking his head off. His arm numbed. Badron was too powerful. The only way Harnin could win was through trickery. Soldiers cheered, calling out to both combatants as if they were gladiators putting on a spectacle.

The king of Delranan forced Harnin back even further, until he was nearly in the ring of defenders. Much to Badron's surprise, and chagrin, the defenders collectively retreated out of the way. Clearly they intended on serving whoever survived. Buoyed by their complacency, Badron renewed his assault. Harnin continued his retreat, hoping to find the gap in Badron's attack. Fate remained fickle. Badron lunged for a vicious swing but tripped on a piece of wood from the palisade. Off balance, Harnin had his opportunity.

One Eye stabbed hard. The tip of his sword bit deeply into Badron's right hip. Blood fountained and ran down his leg. Gasps rang from the crowd. Goblins beat their swords on gnarled shields. Badron staggered back. His face locked in pain. Managing to swat away Harnin's sword, the king grimaced tightly.

"This has been long in coming, *old friend*," Harnin sneered.

He was out of breath. Age had been unkind to Harnin One Eye. Fatigue threatened to drive him to his knees. Badron was larger, stronger. Months of campaigning and fleeing across half of the northern world honed his body. The end was never in doubt.

Badron roared a woeful combination of pain and hatred. Both men collided in a tangle of flesh and steel. Elbows drove into ribs. Badron head-butted Harnin. The crack of bones and spray of blood echoed across the courtyard. Harnin's wild backhand ripped a gash across Badron's cheek as he reeled back, stunned. The larger king ducked in and tackled Harnin. Bones snapped. Axe and sword skittered across the muddied ground. Filled with intense anger, Badron punched and struck Harnin repeatedly in the face and upper chest. Broken teeth spit out. A cheekbone cracked. Badron punched harder. His fists became hammers, crushing Harnin's face to a pulp as the smaller man gradually stopped fighting. Badron attacked harder.

Months of pent-up aggression poured from his muscles. Cold breath plumed in the night. Gasps rose from several soldiers. A few recoiled. Only when Badron could no longer lift his fists did he stop. Harnin's skull was caved in, unrecognizable. The one-eye terror of Delranan was dead, murdered at the hands of the man he once called friend.

Badron rose on unsteady legs. Blood and bits of bone dripped from his torn knuckles. His hands were raw, bleeding. Several knuckles were beaten to the bone. His breathing was heavy, labored. The king of Delranan stared down on the ruined head without compassion. Betrayers got what they deserved. Slowly his hands dropped and he looked out upon those assembled. Semblances of the old king returned. He felt invigorated. Flashbacks from his early days when he'd been forced to prove himself as king peppered his vision.

Killing Harnin was but the first step in the long road of reclamation of his kingdom. Losing the Wolfsreik hurt, but his victory this night showed him he still held power. A commandeering figure by nature, the true king of Delranan came to an inescapable conclusion. He was strong. Delranan belonged to him. Ripe for the taking, he would plunder his way back to Chadra Keep and reestablish his seat of power. The quest began here. Now. He stared out into the crowds and raised his fists high. A long-awaited decision was made. All it needed was the execution.

"My first order to you all," he said, his voice gaining strength, dominating the courtyard. He turned slowly and fixed a malicious glare on Grugnak. "Kill the Goblins!"

The ensuing slaughter last well into the night and when it was ended not a Goblin remained standing.

THIRTY-TWO

A Link Breaks

Maleela cowered in her darkened cell. The world had abandoned her, leaving her prone to the victimization of her own despair. Hate crept in to fill the holes in her heart. Endless nights of misery and wasted hours reflecting on all that had gone wrong since Aurec claimed her from her chambers.

Love became a bane. Love killed her brother, though she'd argue it was his own stubbornness. She began to wonder if it had been in Aurec's plans all along. Getting rid of the heir to the throne was certainly advantageous to Rogscroft. She'd witnessed no evidence of treachery during her brief time with Aurec, however. Yet now that she'd had ample opportunity to think back she found it startling and odd. Her captors whispered, hinted when they thought she wasn't paying attention, of the fall Rogscroft. Of King Stelskor's head on a pike above the city wall. No mention was made of Aurec other than his deceitful heart that caused the downfall two major kingdoms.

Each moment strung into one successive misery. Maleela became her own worst enemy. Her thoughts clouded into miasmic hatred. The blame spread to all involved. She hated her father for never giving her the love a daughter needed. She'd never asked to be born and most certainly had no aspirations to kill her mother during childbirth. She hated her uncle for abandoning Delranan over a private vendetta. While he sailed the seas making a name, the rest of her family languished under disinterest. She hated Aurec for stealing her away in the manner he did. How many lives were lost due to the impatience of his love? She hated Anienam Keiss for concealing important information--information she felt she needed to become the queen her people deserved--from her at every turn.

Hate became her companion. She welcomed the cold embrace, breathing the darkness into the depths of her soul. Revenge became a driving factor. She needed to feel the satisfaction of taking all her rage and recessed emotion out on those who'd wronged her. She ached to feel the blood of her victims slip between her fingers as they breathed their last breath. One by one she entertained the delicious murder of all she now felt nothing but hate towards.

Maleela closed her eyes and clenched her fists. She struggled not to weep. Once, her tears would have flown freely. She was the sort who wore her heart on her sleeve shamelessly. That heart withered and died within the unbreakable darkness of her cell. Trapped and alone, she struggled to push past the obstacle of being kidnapped in a strange land. One day soon she would escape and wreak her vengeance on the north.

A sharp click followed by the sudden rush of wind blowing into the cell told her she once again had a visitor. Maleela slowly raised her head, in no mood for the paltry mind games the Dae'shan seemed intent on playing. Pale, almost absent light filtered into the cell to form an elongated rectangle on the floor. She was forced to shield her eyes from the dazzling light. Long moments stretched into minutes without any sign of her tormentors.

"Come to me or close the door. I am in no mood for games this day," she demanded with what little strength remained in her voice.

Her throat was raw. The words raspy. Muck clogged the corners of her eyes. Her nose ached from the consistent drip she'd suffered during her internment. The Dae'shan delighted in her manipulation. Of that she was certain. Only a being so foul to be assured of condemnation in the blackest of the seven hells could derive any sort of amusement from the suffering of others. Scowling, mind filled with venomous oaths she intended on delivering, Maleela gradually opened her eyes.

The gentle, almost unperceivable sound of the wind answered her demands. She caught herself holding her breath. Anticipation of what might happen had her acting like a child. She was the princess of Delranan. The sole surviving heir to throne. Any evil awaiting her demanded to be met on her terms. Slowly pulling herself to her feet, Maleela wobbled on unsteady legs. Her muscles were underused. She lacked strength, further telling of how long she'd been confined by the Dae'shan.

Grim determination filled her. Visions of murder propelled her from the cell. Her vision swam. Spots peppered between light and dark. Maleela groaned as her stomach squeezed, nearly forcing her to double over. *Cramps. I haven't eaten much lately and feel dehydrated.* None of that mattered. Her one goal was escaping this nightmare and exacting revenge on those listed in her mind.

Dirty, gnarled fingers curled around the door frame. She took her first step outside the cell. The pale light of the moon showered down around her. Without warmth, she began shivering uncontrollably. The sudden whooshing sounds echoing down a long, straight path snapped her head up. Torches flickered to life, marking the path. Instantly suspicious, the princess reflexively reached for her weapons that weren't there. Yet another measure of humbling she'd been forced to endure.

"More games," she murmured. "I am tired of games. Very well, let us add your names to my list of victims. I will break you on the strength of my will. You will be my first trophies."

Feeling her old strength gradually return, Maleela struck down the path in search of answers she knew she shouldn't get. The vagaries of life seemed intent on playing their own games, however, and she was but a pawn. She passed the first set of torches, startled with how they extinguished the moment she passed. Time forced her hand. She was being led to a darker place, perhaps freedom awaiting her at the end.

Maleela took a moment to study her surroundings. Massive thorn bushes lined the way, broken intermittently by a pair of torches. Each thorn was larger than her thumb and secreted an oily substance she subconsciously knew to be poison. The ground was uneven, rocky. Vines snaked across the way, threatening to trip her. She knew that any fall would spell her demise. The vines bore nefarious intent. She sensed it. Traps within traps. Lord Death was coming for her, of that she bore no doubt.

Shoeless, she danced in and around the vines, noticing the membrane-thin spines similar to a caterpillar. *Dead in an instant. It appears I am not meant long for this world.* Maleela carried on, doing her best to avoid the multiple levels of danger surrounding her. She stifled an unexpected yawn. Exhaustion and hunger were as much her enemies as the Dae'shan and her family. *Only I can't kill either of them. My best bet is finding shelter and drinkable water before the dawn. Otherwise….*

She let the thought fade. One step at a time. Anything else all but condemned her to a fate worse than death. Maleela prided herself on the depth of her courage and strength. She was the daughter of kings, a fact few counted among her many qualities. Those doubters would suffer for their ignorance. She was the whirlwind, set to sweep across the northern kingdoms. All shall wither and despair.

The path gradually widened into a semicircle clearing. Conical stones ringed the perimeter. Each was marred with ancient runes. Forgotten languages from long dead cultures whispered hints of what fate awaited Malweir. Maleela cared less. She'd run the gauntlet only to end up in another trap. Worse, she wasn't alone. A hooded figure stood with feet planted shoulder width apart. His head was bowed, doing little to conceal his massive form. A long sword was stabbed into the ground. A second, smaller sword was planted likewise only a few meters in front of her. Clearly she'd been led here for battle.

Maleela's heart quickened. All thoughts of revenge melted in the confines of her mind. *The world is ever against me, but I am strong. All the others forgot that. Treated me like a child. Abandoned my needs and wishes for their own selfish reasons. Today I will prove them all wrong. Today I will break this man over my knee and let his blood grease my desires. Today.*

"You're mistaken," a familiar voice responded to her thoughts. "Today is the last of your wretched life. I should have flung you from the Keep's walls after you were born."

She froze. Impossibility sent her well-laid plans spiraling down, crashing around her feet like so much glass. *That voice. It can't be. It can't.* "Father."

Badron reached up and removed his hood, revealing his time-weathered face. His eyes were hard, reminding her of flint. "You were a mistake. No more than an unfortunate reminder that men aren't as infallible as we like to believe. Have you come to meet your end?"

"How are you here?" she asked, confusion lingering, momentarily blocking her hatred. "Have the Dae'shan captured you as well?"

Badron pulled the sword from the ground. "I should have stopped with your brother. No king wants daughters. Worthless specimens unfit to hold the crown. Your brother died protecting you. It should have been you."

Tears welled. Maleela fought to keep them in. Her slight fists clenched, trembling in building rage. "His death wasn't my fault."

"Of course not. Why should you admit guilt? You murdered your mothe...."

"I DIDN'T KILL MY MOTHER!" Maleela roared at the top of her lungs and lunged forward to rip her sword from the ground. Dirt and stone trailed the tempered steel blade as she brought it around to a high guard and closed on her father.

Badron laughed in her face, daring her to proceed. She did. Growling like one of the wild beasts she'd spied in the Jungles of Brodein, Maleela charged. Badron blocked her first savagely swung blow and used her momentum to shove her further. She stumbled a few steps before stopping and turning. Her face darkened with hatred. Two decades of living like an unwanted shadow changed her core. She attacked again.

Three successive swings struck his sword. Badron grunted once, forced to take a step backwards. Her strength surprised him. He parried, desperate to fend off her frenzied assault. Finally gaining a little space between them, Badron raised his sword for the killing stroke. Maleela was quicker. She ducked under his upraised arms and slashed across his stomach. The widening line of deep red was her reward.

Badron's eyes centered. His sword dropped, clattering against the ground. Large hands fumbled to keep his guts from spilling out. Blood frothed on his lips. He cocked his head, giving her one final look of incredulity before her blade swung through his neck. His head rolled away as she collapsed. Unfamiliar emotions roiled through her mind and heart. Maleela glared at the corpse in triumph.

Any victory was short lived. Badron's body dissolved in a cloud of acrid smoke. The rocks, thorns, and torches followed, leaving her alone in a strange place. An illusion. It had all been an illusion. A haunting orange glow bathed the area. She looked up to see two of the Dae'shan materialize before her. Their robes promised the darkest future while beckoning to her. Maleela stared deep into the hypnotic allure of that darkness and felt the promise of true hope. She meant to become the tyrant queen her people deserved.

"What games do you tease me with?" she demanded.

Amar Kit'han hovered closer, allowing her to witness the horrors of his face for the very first time. When he spoke, his tone was soothing, comforting. "A necessary test. We were …unsure of your abilities."

"You've cheated me, demon," Maleela ground out through clenched teeth. "His death will be by my hands alone. I will kill my father."

Amar Kit'han grinned like a wolf from beneath his hood. At last, she'd been broken. The line snapped. Maleela belonged to him.

THIRTY-THREE

Severed Ties

The ground trembled, rippling for leagues in every direction. Birds erupted from forests of trees by the hundreds, fleeing what came next. Animals ran or burrowed for safety. The very ground struggled to crawl away from the madness working through the world. Lighting struck down from clear skies. No clouds were in sight yet the thunder and lightning was so prominent any unfortunately caught within earshot fell to their knees with blood streaming from their ears.

Wails of long tortured souls echoed on the wind. Pain and suffering trembled from every tree, rock, and bush. The world had gone mad and fifty thousand Goblin warriors with it. They howled. Clashing swords and axes on rusted shields. Boots stomped a wicked song. They sensed their hour had come. No longer would their race be forced to suffer in the cold confines deep underground. Their armies would sweep across the world, destroying Men, Elves, and Dwarves in droves. All Malweir would burn.

Thrask stood atop the small hill surveying his army. They were ragtag at best, the painful reminder of how far his kind had fallen. Abandoned by the gods, Goblins endured through sheer willpower. Reviled across Malweir by all but the worst races, they toiled under the harshest conditions, bereft of the enjoyment others took for granted. Thrask aimed to change that.

There'd been other Goblins with such aspirations. All fell into ruin, incapable of rising to the challenge. Scourd once thought to contend with the will of the Silver Mage and the dragon Ramulus. His death had faded into obscurity, now all but anonymous. The last had been Grugnak. His failed incursion into Rogscroft brought great shame to the Goblins. They washed his memory away, eager to reclaim glory. The bodies of the old would be ground underfoot. Crushed into oblivion's cold embrace. Thrask aimed to wash the stain of the Goblin's failures and build an empire on the corpses of the world.

"This will be a day long remembered by the Goblins," Kodan Bak whispered from behind the Goblin Lord.

"What of the ten thousand who foolishly followed you?" Thrask demanded. His thick chest muscles were exposed to the cold. Harsh, grey skin tinged pale blue. His bottom right tusk was broken.

Thrask was a pure warrior. The Dae'shan went to great lengths to ensure his martial understanding and command of the common tongue were developed well beyond the rank and file of his people. His malice and hatred were natural. They carried him up through the ranks. Hundreds of competitors were butchered during his rise until he alone stood at the top. Grugnak proved an able lieutenant but nothing more. Sending him west with the first wave was the logical move. Hearing of his demise removed a potential rival and paved the way for Thrask to rouse his tribe in a wave of hatred.

Savage as he may be, Thrask had no intentions of allowing his force, the strongest ever fielded by the Goblins, to be wasted on poor tactical decisions. Goblins were not pawns. Not any longer. Their anger threatened to crush the world of men but it was not yet substantial enough to ascend. The battle with the Dwarves and Elves along the riverbank proved that. He'd never seen such weapons as those filthy Dwarves deployed before. The sound of thunder still echoed in his ears. Both field pieces were destroyed before he could claim them, their barrels unsalvageable.

Thrask knew well the treachery of Dwarves. Once from the same genetic stock, Goblins became the lesser kin to a more dignified race. He aimed to change that. It was past time Dwarves were relegated to the dismal pages of forgotten memories. His mind already raced ahead to confiscating some of those terrible Dwarven weapons. Imagining what his army could do with such power blazed hotly in his eyes. First he needed to lose the yoke of Dae'shan captivity.

"Grugnak was capable enough. No one can fully account for treachery," Kodan Bak soothed, his voice a serpent nest of lies. "He played his part in this war. Will you do any less?"

Thrask wheeled on the Dae'shan, ignoring the fact he'd be incinerated well before he ever laid a claw on those foul robes. "My honor is unquestionable. Many have died for less."

"I did not seek to rouse your ire, Goblin Lord. These are troubled times. Uncertainty lies in the minds of most. Kingdoms have fallen. A new order rises. You have the potential to rise above all your predecessors. All you have to do is extend your sword and the world can be yours."

Thrask growled harshly. Spittle dripped from his lower lip as he ground his teeth. "Will you uphold your promises? I want Malweir to burn."

"Our goals align. Amar Kit'han has paved the way for your army to assume control of both Rogscroft and Delranan."

Thrask gestured towards the surrounding forest. "We already occupy the eastern portion of Rogscroft. What has your commander provided we cannot take for ourselves?"

"Perhaps you wouldn't be so smug if Thord and his army from Drimmen Delf had been arrayed against you at the Fern River instead of a mere handful. Look at the damage a hundred Dwarves caused you. How many hundreds dead and hundreds more wounded? A savage waste of fighting strength." Kodan unfolded his arms, anticipating an attack. Goblins were brutal and savage, but ultimately predictable.

Thrask balled his fists. He imagined ripping the Dae'shan to bloody shreds but knew it was next to impossible. They were the chosen servants of the dark gods, impervious to mortal harm. Only a Dae'shan or higher power was capable of killing another. Instead he snarled, "My fight is with the world of men, not you. What promises does Amar Kit'han offer that I cannot achieve on my own?"

Slightly disappointed, Kodan refolded his arms. "Simple. Your army will never reach Delranan in time to be of any value. Our enemies will have already established strong defenses and be prepared for you. Furthermore, crossing the Murdes Mountains in winter is next to impossible. Your entire army would be dead long before you ever set foot on enemy soil."

Thrask growled. "You don't offer encouragement."

"Amar Kit'han plans to…transport your entire army, all fifty thousand, behind enemy lines in the middle of Delranan. Once this is accomplished you will be able to sweep our enemies from the field and claim dominance on the ruins of that kingdom. All he asks is your loyalty when the time comes."

The Goblin Lord contemplated this. It was an unusually vague request with potential dire consequences for his army, but one he couldn't afford to waste. The Dae'shan offered to reduce weeks of foot marches, though how was beyond his level of comprehension. He focused on his army arriving in Delranan in prime fighting condition and with the element of surprise. The world would change in the span of a day.

"Very well," he answered, knowing there was no real option. "The Goblin army marches at your command."

Smoke and electricity exploded between the two, knocking the powerful Goblin backwards. When he cleared his eyes of the grit coating them Thrask stared at Amar Kit'han and a small human female. He snarled and reached for his sword.

"Not my command, Thrask," Amar Kit'han hissed. "But hers."

"Why should I take orders from one I am sworn to kill?" he countered.

Smiling harshly, Amar replied, "This is Princess Maleela, heiress to the throne of Delranan. She has but one desire: the murder of her father, the king."

"She is human," Thrask protested, taking a step forward.

Maleela, tilting her chin back defiantly, pointed an angry finger at the Goblin. "I have fought and killed better than you, mud dweller. You will obey my commands, help me achieve vengeance, and for that I will not set my conquered armies against you."

Thrask admired her audacity, all the while planning her death. "Why should I trust a Human? You have the stench of treachery about you."

"I don't require your trust, only your swords. Disobey me and I'll have the Dae'shan reduce your army to ashes where they stand." Maleela, at barely five feet tall, looked the Goblin in his cold, dark eyes. There was no give in her. Not any longer. She became as tempered as the blade at her hip.

"There will be no alliance between Goblin and Man," Thrask warned. "Your kind has betrayed mine far too many times."

Maleela cocked her head slightly, unsure of what he meant. It mattered not. Whatever deviations her father led them through were his issues to deal with, not hers. She had but one goal: destroy Badron and the Wolfsreik. The Goblins could fend for themselves once they assisted accomplishing her goal.

"I seek no allegiance, *Goblin*," she seethed, her words careful, measured. "I want your cooperation, nothing more. Once I've achieved my aims you can do whatever your black heart desires. I care not."

Recognizing strength, as well as the unfiltered opportunity to slaughter hundreds if not thousands of men, Thrask tipped his head in acquiescence. "It shall be so, *your highness*."

Amar Kit'han watched the scene play out with mild interest. His creation was much stronger than Badron or Harnin ever proved to be. She was the anvil on which a new empire would be hammered, an empire of pure darkness once the dark gods returned to assume their rule. With her as an instrument, the dark gods would slay all who opposed them. Malweir would be theirs once again. It began here in eastern Rogscroft.

"We await you, Dae'shan," Maleela said, turning to Amar. "Open the portal."

"Magic?" Thrask asked suspiciously.

Amar ignored the Goblin. Instead he slid down the hill and went to the largest open area in the vicinity. Ranks of Goblins recoiled, ever eager to be away from the nightmare the Dae'shan represented. Some evils went beyond the scope of mortal comprehension. Amar Kit'han ignored them all. Fools and murderers, the lot. Each Goblin was as insignificant as the tide in so far as he was concerned.

He raised his arms shoulder level, hands extended beyond the cuffs of his robes. Tendrils of electricity bounced across his fingertips. All noise ceased suddenly, leaving the gathered army trapped in a void between worlds. Several Goblins dropped to their knees. Blood streamed from eyes and ears as the Dae'shan built waves of magic within. What he attempted hadn't been done in thousands of years. If he was successful in opening the ways between worlds, there was no promise all Thrask's Goblins would survive the journey. Dark, powerful creatures lurked in the shadow paths, eager to snatch the unsuspecting traveler.

A hole opened in the air. A rent, tearing the fabric of reality. Blackness filled the rent. Gone were the trees and snow-covered fields. Screams rippled through, suggesting violence and despair in equal measure. Such sounds shouldn't be heard by mortals, of that Maleela was certain. Only the strength imbued, without her knowledge, by the Dae'shan allowed her to remain largely unaffected.

Growing larger with each passing moment, the rent quickly became wide enough to funnel ten abreast through. Amar Kit'han gradually lowered his arms. Flashes of red and green power tainted the rent's edges. The surrounding ground was scored, deadened. The Dae'shan returned to his previous position beside Maleela and bowed reverently.

"It is done. Move your army through."

"What awaits us on the opposite side?" Thrask asked. His mistrust continued to rise.

"Delranan."

"This had better not be a trap," the Goblin Lord replied and loped down the hill.

If it is you will never know. Fools. Had you any inkling you were no more than puppets you wouldn't be so eager to march into slaughter. The dark gods have no need of your filth any more than the supplication of men. You will all die upon the whims of your betters.

"Will you not join him?" Amar asked.

Maleela shot him a violent glare. "And risk death at the onset of my campaign? What fool do you take me for, *demon*? Thrask will lead his army into Delranan. Let them deal with whatever force awaits them. I will follow when I deem it wise."

The Dae'shan contemplated telling her the portal led to the largely abandoned southern plains where no major military units were stationed. The way between worlds was relatively harmless. His magic ensured that. So long as Maleela kept her gaze focused on the end point she would come to no harm. *She's stronger than I originally believed. This one will become a great weapon for me to use against her kind.* Instead he remained silent, allowing her the illusion of controlling her own destiny.

Orders barked. Whip masters lashed their soldiers, stirring the Goblin army into action. Oaths and curses snarled back at their overseers, but the mighty war machine eventually formed ranks. Eyes white with stark fear never experienced, the Goblins waited for Thrask to assume his rightful place at the head of their ranks. His tusks gleamed wildly in the witch-light. Sword raised above his bullish head, the Goblin Lord roared at the top of his lungs and marched into the blackness. One by one the ranks followed.

Amar Kit'han grinned savagely from the security of his cowl. All his long centuries of planning were finally drawing to their end. There could be but one conclusion in so far as he was concerned: the total destruction of every race on Malweir. The dark gods would return. All life would wither and die while he and his brothers stood by enjoying the fruits of their labors. *Too bad Kodan Bak has betrayed me. His death will be most satisfying.*

THIRTY-FOUR

A Mighty Thunder Breaks

The snow-capped peaks of the Murdes Mountains struck high into the sky, piercing the fabric between night and day like angry teeth from an imagined nightmare. Wild winds howled between the peaks, echoing ages-old frustration. The mountains grew larger over time, rather than wither away like the rest of the world. Here Malweir remained wild, untamed. Life was rare among the ancient stone. Yet what little managed to find purchase thrived.

Long ago, when memory turned to legend, the tribes of the Pell Darga and Giants fled their ancestral homes and made their way deep into the mountains. The Pell, ever diminutive and cunning, discovered the forgotten crevices and caves, making them a home ever hidden from the rest of Malweir. The Giants did likewise. With no place to fit in, their leaders turned their backs on the rise of humanity and fled to the mountains in search of peace of mind.

Venheim became their greatest secret. Lost amidst the jagged peaks of the southern half of the Murdes Mountains, the greatest smiths in Giant lore crafted intricate tools, weapons, and statues coveted the world over. None but their own knew the hidden paths to Venheim and soon the forges became myth. Hidden against the depredations of the world, the Giants enjoyed the freedoms few experienced. No visitors sullied their smiths for centuries. Not since the time of the Mage Wars.

Once, so long ago there was no recording of it, the Dae'shan and Giants formed a simplistic union. Allies, they roamed the world in search of balance. That balance shifted unsubtly when Amar Kit'han betrayed the gods of light and all sentient life on Malweir to obtain his own twisted enlightenment. The enmity between Giants and Dae'shan grew stronger in the intervening years, until only apathy remained. Joden studied the old texts thoroughly during his tenure in Venheim, growing increasingly more interested after Anienam Keiss visited.

The Giant forge master felt change riding the winds. Darkness was brewing in the west. He felt that familiar ache in his bones. A warning. All Malweir stood in jeopardy and only a handful of hapless heroes formed a wall between good and evil. That worried Joden. Groge was a talented apprentice, nearly ready to accept the responsibility of his own forge, but he lacked the experience to deal with such a threat as the treacherous Dae'shan.

Joden hardly looked up as the air shimmered within his stone house. Colors bloomed and faded, revealing the fragile form of a man in gossamer robes. The Giant blinked, slowly understanding who stood in his home. He whistled quietly. "There are many wonders in this world, but to have one of your kind within these walls goes beyond them all."

Artiss Gran unfolded his arms, smoke lifting off the fabric. "Circumstances have kept me secluded in Trennaron of late. I come bearing ill tidings that cannot wait any longer."

Joden's thick brow rose. "Ill tidings concerning my apprentice?"

"Concerning all," Artiss replied.

Joden nodded understanding. "When last I checked, the Dae'shan had become enemies of the light. How is it you resist that pull so claiming your brothers? Is this some poorly devised scheme to ensnare my people at last?"

"I come only with good intentions, forge master," Artiss said. "The world stands on the edge. The coming conflict will engulf all life on Malweir, whether you choose to ignore it and remained huddled in this mountain refuge. I come not as the perversion Amar Kit'han turned my brothers into but as the Dae'shan the way the gods intended. I am the last caretaker of the light in all Malweir."

The Giant idly stroked his iron-like chin. "A weighty title to claim. One many better would choose, wisely so, to ignore. These are not proper times to announce allegiances to the old ways. You would be Artiss Gran. I've been expecting you."

Artiss recoiled slightly, the shock registering for a split second only. "I did not think to come announced to the vaunted halls of mighty Venheim."

"Be that as it may, I had inklings that one of you would come to sway my clan," Joden answered. A hint of anger tainted his words. The old vows were straining, struggling to remain in place. "What would a Dae'shan, a true servant of the light, have need with the Giants? You must know we long ago eschewed all ties with the lower world."

"Precisely my reasons for invading your privacy," Artiss said. He dared to drift closer, but still far enough out of range to flee should Joden become enraged. "This self-imposed exile is quickly crashing to an end. Nothing you have come to love will remain once the dust from this new peril settles."

"Do not come into my home seeking to cower me with veiled threats," the Giant interrupted. He balled a massive fist.

Artiss brushed the hostility off and continued, "My errant brothers seek to unleash the dark gods. As we speak their armies are converging on the final nexus."

It was Joden's turn to be surprised. "I was under the impression that all three of the nexuses were destroyed."

"A lie Amar Kit'han went to great lengths to perpetuate through the ages but one now exposed. Two have been permanently destroyed yet the third remains active. The hour approaches when the way between dimensions thins. The dark gods will be at their strongest. Amar Kit'han knows this. He has taken every precaution to ensure success this final time. I won't insult you by telling you what will happen should he succeed."

"Why then have you come? And to me precisely?" Joden asked, suspicion now edging in.

The fabled judgment of the Giants. Perhaps we are not so doomed after all. How could I have told Bahr I don't believe he will succeed? That he would perish anonymously as the armies of darkness swept over the lands? More needed to be done. Artiss risked almost certain death by leaving Trennaron. There was no going back. Only one in Malweir capable of maintaining stewardship of the ancient temple. He just didn't know it yet.

When he spoke it was slow, measured. "You trained young Groge for the past few decades. His is a very likeable young man, but that youthful inexperience will turn against him when the darkness rises. Groge has the Blud Hamr in his possession though I don't know if his heart is strong enough to withstand the eldritch energies pulsing through it."

"Have I sent him to his doom?" Joden asked.

"That remains to be seen. My brothers continue to strengthen their position. An army of fifty thousand Goblins has been transported to Delranan in the attempts at preventing Groge and the armies of King Aurec from reaching the nexus in time."

Joden balked. "Fifty thousand? Their filth has not enjoyed such numbers in my lifetime. Do any of these heroes understand what they march towards?"

Artiss shook his head, lamenting the inescapable losses fast approaching. "There is still hope. Once I leave Venheim I will make for the camp of the young king of Rogscroft. He leads the largest allied army in the north. The only field force capable of halting the Goblin aggression."

"But?" Joden asked, noticing the slight hesitation at the end of the statement.

"But it is not enough. They are marching into a trap. Once they cross the Murdes Mountains they will be trapped between the mountains and the Goblins. I can't imagine it taking too long before they are destroyed."

Joden winced. "How many swords does this King Aurec command?"

"Perhaps twenty thousand, but it is a combined army of several kingdoms, not the least of which are the Pell Darga. A much smaller army of Dwarves, aided by the Aeldruin, march out from Drimmen Delf in support. Their cannons and gunpowder weapons will give Aurec the tactical advantage needed to break the enemy lines."

"You fear they won't arrive in time to be of any good," Joden concluded.

"Precisely. My list of options, and allies, grows thin. Desperation moves me now. I am no longer my own being," Artiss ended.

He'd never been one for persuasion. Amar and Kodan Bak excelled at getting others to do their bidding with a simple wave of the hand or the proper string of words. Artiss was more of a thinker. An inventor. His aspirations in his former life seldom included changing opinions or minds. Those days a bitter, distant memory, he pledged his life towards the preservation of all life, no matter how minor or devious. His was the only counter to the ill his brothers intended. If he failed to enlist the Giants…Artiss let the thought drop. There was little point in dwelling on the "could" and the "would" of the future.

Nodding, the forge master added, "So we come to the crux of your story. You wish to enlist the Giants into this war."

"I wish there were another option. One that didn't involve fighting at all," Artiss admitted. "Violence dominates too much of this world. It is past time peace returned."

"Agreed. The very reason we left the lowlands. Convincing Blekling and the others to return to our warring past will be no easy feat. Should you manage, what can we expect? It has been over a thousand years since we last had dealing with Men or Elves."

Artiss spread his arms in a futile gesture, suggesting for the first time he lacked the knowledge of what approached them. *Could I deal with bringing the Giants back into the holocaust of combat? Has their blood thinned enough to leave them vulnerable after all this time? Will they abandon this life of peace and set across the face of Malweir, intent on conquering all lands deemed unworthy in their eyes?* He shook his head. Too many unanswerable questions.

"I make no promises, forge master," he said slowly. "All I can offer is my total assistance in stopping my brothers. Will this be enough for you to take to your council of elders?"

"Me?" Joden was genuinely surprised. "Why should I speak with your voice, Dae'shan? You come seeking our aid. I am content with living my life here, in my forge above the clouds. Malweir has many merits, though I wish no longer to partake in them. My time in the lowlands has come to an end. This is a new age. One for the recklessness of youth, not the overbearing indulgence of age."

Artiss paused, half expecting such a reply. "Should Groge fall without completing his task there will be no other to take his place. It was pure folly to only send one of your kind on such an important task. Will you risk the fate of all life, including your own, on a whim of chance? You and I both know Blekling will not bother with me. I am Dae'shan and he knows us only as enemies. There will be no fair judgment should I step before them."

"Indeed," Joden nodded. "Blekling suffers from brashness. He has potential but remains locked in rigid, antiquated ways of thinking. Younger than most of us, he ignores progressivism and hides behind ancient edicts. His intolerance of outlanders is rivaled only by his supporters. Perhaps it is time to have my voice heard again."

"Joden, will you help me?" Artiss pleaded.

The forge master leaned back in his stone chair and gazed out the westerly window where he watched every sunset for the past hundred and thirty-seven years. He'd grown complacent in his old age. There was a time when he'd have taken up the axe and charged into enemy ranks without second thought. Age made him brittle. He valued life much more than when he was young. A trapping to be sure. Those who lived the longest always seemed to squeeze out their last few years in the desperate hopes of staying alive. He frowned. Leaving Venheim would be his demise, but he could still do his best to convince the others to abandon their seclusion and once again become a part of the living world. The least he could do was try.

"Very well, Artiss Gran of the true Dae'shan. I will bear your message to the council though I will make no promise of their decision," he said at last.

"I can ask for no more. I shall await their decision here if it pleases you."

"I think that best." Joden rose, collected his walking stick, easily twice as tall as Artiss, and headed towards the door while whistling an old lullaby. Times were changing. He felt invigorated to be part of the coming future.

"Joden, I don't suppose it necessary to implore time is of the essence?" Artiss questioned.

The forge master rumbled a barking laugh and exited his house.

For one as ancient as Artiss Gran, he found a decided lack of patience waiting in Joden's home. Meditative exercises failed. Floating back and forth across the smooth stone floor did little to ease the numbing fear growing in the corners of his mind. He wished he might know the workings of the Giant council, but they were the most secretive of all races. Discerning what Blekling and the others thought was an exercise in futility.

The Dae'shan stared out at the massive stone cathedral filling the end of the plateau. Most Giants retained faith in the old gods but a new, disturbing, trend was gaining popularity among the newer generations. The concept of a singular god performing all the functions all the others did was mind-boggling. How any one such being, even a god, could manage was well beyond the limits of Artiss' reasoning.

Still, there was no denying that the gods were the largest source of turmoil in Malweir. Strict adherence to the old ways left the world plunged in a never ending cycle of violence. Perhaps it was better having a singular deity. It would certainly alleviate tension between sects and races though Artiss ultimately decided new reasons for war would be invented and the cycle would continue.

The church itself was wholly impressive. He marveled at the smooth façade and stained glass windows that, when caught just right, reflected sunlight in a myriad of colors. The Giants had taken a relatively inhospitable part of Malweir and turned it into a home. Few others could lay claim to such. Artiss exhaled, mind wandering down forgotten paths. His time was steadily drawing to its conclusion and that frightened him.

Thousands of years on Malweir, mostly squandered by the illusion of immortality, were all behind him now. Life took on new meaning. He'd meant to become something more than the ordinary man born in a backwater village in southern Antheneon. Turning to the Dae'shan had been intensely personal but never in question. For a while he mattered. His life dedicated to the preservation of all others no matter how small or insignificant. That was before the taint crept into the souls of the rest. Artiss broke ties with Amar Kit'han and fled to the sanctity of Trennaron, forever to remain until the final battle between the gods.

No fool, he knew his death rode the morning winds, howling down from the mountaintops to whisk his withered corpse away to his final rest. A well-deserved rest, to be sure. Artiss knew he was ready to die. It was the act of doing so that frightened him. The thunder of heavy footsteps broke his train of thought, dropping him back in the middle of Venheim. He turned in time to see Joden reenter. The sour look on the Giant's face told him enough.

"They wish to speak directly to you."

Artiss followed him to the council hall.

Once inside, he was surrounded by seven Giants, not counting the forge master. They towered over his six-foot frame, diminishing his power by sheer size. Artiss folded his hands in front of him and took in the near dismal sights of the hall. Cross beams ran across the vaulted ceiling like so many spider webs on the morning dew. Torches blazed from all four corners, offering just enough light for business to be conducted. The Giants took seats behind the singularly largest stone table Artiss had ever witnessed. Old and worn, the granite top was smoothed with time.

The Giants were equally impressive. Artiss stared back, noticing their mild and poorly disguised discomfort. He held the upper hand. Everyone in the hall knew so. It was no difficult task to incinerate them all, yet Artiss appeared humbled, reserved before them. It was his one chance at getting them to agree to his plans. He settled his gaze on the young Blekling and waited to be addressed.

The wait was mercifully short.

"Your kind is a stain on Malweir. The painful reminder of what can happen when one places himself above the will of the gods. You are not welcome in Venheim,

Dae'shan," Blekling ground out. "The only reason you stand before us is our respect for the venerable Joden. His voice still carries favor among many on this council. Speak quickly and plainly. Why have you come to the forge of Giants?"

Artiss rose to eye level with the black-haired Giant. Gasps rippled through those assembled. More than one hand reached for a weapon that wasn't there. Artiss ignored them, his eyes fixed on the current Giant leader. "The time of the final convergence is upon us. The time when the dark gods will attempt to reenter our world for the last time. Some months ago you dispatched Groge with a handful of men to claim the Blud Hamr. I do not believe he can succeed without the rest of you at his side."

A scoff.

"Nonsense! He is a Giant of Venheim, even if a mere apprentice. What other being on Malweir is capable of succeeding if not he?"

Artiss frowned. He'd expected resistance. Giants were notoriously stubborn but to deny victory out of sheer obstinacy was madness. "Even the mighty fall or have you forgotten the horrors of the Mage Wars? I come not to you with petty threats while attempting to rope you into doing my bidding. I am not my brothers. They fell from the light long ago. Disgraced into the shadows. What stands before you is the last, true Dae'shan as we were meant to be."

He spun slowly to encompass all their gazes.

"I humbly plead to each of you. Malweir needs your help. If the Giants of Venheim do not march on the ruins of Arlevon Gale I fear the dark gods will succeed. None will be safe. Not even you, hidden amongst the mountaintops. Do not think they have forgotten the injuries suffered by your ancestors' hands. The dark gods will come for the Giants and eradicate you from the face of the world, or worse. Are you willing to take that chance?"

Blekling leaned forward. "We are not the ones to be cowed into action, *Dae'shan*. Our ways may have abandoned the rest of the world but it was through our own choosing.

Not yours. What you see was created by our hands in our fashion. What need have we of the lowland races? Venheim can withstand the dark gods. We have done so before."

"Not like this you haven't. If the rest of the Dae'shan succeed, this world will become a nightmare the likes of which the most-skilled scholar can't imagine. You'll be chained and beaten into submission. If you're fortunate. Carpets of bones will fill the plains. None will be spared."

"He repeats himself too readily," another Giant griped.

"We waste our time. Banish him from Venheim, Blekling."

Frustrated, Artiss raised his skeletal hands and bolts of white-gold power flared across the ceiling. "Enough! This is not a question of who wants to help but who will. I have explained the consequences of inaction. You've hidden away from the rest of the world long enough. Now is the hour in which the Giants need to return and claim what is rightfully yours! Or will you entrust the fate of the entire world to the hands of a singular apprentice? The decision is yours. I obviously cannot force your hand. Yea or nay, choose now for the hour is almost expired."

Darkness crept back across the ceiling. Artiss lowered his arms. He'd spoken his piece, hopefully driving a wedge in the popular opinion. Blekling had great strength if only he chose to use it. Artiss listened as the Giants argued among themselves in their primitive, guttural language. Heated words burst from a few. Rampant gestures towards Joden and Artiss. More than one angry finger pointed his way. It didn't matter. Not when the balance of all life was in the way.

After what felt like hours the Giants ended their deliberations. One by one they fell silent and turned their granite-like gazes on the hovering Dae'shan. Artiss Gran had never felt so small. He heard Joden cough gently from behind, a subtle reminder that he was not alone. Not yet at any rate.

Blekling studied him for a moment, those large, hard eyes desperately searching for any sign of deception. Disdain clear upon his face, he spoke, "This council has decided. It is true, we have abandoned Malweir in favor of a simplistic lifestyle without envy or greed. We live our lives without suffering the indignities of many other races. But as you claim, the end of the cycle draws nigh. We will not, cannot, let it pass without making an effort to affect the outcome. You have your wish, Artiss Gran. The Giants of Venheim will once again go to war."

THIRTY-FIVE

The Black Guard

Boen roared as he slashed diagonally down across the soldier's chest, ripping him open from neck to navel. A second soldier ducked in, hoping to deal the killing blow while the big Gaimosian was distracted. He failed. Utilizing lightning quick reflexes only a lifetime of combat could hone, Boen drove his elbow into the exposed soldier's face. He was rewarded by the crisp snap and crunch of bones breaking. The soldier reeled away in pain, making it but a few steps before Boen finished the job.

Steam rose from the bodies littering the side of the trail. What was once pristine snow melted under the stain of crimson blood. It wouldn't be long before vultures and wolves caught the scent of death. Boen wiped his blade on the nearest corpse and rose, stretching his back in the process. His chest burned. Breaths came in gasps. Each new engagement left him missing another piece of who he used to be. Boen scowled.

"That's all them," Nothol announced, walking out of the small copse of white birch. "Nasty bastards skulking in the trees would have done you in with their crossbows."

Boen spit. "Assassins. The Black Guard."

"I didn't think Harnin controlled any of those units," Nothol questioned. The more he learned upon their return to Delranan the more his mood soured. This was clearly not the kingdom they had left all those months ago. He began to think returning might have been a serious miscalculation of his skills.

Boen gestured to the body at his feet. "This one has the right tools. The attitude. Only an assassin would be foolish enough to keep attacking after he realized what I am."

"We've got to get back to the others. Bahr needs to know this," Nothol said hurriedly. He instinctively scanned the surrounding area for other half-hidden bodies lying in wait in the snow. The Black Guard were the nastiest of the Wolfsreik. Cold-blooded killers who smile as they slide a blade between your ribs. He'd seen their work once before and never wanted too again. Fear was a powerful motivator.

"Bring up the horses. I'll make sure these are all dead." Boen stalked off among the dozen corpses littering the immediate area. The tip of his sword sank with wet, sucking sounds into each body as he walked.

Bahr picked his head up at the sound of approaching riders. The sounds were heavy yet light enough to only be a few. He reached for the blackened crossbow on the wagon driver's bench. Out of the corner of his eye he caught Rekka's brown clad figure slipping behind trees, sword drawn. A bird sprinted from a nearby pine, breaking the building tension. Bahr's eyes tirelessly searched the edge of his line of sight for confirmation of the riders. For the last two days they'd been forced to pick up speed, desperately trying to avoid the increased patrols. Clearly their enemy was searching for them. Urgency drove them on. They'd suffered enough delays since returning to Delranan they couldn't afford many more. Anienam's insistence that time was nearly up forced Bahr to avoid the Wolfsreik rather than engage.

He relaxed when Rekka slipped back into view and waved her gloved hand. It was Boen and Nothol returning from their scouting mission. Bahr spied the dried blood on the Gaimosian's armor as he rode into view. He frowned. *So much for avoiding detection.*

"Did any escape?" he asked after climbing down from the wagon to greet them.

Nothol's face darkened.

Boen, glowering, replied, "One. We didn't find his tracks until after we mounted up."

"It won't be long before that one returns with a platoon at least," Bahr cursed. "We need to move."

"It gets worse," Nothol added without hesitation. "These were no ordinary scouts. They were Black Guard. We're being hunted by assassins."

Bahr said. "We can't hope to fight them off, not if they've brought sufficient strength."

Boen scoffed. "They died easily enough."

"Only because they underestimated you. That lone survivor will know what you are now, Boen. When he returns it will be with enough to kill us all, Groge included." Urgency gilded Bahr's voice. If he still had the *Dragon's Bane* they'd be able to outrun the Black Guard. But on land…thinking of being caught soured his stomach.

"I will stay behind. Draw them off your trail," the Gaimosian suggested.

Bahr was tempted to allow him but Anienam's previous warning blared in his mind. They were all needed at the final battle if Malweir had any chance of salvation. There could be no deviation and, having already suffered two losses, were at a disadvantage. Losing Ionascu didn't bother the old Sea Wolf much, but the disappearance of his niece haunted his nights. Not knowing her fate tormented him to the point he was sorely tempted to abandon the quest. Only his vow kept him on course.

"No," he replied. "The wizard says we're all needed at the end. That means you, Boen. We still have a few hours, perhaps a day, before whoever commands can organize a full war party."

"To what end? There are only so many places we can run to and our tracks will be found easily," Boen countered. "We should stand and fight."

Bahr shook his head. "There is no time. We need to ride, now. Delranan is a vast kingdom with plenty of areas to get lost in. As long as we keep pushing east we should reach the ruins of Arlevon Gale before our enemy."

What then? Don't be so foolish as to think our foes aren't prepared for our arrival. Not if Artiss Gran was correct. We're in for one nasty fight. A fight I don't think many of us are going to walk away from. Bahr blinked his frustration away. *Don't get carried away, old man. We've still got many leagues to cross, an army to avoid, and who knows how many other trials before reaching our final destination. Let the future deal with itself when it arrives.*

Clearly disgruntled, Boen nodded. "Very well, but we need to leave now. There is no time and I don't trust the path ahead to be clear."

"We could be riding into a trap," Nothol added.

"A chance we must take," Bahr said. "Bring in the others. We make for the ruins."

"It's no use. We're cut off," Rekka announced after returning to the wagon. Slightly out of breath, her brown skin coated in a fine sheen of sweat, she bore a worried look.

"How many?" Bahr asked, quicker than he intended.

"Scores. Perhaps a hundred. Captain, we're going to have to fight."

Damnation. So close. Only to have the Black Guard catch us. I should never have returned here. Delranan doesn't need me and I don't need this. "How much time do we have?"

"An hour, maybe less."

"It'll be dark by then," Dorl chimed.

His mood darkened at the prospect of having to claw through yet another battle. Killing turned his stomach. He lacked the necessary conviction required to do his work properly and it was starting to show. The others gradually backed away as he battled his demons. There was only so much a man could take before breaking or changing into something altogether different.

Bahr caught his worried look and decided there was no time for complacency. Dorl Theed could wait. *Or die in the process.* "Making it easier for us to defend. They have to look harder and I'll wager Rekka, Ironfoot, and Boen will take a goodly number out long before they get within range of Groge and the wizard. I want the wagon ready to move.

Keep the horses with Skuld and Anienam. The rest of you break off into teams and form a defensive perimeter. This is going to get ugly."

They moved the wagon under cover of large pine boughs. A small hill blocked the southern approach with a field of boulders that peppered the landscape to the east. Bahr felt the position offered the best, most realistic chance of defense without exposing them needlessly to enemy scouts. Covering their tracks as best they could, the group settled into the mindset that their night was about to get interesting.

Each group was in position just before the sun dropped over the edge of the world. Lost in half light and shadow, they waited. Boen and Ironfoot took the eastern road, fully expecting the main attack to come from ahead rather than behind. Harnin's forces were largely incompetent but these were the Black Guard. The very best, and worst, the Wolfsreik had to offer. Nothol and Dorl headed west, despite Dorl's hesitations. Nothol feared his friend was going to get them both killed, but it was a risk he had no alternative to taking.

Groge took the northern flank. His inexperience was enough to seal off that sector of the perimeter. Bahr didn't expect more than a feint from the north or south. Even should the enemy come in force down from the north they would run headlong into a Giant. Not even the Black Guard had been tested against such. Bahr slipped to the south, allowing Rekka free range further out. At his age and physical impediments he'd only be in her way. She was young yet and agile enough to kill a dozen men on her own.

An owl hooted from the distant tree line. The call was deep and raw as it floated across the snows. Bahr idly thumbed the keen edge of his blade lightly enough not to get cut. He hated waiting for a fight. The prospect that the Black Guard would bypass them was minimal, though he couldn't be certain they weren't being toyed with. Badron's assassin corps was shifty enough to string the group along all the way to Arlevon Gale without forcing a decisive engagement. No, he decided. His gut told him the enemy was crawling through the undergrowth even now, coming to kill them all and recover the hammer for Harnin One Eye.

A twig snapped. Bahr slowly raised his eyes in the direction of the noise. The owl had stopped hooting somewhere in between. The old man's heart quickened. *This is it. Come and show yourselves to my blade, murderers. Let's end this*. Light wind blew loose snow softly around his ankle, obscuring any sounds in the process. Bahr tensed. The first black-clad assassin stalked into the perimeter, intent on making it to the wagon. Bahr paused, trying to discern their goal. His lips pursed when he realized the assassins were going to try to kill the wizard, thus cripple the quest immeasurably. Gripping his sword tighter, he readied to push off the tree to attack.

He was too late. Rekka appeared out of the night, sword swinging harshly across the back of the assassin's neck, severing his spinal column. The Black Guard collapsed with barely a gurgle before Rekka stabbed into his unarmored heart. Jerking the sword clear, she gave Bahr a crisp nod before returning to the night. Message understood, the Sea Wolf carefully made his way back to the wagon. The southern approach was secure better without him getting in the way.

Ironfoot clenched and unclenched his meaty fists a hundred times since taking up position among a group of small boulders. His axe resting within reach against a boulder, the Dwarf used his superb night vision to continually scan his area. Others in the group were growing tired of fighting. Tired of constantly being hounded by one villain or another. He didn't mind. It was a far cry from the relative boredom of living in Drimmen Delf. At least here he got to fill his thirst for action.

His axes already had more nicks and dulled edges than ever in his long career, save perhaps the civil war against the dark Dwarf clans. His muscles ached from exertion. His mind sharpened with each new engagement as the enemy continued to show new facets. Ironfoot knew he was starting to enjoy their running battle with Harnin's forces. It gave him something to do during the seemingly endless leagues of open roads he'd been forced to travel since joining the quest at Bode Hill.

Night vision second only to Groge, Ironfoot immediately picked out the handful of men slinking towards the wagon. He struggled not to grin as his hand grasped his axe. Glancing right, he spotted Boen with his back pressed against a tree. The Gaimosian wasn't moving. Only the faint glow of his eyes could be seen roving. The Dwarf couldn't risk alerting Boen, however, without raising the alarm for the assassins. A slight scrape announced the axe coming free of the boulder.

Ironfoot crouched, shifting his center of gravity to leap forward. His last true engagement was against the river men. The Black Guard were professionals, bereft of the clumsy incompetence of the murdering thieves. The Dwarf knew he was about to be tested. He allowed a savage grin to spread across his weathered face. Ironfoot hefted his axe and attacked.

The assassin had time to swing his head in the direction Lord Death approached before dark and cold claimed him. Headless, the body flopped onto the snow while three others reeled back in surprise. Ironfoot bellowed an ancient Dwarven battle cry and leapt into the middle. His axe wove intricate patterns. Cutting. Hacking. An arm fell. Blood sprayed. Entrails spilled out of torn-open bellies. The Dwarf pressed his assault until all the assassins lay dead in a circle. Breathing hard, he chanced a look to Boen. The Gaimosian had his own struggles.

Towering over the field, Groge narrowed his eyes to slits as cold winds caressed his face and hands. Such simple gifts reminded him of Venheim. Thoughts of home left him melancholic. He enjoyed seeing different kingdoms, visiting strange and unusual places, but the young apprentice began to think it was past time to head home. He belonged in the heat of the forges, not striding aimlessly across endless fields of snow.

Unfamiliar sounds reached his ears, breaking the pull of distant memory. The hammer strapped across his back vibrated slightly, suggesting immense reserves of power. Ancient memories flooded into the young Giant through the awesome power of the Blud Hamr. He witnessed long forgotten battles play out. Armies of his kin marching to war. Visions of past and future collided to distort his reality. The one constant was the whispering of the weapon. It soothed him. Calmed his nerves and warned of battle.

Groge looked down to see dark figures heading towards the wagon. Rage took him. The Giant attacked. His boot caught the nearest assassin in the chest and propelled him through the air. Tulwar in hand, Groge waded into the others. Each swing bore enough force to shatter an oak to kindling. These killers had come for his friends. He refused to allow them. Stunned at the sight of a being many thought imaginary, the Black Guard froze long enough for Groge to slaughter them all.

Their swords barely nicked his leathery skin. Not a one drew blood, even as he brought his tulwar down on the last assassin's head. Bones snapped with sickening crunches. Two managed to escape, already the rearguard. Their tales would reverberate across Delranan within days, though few would give them credence. Groge continued to hammer away at the dead until they became bloody smears. Wicked laughter filled his ears.

"I hate this."

Anienam suppressed the grin he felt. "Be patient, young Skuld. I'd have thought you would have had your desires for action sated by now."

Skuld offered a confused look. The wizard was normally off center, but since losing his vision he rambled ceaselessly about matters few understood. "I've earned the right to hold my own, Anienam. Sitting here guarding the wagon should be another's job."

"Not to mention babysitting a blind, old man? Who else is going to do it? The others are warriors, whether you choose to accept that or not. They are trying to fight off our enemies before they can reach the wagon. Don't be so quick to rush into battle without knowing all the facts first."

"I'm not a child anymore," Skuld protested. "I've been through just as much as the rest. What more do I have to do to prove my worth to Bahr?"

"You can start by keeping your voice down," Bahr's voice called from the surrounding darkness. He stalked out of the night to stand beside the wagon. "The Black Guard have found us. Rekka's already killed one and I'm sure there's been movement on the other approaches."

Dorl and Nothol were the first to return. They were just in time. A score of assassins burst from the surrounding trees, swords bared. Bahr rushed to meet them before the sell swords had the chance to react. Steel clashed as the old man struggled to hold his group. Assassins streaked by to attack the wagon. Skuld stabbed one in the eye before his sword was jerked out of his grasp. A pair of assassins crawled up, knocking him over the head. The boy was in the way. It was the old man they wanted.

Anienam remained still, his mouth innocently moving as words unspoken for generations flew past. His right hand began to glow deep vermillion. Neither assassin noticed. They reached down for him. Anienam opened his blind eyes, the protective wrapping long since removed, and touched each assassin with the tip of his index finger. Each man exploded in a cloud of ash. Exhausted, the wizard slumped back onto the driver's bench.

Their wits recovered, the sell swords charged into Bahr's helpless battle. An assassin was down, holding the stump of his right wrist, but the others circled Bahr, toying with him. Nothol blindsided the nearest assassin, knocking him away and exposing the man to his left in the process. Using forward momentum, Nothol skewered the assassin through the ribs. A gargled scream rippled across the battlefield as that man dropped.

Dorl struck from Bahr's right. With the odds slightly less in their favor, most of the assassins recoiled to adjust tactics. Bright Mage light flooded the area. The smell of burnt flesh choked the air. Forced to parry an overhand blow, Dorl staggered back a step. A blade sliced across his ribs, grating the armor in a shower of sparks. He grunted and swung back. The strike missed and threw him off balance.

Bahr growled as his elbow connected with the nose of the nearest assassin. Blood and cartilage leaked down the man's ruined face. The Sea Wolf propelled into him, crashing down on top with a bone-jarring crunch. Fists hammered. The assassin managed to bring his knee up and threw Bahr off. Dorl killed him quickly with a thrust to the throat.

The battle escalated quickly as Boen and Rekka charged into the assassins from behind. What had begun as a well-orchestrated assault devolved into a bitter contest of wills the Black Guard could not win. Boen's sword reaped a mighty vengeance while Rekka moved much quicker than any of the assassins could anticipate. It was finished in moments.

Being helped to his feet, Bahr looked around at the carnage. *What is it all for? Did these men understand why they'd been sent to attack us? Do we understand the gravity of what we're trying to do? How many more need to die before the gods' lust for bloodshed is slated? I grow weary of this life. So very weary. Even after this nightmare I cannot rest. The wounded need to be seen to. Plans needed to be remade. I've no doubt our enemies will return in even greater force. What fools we were to think we were up to this challenge.*

He sheathed his sword and turned back to the wagon. No words needed to be said. The others paused to watch him, their minds scattered. After several months and dozens of skirmishes and battles, Bahr managed to walk with sternness. Pride wouldn't let him falter. Not now. Not this close to the end. His strength would see them to the end, even if it killed him in the process. One by one they silently followed him. It was past time to move.

Bahr stood at the edge of the sloping hill. Delranan stretched out before him, an endless series of rolling plains untouched by horse or rider since winter began. The morning was still faint, night refusing to let go as easily as it once had. Shadows clung to the world as if sensing the coming conflict. He once found comfort in gazing upon untouched lands. Once, but no more. Delranan had grown wild, untamed since the end of summer. He no longer felt at ease. The peace of his solitude died the moment his brother became seduced by the fell powers of the Dae'shan.

Anienam confirmed their journey was nearly ended. A short, three-day ride to the ruins of Arlevon Gale was all that stood between the increasingly fatigued group of heroes and the end of the quest. What they'd find upon arriving was beyond any guess, even for the wizard. Dark clouds, perpetual as the days shortened, choked the far horizon. Armies were massing. The time of the final convergence was at hand and Bahr aimed to lead his haggard group directly into the heart of it. Only three days left until the final battle for Malweir began. Bahr sighed, crisp in the dawn air. *Three days until we see who lives or dies.*

END

The Northern Crusade concludes in book VI:

Even Gods Must Fall

BOOK VI OF THE NORTHERN CRUSADE
EVEN
GODS MUST
FALL
CHRISTIAN WARREN FREED

Even

Gods Must

Fall

ONE

Dawn. The sun broke the horizon, crisp and bright against the eastern sky for the first time in days. A late winter storm had blown through, covering the lands, yet again, in a perpetual blanket of austere white. While residents huddled in front of sputtering hearths, a sense of prevailing turmoil settled over the world. Rumors of struggles, whispers of titanic battles to the east, reached the villagers of the almost forgotten town. War was sweeping across the northern kingdoms. Yet it was a war that left them largely unaffected. A few favored sons had answered the muster and marched off to join the ranks. The old grieved while the young dreamed. War did funny things to all.

Eldric and Bjorn, eldest of six sons, slipped into their heavy winter clothing and collected their bows on the way out the door long before their mother awoke. They'd ached to enlist when the Wolfsreik recruiter visited back at the beginning of winter. A great, unstoppable crusade was underway that held the implications of liberating the entire north of Malweir under Delrananian flags. Who wouldn't want to become part of such grandeur? Glory was not for the boys, however. With their father long in the ground from an unfortunate plowing accident, their mother insisted on keeping all her boys close. Wars were no place for youth. Not if they expected to mature into decent men.

Abandoning the confines of their home, the boys hurried off down snow-covered trails in search of a stag or brace of rabbits. Winter had been a successive string of miserable storms confining them to the relative security of the house. Eldric grew inspired by the dawn and led the way. All thoughts of war and, given the circumstances, abject misery associated with too many feet of snow, dissipated the deeper into the woods they stalked.

A lone rider had come through the village a few weeks past with devastating news. Eldric and Bjorn learned for the first time of the insurrection against the throne and the destructive civil war raging across Delranan. The sheer incredulousness of it left both boys in doubt. Any aspect of war would surely have trickled down into the minor villages peppering the Delrananian countryside. The rider, claiming to be a messenger from the rebellion, rode off in disgust. Not a single villager answered the call and Eldric and Bjorn watched as their ancestral home quietly returned to the way life had always been.

Still, there was an urgency in the rider's words that inspired a fire within Eldric's heart. Questions of legitimacy sprang forth. He suddenly wanted to know more of what the rest of the kingdom was like. What it was undergoing. Bjorn chastised his older brother for being brash. The impudence of youth was often misunderstood. Why should Eldric's desires be any different? Eventually he calmed down. The rider was long gone, presumably off to other villages in search of able-bodied fighters to join the cause. Eldric forgot his dreams, brief as they were. His life was here, with his family.

"Look," Eldric announced in a hushed voice.

Bjorn knelt to gingerly touch the cloven-hoof print. A light splattering of snow had settled in deeply. Bjorn grinned. "Fresh. These can't be more than an hour old."

"Come on, looks like we're in for fresh meat tonight, brother."

The boys loped off on the hunt. Eldric's eyes scanned the woods as they followed the deer tracks deeper. Both boys stalked with arrows strung. Their stomachs growled hungrily. A long winter of too many old potatoes and slightly rotted vegetables left them salivating over the prospect of fresh meat. This past winter was among the worst in recent history, leaving many old and young naught but frozen corpses stored behind homes until the ground thawed enough to dig their graves. Worsening matters was the intense stir-crazy feeling gnawing away at every villager. It was time for the sun to shine again.

Trees began to thin. They were drawing to the edge of the forest. If either boy was thinking clearly they might have given pause. Deer preferred the security of camouflage, seldom venturing far into the open air. Eldric reached the tree line first and jerked to a stop. Bjorn, more worried over losing the trail, slammed into his brother's back.

"Hey, what did you stop fo…."

"Shhh," Eldric hissed. "Look!"

Bjorn lowered his bow to peek around his brother's solid frame. What he witnessed stole the warmth from his soul. The plain stretching out before them had turned black under the steady wave of Goblins pouring into Delranan. Thousands, perhaps tens of thousands of the vile creatures already choked the fields. Harsh, guttural orders were issued as Goblins slowly broke away into companies. Sword and axe, spear and tulwar gleamed in the morning sunlight.

"Where did they come from?" Bjorn whispered.

Eldric could only shake his head. A flicker of unnatural light caught his eye, drawing his attention to the magic-infused atmosphere on a small hilltop. The very air was warped with sickening shades of rot. Larger than a house, the rent continued to belch forth the Goblin army. Unending waves of infantry flooded Delranan.

"How?" was all Eldric managed to ask.

Frightened yet not understanding what he was seeing, Bjorn nervously clutched his brother's arm. "We need to leave, before they see us."

Eldric continued to stare as the Goblin army grew. He briefly considered killing one, if for no other reason than to brag to his friends, but quickly discarded the notion. Any unwanted attention would draw the entire horde down around him and there'd be no hope of escape. Not against so many. Reluctantly, he withdrew his gaze from the Goblins, creatures he'd only heard of. To see so many in Delranan this close to his home was impossible.

Bjorn, sensing his brother's hesitation, tugged harder. "Eldric, come on. We have to go warn the village."

Shaken free from the horrible scene continuing to unfold around them, Eldric nodded and began to duck back into the trees. Unfortunately for the brothers it was not unnoticed. Three squat, barrel-bodied Goblins emerged from the right and attacked. Bjorn cried out, dropping his bow as his small hands scrambled to draw his hunting knife strapped to his belt. Eldric was not so careless. He quickly drew and fired into the nearest Goblin, more reflex than anything else. The Goblin grunted and fell dead. Eldric's arrowhead punched out the back of the dead warrior, killing him instantly at point-blank range. The other two fell on the young villager with curses and sharp steel. Bjorn screamed as he watched a Goblin short sword plunge into Eldric's stomach.

Eldric fought with as much veracity as a sixteen-year-old boy could but the end was never in doubt. He briefly caught his brother's eye through the punishment. A sad smile followed. Blood coated his teeth. "Run," he mouthed and fell dead.

Bjorn ran for his life without looking back.

The impossible army continued to swell.

Thunder echoed down from the mountaintops, yet no lightning slashed the sky. No storm darkened the world. This was the thunder of two hundred booted feet. Locked in step, the heavy crunch-thump reverberated down through the jagged rock passes, knocking boulder and stone loose in massive cascades. Avalanches filled long-forgotten defiles and ravines. Dust clouds rose to choke the air. Red and heavily mineralized, the dust was the life blood of the very mountains.

Song soon accompanied the baritone of the march. Deep and ominous, the words were lost upon the rocks. Their meaning, however, wasn't. The song returned a forgotten people to old glories they'd abandoned for personal reasons. It whispered of past triumphs and the promise of new glory. There was unparalleled pride drifting on the winds. At last, after centuries of seclusion and the continuing downward spiral into obscurity, the Giants of Venheim were reborn.

Called into action by the Dae'shan and the gods of light, the Giants couldn't abandon the rest of the world to the depredations of the evil threatening. The arguments proved fierce, lasting long into the early morning hours. The outcome was never truly in doubt. At long last the time for Giants had returned. Coerced to march down from the mountaintop fortresses, the Giants headed into Delranan to claim their rightful place in the future history of the world.

Joden, eldest and most revered of the Giant smiths, paused at the rear of the column to give a last, longing glance at the home he'd known for over one hundred years. He knew, deep within the warmth of his soul, that this would be his final look at fabled Venheim. Old and fragile--for a Giant--he'd lived a long, full life. The world was changing, irrevocably moving towards a finale very few even realized approached.

The elder Giant had come to accept that his purpose in life had been to train, mold, and sculpt young Groge into the bearer of the Blud Hamr, the weapon capable of ending the dark gods' quest to reclaim Malweir for good. The war would be fought by blood and steel, the destiny of a dozen races, but the battle for the soul of the world rested in the hands of a young, inexperienced Giant and his small band of companions. That task completed, or at least en route to completion, Joden took his rightful place in the one hundred marching to join the allied army.

Artiss Gran, last of the true Dae'shan, mentioned the momentous occasion rapidly approaching. The world had not seen the likes of such an alliance since the days of the Mage Wars: Giant, Dwarf, Elf, Minotaur, and Man fighting an unimagined army of Goblins. Such prospects robbed the very strong of will and crumbled city walls in anticipation. The Dae'shan offered no promises, no delusions of victory or promise. This war threatened to exceed the reach of all mortals involved.

Unhindered by emotions, Joden accepted his fate. Lord Death rode his chariot straight for the combining armies, ready to reap his terrible reward. The Giant forge master would be among the casualties, carelessly slain for reasons only he valued. Joden grinned as he took in the smooth, stone walls and well-worn paths of Venheim. Content with his inner peace, the Giant turned and joined his troop. The Giants were finally returning to war.

BIO

Christian W. Freed was born in Buffalo, N.Y. more years ago than he would like to remember. After spending more than 20 years in the active-duty US Army he has turned his talents to writing. Since retiring, he has gone on to publish over 25 military fantasy and science fiction novels, as well as his memoirs from his time in Iraq and Afghanistan, a children's book, and a pair of how to books focused on indie authors and the decision making process for writing a book and what happens after it is published.

His first published book (Hammers in the Wind) has been the #1 free book on Kindle 4 times and he holds a fancy certificate from the L Ron Hubbard Writers of the Future Contest. Ok, so it was for 4th place in one quarter, but it's still recognition from the largest fiction writing contest in the world. And no, he's not a scientologist.

Passionate about history, he combines his knowledge of the past with modern military tactics to create an engaging, quasi-realistic world for the readers. He graduated from Campbell University with a degree in history and a Masters of Arts degree in Digital Communications from the University of North Carolina at Chapel Hill.

He currently lives outside of Raleigh, N.C. and devotes his time to writing, his family, and their two Bernese Mountain Dogs. If you drive by you might just find him on the porch with a cigar in one hand and a pen in the other. You can find out more about his work by following him on social media: